THE WAR MASTER'S Daughter

ELLY ZUPKO

sMLX BOOKS

Baltimore, Maryland

SMLX Books
Baltimore, MD

For purchasing or distribution information, contact SMLX Books at SMLXbooks@gmail.com

Front cover photograph by Liquid Squid Productions

Interior plate: Brooke Shaden (www.brookeshaden.com)

Cover fonts:
Porcelain by Misprinted Type (www.misprintedtype.com)
Morpheus by Kiwi Media (www.kiwimedia.com)

Interior font:
Janson by Miklós Tótfalusi Kis, 1685

ISBN: 978-0-9848945-8-1

Printed in the United States of America

10 9 8 7 6 5 4 3 2

To Mom and Dad.

Thank you for everything, but especially for
my first blank sheet of paper.

Note on the Second Edition

Here is a little something I learned in the course of publishing my first book, *The War Master's Daughter*:

That row of numbers on the copyright page of a book—something I had seen innumerable times, and knew I had to have in my own book, but unsure why—is actually representative of the edition. It's called "the printer's key." See, in days of yore, each page of a book was its own typographical plate, comprising hundreds or thousands of individual characters. On the copyright page, editions were marked thusly so that all the printer had to do to indicate an edition change was pluck out or file off the number at the end. This meant less chance for error, less labor, and less cost.

I can't remember now the first typo I found in the initial printing of *The War Master's Daughter*. But I only had to find one to know I was going to revise the interior to fix it, and any others I could find. However, as I pored over every word of the book for what seemed like the zillionth time, scouting for the odd missing space or dropped word, I found so much more that I wanted to change. Obviously, a dropped word would have to be re-inserted. But what about a grammatical mistake, like "further" when I meant "farther"? Is that a mistake or a flaw? What about a confusing sentence? Do I dare clarify it now? Could I take out a whole paragraph that I no longer like? Add a scene I thought of too late? You can see the slippery slope I encountered.

The printer's key is a nod to tradition, and a reminder of how difficult it used to be to change a book. But the reality is that not only can we change the edition number effortlessly, we can change anything about the book—more easily than we can think up what to change. Ultimately, however, I made the promise to myself and my readers that I would resist the urge to change anything about the book other than the typos and true errors. This is the book I set down. And while I am different as a writer now, the book should not also be different, because the book now exists outside of me. It is yours.

The War Master's Daughter also required a second edition so that I could properly thank the people who have helped me over the past 15 months since the book was released, and also so that I could add a map, which many fans requested. Changing the cover was not in the initial plans; I am still absolutely in love with Brooke Shaden's gorgeous photograph. But when I saw the panorama of Rocks State Park that we captured while shooting the trailer, I had no question of refreshing the cover in a way that pays homage to the beauty of my hometown and the talent of my friends.

These additions and the small fixes (I will never admit to how many) are all that have changed in this edition. I am curious to see how other publishers deal with the intoxicating temptation of being able to change any aspect of a book on a whim. But for now, this choice was my nod to the tradition of book publishing.

With that, I give you edition number 10 9 8 7 6 5 4 3 2.

—Elly Zupko, March 26, 2013

"When Adam delved and Eve span,
who was then the gentleman?"

—John Ball, 1381

The Fairgos-Mitoch War (1539–)

Sangeva (see entry for Sangeva, page 15) was a land-locked state in Eastern Europe, located equidistant from the Baltic and Black Seas, adjacent to the areas known today as Ekanta, Barlavia, and Nulle. Like many nation-states in the area, Sangeva dissolved into multiple independent principalities after the death of Mstislav I of Kiev in 1132; the Sangevan schism was a bloodless one, occurring most appreciably along lines of ethnicity and religion.

Mitoch, the northern portion of the former Sangevan state, having declared itself an independent nation in 1132 by royal decree, separated from the remaining southern portion of Sangeva, which became known as Fairgos. Mitoch and Fairgos each created its own separated system of monarchic government with asserted tenets of entitlementism and a noble class. The Sangevan capital city of March was retained as the capital of Fairgos. Only Fairgos maintained a standing military.

To this day, the countries have had the good fortune to make possession of autonomy outside the realm of empiric rule; this is, in part, attributed to the densely wooded and mountainous geographies which discriminate many nations of the former area of the Kievan Rus.

Fairgos and Mitoch existed with one another in peaceful and nonintrusive relations into the 16th century; however, Fairgos invaded its sister country in 1539. The two nations continue their engagement in warfare as of this publication. A narrative detailing the known facts and reliable conjectures associated with this war follows.

—Excerpt from "The Fairgos-Mitoch War" in *Cordrey's Wars That Shaped Our World, Volume V*, London, 1550 A.D.

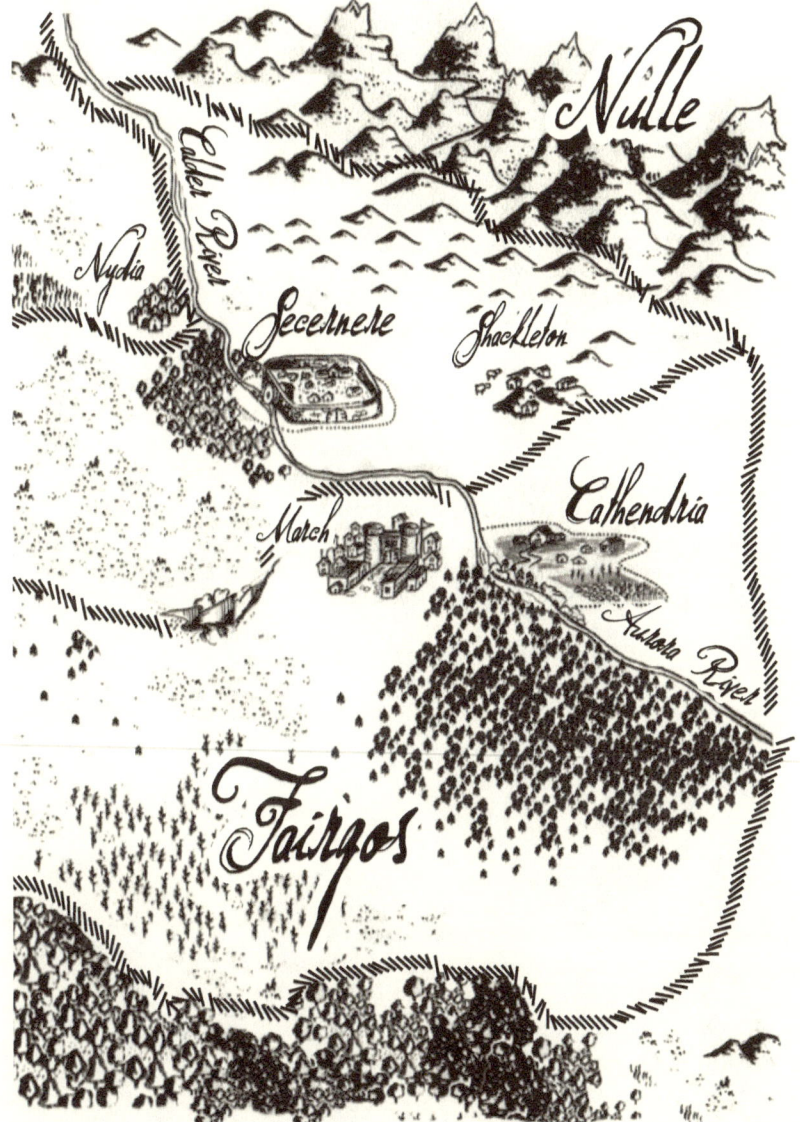

prologue

Stupid dog, thought Storey.

Those damned bloodhound puppies had been freedom-bound since the day they opened their clever eyes in the corner stall of the horse stable.

Don't they know there's no getting out of here?

At the river, he'd finally caught up with it, but only because it had stopped, dead frozen. It stood in a vacillating stance on the precipice of a steep bank by the river—curiosity drawing it forward, fear pushing it away. As the dog rocked back and forth, a low whine vibrated from its throat. Storey tried to calm it in soft tones, approaching slowly. Whatever had the dog scared, Storey only wanted to leash the thing and take it home.

But in one quick motion, the dog launched forward down the scree. Cursing the animal, Storey followed, half-stepping, half-slipping down the loose rocks of the slope.

Then he saw it.

The woman's body lay across the riverbank as if she were only napping in the sun. She was barely dressed, and her white underclothes were transparent like boiled onion, clinging to her alabaster body in all the places Storey wasn't meant to see. The sight chilled him. She was the first woman he had seen in years. And like the last, she was dead.

The dog darted to the body and thrust its nose into the wet brown hair, which was matted with sticky blood. Storey grabbed the puppy by the scruff, yanked it back with a grunt, and gestured for it to sit. The pup obeyed, resigning to sulk and glower at the body.

Then Storey also found himself staring. His mind swayed between noble intentions, and instincts of survival. It was only a body, after all—not something one scooped up and kept around the house. The sharp bend in the river had caught it like a shirt tail on a bramble. It hadn't come up too far on the shore. A solid nudge could send it rolling back into the water.

Who could she be?

If he only let it back into the water, it would meander north for several leagues. It wouldn't chance to go aground again until it was more than a safe distance away from Secernere Manor. Then it would be someone else's problem. No one had seen it. Only the dog, and it wasn't going to tell the tale.

It would be like the body was never here at all.

Storey gestured again for the dog to stay put, then stepped up to the body. As many bodies as he'd buried, he had never gotten used to approaching a corpse. One never should get used to that. His boot sank into the wet sand of the shore, making a soft crunching sound. He took one more step closer, then squatted down. Nausea rose in the base of his throat as he imagined touching the soggy skin.

The body had strange tan lines: the face, the shoulders, the arms were all deeply bronzed, even burned on the extremities, the bridge of the nose. The rest, however, was as white as if it had never seen daylight. It couldn't have been here very long, this dead thing, this inconvenient visitor, or surely it would have grown rancid here in the August sun.

Taking a deep breath of the riverbank's acrid air, he pushed both his hands below the body and began to turn it over on its side. It suddenly convulsed in his hands, and the woman coughed and spit out a lungful of turbid water. Hackles raised, the dog snarled. Storey dropped the body and jumped back.

She was alive.

❧ 1 ❧

Cathendria – 1550 (Present)

The moon had risen very high and the candles had burned very low, and Lady Aurora of Cavalcata was awake in the deep night that engulfed the manor house. Aurora was completely alone on the whole of the darkened Cathendria demesne. In two decades, the manor had never stood as vacant as it did presently. This emptiness was of her own design. Purposeful. She'd even written a plan down on paper. The irony of this fact only served to deepen the rueful loneliness she held around herself like a blanket.

There was no such custom in the country of Fairgos to send one's servants away on holiday. Such a strange and counter-intuitive idea never entered the head of any ordinary person. And yet Aurora had insisted on implementing the practice—in a time of war, no less—because Aurora had to have what she wanted, rest of the world be damned.

Aurora would turn twenty-one in just a few days. After that, it was only a matter of weeks before she would be married to someone she hadn't met. Then she would move away from Cathendria and away from her father, and she would be alone in a new place while her husband was away fighting the barbaric soldiers of Mitoch. A fine Fairgosian law—pass your daughters from man to man, all of whom are away from their homes.

Aurora had never left Cathendria. Her father hardly ever returned to the place. If she could just have one peaceful day alone with him before the rest of her life swallowed her up, that's all she wanted. The war, the world could wait a little while.

She'd been so cunning about it, too, the way she convinced her father it was the greatest idea in history to send the staff away. She developed a case for it, following the form she'd learned as a young pupil: a three-point, logic-based argument, delivered in person to her father in the library.

But really, it was just another self-absorbed demand from a spoiled only child.

She reflected back on the mere two days that had led to this sullen, sleepless night. It began with Aurora standing in the middle of the library with her hands clasped before her.

"Proposition," she had begun. "A vacation for the staff is in the interest of all involved."

She had been wearing a long white dress, and she had styled her hair for the occasion into a low, intellectual chignon at the nape of her neck.

"Premise one," she said. "After a vacation, the staff will be energized with renewed vigor to work—the war has tired all of us. Servants are people of God, and you and I must treat them as such. They, too, require respite, and they will be more loyal for it."

Lord Cavalcata sat in his chair before the cold fireplace, watching his daughter. His hands were knitted together in his lap. A full glass of horilka waited on a nearby desk for the conclusion of Aurora's argument. "In idle time lays evil deeds," he said. "I counter that God commands hard work."

Aurora made a quick change. "Hard work can come in many forms. We should be curious to see how our people choose to spend time away from Cathendria. As we watch them travel many miles to care for wounded relations, as we witness them make pilgrimage to a church and pray for peace, we may be wiser for it."

Aurora felt heat rise to her cheeks, aware of her gamble in logic. Lord Cavalcata nodded.

Relieved, she went on. "Premise two: Giving leave to the staff will provide for us rare time to enjoy one another's company, while we still have time. In the shadow of the insistent requirements of your position, this commodity has become too precious. You always tell me that opportunities multiply as they are seized. This is our opportunity."

Her father's proper title was Royal War Master to the Fairgosian King and His Army. But to Aurora, it might have been Blacksmith or Farmer; it was just an occupation.

"I argue," he said, "that we have a staff in order that we may be free from such domestic responsibilities as Cathendria requires. You have so much leisure time only due the staff, not in spite of it."

"I counter that our staff are well meaning, but are lost without direction. Managing the staff has become a domestic responsibility in and of itself." She paused. "It has become so for me, at least. With just the two of us occupying the manor house, and waning business obligations throughout the demesne and villein holdings, we have many idle hands to fill with work."

Indeed, Aurora desired to see some of the staff permanently relieved, but she did not say this. The war between Fairgos and neighboring Mitoch had been roaring for over a decade, and Cathendria had not been immune to the effects of an economy slowed by destroyed trade routes and the voracious appetite of the military. The complexity of Cathendria's staff was misaligned with the simplicity of their business operations; rather than complementing the Cavalcata status as it was designed to do, the number of personnel had become merely ostentatious.

In all, there were twenty people who personally served the needs of the Cathendria manor house itself, including a personal servant to each Aurora and her father. There were more who worked the demesne within the gates, tending a dairy, a pigsty and oxen shack, two granaries, a stable, a building for visiting clergy, gardens and orchards, and a collection of tenements for the servants themselves. Outside the gates were ten or twelve dependent peasant plots where corn, grain, and vegetables were grown, and more livestock were raised. And of course, there was the small unit of soldiers who kept it all safe.

Nearly all the tenets who remained were women; husbands and sons had departed to become soldiers. Burdened as they were, hardly a soul could afford anymore to pay the lordship in money, so Lord Cavalcata took small portions of their yields and, when the fields were fallow, put them to work on the demesne.

Aurora phrased her next point with care: "I understand that the size of the staff who work on the Cathendria demesne is a symbol of the power of the Cavalcata name and lordship."

She watched for her father's reaction. He made no twitch.

"I shall preface premise three by forestalling a potential argument from your side: You would contend that this vacation may be seen as a blemish on the household, that others may think we can no longer afford to maintain our people."

There. She saw the slight cock of the head that proved she had nailed his position—and had the foresight to preempt it.

"Premise three is that it will appear to those who pay attention that we are nothing but the most luxurious of people, who are able to continue paying a staff when they are not even working for an entire week!"

She saw the smile in her father's black eyes, even as he controlled his stone mouth.

"Premise *four*—" She drew out the word in jubilant awareness that just three sound points were required to make a case to her father. She couldn't hold back her own smile as she exclaimed, "It's my twenty-first birthday this week and I want nothing more than to spend it with you and only you!"

Dismissing all propriety of their mock court room, she ran to his chair and wrapped her arms around his wide, muscled shoulders. This was the wordless and successful closing argument to her case.

The servants were all notified by that evening. The news proved confounding to them. Some, at first, wanted to stay. They did not know anything else in the world but their toil at Cathendria. They feared leaving the boundaries of the property, stumbling upon some battle, being taken prisoner, being killed themselves. There were stories that fields of dead had been left to rot in the sun.

Others did not waste a moment questioning their good fortune. The kitchen manager— "Cook" to Aurora—had a daughter who lived in the village south of the demesne gates. She was ecstatic to go visit the grandson she had only heard about in the letters Aurora read to her. The old man who tended Cathendria's gardens and orchards had no family. He packed a large satchel of keepable food and announced his intention to embark on a long hike, in the peaceful mountains of Ekanta.

"My thanks to you, m'lady," he said. "Now provided the opportunity, my humble aspiration is to spend time in nature without having to cut it down."

Aurora had long ago become proficient in the domestic arts through her own curiosity to learn all there was. Loathe as Lord Cavalcata was to admit it—and to be sure he never did—he had no doubts that his daughter could manage the household herself for at least the week for which she dismissed the staff. There would be only two for whom to prepare meals—an easy feat for Aurora, Cook's young pest of an understudy for long years in her youth. The gardens were stagnant in the heat wave of the potent late summer, and needed no tending. The laundry was a small task, as was keeping tidy the few lived-in rooms. Lord Cavalcata had expressed disgust at his only daughter, only child, stooping to the height of baseboards. But on the eve of her birthday—and thus her marriage—Aurora believed he would soon realize satisfaction at her ability to run an estate all by herself.

But the utopian vacation for which Aurora had planned with hours of her own intellectual slog did not unfold according to design.

On the first complete day free of the staff, Aurora lay tucked in her enormous whipped cream dollop of a bed and dreamily recounted the schedule she had devised. She wouldn't be able to talk him into a swim in the river, but she was sure her father would be game for everything else on her agenda: horseback riding, hiking, a match or three of chess, cooking a meal together in the evening. She smiled to herself, and stretched her thin arms up over her head. What a wonderful world Cathendria was—once the rest of creation dropped away.

She slipped out of the bedding with the grin still on her face. The ivory white of a note pinned to her chamber door was the first and brightest object her bleary waking eyes encountered. She snatched it with the ambivalent anticipation of hope and lessons learned.

Dearest Aurora—

My deepest regrets on foregoing your plans, but an urgent matter has called me away. I am but headed into the capital. I will not be absent more than three days. I shall return in time for your birthday. I promise.

—Your father

She read it twice. Then she crumpled the note in her fist and threw it at the opposing wall, but it merely drifted to the floor. Further aggravated, she picked up a nearby book and threw it. It thudded against the wall, then slapped on the wooden floor.

Anger gave way to sadness, as so often happens when one is worn down from dependable disappointment. Her father had not been present most of the rest of her life—why would this day be different? Something was always more important than Aurora.

She returned to bed and lay there, motionless and staring. It was the first time she had ever been completely alone at the manor. Under different circumstances, the freedom could have been almost intoxicating. But she was older now. Freedom was boring. Solitude was loneliness, and the thought that there was no one for miles save a few soldiers was overwhelming.

So much for her own little world.

She went through most of the day as if in a trance. She wandered through the house, beholding its décor as if she had never seen it, as if it had never seen her. Happening upon some morsels of food in the kitchen, she ate without tasting. She tried to read from the book she'd been immersed in just the day before, but she would find herself at the end of a page not remembering a single word she'd read. She could not even muster the energy to walk down to the stable to take a horse out. The single thought that vaguely appealed to her was a swim in her river. But she felt somehow tethered to the house, as if she should not stray too far.

Perhaps there was a miscommunication.

Perhaps the matter was not that urgent after all. Perhaps he would return home early.

And although she was lethargic from depression, that very fancy kept her awake late into the night. Her father might yet return. His six-month trips to the West had never felt as long as this day had been.

That is why, even far past midnight without a person,

sound, or chore to disturb her sleep, Aurora was nevertheless still awake. If she had succumbed to sleep, she might not have heard the pounding on the path outside the manor house's grand entrance.

She ran out the front door to greet her father.

But an enormous black monster was flying up the path. Long trails of black cloth flapped backward into the wind, like bat wings. As the form came closer, it separated into its two parts: a massive black stallion, and a single man dressed all in black.

He was not her father.

Aurora dragged the back of her hand across her bleary eyes. The man didn't bother to tether his horse and advanced on Aurora. He bowed.

"A thousand pardons for the late hour. May I request audience with the lady of the house?"

He meant her, she realized, and it startled her to remember that she hadn't even dressed or brushed her hair in the morning. In her rumpled state, she must have appeared to be a servant. She ran a hand over her hair then down the front of her dressing gown, trying in vain to smooth herself.

She tilted her chin upward. "I am the lady of the house."

If the man, even for a second, did not believe her, he did not show it.

"You are Lady Cavalcata?" he said. He seemed to be looking straight into her, as if he was charged to describe her in detail later. Then in a lower tone, "Aurora?"

It was shocking to hear her given name in the mouth of a stranger. This man had not even offered his own name. Then a wave of nausea washed over her. If he knew her name, he must also know her father: why was he here without him?

"What's wrong?" she said. "What happened?" She fought desperation rising within her.

"My lady, perhaps we should go indoors, have a seat."

On a different day, she would have bristled at a man inviting himself into her home in the middle of the night. Regardless, she took a step closer to the stranger as she felt her face swell with pressure.

"Where is he?"

He was a head taller than Aurora and half again as broad, yet the man raised his black-gloved hands at her approach. "My lady, please . . ."

She reached him and hit her fists against his chest. "Tell me!"

He caught her by both wrists and pushed her away. Holding her at arm's length, he looked into her welling eyes. "Your father is dead."

"No, he's not. He's just at the capital. . . ."

"My lady—"

"I have a note to prove it—written in his own hand. He's at the capital!"

"I have just returned from there. I am so sorry . . ."

"He's not a soldier!" she yelled. "He's a tactician. He only makes plans! He doesn't fight! You don't know what you're talking about!" Her voice finally broke under the weight of sobs.

With all her strength, she pushed away from the man. He stumbled backward, nearly falling to the ground. The horse whinnied and reared up. The man grabbed at the lead and held the horse while he reached his other hand toward Aurora in a placating gesture.

"He's not a soldier!" She shook her head, and strands of hair fell around her face. "No, no, no," she said with quiet intensity. "He's coming back!" she shouted, then took another lunge at the man.

He sidestepped her while maintaining control of his massive animal. It whinnied again. Aurora retreated, stumbled on the hem of her dress, fell to the ground. She held her head in her hands and slowly shook it back and forth. "I only needed another day. Just one more day."

Shushing and petting the horse, the man tethered it, then

crouched down in front of Aurora. He took each of her hands in his own. She looked up at him, her face streaked with tears and her eyes red and puffy.

"Everyone is gone now," she said. "Who do I have now?" Her shoulders rose and fell with each of her ragged, silent sobs.

The man stood and gently pulled her to stand with him. She wavered a bit on her feet. Grasping her around the waist, he took her hand, and led her up the stairs into the house. Inside, he surveyed the building, then guided Aurora toward the reception parlor. Moonlight flooded into the dark space through ceiling-high windows. Every color in the room was a variation on blue. Still in a daze, Aurora sunk down onto a couch, staring blankly. The man placed a small hard-backed chair before her and sat. He tried to catch her gaze, but she refused to look at him.

He waited a long moment. "My lady, shall I wake a servant to fetch something for you?"

The words wafted up to her reluctant ears, and she finally shook her head. "No one is here but me," she whispered.

". . . Then I will get something for you. Which way is the pantry?"

Aurora's gaze now fell to the floor. "I need nothing. . . . Thank you."

The man did not move from his post and continued to watch her.

She did not look up, but asked simply, "How?"

"A fire at the inn."

Now she met the man's gaze. Even in the dark, she could see that his eyes were rich Fairgosian brown, and his face was deeply sympathetic, as if his pain for having delivered such news was almost more than he could bear. A fresh flood of tears rose to Aurora's eyes and fell from her eyelashes onto her lap. "He was supposed to be here today, with me," she said calmly.

"He told us the same. He spent most of the afternoon in protest of having been summoned."

"You work with him?" Aurora gazed at the man. He was young, handsome. With his close cropped hair and smooth face, glossy boots, shiny metal clasps on his overcoat, he was surely nobility—a military officer. At once, he was her father's kin, but apart from him. Lord Cavalcata was a civilian under Fairgosian law, and this made him different. His obligation to his country was moral, voluntary.

"I serve under him on the High Council of the Army. We have known each other for many years. He invited me often to call on your estate, but the war . . . I never had the opportunity."

"Welcome to Cathendria Manor," Aurora said.

His final statement had confirmed Aurora's suspicion: her father had chosen this man to be her husband. She wanted to laugh loudly, bitterly, to guffaw wildly. A fine first meeting.

"I'm so sorry," he said.

A fire. He had been killed in a fire. Not by the sword of a Mitochian enemy. Not of poor health, old age. His occupation had aged him prematurely; Aurora had worried for his heart. But this—she had never expected this. Rage rushed up inside.

"Why was he even at an inn?" she demanded. "He could have his pick of rooms at court."

"It was a meeting of the council. We meet in unexpected places, and move often."

"What kind of fire was it? Was it arson? A topped candle?"

"I don't—"

"You're here. How did you get out and he didn't? Why could he not get free?"

"He went back."

"Why would a person run into a burning building? Why would—"

"He went back to help others escape."

Aurora felt a pain shoot through her chest, and fell silent.

Of course he did. She cleared her throat. "What is your name?"

"Kynton." He did not offer his house or his title. That wasn't what she was asking, and he seemed to know that.

"Kynton, I am tired of being alone," she said. "Will you stay with me until the morning?"

At dawn, Aurora stumbled into the parlor where she found Kynton sitting stoically in the same chair. Even though she had not slept, she had almost forgotten the events of the night. But his dark brown Fairgosian eyes brought it all pouring back. What now? If this man was indeed to be her husband, was her home now his? Was *she* now his, passing from father to husband? She shook away the thoughts, realizing answers would not change anything.

She offered breakfast, was politely declined, and politely insisted. In the kitchen, she also packed a meal for Kynton's trip back to March.

Reluctantly receiving the satchel, he said, "I think it is too soon for you to be alone."

"I will be alone whether or not you are here." Feeling the pressure of decorum brought by the light of day, she added, "Please, take no offense."

She steered him toward the door with a light touch on the shoulder.

"You are an important man, and I know you left important business to deliver this news when you could have sent an envoy. I thank you for that. You would do me a comfort by returning to your work."

He nodded. "I shall return in a few days. There will be affairs to attend to—"

"It is absolutely not necessary—"

"Please. Let me help."

She finally agreed, if only to make him go.

She watched him atop his horse, riding toward the horizon, until she could no longer see the figures. She floated up the stairs to her bedroom, stripped herself of clothes, and washed herself. She dressed herself fully in a long, elegant gown, leaving her hair to fall down her back, full and curly, its dark color streaked golden by the sun. She folded her dressing clothes into neat packages and stowed them in a bureau. She made her bed and fluffed the pillows. Retrieving the crumpled note from her father, she smoothed its creases along the surface of her reading desk. It lay there, white and imperfect and hateful, its edges in precise alignment with the planes of the desk. She floated back downstairs, tidied the parlor and replaced the hard-backed chair, then cleaned the kitchen and put everything away. All signs of the late night visitor were erased.

She walked out the front door and latched it behind her.

Then, she began to run. She ran and ran, ran for miles, ran until, exhausted, she collapsed on the ground, dead to the world.

❧ 2 ❧

Twelve Years Earlier

The boy huddled in the corner of the stall, bracing himself against the night-brought chill that filtered in around him. He scraped hay up around his body, creating a half-nest, half-blanket to protect his small body from the cruel autumn evening. His belly rumbled. It had been a whole day that he'd hidden here, and he was no longer sure anyone was coming to find him; maybe there was no one left in the whole world. Only he and the horses existed. But even in the face of such terrifying lonesomeness and intoxicating freedom, he had no plan for where he would go or what he would do. He knew only that he would sleep here in the hay, slumber hanging its heavy mantel over his shivering body. What the morning would bring was a frightening mystery.

He could not even ride a horse; how would he get anywhere? Even if he knew how to get somewhere, he didn't know where that would be. Abandoned here, among angry violent strangers, no home to which to return, he was utterly lost. He

18

was caught amid a discomforting past and an unknown future, like being stuck between someplace not as bad as hell, but from where heaven was unattainable.

As his eyelids began their drooping descent toward sleep, they soon popped open at the sound of hay-crunching footsteps out in the stable corridor. A horse snorted and stamped at the ground. A strange soothing voice whispered for the horse to calm itself, and the horse obeyed. The footsteps, accompanied by the glow of a weak lantern, made their way down the seemingly mile-long corridor, stopping at each stall, until they were just outside of the boy's hideaway. He hunkered down, pulling his shoulders up toward his red tinted ears, as if he could pull his head into a shell and hide like a turtle. He also held his breath. He was good at that after years of practice at the river with his friends. Maybe he was well-enough covered with hay that, if he remained perfectly still and took not a breath, no one could see him in just the dim light of a lantern.

Inch by inch, the stall door creaked open. It took a maddening eternity to fully expose the boy's seeker. Finally, he was revealed: an old man who was bent forward like a shepherd's staff, dangling a tarnished metal and glass lantern in the crooks of his gnarled fingers. The boy had seen him earlier. He leaned heavily against the doorframe and peered inside the stall, his myopic eyes squinting in the boy's precise direction.

"I knew Lord Gomery was trying to breed new kinds of horses, but you are by far the strangest variety of foal I have ever laid my old eyes on." The man's voice lilted along as if on a formless melody.

The boy, green eyes wide, stared up at the man and continued his tactics of breath-holding and turtle-shelling. The man stretched out his arm and held the lantern deep into the stall, illuminating all the dark corners, and the boy finally had to exhale.

"Please do not kill me, sir," he whispered, hugging his knees to his chest. "I am just a boy, sir. I am just a boy, sir."

"Do I look like a man here to kill you?"

"I do not know what a killer looks like," the boy said, still frozen.

The old man entered the stall and offered his hand to the boy. Gingerly, the boy took it and allowed himself to be tugged into a standing position. The man huffed at the exertion.

"Son, none of us do. Most of us, however, are lucky enough not to decipher that fact until we are old men. Are you frightened?" The man leaned forward and picked a piece of hay from the boy's shaggy auburn hair.

Eyes fixed on the ground, the boy shook his head no.

"You've done nothing wrong. You have no reason to be frightened."

This was the kind of lie adults tell children. He knew this. But he also understood completely the truth of the remark, here. In some places, there existed a morality as stark as a cast shadow across the snow, where all wrongs were wholly black, and all were wholly punished.

The old man gripped the boy's shoulder and lifted the lantern as if to illuminate the entirety of the stable, though much was still left obscured. "What are you called, son?"

"My name is Storey, sir."

"Storey, I am called Abern. Tell me, do you like horses?"

"I like them all right, Mister Abern, sir. But I have had no occasion to gain experience with them."

"Do you have anywhere to go, young Storey? Have you family elsewhere?"

The boy shook his head. He felt the tears burning his eyes, and tried to blink them away, sniffling.

"Sir, I have had no occasion to gain experience with horses, but if you were in need of the services of a stable boy, I could learn. I am very smart and I learn new things very quickly." He turned his head away and swiped at his teary eyes, then looked back up at Abern.

"This is an awfully big stable, son." Abern held his lantern aloft again to demonstrate the vastness of the undertaking. "And these are big horses. Very tall. Eighteen hands high, some of them."

"I am getting bigger every year, sir. I would take care of the horses and you would hardly know I was here. I could even sleep here, in the stable. You would hardly know."

Abern guided Storey out of the stall, and they stood together in the middle of the barn, motes of hay dust floating up into the orange light of Abern's outstretched lantern. The horses were still. Outside, the sky was the soft, low-hanging black of a plush velvet drapery.

"Son," Abern said, "I know you are frightened. You saw things today that not even a soldier should have to experience. To stand here with me talking about such things as horses, that means you are a very brave young man."

"I am not brave, sir. I was hiding."

"We all hide when the time calls for hiding. But we are not all brave when the time comes to be brave."

"You are brave, sir. You do not seem frightened at all. We saw the same things today."

The old man heaved out a weighted sigh, and his chest rattled as he did.

"Sometimes I think my heart is just a shriveled up prune," he said. "And my soul is like a vapor of morning mist that burns off in the sunlight. My mind still works with all the regularity of a clock, but a clock has no space between its gears for things like horror or fear, or even sadness, or joy. There is not much left of me but creaky bones and sagging skin. I have seen such things all my life. One knows one is ready for death when one no longer feels pain at the deaths of others. I am sorry, son. I offer a thousand apologies, and I hope you will pardon me a thousand times for my blind heart. I simply do not see it anymore. It happens before my very eyes, and I do not see it."

They stood together in the middle of the stable in silence, both staring out into the abyss of sky that looked equal parts expansive sea and towering wall. If one could fly up into it, one was as sure to drown as to crash.

"God sees it," Storey finally said, breathing the words out in puffs of silver smoke that floated up toward the rafters.

"No, son. God does not come to Secernere anymore."

"I am not frightened, Mister Abern," Storey said. "God will return. It is said, God does not live for God's own self. God exists for us, and because of this, God can never be separate from us. I will take care of your horses, and you will hardly know I'm here. God will take care of us—and we will know when God is here."

Abern encircled his boney arm around the boy's slender shoulders and brought him to his side, gently hugging him. Storey looked up and saw the old man was crying. He reached his own arm around the man's bent back and held him there. The horses slept, and the sky opened up.

Cathendria – Present

Vultures, desperate and gaunt, circled overhead. Like black gashes before the bright white sun, they rode the columns of rising summer air. Their eyes were on the ground below, watching the corpse-like body baking in the high afternoon heat. But as much as she wanted to be, Aurora was not dead.

A violent dream cut short, Aurora heaved into a sitting position. She doubled over, jerking with coughs that racked her aching ribs and shoulders. Her eyes were dry and puffy as she blinked them against the aggressive blueness of the sky. When she ran her thick, desiccated tongue over her lips, they felt cracked, like the scales of a desert lizard. She needed water. It was calling to her, pulling her. She needed to get to the river.

Maybe it will take me away.

Grunting, she contracted the thick muscles of her thighs

and rose to her feet, still coughing. Her throat was raw. Arid bits of earth and broken wheat berries stuck to her dry red cheek and in her tangled nest of hair. She moved one leg forward, then another. Her boot caught in her rumpled petticoat and she fell hard onto her outstretched hands, pain cracking through her wrists.

With a heave, she flopped onto her back and yanked off one knee-high suede boot, then the other. She sat up, and began to unfasten the innumerable buttons on her gown, but her fingers felt fumbling, numb. She grasped each side of her bodice and tore it open, popping the tiny pearl buttons to the ground, then wriggled out of the black satin dress like a shedding snake. Standing, she shoved her petticoats down off her taut waist and stepped out of them. Then, wearing only her white and clinging undergarments, she ran toward the calling river.

Behind her, the rising stone walls of the ivy-covered manor house became smaller and smaller. By the time she reached the river's edge, the place called Cathendria would disappear completely. And that's what she wanted. There was nothing back there worth returning to. Not anymore.

Beyond the boundaries of the wheat field, a thick stand of trees lined the river's edge. A distinct path of trodden earth cut through dense overgrowth of withered may-apple parasols and curling ferns and spiny, thorny things. Lord Cavalcata had borrowed the gardener's axe to cut the path when Aurora was just a tiny girl, and her constant passage over it had stayed the fecundity of the forest. As her feet turned over and over on the trail, Aurora realized that even in death her father was omnipresent.

She halted at the river, wary.

The river had seen her sadness many times. All the saddles of youthful disconsolation had weighed on her back at one time or another. This or that mood swing would send her running to the comforting solitude of the woods and water, but she had never approached the river with such desperation. The death of her sole living parent, her sudden and irrevocable orphaning, was more than she had ever endured. The river's call was different this time. A siren's call.

Aurora stood on one of several rocky bluffs that jutted out of the forest, breaking up the eastern bank along several miles. This was her diving platform. She stepped to the edge and curled her bare toes over the knobby lip of the flat, gray rock. Raging in some places along the river, the water pooled here, quiet and still.

Thunder rumbled somewhere north. On the opposite bank, a raven shouted a raspy call and ascended from a tree branch in a flutter of leaves and beating wings. Then there was no sound but the trickle of water below and Aurora's own heaving breaths. The sun overhead burned her bare shoulders and the tip of her nose. The crown of her head was smoldering, and the soles of her feet seared on the calescent crag beneath her. Was it to escape the terrible heat of the terrible sun? Was it to escape everything else? The river was calling to her, and she threw her body into it.

Plunging deep into the pool, Aurora let herself become enveloped in the chilling water. She floated in limp suspension halfway between life and death. The surface of the water was like a window pane, and one deep breath on either side of it would make her choice.

She resisted until the last instant, then pushed back to the surface. By the time her face broke through and she took a gasping, hungry breath of air, the rain had already started. The storm's power and presence were immediate. Aurora was assailed from above with needle-sharp raindrops. She sought refuge underwater, diving as far down as she could go until her lungs burned. Only then would she surge upward, exploding into the rain.

Aurora soon found herself farther downstream than she wanted to be; she was out of the pool. The river tugged at her with alarming strength, and as she traveled around a sharp elbow, rocks blocked her view. She could no longer even see the pool.

In much shallower water now, she could feel her feet banging against the rocky river bottom. The water was much swifter, too. She tried not to panic. She recognized the land above her, the trees, the rocks. But the water, she did not recognize the water. The river had always been her element; she had been born there. But this thunderstorm had delivered strange, unfriendly water into the river and it was fighting against her. The muscles of her arms taut like rope, she pulled hard against the current, trying to find her way to the edge or to a rock or a tree branch. But the river yanked her farther and farther downstream.

Ahead, rapids. Ugly peaks of gray covered the river's surface. The water was muddied from churned up silt. The rapids snaked around a maze of rocks. Aurora was approaching a gauntlet.

She wouldn't get through those rocks without being badly wounded. Digging her heels into the bottom shredded the soles of her feet. She grabbed at branches but only stripped them of their leaves as they sprung out of her grip. The rocks were slick and slimy. Nothing to grab.

A current wrenched her down. Her head submerged. Panicking, she gasped. Burning water shot up her nose, into her lungs. She pushed above the surface, coughing, almost vomiting, then fell under again. She had lost control. Another cough forced her eyes shut. When she opened them, a large rock was suddenly ahead of her. She braced for impact, but a swift eddy tossed her body around the rock. Eyes wide with fright, she looked back at what she had narrowly missed, and another rapid slammed her head into a stone, invisible just below the surface. Blood flowed from a gash in her head, mixed with the water of the river. Everything turned red. Then black.

$\approx 3 \ll$

Present

Whispers, ghosts of speech, slipped through the door and finally awoke Aurora. She felt the wakefulness wash over her body, drawing her from the foggy sleep that had held her for untold hours. She didn't want to open her eyes. She didn't want to be awake. She didn't want to feel the throbbing pain that emanated from the back of her head to the space behind her eyes. It was the pain that told her she wasn't in Heaven; it was the pain that told her she was still alive.

Even before she opened her eyes, an overwhelming and unfamiliar scent of clean linen surrounded her. She blinked into the stabbing brightness of daylight, squinting as her eyes adjusted. Her head was throbbing. She reached up and felt stiff bandages encircling her crown. Her hair had been washed and combed.

At first she thought she was in the boudoir of her late mother: white sheets shrouded all the furniture in the grand bedroom, everything save the bed in which she lay. The torrid river flashed into her mind. She winced at the image. No, she was not anywhere on the Cathendria manor. How far had she gone up the river? The river flowed north, toward Mitoch.

Her father's words from a long ago speech echoed in her mind: *What kind of people is this? Are they people at all?*

She felt her heart squeeze in her chest. She had to figure out where she was. If she was in Mitoch, this could very well be the last day of her life.

She surveyed the room, searching for a clue. As her eyes happened upon a tray of food, the more immediate need of hunger won her over. The tray contained a silver pitcher of clear water, half a loaf of crusty white bread, and the plump segments of a tangerine. She reached for the bread and tore off a large piece with her teeth. Crumbs spilled over the white comforter as she gnawed, famished. She would eat first. Then she could gather a way to find out what this place was.

She reached for the tangerine and sent the pitcher clattering to the floor. Water splashed and spread all over. Before she could even get out of bed to mop up the mess, the chamber door creaked open.

A gnarled, bent twig of a man lurched into the room and shut the door behind him. A long scar hatched his face, starting on his forehead, crossing his eye, and ending on his sunken cheek. He was the oldest living creature Aurora had ever seen.

"You are awake," he rasped. The man's wizened face was puckered into an unmistakable look of disapproval.

Aurora snapped upright and clenched all the bedding she could grab up around her throat. She didn't know whether to apologize or scream. The man approached the bed, then began to bend toward the floor, a motion that took him an eon, every joint popping and cracking. He dabbed at the water with a rag. Then, with a heavy grunt, he stood and shuffled toward Aurora.

She dug her heels into the bed and thrust herself to the far edge, staring at the intruder. Was this a Mitochian?

"Who are you? Where am I?"

"M'lady—"

Clutching a clean, white cloth in his knotted fist, he reached toward her head.

Aurora dodged. "Stop that!"

He made a sound that was something between a growl and a sigh.

"M'lady—" He reached toward her again.

"No!" She all but smacked his hand away.

The old man finally retreated, folding his arms across his protruding rib cage. The scar-like wrinkles in his filmy skin deepened as his mouth folded into a frown.

"All I have done is break my aching bones to help m'lady, and the first thing m'lady does when she awakens is tell me to stop that." His red-rimmed eyes scrutinized her. "May I remind m'lady that *she* is the stranger here?"

"What do you want from me?" Aurora's tattered fingernails were digging through the sheets into her palms; her body shook with nerves.

"M'lady, I take care of things. That is what I do. The world tries to destroy things, beats them down, and I take care of them in the small way that I can. I take care of this place, and if you are here, I take care of you."

He reached again, and again she evaded him. Never had a strange man touched her. Never had any man but her father. The speed of her own breath frightened her.

"I beg of you, tell me where I am." *Please, not Mitoch. Please.*

The crooked man exhaled another vexed sigh and threw his cloth at her lap.

"I do not miss the women of Secernere." He shambled back to the door and left.

Again, Aurora heard indistinguishable voices waft through the door, then quiet. Footsteps, then nothing. She was alone once more.

Her breathing calmed. If she was being cared for, it was clear she was still in Fairgos. That a man would dare touch her was shocking, but at least her life wasn't in immediate danger. As the tension dissipated from her body, it was replaced with the dull ache of deep bruises across her shoulders and back. Her legs were fatigued and sore. She could tell even before standing that she would have difficulty walking. No matter where she was, there might not be a way for her to leave until she healed a little.

Lifting the bed sheets, she regarded the new garments in which she had been dressed. The long smock was much too large for her. Her feet were bound in bandages, under rough knit stockings that covered her calves up to her knees. These were much too large, as well. The most bizarre discovery, however, was that she was wearing a pair of man's undershorts, like those she had sometimes seen hanging on the laundry line at Cathendria. Had some stranger stripped her nude, bathed her, then dressed her in a strange man's clothing? Was it that knotted old man? The thought undid every sense of cleanliness. She spied a robe on a nearby chair. At least some attempt at modesty was possible.

With a great heave, Aurora threw the duvet and sheets off, leaving herself exposed on the open bed. Both her knees were red with scrapes. Yellowing purple bruises splotched her white legs. She had been hurt before, bruised and beaten up by her recreation. But horseback riding, swimming, running, falling—nothing had ever taken her apart like this.

Gingerly, feeling every movement like lightning through her muscles, she swung her legs over the side of the bed. She placed one hand on the bedside table, then reached for the chair back with her other hand and pulled herself into a standing position. Now with her full weight upon them, her feet stung. The tiny cuts felt as if they had glass in them. Her legs seemed to vibrate under her weight. She put on the dressing gown and hugged it around herself.

Grasping the chair back again, she took one step forward and winced. She found herself longing for the boots she had left behind in the wheat field. They'd been her favorite: knee-high suede with soft but durable soles. Intricate flowers and foliage had been embroidered along the calves in dyed silk thread by the northern artisan from whom her father had purchased them. Even though they were his gift to her, he criticized her for wearing them so often, "like a peasant with only one pair of shoes." Aurora owned several dozen pairs of shoes, but almost all of them lay unworn after the first day of the arrival—from every corner of Fairgos, from neighboring Barlavia, from Mitoch before the embargo. The boots would have been something familiar in a strange place.

They might have let her run.

She took a few more steps forward, steadying herself with a hand against the wood-paneled wall. Stumbling, she grabbed a nearby piece of furniture for balance, and the white sheet slipped off of it, pooling on the floor. Beneath was a luxurious sofa, upholstered in rich, soft green velvet. The arms were studded with polished brass rivets. The piece was in gorgeous, perfect condition.

Her curiosity piqued, Aurora staggered around the chamber, pulling the sheets from all the furniture. Every piece was of similar richness and quality. Even the presence of the humble tangerine signified wealth and culture. A soft relief came over her; this was certainly Fairgos.

She pulled the sheets off an enormous golden vanity and cushioned stool, then sat and looked into the mirror to examine the damage. She was slightly horrified, but unsurprised, at the face looking back at her. The bandage wrapped from the back of her head to the fore. It was free of blood, must have been new. Her face was sunburned to a deep rusty brown. Even her unfashionable tan hadn't protected her from the hours she lay almost comatose in the sun. Raising her index finger to her face, she touched her cheek tentatively. The skin was tender and raw under her finger. She pressed a bit harder and left a fading white fingerprint.

Pulling the robe and dressing gown aside, she saw that her collarbone and part of her shoulders were also burned. The bright red against the stark white skin looked like a bitten apple. Her eyes, too, demonstrated an alarming contrast of red against white. Beneath, her eyes were cupped with dark pouches. She looked as if she had not slept in days, belying the hours upon hours of recent unconsciousness. Plainly, she was not a pleasant sight to see. And even more plainly, she needed the nursing that her fear had caused her to reject.

In the mirror's reflection, Aurora caught a strange image behind her and turned to look full on at a large rectangle hanging high on the wall. It, too, had been covered in a sheet. She rose from the stool, hobbled over to the wall, and tugged at the veil. The sheet slid partway down and revealed the top half of a face. The painted portrait was a young woman with white-gold hair, milky blue eyes, and a ghost's skin. She appeared close to Aurora's age. The sheet slid down all the way. A long knife slash sliced from the woman's ear, across her chest, and all the way down to the bottom edge of the painting. Aurora gasped.

With renewed immediacy, she ran to the door and jiggled the latch. It was locked.

"Hello?" she called. The silence outside offered no reply. "Hello?" This time louder. She slammed one palm flat against the wooden door. "Hello!"

She ran to the window and it, too, was locked. Looking out, she saw a long view of the patchwork demesne and farm holdings. She was on an upper floor, and the only reason the window would be locked from the outside would be to keep her prisoner.

Anxiety rising, she looked around the room, seeing many locks—the drawers in the vanity cabinet, the enormous armoire, a hefty chest against the wall beneath the portrait; there was even a keyhole in the fireplace door. She tried them all.

Every opening was locked up tight—except one: the bedside table beneath the tray of food was unlocked, and the sole contents of the cabinet was a clean chamber pot. She snapped the door shut and returned to stare out the window.

As she surveyed the strange property, a horse saddled with rider galloped out from a stable. The horse's black coat sparkled in the dusky sun as if spangled with constellations. The man had shaggy copper hair and wore a billowing white shirt, but that was all the detail she could discern. She banged her hands against the window, shaking the blurry panes of glass.

"Hello!" she shouted. "Hello! Help! Help me!" But he did not turn and he did not look, and she had not expected him to.

Could he have been the one who found her, who carried her from the shore? She'd had just a flash of consciousness during the rescue. She remembered that he had green eyes. And that he was strong enough to carry her.

Perhaps he would come unlock the door. Someone would come back eventually; they had to. They would not let her starve in here, would they? They would not let the chamber pot overflow. However pure or sinister the designs of the people who loved locks so much, someone had to come back.

Sleep was full of violent and random images, like her father's face engulfed in flames. Then, she was falling, tumbling down from the top story of the Cathendria manor house. Tumbling, tumbling, then landing—abruptly she was back in bed, sheets twisted around her legs like chains. Her pillow was damp with cooling sweat. Her breaths came fast and short. Where was she? She stared frantically around, confused, lost. She noticed the pooled piles of sheets on the floor, the slashed painting, and remembered the strange room. A new addition floated at the foot of Aurora's bed: a pale white specter, with white-gold hair and white dress.

The girl, age twelve or so, stared at Aurora like a child would stare at an unusual bug. Aurora's eyes shot toward the door and she saw it was open. She looked again at the apparition.

The girl said, "You were calling out in your sleep. You called for your father."

Every part of the child seemed transparent, like paper, and she was so thin she looked malnourished. Her dress itself looked half-starved, a cotton sheath hanging limply on her frame as it would hang from a laundry line. Sunken into the middle of her buttery face were two enormous blue pools, shrouded beneath golden-white lashes. As Aurora watched her, she caught the girl's eyes dart covetously at the rich plate of food. Aurora sat up and held the last remaining piece of bread out. The girl tentatively took it, then ate greedily.

"Hello," said Aurora. "Can you tell me where I am?"

The girl finished chewing her mouthful, then said, "Are you going to stay?"

"What?"

"Are you going to stay?" she repeated. "I've never seen any-one like you before. Everyone like you always goes away."

What did she mean, like you?

"I would gladly be on my way, but last night that door was locked." Aurora pointed.

"So many people go away," said the girl. "But mostly they just don't come."

Aurora had no immediate response for this. She hadn't come; she had arrived, and not by choice. Finally she said, "And when they *do* come?"

"They never stay long."

The girl's impassive tone lent a hollow ominousness to her simple phrase. This place was not an inn. *Stay* and *go* had dif-ferent meanings here.

"Do you know why I'm being locked in this room?"

"Sometimes locks are to keep things out," said the girl. She turned and walked to the door. Aurora saw she was barefoot.

"You should stay. I think you could help us. You could help me."

The girl exited, closing the door behind her, and Aurora heard the soft metallic sound of a lock clicking shut.

"Wait!" Aurora cried. But as to every question and shout before, no answer returned.

Aurora thought she would never feel so helpless as the moment Kynton delivered the news about her father. But every question she faced in this room heaped measures of trial onto her. After a loved one dies, one finds oneself trapped in a room: lonely, frightened, anxious, desperate . . . visited by ghosts. The metaphor was not meant to be real.

❧ 4 ❧

Hours spent alone in waning, purple light, Aurora found that the four walls of the shrinking room elicited her darkest musings. She was shouting conjecture down a well: her thoughts ricocheted against stony walls, then echoed back to her, distorted and strange.

She squinted, trying to remember the geography of northern Fairgos. Perhaps this place was part of a slavery ring? She could have been carried near the mountain foothills, close enough to the border with Nulle where the slave trade was routed. That would explain why they had so carefully dressed her wounds, why they were feeding her. She would have to be in perfect physical condition when she was stripped, bound, and forced naked onto an auction block. Less likely but possible, someone might have recognized her as Fairgosian nobility and was holding her for ransom. She would be the pathway to the Cavalcata fortune only if she was returned unharmed.

After the sun set, the passage of time lost definition. As she sat without even a candle to illuminate the room, she knew not whether hours or minutes ticked by. The distortion was painfully different from the way she would lose time to leisure: horseback riding or reading in a field of wildflowers, or swimming in her river. Out on the demesne, sometimes her only signal that it was time to return home was the sudden onset of dark. With a satchel full of kitchen leftovers that Cook would set aside for her, Aurora never even returned for meals.

The entrapment in this room was so much like bitter Cathendria winters, when she was not as free to roam the countryside. She would bundle herself like a large furry animal and brave the outdoors, but always found she could not stand it for more than a few hours. Reluctantly, she would return to be warmed by hot chicken stock and Cook's handmade tea, blended from exotic spices Lord Cavalcata sent from far away. When she was a small child, she would select a musty volume from her father's massive library collection, then curl up on a sofa by a fireplace. Before long, however, her father caught on to her habits.

Her memory of a particular altercation was like an oil painting, a frozen moment that had changed so much for her. It was three years after her mother's death, three years of running rampant without a governess, a tutor, or a present parent. Cook had said to her once, "How do you play so when you mother has died?"

"How do you work?" Aurora returned. That was the extent of Cook's attempt at discipline.

The month was January; the day was a few after the New Year. Aurora had been out in the snow all morning, building caves into the drifts and hiding like a hibernating bear. She sculpted men out of snow and decorated them with whatever scraps of nature she could find that had not been buried in the white. She was bundled in animal skin from head to foot like a Northlander, in an incredible outfit the likes of which she'd never be permitted to wear in public.

On winter days, she did return for meals, for warmth and

strength. When stomach pangs hit her late that morning, she trudged through the knee-high snow right to the kitchen. The building was hot like a furnace. Clambering onto a rickety stool at a massive table in the middle of the room, she did not have to say a word: Cook was already ladling her a crock of venison stew that had been simmering all night in a fat-bellied kettle.

"The buck from Mister Swain," Cook said, presenting the bowl. Mister Swain's Yule donation had provided venison steaks and sausages already. The very last shreds of meat, under Cook's prudently parsimonious ways, turned into stew that would feed the household for half a week. Aurora stripped off one coarsely-knitted mitten, then the other, and flexed her stinging fingers. She fumbled through each of the buttons on her coat and let the front vent open. Placing her palms around the rugged pottery, she began to thaw. She brought the crock to her chapped and broken lips, sipped the rich broth, tasting the familiar gaminess of venison and the strange wonder of Cook's gastronomical alchemy. Cook next served a dainty cup of peppermint tea on a delicate porcelain saucer. Aurora let the steaming tea, sweetened with one lump of sugar, glide down her throat in just a few gulps, then returned to the stew. Warmer now, she let her coat fall from her arms and hang limply behind her, just short of dragging the dirt floor. She kicked her booted feet back and forth, and hummed a little carol.

She'd just taken another mouthful of soup, when she heard her father's manservant, Baston, at the kitchen door.

"M'lady Aurora," he said, "your father would have a word with you in the library."

"But I'm *eating*." She knew her power over both the servant and her father.

"I believe he means presently," Baston said. The implication was subtle, yet unmistakable: there would be no bargaining this time.

Aurora gave an exaggerated sigh and a roll of the eyes. She did not miss the look exchanged between Cook and Baston.

She'd heard the conversation among the adults. She was now of a "certain age" (that age was twelve, apparently), and would become more of a handful than ever unless she was somehow disciplined. Discipline was for slaves, she always thought, not for little girls who like to read books and play outside.

She reluctantly left her soup, climbed down off the stool, and followed Baston outside, then into the manor house toward the library. She knew her way blind—and protested as much—but he insisted on escorting her. Baston would not have gone so far as to grab Aurora by the ear (her father would nigh kill a man for putting hands on her) but she knew better than to give him cause.

Baston walked her as far as the west library door, then took his leave. Aurora stood in the doorway looking into the library. It was a magical, shape-shifting room; it could change from welcoming to foreboding with frustrating ease. She spied the back of her father's head, his right arm laying on the arm rest of a great oaken chair. The room was aromatic with the sweet burning of the fireplace.

"Father?" she said tentatively.

Under the intimidation of his presence, she began mentally to recount all her recent transgressions. She had spoiled her supper once again with the venison stew. She had drawn a horse's portrait on a stable wall with charcoal. She had used an expensive vase to dig faster in the snow. Nothing was new. She had been bending and breaking rules in the same ways as always; she could think of nothing egregious enough to warrant this summons.

"Come over here, Aurora." She obeyed and stood in front of him, her back to the flickering fireplace. He continued to stare into the fire, and the orange flames reflected in his black eyes. His hand rested idly near a chessboard beside him. "I have been ruminating lately, young woman."

"Yes, Father?"

"I have been *ruminating* about how you spend your days."

"I hope you have been ruminating about how much fun I'm having or how healthy I am because of all the exercise I take."

"I think you have become idle."

"*Idle?* How can one who does so much be *idle?* Have you not seen my snow fortifications and sculptures?"

He touched the tip of his index finger to the crown of the black king on the chessboard and slowly rocked the piece to and fro. "In idle time lays evil deeds."

"I have exercised the horses, who do not have much opportunity to be outside in the wintertime. I have cleared walking paths so our old and infirm do not slip in the snow. And when I am indoors, I spend my time reading. I have finished reading three volumes of *belles lettres* since the new year."

"These are not appropriate deeds for a girl of your age and station," he replied. "And not for a girl of the Cavalcata name." His finger moved to the white queen as he planned his next words.

But Aurora cut him off before he could continue. She was not even sure for what contravention she was being scolded, and yet her defensiveness flared.

"What then? You would have me attending tea parties at court? Shall I don pretty dresses and sit for hours posing for portraits?"

At one time, such impertinence would have gotten her mouth slapped. But she knew her father was growing wearier by the day and he no longer had the vigor to reprimand her with the hard hand she so often deserved. And so she pushed even further.

"Shall I find a gentleman to court me? Shall I wed, then drop babies from between my legs year after year? Is that how I should fill my days?"

"Lady Aurora of Cavalcata!" He stood abruptly, sending the chess board rattling to the floor.

Aurora retreated in fright. She felt the heat of the fire, now much too close, burn at her back. Deep trenches of age on her father's face seemed magnified in the dancing flicker of light.

"I have not done my duty if you feel the necessity—or the comfort—to say such things to me."

"Father . . ." She dared not meet his eyes. "My every apology. I did not mean—"

"It doesn't matter what you meant or why you said it. Your words would not change my decision. Indeed, they have confirmed it."

The white queen was still in his hands and he rolled it between his fingers. He seemed to calm.

"We have servants to exercise the horses and clear the paths. Cook should be left alone in the kitchen, to tend her work; she is not to be interfered with by little girls with no respect for boundaries. Even your so-called 'art' is transient and impermanent, melting by spring, if not afternoon. These things are not worthy of your time or talent. They will certainly not win you favor with a husband."

Her father saw no merit in the creation of any art, whether a snowman or the ceiling of a grand cathedral. People of the Cavalcata name purchased art; creating it was for the lower classes.

He continued, "And finally, I know that you read, but I've also taken note of *what* you read, and it has been those nonsense fairy tales and romantic stories that . . . that your mother kept here. They have already started to fill your head with lies and illusions, and it is time you were grounded in reality—hard science, mathematics. The history of our great country."

He gently placed the queen on the table beside him, then sat back in his chair. Aurora cleared her throat, then glanced up at him. He was looking at the fire.

"Father, I've read more than that. I have read Erasmus and I have read More. I am familiar with the physics of Archimedes, the mathematics of Pythagoras, and the astronomy of Aryabhata. I know the history of our family back a hundred years, and I have finished Luther's entire translation of the *Bible*." She offered meekly, "Is that not enough? What would you have me do?"

When her father responded, his voice was even softer now. She felt his retreat: guilt from her, and a hundred unknown sources, eating at him for never knowing which decision to make when it came to his daughter. In his rise in military power, he made decisions daily that affected the very lives of men. He could lead the country, given the chance. But when it came to a little twelve-year-old girl, he was nigh without an idea in his head. He turned his gaze to Aurora and said, "I have been interviewing tutors."

That explained the recent parade of strange visitors. She had assumed they were court associates; though, there had been too many female guests for Aurora's liking.

"But, Father—"

"I have finally selected one."

Aurora's first thought was her hope that it was not the young, pretty one. There oughtn't to be that kind of temptation walking around the house. "But, Father—"

"My men have captured Mitochian scouts at the northeastern border. I will be leaving again to survey the territory and plan. If they mean to enter up there, we will be prepared. While I am gone, it will not sit with me to have you at your leisure for more months still. Therefore, she shall be moving in for the duration of the winter, and will stay through the first thaw. It is then we will decide how we shall continue."

It was a curious use of the word, *we*. Aurora knew her father would not be perched at a cramped little desk right there next to her, reciting multiplication tables. "But, *Father*—"

"No, Aurora. I know all the creative arguments you've no doubt already concocted, and the answer to all of them is: It is done. She arrives this afternoon from the royal college. She comes with excellent credentials directly from the King. I will reexamine the situation after the thaw. Only then will I withstand my ears to any protestations from you, and I will warn you now you had better prepare a case solid enough for a court judge if you want me to consider other options."

"Yes, Father."

"I expect you in the classroom at dawn tomorrow."

"Father!"

"*Dawn*, Aurora. Opportunities multiply as they are seized. Learn to identify opportunities, for they are hidden from those who do not seek them. Do not be late for this opportunity."

Aurora murmured another objection under her breath.

"And I will not stand mumbling! I hope this new structure will put an end to your impertinence. I do not know if it is your age or your unfortunate lack of a mother or that you just have her rebellion seeded inside you. But I am going to do whatever it takes to weed it out!"

"Yes, Father."

"That is all, Lady Cavalcata."

He turned his eyes back to the fire as if she had already left.

Though bleary-eyed and choking back yawns that fateful morning, Aurora still recognized instantly that the new tutor was not the young applicant. Rather, presiding over a make-shift classroom in the east wing (far from both the kitchen and library) was a hunched eagle with a beak nose, white head, and talons that shredded through fish and books and little girls. Aurora pushed the door closed behind her and surveyed the trappings of the cell. The former storage room had been emptied of anything of interest. The only remaining furnishings were a large, important escritoire for the tutor, and a meager woodchip of a desk for herself. Books and papers were piled on the escritoire in precise stacks, like buildings in a town.

The eagle woman stood behind her desk, holding a long, whippy rod that protruded from her crossed arms. The way she squinted at Aurora, fans of crinkles radiating out from her eyes, she appeared in need of spectacles.

"Good morning, my lady. If you would, please take a seat."

"I prefer to stand." Aurora stepped into the room, clasping her hands behind her back. She was still wearing her sleeping tunic and had not tended to her night-ravaged hair, which sat atop her head like a bird's nest.

"Indeed." The tutor coughed nervously. "Then I shall begin. Our lessons will commence with that which is most pressing to the Fairgosian people. Can you guess to what I refer?"

"Candy." Aurora yawned broadly.

"If you are referring to the sugar shortage we are experiencing because Mitoch has cut off the major trade routes with Barlavia, you would be correct . . . somewhat. We will begin today's lesson with the war."

"What on earth could a woman have to teach me about war?" laughed Aurora. "Have you ever fought in a war? Have you ever seen a war? How do you know that war is not a toad, that it will not give you warts? My father is Royal War Master to the Fairgosian King and His Army. Why would you think I would need to learn about the war?"

The tutor clucked once, then opened her mouth to speak, but Aurora was already asking another question: "What has my father told you about me?"

She cleared her throat. "You'll be glad to know that he offered no fodder for prejudice. Now, if you will—"

"He didn't tell you that I'm a Tom? A disobedient wretch? He didn't tell you I break things on purpose and swim in a filthy river and ride with one leg on either side of the horse? He didn't tell you that you won't be able to teach me a thing and not to bother trying?"

"Of course he did not tell me such things. I would—"

"He told me about *you*. He told me you were his twenty-fifth choice and he only hired you because you're cheap and too stupid to know your own worth. He said you were skinny and we wouldn't have to feed you much. He said you were old and ugly, so he wouldn't have to worry about the stable boys fighting over you. He also told me to be nice to you, but I don't listen very well."

The tutor's brow lowered over her eyes, giving her an even more aquiline countenance. Suddenly, she whipped her switch downward. It whistled through the air and snapped atop the wood of the desk. "I will—"

"You will . . ." began Aurora, walking directly up to the tutor. She pried the switch from the woman's hand, then snapped it in two. ". . . not last until the thaw."

The woman blustered something incoherent then flew out of the room. Aurora smiled to herself and turned the splinters of switch over in her hands, giving the tutor some time to get out of the house before heading back to bed. But when she finally tried the door, she found it locked.

"Oh . . ." She knocked on the door. "Hello? Madam? You locked me in."

No reply. She turned back to the sparse room, frustrated at being foiled—but, even so, a bit impressed. Aurora did not have all the power after all. And right she shouldn't.

She sighed and collapsed into the chair behind the escritoire. From atop one stack of books, a glint of gold caught her eye. She snatched the book and read the emblazoned, illuminated title: *The King's Official History of Sangeva*. This wasn't a volume from her father's library; she'd read all but a few of those. This was something new. Sangeva was something new. She immediately began to read.

Hours later, Aurora felt a hand shaking her shoulder. She lifted her sleepy head from the desk and swiped at a rope of drool hanging from her lip. The tutor had returned, and she was eyeing the pool of saliva on the last page of her golden history book with a look of utter shock.

Abashed, Aurora said, "I am sorry if I ruined your book."

The tutor did not reply, her mouth hanging agape.

"I am really awfully sorry too that I broke your switch."

The woman's arched eyebrows strained toward her hairline.

"And I was quite cruel," Aurora said. "I am not accustomed to such structure, I know."

Shaking her head back and forth, the tutor said, "No . . . no. It is only . . . you finished that book?"

"Of course."

"The whole book?"

"I did not pore over all the maps. But neither did I skip any parts, if that's what you mean."

"That book is over three hundred pages long."

"It was very good."

The woman was struck speechless again.

"If everything you have to teach me is as fascinating as this, I do think we shall get on." Aurora began to search through the pile of books, scattering them all over the acre of desk. She lifted a copy of *Rhetoric* and held it up to the tutor. "This one next?"

When the thaw finally came, Lord Cavalcata summoned his daughter back into the library, which was not nearly so ominous this time. Aurora was prepared.

"Proposition," she said. Her father's eyes glittered with amusement, and Aurora stifled a grin. "It is in the best interest of the staff, yourself, and myself that I continue—in a *limited* way—under tutelage, during the winters only. I will prove this proposition with three premises of logic, culminating in a conclusion, after which I expect you will rule in my favor."

He did. Every time.

Secernere – Present

As he approached the chamber that housed the unwelcome woman, Storey saw Abern standing outside the door, clearly reluctant to go back inside. Knowing Abern had not yet seen him, Storey watched him for a moment. The old man was like a crystal ball's view of Storey's future self, he sometimes thought. The years at Secernere had passed by so slowly and yet so quickly, like when one walks down a long, straight path where the trees all look the same. One is aware of moving forward, and yet nothing changes. Storey felt the weight of time press him whenever he saw Abern, who himself had been stooped, crumpled, crushed by his long life tending to Secernere. Storey was Abern's successor in occupation; he worried that continued stagnation in this place would lead him to be successor in character as well. But it wasn't time yet. It wasn't time. *When would it be time?*

Storey puffed himself up, crowding the narrow corridor, and moved toward Abern. He could make himself look so powerful, on the exterior. The old man turned at the sound of a creaking floorboard, and cowed at Storey's approach.

"Mister Storey . . ."

How their roles had reversed. In old age, some men retreat toward childhood, growing smaller, weaker of will, ignorant. They relinquish their power in order to relax in the laze of irresponsibility as their lives near their end. This was Abern. Once a powerful man, a father's father to Storey and a mentor, he was now simply old. He had given up. As Storey had grown tall, grown broad, grown strong and wise, he had taken up the fallen reins as steward of Secernere, as the only one who cared much anymore.

"I beg of you, Abern," said Storey, restraining his words into a hush. "I cannot ask anyone else to go in there. No one can know about her, and she needs care."

"She will have so many questions." Abern shook his head sadly.

"I suppose we might answer some of them then—those that *can* be answered."

"I fear I may say something I should not."

"Then think long and hard about everything you *can* say before you go back in. Simply . . . calm her fears, Abern. I saw

46

her banging on the window yesterday. That simply cannot be. If Cashel returns early—"

The old man wheezed out a noise of exasperation, but nodded.

"Say no more. If Cashel returns early, I shall be as liable as you, and these bones need no whipping. I yet do not understand why I agreed in the first place."

A smile broke across Storey's face, and he clapped a large hand on Abern's protruding shoulder. The old man could yet be swayed, even in such a gamble as this.

"Because you know it is the right thing to do. We will get her on her way shortly. Simply . . . check on her. One face is all she needs to see. She'll be gone soon enough."

"It is too late for soon enough, Mr. Storey." He shook his head again. "It is too late."

❧ 5 ❧

Aurora woke to a bump outside her door. She froze, staring at the latch. There followed the sound of a key in the lock, the lift of the latch, and the slow creak of the door. Though she had tried to lull herself to sleep with pleasant memories of home, she had dreamt all night of being bound and beaten, enslaved in Nulle; her anxiety was freshly manifested in a quick pulse and moist brow. She knew not whether to yell, try to run out the door, or just remain calm. Wrapping her robe around herself, she stood and waited.

The gnarled man had returned, and he was bearing yet another silver platter, toppling over with food. A grim smile was smeared across his mouth; his eyes did not smile.

"Hello," Aurora said quietly. She wanted to scream and run for the door, but she held fast. Her father had told her that the most skilled warriors were those who could prevail without even a fight. She wanted no fight.

"Hello." His response was strained. He glanced about the room at the sheets all over the floor, and his gaze caught long on the slashed painting. Something distant and disturbing flashed across his face. He swallowed, but said nothing.

Aurora took a deep breath and forced a half-smile.

"Sir, I do beg your pardon and offer my apology." She clenched her robe and tried to look sincere. "I was frightened and confused." Her back teeth ground together.

The man set the tray on the bedside table then turned to face her; his manner seemed rehearsed. He sighed heavily, and the expulsion made something liquid burble in his throat. He cleared his throat and displayed his own half-smile.

"I appreciate the kindness, m'lady, but I am no sir. I am called Abern." His craggy face had softened in the smallest way. He gestured to the bed. "Please, m'lady, you oughtn't to be up and moving about."

Aurora remained standing. She was taller than he, and she knew it made her seem more powerful than she felt. They were having a dance, she and this man. If she made the right steps, maybe she could get the information she needed.

"Mister Abern, sir, I do beg of you, tell me why I have been locked in this room?"

"Please, m'lady, if you will not return to bed, please sit, at the least. You should eat something. . . . I have boiled kid and soft cheese."

She continued to stare at the man, feeling the sincerity on her face melt away. *Answer me.*

"What place is this?" she asked, this time more firmly.

"An exotic pomegranate as well," Abern replied. "I hope it is to your liking."

Abern picked up the empty silver tray from the previous meal and handed it to someone just outside. He made to continue this game of hospitality. She could play along until he was ready to talk. She obliged him and perched precariously on the edge of the mattress, the farthest from Abern as she could. His demeanor had changed substantially, she recognized this. But he was still a stranger—still a man in her chamber—and still the bearer of the key that kept her locked here.

Abern sat in the chair near the bed, crossed one leg over the other, and knitted his fingers together in his lap. He looked down at the floor for a few seconds, then took a deep breath and launched into a monologue without once looking directly at her eyes.

"M'lady, you must know that you are a stranger to us, and though it appears you would do us no harm, it was simply not the safe choice to let you roam wherever you wished on our manor, not in this time of war. I beg your understanding, and I beg it on behalf of my master. We are quite the skeletal household. We cannot afford the staff to have someone watching over you constantly, so we required the security of knowing you are in this room.

"Moreover, we were worried that, in your state, you could possibly be confused, and therefore would become lost in this unfamiliar manor. We were keeping wary of your own benefit, as well as ours. It is important to us that you heal and become well so that you may return to your home, and my master thought the best to keep you in a room with the many comforts of a large bed and delicious food that would promote your health." He paused, squinted his eyes, then finished: "I beg your understanding, m'lady. We were only trying to help."

Aurora began to speak, but Abern held up one finger to quiet her. He was a curious, effeminate man, the likes of whom Aurora had never met. He was silent for a moment and closed his eyes as if trying to find words at the tip of his tongue, then began to speak again, rapidly.

"Also, there are curious minds around the premises who might like to peek in on such a beautiful young woman as yourself, and we only wanted to be sure of protecting your modesty. I beg your understanding, m'lady. We only want to help."

Abern sank backward into his chair, exhausted. Aurora waited in case he remembered more of his speech.

"M'lady?" Abern prompted after a time.

"My apologies, sir," she finally replied. "I seem unable to find the right words."

She cleared her throat and looked around the room, her eyes falling on the milky blue eyes of the portrait. She half-coughed. As much as she wanted to protest further, his three points were inarguable. *Well done.* But it was apparent he would answer questions, so long as she remained polite.

"Sir, pardon if this be impropriety, but why . . . I mean . . . Sir, this be no offense to you, but . . . I am unaccustomed to the bedside servitude of . . . someone such as yourself. . . . Was there no lady in the house to serve as nursemaid?"

At this, Abern expelled a phlegmy laugh that turned into a cough. He caught his breath and looked back at her, his eyes twinkling.

"One does forget what it's like to have a woman in the house. My every, every apology, m'lady. No, there are no women in the house at this time." He laughed again, but was quick to stifle it. "No, indeed. I am quite the only person here equipped to care for the injured or ill. Please, I assure you, there has been no impropriety; we just do things differently at Secernere."

Aurora did not understand how he could claim there had been no impropriety when clearly there had. She reminded herself that she had more questions to be answered—and that she was lucky to be alive. Arguing the point he made so lightly would not serve her.

"I am unfamiliar with any manor called Secernere. What family lives here?"

"Oh, it is but the master, Lord Gomery. His only family are we, his staff."

Aurora felt her heart leap in her chest. An unbidden and immediate kinship with Lord Gomery, whoever he was, bounded up within her. They were two of the same, the last of a family name. Alone.

"If there are no women here," Aurora said, "who cares for the little girl?"

"The little girl?" Abern looked at her quizzically.

"Oh yes, the one who came to visit me yesterday. Odd little thing. She could stand to eat some of the food you bring me."

Abern narrowed his eyes, tilting his head to the side in an almost imperceptible way. "How does your head feel this morning, m'lady?"

Aurora reached toward her bandages.

"It must have been a dream, then." She forced a little laugh. "How strange I must sound. I do feel quite well."

Lurching to the bedside table, Abern prepared a small plate of food and handed it to Aurora. She accepted, slowly chewed a shred of meat, and he returned to his seat.

"If I may be so bold," he began, "all these words, and still I know all but nothing about m'lady. Who is your family?"

The question stung. The true answer was that she had no family, not anymore.

"I'm the Lady of—of the Venclova family. We keep the Peregrine Manor, just a ways up the Aurora River." She made the decision to lie without any reason or forethought. She could always play forgetful later, blame the bump to her head. For now, she was not yet sure of what identity would serve her best.

"The Aurora River. I know it not."

Aurora returned Abern's look of perplexity. "The Aurora River? It must flow right through your land." Abern continued to stare blankly. "It's where I was found yesterday."

Abern shook his head. "Four days have passed since we found you—at the Calder River. M'lady, perhaps I will take my leave so you can rest. . . ." He stood.

Aurora stood, too. A tightness stiffened her entire body. "Where am I?"

"M'lady . . ."

"Where am I?" Her attempted propriety was strained now, cracking. "What country is this?"

"Mitoch, of course."

Mitoch. She forced herself to count to five with each breath in and each breath out. It was essential she maintain every appearance of calm.

"Ah, Mitoch," she sighed. "I feared for a moment I had landed in Fairgos." She forced a smile onto her face and sat again, though her back remained rigid. Her head threatened to spin right off her body.

"Oh no, m'lady, you're certainly not in that awful place. We're very far from the border. The Calder River will only take you north, toward Ekanta. Though if that is your destination, I recommend a boat for your next trip." Abern winked a crinkled pink eyelid.

There was no dance now. Aurora was in a different ballroom entirely.

"I really do think I should rest now, sir, if you would be so kind."

"Indeed, m'lady. Just one last question, one of total impropriety, if I may be so bold."

"Of course," Aurora replied absently.

"Your name? Your given name? I am but a curious old cat."

"Oh . . . my name. Inna." It was her mother's name. And it would now be hers. Even if Abern did not know the Aurora River, someone would. The name Aurora was certain danger in this place. "I am Lady Inna of Venclova."

And so saying, she was. Aurora felt something shift inside her. There was no going back—there was a new truth to live. She felt completely electrified, every piece of her brain sparking and sizzling. Her wits would be everything as she stepped into this role and moved forward into known and unknown danger. She inhaled deeply and gripped her dressing gown.

"Mister Abern, sir, I beg your pardon, but I do not feel it is prudent for me to share with you all the circumstances that brought me to your estate, especially while our country is at war." Near the door now, the man nodded, and Aurora continued. "I must request an audience with Lord Gomery."

"Of course, m'lady. As soon as you are well enough."

"I am well enough *now*," Aurora said.

Abern, quietly stunned, attempted a small smile.

"M'lady, please eat your meal. It will give you strength. I will return soon, and we shall see what we can do about removing that bandage, if you'll allow, and getting you suited for a meeting with Lord Gomery." He lifted the latch and opened the door. "He will be returning in a few days."

"My thanks, Abern. My thanks. Oh, and one more question. Who was that man who rescued me? I would like to thank him in person. . . ."

But Abern was already gone, and Aurora heard the lock click shut once more.

Storey sat cross-legged in the middle of the floor, mumbling prayers to himself. His quarters were small, austere, even for a servant. Standing, he could touch two opposite walls at once. But this room was his. It had heard his every chanted prayer, seen every tear he'd shed in frustration, fear, and anger. It was his womb, his armor. No one could penetrate this room any more than they could get inside his head.

He had almost no personal belongings, save his clothes. A pencil sketch of his mother, the way he remembered her from twelve years ago, was tacked to the wall above his pillow. It did not much look like her, but it felt like her.

His eyelids were closed most of the way, but fluttered, letting in bits of light.

"I must look into myself without seeing myself. I will only understand the teaching if I find it within."

The floor was hard beneath him and he grew sore of sitting, but he tried to let go of the pain; the pain was the self.

"I will be serene in the midst of my own sorrow. Then, no Evil can enter my heart."

His back felt stiff. He willed the ache to melt away.

"Whoever can see through all fear will always be safe. There is no greater illusion than fear. There is no greater wrong than to be defensive. There is no greater misfortune than having an enemy."

This last was the hardest. *No greater misfortune than having an enemy.* If an enemy was a friend, was he then fortune? Did he cease to be enemy? What if enemy is caretaker, provider? What if enemy is brother?

"Whoever can see through all fear will always be safe. Whoever—"

Abern's gait was thumping down the hall. Storey quieted himself, slowly opening his eyes. As the steps came toward his door, he stepped out of his room and caught Abern by the shoulder.

The old man gasped and wobbled a bit on his feet, nearly toppling backward.

"Mister Storey! Have you no instinct as to the age of my heart? You'll soon have to feed Lady Venclova with your own hand."

"*Lady* Venclova? She is nobility?"

"And then some."

"My God, Abern. What have we gotten into?"

" 'We,' Mister Storey?" Abern removed Storey's hand from his shoulder.

"I should have just sent her back down the river." Storey folded his arms across his broad chest and took two paces up the hallway, staring down at the planks of hardwood in the floor. Why had he not acted? Why could he not rend the mind from the heart, when it was necessary to do so? To bring this woman into Secernere had not only jeopardized her safety, but theirs as well, all of them. To have let her stay this long was madness.

"The opportunity has not passed entirely, Mister Storey."

Storey looked up and saw Abern's glazed eyes staring straight into his. He nodded. Sometimes the impetus of another's petition was called for, and Storey would not ignore it.

❧ 6 ❧

The revelation that she was in Mitoch refreshed the devastation of Aurora's circumstance. Whether or not she desired to return to her empty Cathendria, it was now an outright impossibility. Merely requesting Fairgos as a destination would raise unanswerable questions. Even if she could secure some kind of unscrupulous travel, for which—despite her wealth—she had no currency, there would be no way to cross the border without being discovered. She was likely only able to cross in the first place because she appeared to be already dead. Thinking of what she must have looked like, bloodied, bruised, nearly naked, and almost dead, floating by drunken border guards who did not even notice her, let alone know who she was—the thought was disgusting.

The border crossing at the river was held by the Fairgosian army; the enemy soldiers had been pushed back beyond a canyon that cut through Mitoch at its southernmost point. That much, she knew. It was almost all she knew. She cursed her incomplete knowledge of the war, cursed all that had been withheld from her. Lord Cavalcata had balked at the idea of his daughter studying the subject, even after she so carefully presented the syllabus.

"The intricacies of war politics will not serve the needs of a woman's education," he had said to Aurora. To the tutor, he warned, "I am making it perfectly clear that I forbid Lady Cavalcata's study of the war. She may study what books you have regarding Mitoch and I believe she will draw clear conclusions."

The tutor, submissive to the Lord's ruling, withheld any education on the war. But knowingly or not, she did not remove any of her volumes from the manor. Aurora scrutinized every history and geography book the tutor provided from the Royal Library, trying to glean pieces of information that would help her understand what she really wanted to know. The books fully illuminated the nation of Mitoch and every issue that caused its strife with Fairgos. She even read a copy of the King's enlightening *Declaration of War*. She remembered, always remembered, the beginning: "I am a new leader in an old country."

I am a new leader in an old country. It is incumbent upon me to pay diligence to Fairgos' peaceful history and to respect the honorable efforts of the former regime. But as well, it is my duty above all else to protect Fairgos from threats not invited by our nation. I have sworn the oath.

The current plays of Mitoch have overcome the final strains of indecision. Peaceful efforts to repair the torn moral fabric of their ideology have failed, again and again. I will now lead us toward action before the risk of inaction becomes the downfall of our nation.

But this war had lasted many years. There was more to the

story. Inaction was the downfall of any nation, peaceful and violent alike. There was a *why* that wasn't written in any document. The politicians and the militants alike spoke and wrote in such grandiose metaphor, vacant idiom, that it was almost impossible to translate anything more substantial than "Faigos: good. Mitoch: bad." Somewhere, there was a humanity to this war the impelled Fairgosian men to continue taking up arms. And Aurora wanted to understand it.

She bristled at the constraint on her education and bore her grudge hard. She and her father had agreed on the terms of her tutelage; this ban was not part of the deal.

And so she had studied in secret, pilfering what books, letters, and documents she could. Despite what she assembled from these sources, most of her knowledge about the Mitoch War, and the men who waged it, came from a particularly informative eavesdropping session.

Cathendria was holding a banquet. It was of a type that would kill old Cook if it occurred today. Over thirty guests attended, members of her father's council and their respective wives. For each of five courses, there were over thirty different dishes for the guests to sample. A servant stood in the shadows behind the chair of every person at the table. Sixteen-year-old Aurora, as lady of the manor in the absence of her mother, had a place at the foot of table, a social anomaly that gossip would ignore in the shadow of her father's station.

The last course served, Lord Cavalcata stood and pounded his goblet against the table in a percussive rhythm. Idle and profound chatter alike fell into silence, and all attention turned to the man at the head of the table. With his black hair and olive skin, the epitome of pure Fairgosian blood, with his imposing stature, and cave-deep voice, Lord Cavalcata was every bit a king holding court.

"I would first offer my thanks to my cook, the greatest magician of food Fairgos has ever seen. We would not be such a skinny people if all had such wonderful help in the kitchen."

The guests pounded their forks and goblets and fists atop the table in applause. Cook, who had been waiting in a shadowy corner, bowed her head low in humility. Aurora caught the smile that toyed with the corner of her mouth.

"I would second offer my thanks to the beautiful women in this room, to be so generous as to provide me with these men, these greatest minds in the nation, who will, in this coming retreat, work together to form the greatest strategy war has known—that which will win the greatest and most horrible war our nation has ever fought."

A second, greater wave of applause rose from the audience.

"And I would third and finally offer my thanks to Mitoch."

Hisses and boos throughout the room echoed on the high walls. Aurora's father pounded his goblet and regained control.

"Hear me out, ye soldiers of the mind! Were Mitoch not to strike at us, to endeavor to undermine the very fabric of our government and society, were Mitoch not to challenge the means by which we protect the lives and futures of our wives and sons and daughters—" at this, he looked straight at Aurora—"we might not have had the chance to prove that Fairgos has always been, and always will be, the greatest nation in the world!"

At this, the whole of the room rose to their feet, shouting, clanging flatware, banging dishes and goblets. Even Cook, still in her corner, could be seen clapping her fat hands together. Aurora rose like the others, but her continued lack of understanding palliated her excitement, even at her father's most poignant speechifying.

Lord Cavalcata raised his goblet to each man in turn, beaming in happiness, glory, and camaraderie. Every man returned the emotion and gesture, though each was merely a pale reflection of her father's greatness.

"I would take this opportunity to invite you, gentlemen, to retire with me to the library. My fairer guests, Aurora will show you to the parlor for dessert and digestif."

This was the first Aurora had heard of her duties. She threw a dark glance at Cook, who only shrugged. Lord Cavalcata's gaze avoided Aurora's eyes, and he was gone from the room without another word. At once the central focus of fifteen pairs of heavily made-up eyes, Aurora forced an ingratiating smile and led the way to the parlor.

A woman lightly took Aurora's arm along the way. "What it must be like to be Lord Cavalcata's daughter!"

Aurora only smiled.

Cake and brandy were waiting, and the guests did not hesitate. Without taking any for herself, Aurora made straight for the harpsichord. She took a place on the bench, opened the cover, and began to play the only tune she knew by memory. She played it as if she'd written it.

Her mind drifted as the melody began to haunt the room. The piece was written by an Fairgosian priest with whom Lord Cavalcata boarded for several weeks while traveling in the West. He presented Aurora with the sheet music as a gift, as he often brought her gifts after he was away for long stretches. As the war intensified and his absences grew longer, he ceased bringing her presents; rather, he would send them. This hurt the most, because she could not see the joyful anticipation in his eyes as he watched her open the packages. Once, when he had been gone for over eight months, she stopped opening the packages entirely. Instead, she stacked them in a room to see just how high the tower would reach. It did not make it to the ceiling, but it came close.

She found herself pounding at the keys as she played and willed herself to calm.

When she finished the last strains of the Western melody, the room had hushed and women held half-drunk snifters of brandy in their still hands. After a few moments, one woman began to clap quietly and was soon joined by the rest of the audience. Aurora bowed her head graciously.

Lady Winifred of Kerala was the first to speak. "My, Lady Cavalcata, what a talent to have!"

"My thanks, Lady Kerala." Aurora bowed again. Winifred had responded exactly as planned. "It is my understanding that you are a musical one as well."

"Oh . . ." Winifred batted her eyelashes and shrugged her shoulders. "I don't speak about it on regular occasion. . . ."

"But you do sing, do you not?"

"We all know we are forbidden from singing in church. . . ."

Aurora rose from her bench and lightly placed her hand on Winifred's shoulder, giving the woman a subtle wink. "There are no men here. Your secret is safe. It would honor all of us so much to hear you sing a hymn in His name."

"I could never . . ." Winifred was blushing and shaking her head. Aurora was gently pushing just enough to turn her to face the other women in the room.

"Oh, please do!" piped up a voice from the back.

"Would you?" came another.

"Lady Kerala, we've heard so much of your angelic voice!"

"Well, I suppose . . . if it is in His name."

Winifred began to sing, and Aurora was already backing out of the room, unnoticed and profoundly relieved.

She slipped her shoes off her feet and scooped them up into her hand. Her shoulder brushing the wall as she walked, she made her silent way along the corridors to the library. The main entrance was closed up tight, but Aurora kept moving to another door. This one opened onto another narrow corridor that ran parallel to the library. Halfway down this dark hallway was the library service entrance, which allowed servants to stealthily exchange glasses and empty plates as the guests went about their business. Aurora lifted the latch with careful, practiced precision, and opened the entrance door several inches. Conversation punctuated with laughs and hurrahs poured out of the opening. She peeked inside and confirmed that she saw only backs. She was unseen, but could hear their voices clearly;

it was the most perfect eavesdropping location she had discovered in the house.

As in the dining hall, conversation subsided when Lord Cavalcata stood and took command. Aurora slid down the wall until she was seated on the floor beside the ajar door, listening, but not looking.

"My friends," he began, "I desire once again to welcome you warmly to my home. I know many of you traveled a great distance to meet here today, while also subjecting your wives to the discomforts of long carriage rides and strange beds." Chuckles reverberated throughout the crowd. "I hazard that some of you rather enjoy an excuse to get your wives into a strange bed."

The chuckles became honest guffaws, and the tension dissipated entirely.

"Though an uncommon practice, I felt the necessity to invite each of your wives along to this retreat in an effort to demonstrate how much we care for them and their roles in our lives. They are not to be relegated merely to the home life! They are our partners. They feed us when we are hungry. They nurse us when we are sick. They tell us jokes when we are melancholy. Without our wives, are we men at all?

"As most of you know, I lost my own wife many years ago. Despite my lack of an heir, I have chosen not to remarry, because I believe there could be no replacement for my Inna, and I do not make a habit of vain pursuits. Besides that, the search for a quality woman would take too much time from the most important matters of our nation, on which I must focus my attention."

Aurora held her breath. She had never heard her father speak so intimately.

"I feel the empty space left by Inna every day. My love for her and my love for my daughter are the driving forces in my life, and the very reason I feel so strongly about this war effort. We *must* protect our way of life from those who would destroy the very moral fabric of our family and society.

"The Mitochian people have no reverence for family. The very power structure of their government is a frightening aberration in the eyes of God. What they do not understand is how much we love and respect every woman in this nation, and the powerful role our wives and daughters have. They would send their daughters to fight and to *die!* What kind of people is this? Are they people at all?" Hisses and hushed assent whispered through the audience. "Do we want to see the day when we send *our* daughters to war?"

"No!" came the choral reply.

"No!" repeated Lord Cavalcata. "And that, my gentlemen, *that* is the reason we send our sons and brothers to fight. *That* is why we meet tonight. It is not enough that the fighting stop, though the bloodshed has cost both sides dearly. Nay, our mission is a higher call: we must enlighten backward Mitoch to a new system: a system that has been proven to serve both citizens and leaders toward progress; a system thar leans on the lessons taught to us by God; a system that leverages our natures and strengths and humanness, *both* masculine and feminine—the *Fairgosian* system of rule.

"We must aid Mitoch so that they may thrive in these modern times. We must seize this opportunity. Opportunities multiply as they are seized! In this neighboring country of ours, we may find an eventual ally, and a bountiful trading partner. Perhaps—dare I say—unity after 500 years is possible. But most importantly, we must once and for all find a way to put a stop to the influence Mitoch would have over the easily swayed citizens of our country.

"My friends, we will accomplish all of this and more. We *will* win this war, and we *will* make the world a better place."

The crowd erupted with shouts and applause.

Over the din, Aurora's father raised his voice once more: "At dawn, we begin."

Secernere – Present

Despite an appetite that had evaporated, Aurora forced herself to eat the provided food. Abern was right: she needed her strength—especially with what she had gotten herself into now. The rich velvet of the couch, the juicy pomegranate on her tray, the surprisingly banal conversation with the old man, these had almost made her forget where she was. Request an audience with Lord Gomery? Had she really bumped her head that hard?

Mitochian nobles, she knew, were primitive beasts. It was insanity to think she could put her fate into the hands of someone like that. It was a misstep on her part to think for even a second that they were as humane, as human, as she.

In the remote possibility he was an educated man, someone with couth, could she carry on a lie to his face? Her father had never stood for lies. Even if he were a complete dunce, Lord Gomery would know there was no such Mitoch family as the Venclovas. She had plucked the name from a fairy tale. Chances were greater that he'd read the self-same story than that there existed an actual family of Venclovas into which Aurora could believably insert herself.

She sighed in frustrated defeat. Delivering an entreaty to Lord Gomery in person was her only hope in the face of dark alternatives. Either she found a way to stay at Secernere until it was safe to cross back into Fairgos, or she took her chances finding a brief means to life in a Mitochian town. With all her books' worth of knowledge, her head might as well have been empty. If she didn't know where she was, she had no notion of the closest town, somewhere she could find food, shelter, even work. With no real name, no wealth, with her tan skin and thin arms, she would be taken for no more than a commoner—and there was nothing lower than a common woman. She suppressed the thought that the only paid work she might find would be in a brothel.

Biting into another piece of kid, which at first taste had been delightful but which now was nothing more than wet leather, she began to plan her appeal. Would logic work on a Mitochian? Perhaps she could rely on sympathy. She would be Inna of Venclova. The lie she'd already told would be just as good or terrible as the lie she hadn't yet made up. Her parents . . . what could she say about her parents? Prisoners of war? Victims of mountain piracy? Somehow, they would have to be gone, dead, so no one would look for them.

But how? To garner the sympathy she needed, it would have to be violent and sensational. Her father really had died a violent and sensational death. Though, he could have died in his sleep and it would have seemed just as horrific. Aurora remembered it happening just the night before last, but Abern had revealed that it was actually four days ago. The sting was still sharp and the wound felt even fresher than those on her body.

She shook the thought from her mind. She did not have the luxury of time for grief. Neither could she afford indecisiveness, not when the occasion so strongly called for a choice to be made, a choice to be adhered to at any cost. She had requested audience with Lord Gomery. No matter who he was, she needed his help and there was nothing to be changed about that circumstance. The result of their conference, whatever it was, would be her fate.

❧ 7 ❧

Waiting for Abern's return with news of Lord Gomery (for what else had she to do but wait), two thoughts occurred to Aurora in the wake of learning she had been found not one, but four days earlier.

First, Kynton would have returned to the estate and found her missing. He served in the Army, and Aurora knew there were certain arts in which he would have been trained. She knew also, even from their brief and intense interaction, that he was intelligent and compassionate. Her disappearance would not have left him unaffected. She wondered what course he would take. The servants gone, he would have been free to search the manor for her. He'd probably have discovered that no horses or equipment were gone from the stable. He might even have tracked her to the river. But dejection dawned on her: even if he gotten as far as the river, the trail would have died there.

Second, she realized it was her birthday.

She was twenty-one today—marriage age. In an ordinary

life, this day would have been extraordinary. Fairgosian noble-women were married much later in life than their common counterparts, whose poverty necessitated the early bearing of worker-children. This was a day of fantasy, anticipated and idealized by privileged women who waited for over two decades, not without impatience, to be freed from their families and enter new bonds with husbands.

For Aurora, it was the day for which her father had promised to return home, but hadn't.

A birthday. What did she expect, a cake? It occurred to her with bitter amusement that Lady Inna of Venclova might not even have the same birthday. Then upon reflection, Aurora realized that she did indeed share the day with her new persona, who had just been brought into the world.

"Happy birthday, Lady Venclova," she mumbled. "Why thank you, Lady Cavalcata. Happy birthday to you as well."

In the stove-hot Secernere kitchen, Storey leaned forward against a wooden table, clasping his hands together with force enough to cramp his knuckles. His hands held each other back from throwing the crockery around, or worse, trying to choke the old man. He did not look up as he spoke. "Allow me to summarize."

"Mister Storey—"

"No, please, Abern. Indulge me."

Abern was hunched over the table as well, but only because his ancient back would not allow him to sit upright. His balding head, however, was bowed in ignominy, and beaded with sweat.

"This woman, who told you she comes from a manor of which neither you *nor* I have any recollection, requested an audience with Cashel."

"Yes, sir."

Storey knotted his fingers even more forcefully, and lightly closed his eyes. He enunciated his next words with measured intensity. "And . . . you . . . told . . . her . . . *yes.*"

Abern remained silent.

"And *you told her yes.*"

"Yes, sir." Abern's wet voice was nearly inaudible.

Storey slammed his palms flat against the table. Abern jumped at the noise, but did not look up. "For God's sake, Abern!"

"A thousand apologies, Mister Storey. She seemed so frightened and confused. I thought such assent would calm her. We do not have to fulfill her wish. . . ."

"Obviously, Abern!" Standing, Storey rubbed his eyes and paced the width of the room. "All things considered, it matters not."

He continued to pace, the heavy tread of his boots punctuating the discordant music of Abern's wheezing lungs. That she had spoken, conversed with Abern, that she had made a request, one at once so plainly reasonable and patently impossible, that Abern had sought to ease her anxiety and comfort her confusion, these made her seem more real, more human than Storey had been prepared for. She could not be a person. She was not a person. She was to be an object, a parcel on a stopover at Secernere that was ultimately to be delivered elsewhere.

She was rubbish to be turned out. Rubbish could not merely sit in a place and be ignored. With time, it would grow rank. It would stink up the room, seep into the floor, become a bigger problem that was not so easily cleaned up. She had to be turned out.

Aloud, he spoke to Abern: "Is she well enough?"

"Well enough for what, sir?" Abern looked up.

"I don't know. Well enough . . . to be on her own?"

"On her own, sir?"

"Would you have us continue to care for her? How long do

you think she can remain undetected once Cashel returns? She is not our problem."

"She has been our problem since you brought her up from the river."

Storey placed his palms flat on the table and stared at the old crooked man sitting across from him. He swallowed hard. *Rubbish.*

"Then I suppose it is my duty to remedy the situation once and for all."

Some hours later, as Aurora stared out the window, she heard the bedroom door being unlocked again. She turned to greet Abern, but instead found herself flying to the bed to snatch the comforter up in front of her body as a young man came through the doorway.

She gasped, and at first found she had nothing to say and could only stare in aroused fright. Every hair on her body stood perpendicular to her skin, electrified. Her mouth fell dry. This man looked strong, virile, at the peak of his life. He was someone who could swallow her up, and for a second, as she stared into the deep green pools of his flashing eyes, she felt she could allow him that.

She sputtered at him: "You too would enter a lady's chamber without even knocking? What kind of place is this?"

The man did not turn away and he did not leave. Glancing around, he said, "You've been redecorating." He shut the door behind him and locked it from the inside.

"I'll scream."

The man smiled slightly. "Why would you scream?"

Aurora felt ultimately vulnerable, naked. Her skin was searing. She pulled the comforter farther up on her chest, casting a brief and bitter glance toward the locked wardrobe that likely held something to cover her better than this flimsy smock.

"What do you want with me? I'm stronger than I look."

The man continued to stare at her, bemused. His clothes were dirty and ragged, common. Though youthful, his skin had the weathered look of outdoor labor. This was not Lord Gomery. Slung across his right shoulder was a large grain sack. A frayed end of rope stuck out from the closure.

"I swear to you, I will scream." She retreated a step. The air between them seemed to push insistently against her. "What do you want from me?"

"You do not recognize me? Lady, I am hurt."

"I recognize nothing about this place. I do, however, recognize that you are a strange man entering a lady's bedchamber, and you have locked the door behind you."

Aurora felt her breath quicken. Even if she did scream, was there anyone to hear her? Would they even care? Would she really even scream?

"Abern has a key, and he shall return any minute," she pressed. No explanation from Abern made the threat from this new man, this broad-shouldered, thick-armed farm hand, any less terrifying. Was this someone Abern was trying to lock out?

"This key?" The man dangled a long iron skeleton key in front of his face. "You think *Abern* would be able to rescue from whatever sordid fantasy you're imagining I'm going to act out?"

Aurora bristled, coughed. For a moment, she felt caught, as if he could see directly into her. "*Fantasy?* Who on earth do you think you are!"

She retreated another step and found herself backed up against the wall, fumbling with the comforter as she tried to retain her balance.

"Around here, I am called Storey, but you can call me the man who saved you from drowning in your own vomit when you washed up on the shore of the Calder River four days ago. I believe you *requested* my presence?"

70

Mortified, Aurora clenched the comforter around her body and fought the bloom rising in her cheeks.

"You seem to be nearly naked every time I show up."

Aurora opened her mouth to speak, but shut it again without a word. She closed her eyes and took a slow breath in an effort to calm herself. "I beg your pardon, Mister—"

"Simply Storey will be suitable. No pardon necessary, but I will take a thank you."

Again ashamed and offended, Aurora had to rein in another snappish retort. "Thank you," she whispered. "I . . . I would reward you, if I were in circumstances to do so."

The man's face seemed to go dark for a moment, but then returned to its state of bemusement.

"Lady, I promise you, I am not deserving of any reward."

He flopped the sack to the floor.

"I am paying you visit today because we two need to have a conversation. The way I have planned it, I am going to say a few words, and you are going to agree with them, and then we shall be finished. Now, look at you backed up against the wall like some cornered animal. Would you like to take a seat so we can talk like civilized folk?"

Aurora eyed him, but did not move.

"Look, you sit on the couch, and I'll sit way over here." He motioned at the green sofa nearly on the other side of the room and sat himself in the hard-backed chair next to the bed. "You've so conveniently uncovered all the furniture, it would be a pity not to make use of it."

Keeping her back pressed against the wall and the man within her sights, Aurora dragged the comforter off the bed as she slinked toward the couch. Nearing it, she took three quick strides and dropped down. She wrapped the comforter around her body like a shield, already feeling the sweat start to make her body sticky. But she did not dare let it fall, even a little.

The man made to sit, then in one fluid movement, grabbed the chair, placed it directly in front of her, and sat, his face less than a foot from hers. She could smell his hot breath. It at once repulsed and attracted her, like pungent, roasting meat. She instinctively backed up on the couch as far as she could. This man was the very beast she had feared. A true Mitochian animal.

"These are my few words," he began in low, hushed tones with startling intensity. "I do not know who you are. Even if you told me, I'm fairly sure it would be lies, and frankly, it matters not. The very crux of this matter is that you do not belong here."

She studied him and recognized that he was not mocking her; his statement was more advice than dismissal.

"Now, you agree," he said.

"Yes, I agree that I do not belong here."

"Wonderful. Now, I shall go on."

"If I don't belong here, why have you locked me up like a prisoner?"

"Sorry, Lady, that's not part of the conversation. The next part of the conversation is this: you are going to leave. Now, agree."

"I cannot."

The man expelled a wry laugh. "You would *stay*?"

"I cannot leave, because I haven't anywhere to go."

"Your logic is backwards, Lady. The truth is, you haven't anywhere to *stay*, and therefore, go you must."

"Please . . . *sir*. I must have audience with Lord Gomery. Has he yet returned?"

"An unfortunate thing, but Abern's assent to your 'audience,' as you call it, was mistaken. You will not be afforded a meeting with Lord Gomery, and *you must leave*."

"Please . . ." Aurora searched the man's face. His emerald green eyes were hooded in black fringe. It looked soft as mink. His voice was angry, but those eyes were concerned, protective. She was sure that her entrée was through his sympathies rather than logic. "I haven't anywhere to go. You are the only one who can help me. Please, let us continue to talk and you will see . . ."

She trailed off, examining his expression for evidence he was softening further. He gripped the sides of the chair for a moment as a dark, pained shadow crossed his face. In a flash it was gone.

"Very well. I can see that you will not participate in your assigned script, in which you agree with what I say. In that event, the second plan is called for." His face was hard again, and he was standing.

"Second plan?"

The man was at the grain sack, crouching down in front of it. Aurora tensed.

"How are you feeling today, Lady?"

"Feeling?" She hiccupped as her breath caught in her throat.

"Are you well?"

She hesitated. Where was he going with this? "I am well enough. . . ."

When he stood again, he was holding the length of rope in his hand. "Wonderful news, that. You should be fine."

Aurora jumped to her feet, leaving the comforter to fall to the floor. She pressed herself against the wall. The man stood between her and the door. The window was locked. There was nowhere to run.

"I don't understand. What do you want from me?" The muscles all over her body began to ache simply from the effort it took not to shake with fear.

"Want, need, force. What is the difference really? With *want*, I require your assent to fulfill my desire. With *need*, I still require your assent, merely with more urgency. With *force*, I do not require your assent." He took a step toward her.

"No, please!"

Another step.

"Help!" She screamed as loud as her voice would allow. "Help me! Help!"

Her shout deteriorated into a broken sob, and the man was upon her.

❧ 8 ❧

Aurora woke with the feeling of weightlessness, like she was flying or floating.

Then her body slammed down, and she pressed out a grunt like a squeezed pair of bellows. She was blind—blindfolded. She was stomach-down across a horse's back, and there was a body, the rider—that man, Storey, it must be—behind her. Her hands were tied in front of her. She was not gagged, but she did not bother to scream.

"Oh!" Storey called out above the drone of horse hooves on the hard ground. "You are awake! My apologies—I'd hoped to knock you cold for the duration of the trip."

"You are a bastard," she hissed.

"What?" he called.

She contracted her abdominal muscles to lift her head up farther. "You are a bastard!" she yelled.

"Lady, you have no idea."

They continued to gallop along, the three of them, and with each bump, Aurora felt her ribs would crack like chicken bones. However she was bound, though, it was securely, and she had no fear (or hope) of falling from the horse.

"Don't worry, we are soon there!" Storey called.

It was not soon, but the horse did finally slow to a stop, and Storey dismounted. Undoing some of her bindings, he grabbed her by the waist and gently lowered her to the ground. She took an awkward blind step, then spun at the sound of a twig snapping behind her. She heard the man laugh and turned toward his voice, but her toe caught under a tree root and she fell hard to the ground. Her hands still bound, she crashed onto her hip.

"A thousand apologies, m'lady," Storey said. He took her by the shoulders and helped her to her feet, then peeled away her blindfold. Aurora squinted as her pupils contracted in the dim, filtered light. They were in a forest. She spun and looked in every direction for something familiar—a path, the river—but found nothing except an army of soaring trees, vertical as fence posts. She looked at Storey, who was winding rope around his forearm, seemingly oblivious to his hostage just yards away.

"Where are we?" she asked, her voice husky.

"Wrong question!" Storey proclaimed, concentrating now on his saddle. "But I am happy you brought it up. Correct question: Where are we not? Correct answer: We are not at Secernere!" His pronouncement seemed to please him immensely. "Far away from Secernere we are! But not so far that I cannot arrive back before the sun goes down."

"You mean to leave me here?"

"It's funny that you mention leaving. *You* are doing the leaving, not me. In fact, you have already left!" He looked directly at her and made a small bow. "I thank you, dear Lady."

"You are a mad man." She seethed, berating herself for allowing even the tiniest vacillation in her judgment of the Mitochian people. "You are the worst sort of villain, a caricature of how the world views this country."

"On the contrary, I am a man of quick decision and sober

action. I should make a sound queen someday." He chuckled at his own confounding joke, then threw his sack to Aurora's feet. "Food. Also, a knife is within. I trust you'll have dexterity enough to reach it not long after I am gone, to cut yourself free and kill whatever woodland creatures strike your mealtime fancy."

Aurora stepped toward him. "Please. My name . . . is Inna. I am a Lady of the House of Venclova."

"There's no such house as Venclova, and no manor called Peregrine."

So, he had heard from Abern—and Storey knew more than the old man. But Aurora did not waver.

"It's been burned to the ground." She choked back the rising lump in her throat and tried to lose herself in a fantasy that was more horrible than her own reality—if that were possible. "Peregrine was right on the border, near the canyon."

"I know the Fairgosian border well; there is no Peregrine."

She nodded. "Yes, near Fairgos. Rogue soldiers somehow slipped through the border patrol and made it all the way to our manor. It was late at night, and they demanded quartering. My father . . . he was so brave, so hardheaded. He refused, and they left."

"Quite a sob story, Lady." Storey tugged the saddle belt and patted the horse's hind flank.

"Before we knew it, the buildings started going up in flames. A few made it out alive, but most were asleep in their beds. They were consumed before they could even open their bedroom doors. My mother . . ." Though the memory was false, Aurora's voice began to crack as she continued. "And my father . . ." Now she was crying outright. "He was trying to get everyone out. The Cook, she made it out. She told me that part of the servants' quarters had collapsed. He was trapped. He died in there."

Her body shook as she sobbed.

Storey continued to busy himself with his horse's tack. He

did not look at her. "And you?"

Aurora took a breath, then another step forward, and continued, holding her bound hands before her in appeal. Was there softness in him yet?

"I could not sleep that night. I was not in my bed. I had walked down to pay visit to my horse. I often do so when I cannot sleep. When I noticed the flames start to go up, I released all the horses and rode mine to the edge of our property, near the canyon. . . . I was a coward."

She looked at Storey. He had stopped working at the tack, but still withheld his gaze from her. She plunged forward with her exhausting lie.

"It was so dark that night. It was too dark. Behind me, I could see orange flames consuming my home. It was like the sun rising right out of the ground . . . an aurora. . . . But in front of me, it was like there was a black wall. I think we must have gotten too close to the edge of the canyon, because my horse balked. I was tossed off his back, and that's all I can remember until waking up here. I think now I must have hit my head on a rock when I landed, then tumbled down into the river. I cannot believe I am even still alive."

"But you are alive," Storey said after a brief silence. "That means you are a survivor. You should do well out here. Do mind the wolves, though. Just remember they will not bother you if you do not bother them." He gestured. "There's a cave a few steps that way. It will shelter you, if you need it. But it should be rather a beautiful night to sleep beneath the stars."

"Please!" Aurora begged. "You can't do this! Why would you be so horrible to a woman you don't even know?"

He placed his foot into a stirrup and mounted the horse. Turning, he finally looked at her. His eyes were flat and his face betrayed no joy in his task.

"Lady, you answer your own question. Now, within the bag, there is also a map. I've marked what you need to know." He pointed to his right. "That way is mountains. Do not go that way. You won't make it through the mountains. Even if you do, you would only end up in Nulle, and someone as beautiful as you should never find herself in Nulle."

He pointed behind him. "To the north, you will find the town of Nydia. That is where I recommend you go if you need sanctuary. They are a border town, near Ekanta. It should take no more than three days on foot."

He pointed to his left. "In that direction, you'll eventually come upon the Calder. You can follow it southward to the canyon and your precious imagined Peregrine. I do not advise you, dear Lady, to choose that path. You have food enough for three days, and that journey would be over a week. Moreover, latest news is that a fierce battle is waging for a river crossing along that route. You will not want to find yourself among soldiers who are operating from the very basest of their animal natures. To be killed would not be the worst of your fate. . . . But besides that point, why would you choose as your destination a place that exists only within your mind?

"Finally, do you see the direction my horse is pointed?" He looked at Aurora. "Do you?"

She gave a slight nod.

"In that direction is Secernere. You are forbidden from returning to Secernere. I repeat, do *not* travel in that direction. If you travel along the river in search of lost Peregrine, cross to the opposite bank. Do *not* return to Secernere. You are not welcome."

Aurora reached toward him, tears streaming down her face. "Please, don't do this to me!"

"It is done."

Storey kicked his booted heel into the horse's side, and the two bolted forward through the woods. Aurora fell to the ground, heaving with sobs, and she watched the figure on the horse vanish through the fog of her teary, blurry eyes.

Abern heard heavy breathing and dragging footsteps, and turned to see Storey. He slinked into the kitchen as if someone had extracted his spine and replaced it with string. His shoulders slumped and his head hung low; if not for the wall against which he leaned, he would have fallen straight to the ground. He dragged a dirty hand across his face and left a smudge there, where the trail dust mixed with the tears on his cheeks.

"Mister Storey?" Abern glimpsed in him the frightened little boy who had seen too much for this life.

"It is done."

9

After finding the knife and awkwardly cutting free her hands, Aurora rifled through the bag. Indeed there was food enough for several days, and a large canteen of water that would be serviceable if she rationed it. There was the promised map, and also an unmentioned dress, pair of tall leather boots, and a woven blanket. How was he at once so cruel and so thoughtful? The smock she still wore was filthy and torn, near shredded around the back where she had been tied down. She doffed the strange clothes and put on the long, green gown. It was beautiful, new—a strange item to have at a manor that boasted no women. The dress had been made for someone thicker around the middle than her; in fact, the empire waist and extra material that bunched at the belly indicated it might have been an elegant maternity gown. The dress was cold inside, as if it had been worn by a ghost.

The boots were also too large, so Aurora tore strips of cloth from the smock and wrapped them around her feet until she achieved a snug fit. As she stood to test the boots with a few strides, she was still crying fitfully. It seemed anymore that she cried more than she didn't. She walked a few steps forward, turned, and walked back to the spot where her bag lay. The boots would do.

She was still undecided, however, about a destination. As the man had indicated, the town really was the only viable answer. Though the river would lead her back to Cathendria, the duration of such a journey was unknowable; she knew not how far she had traveled. Was there really a battle waging? How would a farm boy on a remote manor even hear such news? Granting that she could make the journey, the border crossing would be impassable. Granting that she could bribe the guards . . . with . . . she quelled the thought. Granting she could cross the border, what would she find when she returned to the manor? She had been gone half a week already. What would happen to the servants when they returned from holiday and found no one there? Would they continue to prepare meals, launder the linens, beat the carpets? How long before they realized no one was coming back? How long till the food ran out and they were forced to sell the valuables that sat uselessly around the manor house? Would they pack their belongings, steal horses, and leave to seek their fortune elsewhere?

She imagined the day she could return home safely, maybe after the war's end, and all she could think about was the empty shell of an estate, abandoned and fallen into disarray. The furniture, the valuables, perhaps even all her gowns, hocked for food. The horses gone missing from the stables. The livestock loosed out into the wild, or torn apart by wolves. Would she then wish she had taken her chances in the mysterious Nydia? Invisible walls surrounded her on three sides. And north—away from Cathendria, away from Secernere, away from everything she had ever found familiar, if only fleetingly—was the only direction open to her. So, she began to walk.

The trees around her seemed miles high, reaching up toward an obscured afternoon sun. Had she never spent time in the woods before, she might have easily walked herself in circles, but Aurora had a keen sense of direction, and kept the moss to her back. As alone as she felt, an abundance of wildlife seemed to surround her, unfazed by her presence. Squirrels and chipmunks darted across her path, while the flapping of bird wings sounded overhead. After a time, she glimpsed the white flash of deer tails—a family of four—as they leapt away into darker parts of the forest. She hoped the mention of wolves was just another cruel joke. She tried to remember whether bears lived this deep into the woods. Flashes of every breed of dangerous animal flew through her mind; indeed, what animal could not be dangerous if frightened enough?

Aurora herself: she was no dangerous animal. As brave and strong as she imagined herself to be, in the face of mortal danger, she'd cried, pleaded, prostrated herself. She was, indeed, a coward as she had labeled her false self in her false story. If that lie had been truth, would she have reacted the same way, fleeing? And her father, would he have been as brave as she'd created him to be? Of course. He no doubt would have risked—and given—his own life to save others. But telling that story, no matter how flattering, had been disrespectful to her father's memory. She was a cowardly, horrible girl. For all her education, for all her athletics, for all her riches, for all her name, she was nothing more than a lonely figure lost in the woods, surely on the way to her death. No one was left to miss her. She had no one left to miss. Each step forward was a painful reminder that she could never really return home.

As the hours passed, Aurora tried to concentrate on the sounds of the woods and the feeling of her body as it moved forward—anything to keep her brain from wandering onto fearful, ugly topics. As the trail grew longer behind her, the spot on her head where she'd been struck by Storey was growing increasingly sore, pulsating in time with her heartbeat.

When the sun finally began to set, the forest grew dark very quickly and Aurora knew it would be unwise to try to continue into the pitch. Sitting, she removed her boots and unwrapped her feet. With the sharp ends of her fingernails, she carefully pierced her blisters and drained the liquid. She removed the dirty clothing from her bag, shaped it into a makeshift pillow, and set it against a mound of moss. The bag, with food, water, and map, she hung from a tree branch. Clearing a few stones and twigs from her makeshift bed of pine needles and leaves, she spread out the blanket and lay down, curling into a fetal position. The temperature was dropping. She wrapped the blanket around her body, and curled even further into herself.

The dark was always her signal to go home; she'd never spent a night outside before. The further the light waned, the louder the forest sounds echoed, and she picked out the calls of bullfrogs, crickets, and cicadas. But after moments, friendly calls became more sinister. An owl hooted. A faraway wolf howled into the night. Wishing she had not walked so far from the cave Storey mentioned, Aurora pulled the blanket tighter around her body and fancied it was chain mail. At this moment, she knew she no longer had any sliver of control over her life. She was fate's ragdoll and all she could do was wait for what came next.

Curiously, the intense feeling of powerlessness relaxed her. She'd had to prove so many points, always know the answers, *decide*. Now that she knew she couldn't make a choice about what would happen to her—even if for just the night—the tension left her quivering body. If in the morning she was no longer in the world, it was of no consequence.

The owl and wolf soon quieted, and the forest noises melted into a drone. Exhausted and empty, Aurora slept.

Aurora was alone in her dreams, as well. She found herself trapped in an enormous, labyrinthine mansion. Doors everywhere, all of them were locked. She tripped over piles of keys spilling across the hardwood floors of the hallways. Scooping up a handful, she tried each one in the lock of a tall wooden door, but none fit. When she called out, no one answered. She called mostly for her father, forgetting he was gone and could not save her from the world. Some of the doors had windows, and through one window was her bedroom. Through another was the room in which she'd slept at Secernere. Through yet another was her river, the Aurora River, whose traitorous waters had brought her to this place.

A horse whinnied from afar. She could hear it through the window, and it soon came into her view. It was her horse, running toward her from the banks of the river. She heard the hoof beats pounding. In her lie, she had made him to buck and betray her too, but now he was running toward her. He could break down the door. The hoof beats became louder, and then thunderous. The horse was feet away from the window. His hot breath fogged the glass. He whinnied again and Aurora's eyes snapped open.

An enormous black horse neighed and snorted, pawing the ground. It was tethered to a tree nearby. Aurora sat up abruptly, blood rushing to her pounding head. Where was she? The forest. The man . . . God damn this life! A horse? How was there a horse?

Aurora rubbed her eyes and smacked the side of her head with the tips of her fingers, as if tapping something out of a jar. A horse? She opened her eyes again, and the horse remained. He neighed. It was dawn in the forest. The light was gray, and a white mist hovered low over the ground. Her blanket was wet, her face moist with dew. A horse? She stood, holding the damp blanket around her.

"Shh," she said, raising her hand in a placating gesture. The horse shook his head and snorted again. "Shh. Hello there, sir horse. Calmly now, calmly now. It's all right. It's all right. Shh."

She moved forward slowly, hand extended. The horse turned

his head away, then turned back and allowed her to stroke his nose.

"Hello, sir horse. There, there. That's a good horse. Where are you from?"

Running her hand along his cheek, then down his neck, Aurora moved to his side where she found that he was outfitted with an oily, black leather saddle and two empty saddle bags. There was a smaller cloth bag pinned to the saddle.

"Shh, sir horse. My name is Aurora."

She continued to stroke and sooth the nervous horse as she unpinned the small bag and loosened its drawstring. Inside was a folded leaf of paper, which she extracted and read. The words—written in the crooked, scrawling hand of a child—said:

You must return to Secernere.

❧10❧

The members of the Fairgosian General's Council were huddled in a cramped back room at a tavern frequented mostly by transients and criminals. The majority sat dutifully around the rugged wooden table, each maintaining a stoic soldier's visage. But some did not make the courtesy of hiding their exasperation. Several paced the room. One looked out the window. Kynton, spurred on by the two men who seemed to find merit in his argument, stood at the head of the table, leaning down with his weight on his palms.

"I must entreat once more—"

The man at the window, called Volker of Gellert, cut him off in a bored voice that flowed out slowly from his mouth.

"Please, spare us the reprisal, Lord Sebastia." He turned from the window and faced the room, arms folded across his open jacket. Volker had a barrel chest, spindly legs, and an incessant expression of sleepiness. "We all know how your chorus goes; we have given ear to your argument for nigh half of an hour now. I think it is no secret that we, democratically, are *not* in favor of your proposition."

Titters of shy, indistinct agreement moved through the room.

A man at the table, Cort, spoke up. "Kynton, it is not that we do not have empathy for your situation, or that of Lady Cavalcata—"

"—Your *betrothed*." Volker drew out the word in a contemptuous sneer.

"We simply cannot afford the loss of resources," continued a man called Farhan, also seated at the table. "We have absolutely no soldiers available, and what we have of officers must continue to lead where Lord Cavalcata left off."

Kynton pressed off the table and stood upright, looking at the ceiling. "Is it not a significant coincidence that Lady Cavalcata has gone missing only the day after her father was murdered by a Mitochian attack?"

"Naturally it is a significant coincidence," said soft-spoken Cort. "But the meaning of her disappearance does nothing to unbind our hands."

"What are the possibilities?" said Farhan. "One, she too has been killed." Kynton snapped his head forward with a malevolent look at Farhan. "My apologies to bring it up, sir, but it *is* a possibility. If she is in fact dead, our search would be wasted on a mere body.

"Two, she has been captured and is being held for ransom. In that case, what do we have to offer? They do not desire money. They would want concessions, or military secrets. We have none to give that outvalue Lady Cavalcata."

"Curse your words!" Kynton spat.

"*Three*," Farhan continued, undeterred, "her disappearance has nothing to do with the war. A distressed daughter of a dead father takes an unannounced leave of absence to *grieve*. There lies no surprise in that act, no actionable wrongdoing."

Volker hacked out a cough and drew the attention of all eyes in the room. "Lord Sebastia," he droned, "I might also add—and I think our council will agree—it would be unacceptable for you to take your own leave of absence to form a search party of one. A person might consider that to be desertion."

Incredulous, Kynton searched the faces of his men for solidarity, but only found downturned eyes and sidelong glances at Volker. "Curse you all!"

Cort rose and moved next to Kynton. He was a tall, rangy man, made to seem near reed-thin as he stood next to the broad Lord Sebastia. Tempered compassion shone in his eyes.

"My friend," he said, placing a hand on Kynton's shoulder. Kynton shook it off and stared at the floor like an impudent child. "My friend," Cort continued in a low voice, "you are our general. We—all of us—" He glanced toward Volker, who was again staring out the window. "—trust you to put proper priorities first in this dark time. We have all lost loved ones in this war. Not all of us are so lucky to have the possibility that our loved ones may return to us. Let us move forward, holding onto the thought that your Lady Cavalcata is alive, well, and simply grieving her father somewhere far from the place where she received the horrible news, and from where all her fond memories of him reside. Let her be sad, let her be alive. Let it be so."

"Let it be so," echoed the men.

Kynton finally looked into Cort's face, hugging his arms around himself. "Let it be so," he whispered.

The room expelled a collective sigh of relief.

"Have we another order of business?" prompted Volker. "I know I am not the only one who thinks it dangerous to have all of us in one room together so soon after the last attack, even if it is such an . . . *unpredictable* place."

Kynton cleared his throat. "You are right, Lord Gellert. Let us disband."

One by one, the men approached him, shook his hand, patted his back, and offered a word of comfort before quitting the tavern. Volker approached him and offered his hand. When Kynton took it, Volker yanked him close and whispered in his ear: "Watch yourself, Kynton of Sebastia. I would not want to take over your position at such a crucial time."

"Have no worry, Volker of Gellert. I remind myself daily who would take my place, and it guides my every careful move. Trust me when I say I want it less than you." The men held eye contact, broken only when Cort placed his hands on Volker and steered him from the room.

Returning, he pulled out Kynton's chair and offered it. The two men were now alone.

"Let us sit."

Kynton did. "I thank you for your friendship," he said. "I have been lax in expressing that to you. I would you were my second in command. I do not believe you would play the rival to me so brashly as Volker."

Cort took his own seat, leaning back in the stiff wooden chair. "I do not have the right blood. Anyway, I could not lead as you, or even Volker. It is best as it is."

"I suppose."

They fell silent. Muffled laughter filtered in from the adjoining pub. The sun was setting, night was falling, and activity best reserved for the cover of dark was just beginning.

"Tell me about her," said Cort.

"I know her not." Kynton leaned forward, resting his thick, tanned forearms on the table. ". . . But I know her." His shirtsleeves were rolled up in the manner of a commoner. "Lord Cavalcata talked of her to no end. 'Aurora did this. Aurora did that. Aurora finishes a book in a day. Aurora can swim two miles. Aurora bested me at chess once again. . . . Aurora could lead our country.' "

"Nearly a traitorous thing to say."

"If Lord Cavalcata is a traitor, then I am the Queen of Mitoch," said Kynton.

Cort gestured deference.

"He loved and praised her without limit, and the more time I spent with the man, the more I felt in my heart a growing place for her. We were to be wed at the war's end."

"A fine a reason as any to seek victory."

Kynton chuckled. "Indeed."

"You'd not met her even once?"

"Not before the night of the attack. I had not even seen her portrait. Lord Cavalcata downplayed her beauty. He did not desire me to have false expectations about milky skin and thick hips. But the minute I saw her, she was everything and nothing I expected." He smiled to himself at the memory. "She wasn't dressed; her hair was everywhere. Indeed, her skin was deeply tanned, but it was such a beautiful copper color, and it made her blue eyes almost glow. Her beauty was so exotic, so breathtaking, I only wanted to take her in my arms. Seeing her was the culmination of years of anticipation—and she had no idea who I was."

"You did not tell her?"

Kynton shook his head. "It was not the time. Even now, I am pained that I had to be the one to break her heart. But it would have pained me more for someone else to tell her. I offered my given name and nothing more. I promised to return the next day to help put her affairs in order; I would have told her everything at that time. Only, that time never came." He sighed heavily and tucked his chin down to his chest, looking back up at Cort from beneath his dark brow. "She *is* alive, Cort. What do I fight for, if not for her? They do not understand."

"Some of them do, my lord. Some of us."

A crash of breaking glass sounded through the door, followed by a loud cheer, and then the din settled again.

"My lord?" Cort said.

"Yes, my friend?"

"If I were absent for a time, from the ranks I mean, I would not be missed."

Kynton looked up. "Indeed you would! You are our finest tracker!"

"I do not mean my services, sir. I mean *I* would not be missed. I take no umbrage to the fact that I often blend into the background. A few days, a week at most."

"I am afraid I don't understand." Kynton's brow furrowed. He understood very well.

"If she is alive, she left a trail. If there is a trail, I can follow it. You know as much."

"Alone?"

Cort nodded.

"I could not allow it."

"I do not believe I am requesting permission, sir." Cort held Kynton's gaze.

The sun had fully set, and the room was lit by a single candle burning low. Light flickered across the men's faces, highlighting lines that had appeared only since the war began.

"Find her."

Cort nodded once, stood, and shook Kynton's hand. As he opened the door to leave, celebratory cheers, laughter, and hurrahs flew into the room, then hushed again as the door closed. The war had done nothing to diminish the numbing effects of alcohol on a people weary of losing their sons. Kynton sat, and the candle burned lower. He sat until well after it had burned itself out and the room and the night and everything about the world was very, very dark.

11

Continuing to stare at the horse, the all-consuming fear within Aurora seemed to fall away for the first time in days, replaced by a very heady feeling of absolute absurdity. A horse. Yes. She had come to terms with the very believable, very pungent and snorting reality of a horse, saddled, bitted, and reined, tethered to a tree next to her forest bed.

But worlds more ridiculous, an *invitation* to return to the very place from which she had been forcefully and indisputably ejected just the night before. She was certain this was not the doing of that malicious madman. Neither could it be the work of Abern, who would break in half at the first jarring step of a horse's trot. That only left the ghost of a girl who had visited her. No one else seemed to know about her. Could this be her folly? Could such a small, frail thing even ride a horse, let alone guide a second horse along with her—and in the pitch black, when Storey himself didn't wish to ride after nightfall?

Aurora stared at the note, imagining a quill in the girl's small fist as she scratched out the words. It could be a plea. It could be a cry for help. Abern claimed no knowledge of the girl. Was someone taking care of her, or was someone doing the opposite? She remembered the girl's soft words: "You could help me."

Then Storey's words echoed through her mind: "Do *not* return to Secernere. You are not welcome."

You must return to Secernere.

Do not return.

You must return.

Her feet bare on the damp pine needles, Aurora absently stroked the horse's neck as her brain flew over the possibilities. With a horse, everything changed. She could travel west to the river and follow it south to the border in much less time. But what then?

She knew of one town, but it was far from the river border crossing, eastward near the mountains. The mountains should have been an essential strategic holding in the war, but neither side had succeeded in capturing them. The paths were too treacherous for horses, and many of the areas were too dangerous even by foot. In August, soldiers did not have the blizzards or avalanches to contend with, but those would return with the full force of nature as early as October. But the mountains also belonged to the Nullean slave traders, for whom borders and wars did not exist. They waged their own guerilla offense against both armies, and it proved too problematic for Mitoch and Fairgos to be struck at by an unknowable second enemy who was at home in the mountain passes. Defeated not by each other, but by Mother Nature and the barbaric slave traders, the armies had ceased playing their bloody version of King of the Mountain, and devoted their energies to gaining control over other strategic stakes around the border.

Fairgos had made some progress in the east, breaking north into Mitoch. They'd taken over a fort, and had a nearby town living in fear. The way her father told it, their occupation of that little city was the key to turning the tide in their favor.

But, as Aurora discovered in a stolen correspondence, the town housed a population of less than fifty people—mostly craftsman and small-time merchants who served the needs of foothill fur trappers and southern Mitochian farmers. It was no great coup. And the soldiers' tactic of intimidation, progressing to pillaging and looting (and rape and murder, Aurora imagined) was no shining badge of honor for the Fairgosian army.

Aurora had not thought of that little town until now—what was its name? Shackleton, they called it, though that could have been a nickname. If it was still held by Fairgos, it would prove a safe haven for her, and a way back across the border. If Mitoch had recaptured the area, it was no safer than anywhere else. There was no way to know.

Another option for her was to try her luck in Nydia, the town Storey mentioned. While she had no reason to trust him other than the fact that he did not kill her, such gifts as the map, boots, and blanket proved that he had fair intentions. Nydia could very well be a sanctuary, as he suggested. But while he seemed to know she was lying about her origins, did he know her nationality? Perhaps he had pegged her for a Fairgosian ex-patriot, by her accent or some other mannerism; perhaps that was the reason he was so eager to rid his manor of her. What would the townsfolk of Nydia think?

Do not return.

You must return.

To think that last night she believed she had no more decisions to make.

A ghost could not have brought this horse. Aurora pet the horse's coat again, as if to make sure it still stood before her. A ghost could not have written this note. She turned the paper over in her hands. *You must return.*

"What does she want from me, sir horse?"

The horse snorted.

"I know that is not your name, you silly thing. What shall I call you then, if we are to be friends? I shall call you Nocturnus, because your black coat is deep like the night sky, but still shines with stars." She patted him on the roundness of his velvety cheek and turned his face to look into his brown eyes. "Where shall we go, Nocturnus? Do you wish to visit faraway cities? Could you protect me if the residents find me as disdainful as your man Storey did?"

Perhaps this magical horse could answer her, answer every question, free her from choices and the consequences thereof.

She retrieved her bag from the tree branch, removed an apple, and handed it to the horse. He pulled back his lips and gently plucked the red fruit from her hand with his big, yellow teeth.

"I suppose if you can get me everywhere twice as fast, half my food must belong to you."

She extracted a piece of bread for herself and ate it in small bites, chewing slowly, willing the food to linger long in her stomach.

"Or would you rather return home? I would, if I could. No one wants to be forced from their home, not even a horse like you."

Aurora was positive now that the strange little girl had written the note. She was so cryptic. So pale, and so thin. Could she be a fugitive, like Aurora? What situation was so desperate that she would find Aurora in the woods, but not remain to offer explanation? The longer she considered, more questions than answers rose to the surface of her mind. She could not spend forever not knowing.

But curiosity was merely a spark thrown by the candle newly lit: someone out there needed Aurora. She felt the warmth and light inside her chest. Her choice was not one of four compass points; it was to disappear completely or to matter.

Aurora was suddenly certain that this horse was only going in one direction: back to Secernere.

She gathered her few belongings and repacked the grain sack, then stuffed it into one of the saddle bags. She adjusted the stirrups upward; they'd been placed for someone much taller. Donning her boots and makeshift socks, she hiked the skirts of the dress up to her waist, put one foot into a stirrup, then swung her leg around to the other side of the horse. The dress puffed out ridiculously around her body. Threading the reins through her fingers, she lightly kicked into the horse's ribs to turn him in the direction Storey had forbidden. All the trees looked the same, dark vertical lines like the bars of a prison. No trail was evident at all. Aurora kicked again and proceeded very slowly, staring down at the forest floor in search of the telltale hoof prints of Storey's massive horse. She saw nothing.

"Nocturnus, I hope you know the way home." She kicked him hard and whipped the reins. "Hee-ah!"

Nocturnus broke into a full gallop and ran expertly through the dense trees. Aurora kept the reins loose; the horse knew the path. Trees flew by so fast they blurred into a streak of green and black. Birds protested and flew from the trees at their approach. Aurora leaned forward over the horse and called again.

"Hee-ah!"

Nocturnus obligingly accelerated, and Aurora smiled into the wind, eyes closed as her hair blew back behind her. It felt like heaven to be on horseback again. Horses were fully innocent and trustworthy animals, more so than any other creature she knew. Just looking into their eyes offered a kind of peace and comfort so rare in the world. A horse would never let you down. This horse, this nameless horse called Nocturnus did not let her down either: he brought her at breakneck speed all the way back to Secernere.

The horse slowed to a walk, and Aurora could tell they had arrived by the enormous stone wall that rose up before them. Such a lock-filled place was certain to be walled all the way around; it was no surprise. Yet another sign to turn back, Aurora ignored it.

The wall was much too high to scale, probably forty feet. There would be gates, but surely locked and barred from the inside. She wondered if the "skeletal staff" would have guards. Perhaps the wall was sufficient by itself. But there had to be some vulnerability she could exploit. Her eyes roamed all around the landscape, looking for some clue. The Secernere demesne abutted the river, like Cathendria. So then, did Secernere too have a mill? She thought of Storey's grain sack, the freshness of the bread. It would be a foolish lord not to harness the natural power source of the moving water—it was one of many reasons that lands along the Aurora River were held by the most powerful men in the country. If there was a mill, there might be a window or a door, some opening through which she could re-enter the manor.

She guided Nocturnus to within yards of the wall, then steered him to walk parallel with it. As they approached a colossal wooden portal, Aurora dismounted and walked up to the handle. The iron ring welded to the door was the thickness of her wrist. She grabbed and pulled in a requisite attempt, but she was not surprised when it didn't budge.

Leading Nocturnus by his reins, she continued walking along the fortification and found that the space between the wall and river was narrowing. When the strip of land became too narrow for the horse, Aurora left him and continued on her own. Then she came upon a place where the wall was built down into the river itself: there was a mill after all—it was a seamless part of the wall, but a waterwheel that protruded from the stones lazed round and spilled the secret. The gigantic wooden wheel seemed beneficent in its familiar simplicity.

But it was no solution. The mill wall boasted not a single gap—door, window, or otherwise. . . . Or did it? Aurora lay on her belly and crept out as far to the edge of the riverbank as she dared, trying for a good vantage on the waterwheel's axle. She squinted against the sun, and saw the dark space she was looking for; the axle jutted out from its inner machinery into the open air through a square window set in the wall.

It would be utter insanity to try to squeeze through that opening, to return to the potential wrath of an entirely illogical man—a man who could be the sanest person on the property. Aurora looked back at the patient Nocturnus and her every option to escape this place. Here she was, yet again at the river's edge, somewhere between suicide and salvation.

Her heart jolted as the image of the little girl returned to her mind. Without another thought, Aurora pivoted and began to lower herself down the steep bank, into the river. Something about this water made her crazy. The river flowed in only one direction, and it would forever be the wrong way—and yet she was in it.

It was deep here; she couldn't touch bottom. The current was already jerking her toward the waterwheel. The storm flashed through her mind, the ripping white caps, the penetrating rain. Water roared around her ears. From within the mill, the massive machine grinded and groaned. The thing no longer seemed docile as it sucked her toward its multi-mouthed wheel. She gasped and flailed her arms. She stroked against the current, trying to tread water and buy time. But she was at the point of no return. The bank was too sheer to climb back out. Her choices were to find her way through the window, or find herself farther up the river, again.

She let herself go. She floated directly to the wheel, fast— too fast. She tried to grab at a spoke but cut her hand on the splintery wood. Blood in the water, again. One more chance, or she would be gone forever. She lashed forward again and caught part of the wheel, holding to it for her life even as the wood cut into her. The wheel continued to turn. She was about to go under, but if she tried to adjust her grip, she might slip off completely. She held her breath and let it drag her underwater. The memory of drowning flooded her mind and her body briefly lost control, thrashing in horror as if in a nightmare.

When she burst back to the surface, she gasped for breath,

then wedged her foot into a blade and reached high above to grab another. As the wheel spun her upward, she climbed the blades like a ladder. When she was near ten o'clock on the wheel, she swung herself around to the back and grabbed the wheel's outer rim with both stinging, bleeding hands. As she approached vertical orientation, she let her lower body dangle loosely. She would have only seconds to step onto the axle and jump through the window before its spinning action threw her back into the water. The machinery was deafening.

She was too high to lower herself onto the axle. Her breath was coming so fast now she could barely see straight. When she was at midnight on the wheel, there was no time to think. She let go. Her feet landed on the slippery spinning axle, but slid out from under her and she fell. Crying out, she caught the axle with her legs, gripped it like the bare back of a horse as it continued to turn. She twisted herself around and thrust her upper body through the wall opening. Pressing her arms against the window frame, she launched herself off the stones into the building. She crashed down, and lay prone on the floor like a rag doll, soaking wet, her lungs heaving and coughing, spitting river water.

It was done. By flagrant and brash decision, Aurora was once again within the walls of unfathomable Secernere.

She felt as if she had been put between the two millstones. Everything felt broken. The skin on her hands and legs was gashed, bleeding. She forced open her eyes, just in time to catch a glimpse of white disappear through a door across the building. Pushing herself upright, she called out.

"Little girl!"

When nothing came in return, she wondered if she had seen anything at all.

The mill was empty, almost rotting with abandonment. The waterwheel turned the axle, which turned another gear mechanism inside, but the mechanism was uncoupled from the mill itself, and the stones lay still. Aurora pulled off her boots and poured river out onto the floor, then wrung the water from her dress and hair. Her gaze hit upon a glint of gold shining out of a pile of dust in the corner. She wiped away the debris and found that it was a book with gold-embossed title: *The King's Official History of Sangeva.* She gasped.

"Little girl?"

Still nothing. She replaced the book in its bed of dirt, then found her way outside.

Before her, verdant grassy plains stretched out for acres and acres. There did not seem to be crops growing on this side of the demesne, which was curious in light of the river's proximity. At Cathendria, the manor crop holders had established a complicated system of irrigation to bountiful ends.

She surveyed the property and her eyes fell on the giant door she'd seen from outside. *Nocturnus.* At the colossal entrance, she strained to unbar the latch, then heaved the door open. Nocturnus was a few paces away, grazing on grass. Aurora whistled and he ambled over to her, entering the property.

Farther ahead, enormous, twisted trees took over the grassy field. Even farther, almost out of her scope of vision, she could see a stand of low, squat trees—probably an apple orchard. So there were crops after all. Beyond the trees, in the center of the horizon before her, were several stone buildings with a small cemetery off to the right. The headstones and markers were enormous. Monuments to the dead.

The sun high in its late morning station, the sky was a beautiful, gladdening azure. Nothing about the appearance of this place matched the ominous tone that weighted Aurora's heart. She knew not where to go from here, so she stood dumbly out in the open of this field, exposed, while the horse benignly munched at the ground. What had she expected, for the little girl to be waiting there to greet her, to answer Aurora's every question? No aspect of her task, whatever it was, was meant to be easy. It was the diametrical nature of adventure that always piqued Aurora deep within her loins: the task was at once possible and impossible. If it was not possible, it could not be accomplished. But if it was not impossible, it would not be exciting.

"Come on now, Nocturnus. Let us discover our fortunes in this place."

Grabbing his reins, she lifted his head from the tasty meadow, and together they began to walk. The field was enormous— flat and wide open. The tree line did not begin for a hundred yards. Nothing offered shelter or cover or a hiding place. Aurora reminded herself that she chose to be here; she would face the consequences of being discovered. In fact, finding another soul to talk to might be the only way for her to discern why she was even here.

You must return to Secernere.

She had returned. Now what?

❧12❧

Storey kicked into the horse and drove it as fast as the thing could go, rocketing forward toward the edge of the demesne. There was no way to sneak up on her, so speed was his only ally. He could risk her seeing him and fleeing—away from Secernere; that was a suitable ending to this matter— but not to any other part of the property. Cashel would be returning from the west, using the northwestern entrance. This woman, Inna, was in the southeastern corner. Storey could prevent any meeting between the two if he just rode fast enough.

There. She'd seen him on his horse careening toward her like a loosed carriage rolling down a mountainside. She leapt onto the horse. She was riding. Damn it! Where did she get that horse? It was *his* horse! Damn! He kicked and kicked.

"Hee-ah! Come on!" He leaned forward, clinging to his horse's massive neck. "Come on, boy! Hee-ah!"

She was riding towards the west, along the wall. He was closing the gap. He was on the faster horse. He'd reach her yet.

Gap closing. Closing. He was close enough to call out.

"Hey!"

Save breath, time for talk later. He had to let instinct take over or who knows what poor decisions his intellect might make.

"Hee-ah!"

Kick. The ground dropped away and the horse was flying. The gap was gone. He was beside her. She was leaning down, arms whipping at the reins. Turning her head, she looked directly into his eyes.

"Stop!" he called.

She whipped and kicked. Her horse sped up.

"Leave me alone!"

His horse sped up. They ran parallel. With his right hand, he whipped his reins. His right foot kicked, nudging his horse close to hers. Closer. Closer. Close enough. He reached toward her. She looked again, eyes wide. She tried to pull away.

"No you don't!"

He reached and leaned. Caught her. He felt the dress rip as he tugged. She pulled away, but he was stronger. She was on his horse. She was across his lap.

Her horse angled off to the northeast. He would capture it later.

He had her.

"You goddamned bastard!" she yelled.

She was kicking, struggling. Storey had his hand twisted in the back of her wet dress, but it was far from a firm grip. If she just struggled hard enough, she knew she could get down.

"Stop!" he shouted over the thunder of hooves. He hadn't slowed his horse from the throttling speed at which he'd approached her. They were flashing across the fields. "Are you really that insane? You'll break your neck! Just hold on!"

Reluctantly, she obliged, and wrapped her hands firmly around the saddle belt. It was a terrifying and painful position. She had no control.

"Slow down!" she pleaded.

"I can't! We're almost there!"

She could see nothing but the smudge of ground beneath her, its rushing movement nauseating her. But soon the horse slowed, and the light dimmed; they had entered a building. As Storey dismounted, she let herself slip off the side of the horse onto the ground. Immediately, a hand was across her mouth, and she tried to call out in protest.

Storey's hot breath was in her ear in an forceful whisper: "I promise you, Lady, if you speak, if you make a sound, you *will* die. Not a sound."

He released his hand. She remained quiet. At once, his arm was across her back, shoving. She was thrown into a stall, and fell hard against the wooden partition, then down to the musky ground. Looking up, she saw Storey meeting her eyes with hurried intensity. He placed one finger up to his lips, then mouthed the words, "Not one sound." The stall door closed and clicked shut.

Almost immediately, Aurora heard another clamor of hoof beats, as well as the rumbling of a carriage entering the stable. With the greatest of care not even to crack a piece of hay, she crawled on her hands and knees to the front of the stall, where there was a narrow gap between the door and doorframe through which she could look. It was a terrible vantage, but at least she could see part of what was happening. Storey's long legs and tall black boots passed by. The hoof beats and carriage came to a halt. A door creaked open, and someone exited, thudding onto the ground.

"Storey!" It was a deep man's voice. Aurora shifted to see a different angle. All she could make out was a second pair of tall boots. They were of a finer, glistening leather—traveler's boots, not rider's boots. And a long scabbard hung down beside them, its pointed end brushing the boot cuffs.

"I am here!" Storey called, breathlessness still evident in his voice. Storey's boots crossed Aurora's sightline as he moved toward to the new arrival. "Welcome home. What news of Barlavia?"

"Fools!" the man replied. "It is good to be home, among Mitochian men."

"It is good to have you back, Cashel," Storey said. "I must say it lightens my heart to know you were on a mission of ambassadorship. There are many ways to reach an objective, and your acumen allows you to choose that which is best. "

The man strode over to Storey and pulled him into a sharp, masculine embrace. He said, "I have missed you, my brother. Your familiar face is a welcome sight for me, and your wise words hit my ears sweetly." He pulled back, cooled. "Take care of the horse, will you? Park the carriage. I trust there is a meal waiting."

"Of course," Storey said.

"Fools." The man paced down the center of the stable, scabbard swinging at his side. "They would be such powerful allies. Did you know every male citizen of Barlavia must enlist for two years, whether or not they are at war? Such patriotism, such organization and discipline. I am very close to bringing them aboard. I shall meet with the ambassadors again in a week's time."

Aurora watched Storey's boots move over to the four legs of a horse, which he appeared to be unbridling.

"I thought your meeting had a different purpose. . . . But I do not pretend to understand. Why bring another party into the war? That seems the way not toward peace, but to more war. Are we not strong enough without allies?"

"You *would* have to pretend to understand. It is not your job to understand. That is why I am in charge, and you shovel dung." The man forced a stilted laughed to show his insult was only in good fun.

Slinking down lower, Aurora tried to get an upward angle, to see the face of the man speaking—Cashel. Lord Gomery. She could see up to his chest, but no farther. His all-black clothing comprised various rich fabrics with no visible seams. The intricate gold and silver handle of his sword glistened and sparkled in the sunlight that filtered into the stable. In front of his torso, his hands removed bejeweled leather gloves from each other. Lord Gomery. What should happen if she were to burst out of the stall right now? This man was the man in charge, not this stable boy, Storey. Moreover, he *sounded* like he was in charge—not like he was desperate and mad. But she resisted, and continued to wait in silence, breathing through her mouth.

"I saw you as I was on my way onto the property," Cashel said. "It appeared as if you were carrying a person on your horse." He laughed. "You haven't entered the league of slave traders while I was away, have you?"

"A person may have been more profitable. It was merely a bag of rye. I was returning from the mill."

"Where is it now?"

"Kitchen."

"You are a fast one on that horse. I'll give you that," Cashel said. "That damned Barlavia. The fools frustrate me to no end. You know that they want to intervene as *negotiators*? Is that not preposterous?"

"Negotiators?"

"They offered—" Cashel was breaking himself up with laughter—"they offered to help us draw up a treaty." He guffawed. "As if I am even close to that!"

"Would it not suit us to have a third party to bring the countries closer to a solution?" Storey asked.

Cashel turned serious. "The only viable solution is that I, once and for all, crush the barbarian nation that monstrously attacked us on our own soil. What have we, as men, if we are not free within our own borders? And what is freedom if we are not secure? Such attacks will *not* be tolerated, and Fairgos will *not* be bargained with. I fight until we win. There is no other way. If Barlavia will not be our ally, they will be my enemy, and they will feel the full force of my wrath. I have already been to the blacksmith, and he is preparing four-yard pikes for the heads of the ambassadors."

At that, Aurora heard Cashel's boots treading out of the stable. He called back, "Polish the leather within the coach! Wash the doors and the wheels! It is filthy with the mud of Barlavia."

Storey sighed deeply, just outside of the stall in which Aurora waited. The door shifted as he leaned against it.

"Dear God, help us in these trying times," he whispered. "Thoughts weaken my mind and desires wither my heart. Help me to trust my inner vision. Help my heart to be as open as the sky. Bring us peace so that we may enjoy your gift of life, instead of each and every day fighting against pain that would threaten to kill us from inside our hearts."

"Let it be so," whispered Aurora to herself.

The stall door opened, and Storey stood in the frame looking down at her, one hand on the door, the other balled into a fist on his hip. His expression was one of exasperated defeat. Looking down at her, he sighed again.

"Don't get up just yet." He said it like she was lounging on a sofa.

Aurora had no intentions but to do exactly as he said. Remaining silent, she watched him. Again, she saw his face flash softness, then darken as if he had pulled a shade down over it.

"I would ask you why you returned."

"I was asked to return." She almost said more, but decided she would not mention the little girl until she had a better understanding of whom she could trust.

"Aha!" he exclaimed. "You misunderstood. What I said was do *not* return." He laughed bitterly. It was evident even he was growing weary of his own swaggering guise. "You must have been *awfully* confused as to why I took you into the woods. I must be certain to speak more plainly this time."

"Not by you," she said.

"Oh, was it Abern then? Let me tell you, he likes those of the female persuasion about as much as old Cashel. Or maybe it was the voices in your head. Oh wait! The Friesian. The horse told you to come back."

"Don't be obtuse."

"Please, Lady, help me understand. Why come all the way back to Secernere, what was probably a night and half a day's walk, just to steal a horse, when you could have reached Nydia in nigh the same time?"

"I did not steal the horse. It was given to me."

Storey laughed derisively. "I would venture by the same person who asked you to come back."

"That's right."

"You are quite insane."

"No more than you," she said. A liquidy warmth began flowing through her veins, as if the repartee had opened a small valve.

"What's your real name?"

Her eyes sparkled. "If you would like to talk, perhaps we could find someplace less . . . aromatic?"

"I happen to like where we are," Storey said. "And I particularly like where you are. Watch that right hand."

Aurora looked over and saw a formidable horse patty in the hay. She jerked her hand back in disgust. Storey laughed.

"Indeed, this is the perfect place. Besides, Cashel only visits the stables when he is coming or going. He's come, and won't be going for a week, so we can have our little rendezvous in private. Save the talking horses, of course. Or is it just the Friesian that talks?" He cocked his head.

"Why is it so important to you to keep me away from Lord Gomery? I could offer you at least three good reasons—"

Suddenly Storey was inside the stall with her, squatting down directly in front of her. His brow creased low over darkening eyes. "Because Cashel would kill you on sight before he took the time to exhale a second breath."

Aurora stared back into Storey's flashing green eyes, dumbfounded.

Storey stood again and paced the stall. "You are a terrible spy, or assassin, or whatever you are. Whatever you are, you are terrible at it."

Aurora allowed herself a small laugh. "What makes you think I am an assassin?"

"Just because I fulfill the role of a manservant, don't think me stupid."

"It is you who use the word 'stupid' to describe yourself. I describe your idea as ludicrous!"

"You continue to pretend you do not know who Cashel of Gomery is, which is about as believable as the talking horse. Obviously, caught, you are overcompensating in your story. Coming to kill him, instead, you pretend not even to know him?"

"It wouldn't make sense for me to kill Lord Gomery. Why on earth would I want that?"

"The same reason anyone would. You cannot stand to see a man with so much power, so much malicious power."

"I seek asylum from Lord Gomery! I have nowhere to go. If I cannot stay here, I do not know where I shall end up." She stood, taking advantage of a rush of momentum in her speech. "Abern implied you were short staffed. Surely, you could use the help. I can cook, I can do laundry, I can tend horses. Anything you need, I'll do it—if you promise not to turn me out into the wilderness again."

"You're telling me you returned to Secernere so you could do laundry?" Storey was incredulous. "You poke ever more holes in your own story! Does the Lady of Venclova muck her own stalls at Peregrine Manor? You really are the worst liar I have encountered, and that is saying quite a lot."

She held her hands out before her and took a step closer to Storey. "What I mean is that I shall learn. Surely, someone could teach me. I do not expect to stay for free. . . . I cannot even prove my title—I could just be a lowly servant from the Venclova House. Why should you believe me? I would not believe me."

Storey simply shook his head at her. If nothing else, he was confounded. So strange that he no longer seemed dangerous. He seemed just . . . confounded. She could not blame him; she sounded insane even to herself. And the truth made even less sense than the lies. What a stupid mistake to return.

Storey expelled a small wry chuckle. "I honestly, honestly cannot fathom that you are here, standing in this very horse stable." He looked her up and down, foot to face. "A woman, a titled lady—or so you say—at Secernere. I wondered about my eyesight when I first saw your body by the river. I wonder again. Is this a dream?" He reached forward and lightly touched her cheek with his index finger. "You feel real."

She felt a flash of heat where their skin met, like a struck match.

"I am real," she whispered.

He stepped away from her, rubbed his rough hand over his face, and emitted a quiet growl. "You will not leave. I take you into the woods, half a day's ride from here, and you return. So what shall I do with you?"

Let me see the little girl. She will have answers. But she didn't say it.

"Please, just let me have audience with Lord Gomery. I would not be your problem."

"I told you!" Storey shouted. "He will kill you."

"Surely, you cannot be ser—"

"I *am* serious." He threw up his hands. Aurora cringed slightly as he raged around the stall. She had pushed too hard. "I am serious! Do you think I would abandon a strange, injured woman in the woods because I am some sort of fiend? Do you think I *enjoyed* that?"

Aurora looked downward, abashed. "I . . . did not know—"

"Of *course* I did not enjoy it! I did it to save your life!"

"I—"

"Just . . . shush," he said. "I have to think." He paced again, continuing to rub his hand over his stubbled chin. "Is there nowhere else you can go? How far to your home?" He looked at her. "Your *real* home."

"I told you, my home is gone. I cannot return to it."

Sighing in exasperation, he said, "All right, continue in this story that you cannot return home. Surely you must have family somewhere?"

Aurora shook her head.

"A suitor? A betrothed? Perhaps the wedding can be conducted sooner."

Again, she shook her head.

"Nowhere?"

"No."

"What are you not telling me?"

"What are you not telling *me*?"

"Revealing secrets will not change our circumstance," Storey said.

"I agree entirely." She thrust out her chin and eyed him hard. He returned her look with his own shrewd examination.

"So what do we do now?"

Storey shrugged. "I find somewhere to hide you. What is one more secret?"

Indeed, thought Aurora.

"You shall stay in the stable until I can find a way to make more comfortable arrangements," Storey said. "But I promise you, this is no long-term solution. On my next trip into town, I shall secure you a service with someone trustworthy. Then I can take you there the next time Cashel is away. From there, you will be on your own."

Such an arrangement would suffice until she discerned her next course. She could be a servant; her hands were not tender.

"I thank you," she said. "I thank you a thousand times."

111

"I abandon her in the woods, she returns. I quarter her in a stable, she thanks me. Perhaps I am ever more dashing than I give myself credit for." Storey moved to the stall door. "I shall bring you what food and bedding I can. This shan't be for more than a night."

"Thank you."

"And one more thing," he said.

"Yes?"

"I am not doing this for you. I know you not. I care for you not. I am doing this for me, because I am a peaceful man and because I believe in the sacredness of life. I will do as much in respect of your security and safety as I am able. But you are the stranger here. I owe you no favors. Do not forget your place."

Aurora said nothing and watched him leave the stall and latch the door shut. She listened to his boots on the dusty ground as he walked out of the building. She was alone again.

❧13❧

Aurora was becoming a veteran at spending cold, uncomfortable nights on the ground. Moreover, the luxuries of a door and roof, and being surrounded only by animals of the non-carnivorous variety gave her a sense of security that allowed a hard, deep night's sleep. She awoke finally to the sound of banging on the stall door. Storey entered just as she was opening her foggy eyes.

"Morning," he said.

Aurora smiled weakly. She pushed herself into a sitting position and began to pick stray pieces of hay from her hair and ravaged dress. "Hello."

"My apologies for not returning last night. Cashel detained me for much of the afternoon, and I had my regular duties to attend to, and why am I making excuses?" He tossed a small burlap sack at her. "Here."

Within, Aurora found a hunk of dark bread, a wrapped piece of ham, and a tomato. She tore into the bread without hesitation.

"I believe I will be able to move you within a few hours."

"Move me?" she said, her mouth unabashedly full. "Like I am chattel."

"Pardon, m'lady. Your accommodation shall be suited for your arrival by late morning. The maids are making up your king-sized bed and drawing you a bath as we speak."

"What I would not give for a bath . . ." she mumbled. "And in the meanwhile?"

Storey disappeared from the stall, then returned holding a bucket and rag. "You can make yourself useful. It is safe enough for you to be out in the stable today. The coach badly needs washing after Cashel's journey—not so badly that he could have let me go to wash it yesterday instead of regaling me with hideous war stories, but badly enough that it should be done today. Need I demonstrate?" He pantomimed a circular washing movement. "It goes like this. Apply pressure, remove the dirt. Simple enough."

Aurora frowned at him. "I know how to wash."

"Good!" He flopped down the bucket, sloshing soapy water onto the floor of the stall. "Enjoy breakfast, but not for too long. I expect that coach to sparkle by the time I return. Remember: let *no one* see you. I cannot protect you if you are seen." And again, he was gone.

Aurora wrapped a piece of bread around the scrap of ham and stuffed it into her mouth, following with the tomato, which she ate like an apple. The juice ran down her chin and she lifted a corner of her gown to wipe her face. The air in the stable was pungent with hay, manure, feed, and the pure musky scent of the animals themselves. Aurora was sure she smelled the same way. Before beginning on the coach, she wrung out the rag and wiped her face, then reached into the bodice of her dress and scrubbed under her arms. Finally, she reached under her skirts and cleaned between her thighs. It wasn't much, but it would do.

She rinsed the rag in the bucket then brought everything

out of the stall, and she could finally see the enormous livery stable in its entirety. The vaulted roof must have been thirty feet above her head, with hay lofts lining either side. A wide corridor, carpeted with hay ran down the middle of the building. Large doors open on either end let in sufficient sunlight so no lanterns were needed. Lining the corridors were more horse stalls than Aurora had ever seen in one place. She walked slowly down the corridor. There were forty stalls, but only six horses.

Beyond the horse stalls, at the far end of the stable were two larger garages, housing coaches and carriages of varying sizes. The object of her duty was obvious; a small personal travel coach was parked in the corridor between the two garages. It appeared rawhide colored when the coach underneath was clearly black. The dirt and mud, thick as dough, caked the wheels, undercarriage, and the sides halfway up.

"He gives me one measly bucket of soapy water for this task?"

From nowhere, her father's voice drifted through her mind: "Opportunities multiply as they are seized."

She wondered whether she had seized or squandered the opportunity that was the horse. Yet again forced into an unpleasant situation about which she had no choice, she did not spy any of opportunity's offspring. As she scrubbed, the dirt on the coach became a thick, goopy sludge that fell to the ground. Her water was already sullying. Soon she would be washing dirt with mud.

She could see outside that it was once again an incredibly bright, blue day. It was such a shame not to be able to take one of these beautiful beasts out onto the gorgeous green property. Was it not unfair to keep them in on such a day? She let herself, for only a second, become entranced with the gorgeous sky and the sweet smelling breeze that wafted in. But that spell was soon broken at the sound of a barking dog, quickly approaching. Behind the sound were the voices of children—

girls—calling after it. The dog was inside the stable before Aurora could even drop the rag into the bucket. It froze in front of her and began to bark wildly. The girls were approaching. She wasn't close enough to any stall to hide, so she flung open the coach door and threw herself inside, slamming the door in the dog's face. It continued to stand outside and bark. The girls' voices were now in the stable. Aurora stuffed herself as far as she could beneath the minuscule coach seat and tried to slow her breathing and her racing heart. That damned dog.

"C'mon, boy!" said one girl. "What are you barking at, you silly pup?"

"He's barking at that carriage!" said the other girl. Her voice had a deeper, more mature tone, going through the changes of adolescence.

"It sure is dirty!" said the first girl. "Stop barking, you dog!"

"Hey, look at this." The older girl's voice was directly outside the coach. Aurora felt the door move. She held her breath and closed her eyes. "Look, you can write in it, it's so dirty."

"Awww! You oughtn't to write such bad words!"

The dog was barking. Aurora felt tears squeezing out from the corners of her eyes as she strained to stay still.

"A dirty word for a dirty carriage," sang the older girl proudly. "Go on, write something. Write your name or something. What are you barking at? That dog is crazy."

"Hey, you girls!" A man's voice approached the stable entrance. It was Storey. Aurora allowed herself a slow, relieved exhale. "What are you doing here?"

The older girl answered with audible remorse. "A thousand apologies, Mister Storey. We were just playing with one of the puppies."

"You know you are forbidden this close to the manor house when Lord Gomery is home!" His voice was furious.

"We're sorry, Mister Storey," squeaked the younger girl.

"Yes, we're sorry."

"And you know you should never bring such an excitable

pup around the horses. You'll frighten them out of their wits. What then?" he snapped. "Where did you learn that word, Kinga?"

"I heard it from Mister Abern once," the older girl replied sullenly.

"There's a rag. Wash it off." The dog barked again. Storey shouted at him, "Quiet, boy!" The dog was quiet.

The coach rocked back as the girl scrubbed away at the mud. Aurora's shoulder began to ache from the position she had contorted herself into. She tried to shift, but found any small movement she made caused the floor of the coach to creak.

"I think you girls need to wash the entire carriage," Storey said, "as penalty for breaking our rules. What would Abern say?"

"Probably the word I wrote in the mud," mumbled the girl.

Aurora remained perfectly still for the next hour while the girls washed the coach, shaking it back and forth as they scrubbed so hard. Storey seemed to be taking care of various tasks around the stable, while questioning the girls about working at the dairy, and how their mother was doing.

"How old are you now, Kinga?" Storey asked.

"I shall be fourteen in a fortnight, sir," the girl replied. "Then conscription to the army."

"At fourteen?" Storey was clearly shocked. "Is not the age sixteen?"

"It has since been lowered, sir."

"I get to go in four years!" exclaimed the younger girl.

"Disgusting," Storey said in a low voice, more to himself. "Listen, you girls have done a fine job. Do not let me catch you here again, I mean it. If you behave, I shall bring you a pup of your own very soon."

"Brilliant! Terrific!"

"Don't make me escort you, now. Off you go."

"Good day, Mister Storey! Bye!"

Aurora heard the feet scamper out of the stable, and their

youthful shouting commenced once again then faded with distance. The door of the coach opened, and she craned her neck upward to see Storey standing above her with a half-smile on his face.

"The Misko girls," he said. "Forgive me."

Sitting up slowly, Aurora raised a hand to her left shoulder and began to rub.

"Yes," she said, "of course. I wonder, however, if the 'maids' have finished with my suite?"

"Let us wait a few moments, to give the girls time enough to leave the property. Then I shall take you." Storey offered his hand and helped Aurora step down from the coach. "Just little girls, they are. They've lived their whole lives just outside these walls—the only visitors I ever get. If Cashel knew, he'd kill them and then me."

Every time Storey used the word "kill" when he talked about Cashel, it seemed at once more and less like a euphemism, as if there really were a deadly violence at play, but that it was commonplace enough to be daily discussion. Aurora shuddered. No, that couldn't be it. It was certainly more of Storey's pomp and pretense.

". . . I can't believe they'll be going off to war," Storey was continuing.

Aurora's thoughts turned away from Cashel. *Little girls going off to war?* She couldn't imagine that frail thing she'd seen in her bedroom fighting as a soldier. Not now, not ever. The idea made no sense. Aurora so desperately wanted to ask a thousand questions. Then the memory of her father's speech flooded back: *They would send their daughters to fight! What kind of people is this? Are they people at all?*

"I think this war may last for generations," said Storey. "It is the kind of fight that will be bred into the next generation of children, who will grow up knowing nothing but hatred for the Fairgosian people."

"Why are you not in the war?" Aurora asked.

"Cashel's position has afforded me exclusion from duty. I stay to be manor steward while he is so often away."

His remarks had practiced offhandedness, and Aurora knew he was lying.

So many questions, and no answers. The answers she did get were falsehoods, and she was treading a thin line of inquiring too much, making obvious her utter lack of knowledge about the country of whose origins she claimed to be. Though she'd studied her country's greatest adversary with the intensity befitting the War Master's daughter, with every word Storey uttered, Aurora began to believe less and less that she actually knew anything truthful at all about the nation of Mitoch.

∽14∾

Secernere – Twelve Years Earlier

The stairs creaked, and Abern creaked, as he and the boy Storey slowly climbed up a narrow corridor toward an empty room where Storey could spend the night. The boy had protested that the horse stall would be just fine, but Abern would hear none of it.

"You are a man, not an animal," Abern said. "Not all men are one or the other, but you, son, are not an animal. You shall not sleep among them until I do."

At the top of the stairs were four doors, and Abern opened the last on the right. He stood to the side, held the lantern into the room, and gestured Storey to enter.

"It is not much, but it may be more than you are accustom—" He stopped short with a sharp intake of breath. "M'lady!"

He bowed deeply. Storey stared in horrified awe, eyes like saucers. He felt a hand pushing on the back of his head, and he, too, bowed forward, stealing a confounded glance at Abern.

Before them, huddled next to the wall like a wide-eyed

rabbit cornered by the barn cat was a woman. She glowed in the moonlight that flooded the room. Her luminous skin was ivory, and she wore a gown of the same tone. It was spattered and stained all over with darkness—blood—and torn to tatters around the waist and bodice. Storey knew at least some of the blood on that dress was her own. Clumps of hair had been torn from her head and lay scattered on the wooden floor around her. The glowing woman shook, hugging her arms around her body as if to protect it from an invisible attacker standing right in front of her.

Abern slowly rose and took a tentative step into the room, setting the lantern on the floor.

"Lady Gomery . . ."

He stepped forward again and reached his hands out, palms up, as one would approach a strange dog. The woman hugged the wall even more tightly, her wild eyes glued to Abern or some spot just in front of him.

"I tried to get her out so she could run away. I tried. I tried to get her out."

Not taking his eyes from Lady Gomery, Abern reached a hand behind him and shoved at Storey, motioning for him to stay back. Storey continued to stare. The blood. The blood was all over this place. It dripped from the walls. It flowed in the river. Every white flower ever to grow at this place . . . Secernere . . . would be fertilized with blood.

The woman suddenly jumped up. She pressed her back against the wall and rolled her head from side to side, moaning toward the ceiling. They could see now that an arterial spray of blood had shot across the bodice of her dress—it was the blood of another. But the large stain around her abdomen that seemed to be spreading was undoubtedly coming from her own body.

"I tried," she moaned. "She remains!"

In another sudden motion, she bent forward, grabbed the hem of her dress, then yanked it above her head. Hanging over the bunched waist of her pure white petticoats was the shiny protruding belly of an early pregnancy. The skin on the left side of the bulge had been clawed to bleeding shreds.

Abern rushed toward her, but the woman struck out her hand, fingers bent into talons. He dodged and stumbled backward. Storey leapt forward to catch the old man, but Abern's body crashed into him. Storey tumbled onto the floor, knocking over the lantern. Oil spilled out and ignited. Flames licked up, and the orange light danced across the vibrating figure against the wall.

She shrieked, "Hell is here!"

Storey tore off his shirt, threw it onto the fiery puddle, and stamped out the flames. The room was dark now but for the bluish moonlight and the radiance of the woman's whiteness. Storey watched as she slithered back down to the floor, her dress pooling around her like milk and raspberry jam. He grasped Abern's arm and helped the old man to his feet.

Abern nodded almost imperceptibly at the boy, then said to the woman, "Let me help you, m'lady. It is I, Abern. Your faithful, loving servant, Abern."

"It is not I who needs help," the woman breathed in a suddenly lucid and disturbing voice. "I can die. I will die." She looked at Abern and Storey each in turn and said, "You will die, and you will die. It is she who must be saved."

She cradled her blossoming belly in her hands and looked down at it with mingled worry and affection.

"We will help you save her, m'lady. But you must let me attend to your wounds. We must get you to your room." Abern again reached and stepped forward. Lady Gomery seemed unconcerned now, and continued to caress her stomach. "I was sure you had run away forever, m'lady. I am so happy you are still here, and you are safe."

She looked up at Abern, her pale blue eyes reflecting the moon back at them. "No one is safe here."

She shifted her gaze to Storey. The shock of her sudden

stare caused him to gasp and hold his breath, frozen.

"You," she said.

Storey nodded.

"You are not my son," she said. "And I am not your mother."

Storey felt the lump begin to form in his tightening throat. He shook his head.

"But you will be her brother."

Terrified and confounded, Storey looked to Abern for assurance, but Abern was staring at the woman, transfixed, frightened.

She was looking down now at her wounded belly, rubbing it in slow, affectionate circles that would have caused stinging pain to any sane person.

"And she will be your sister."

"M'lady—" Abern began hesitantly. ". . . might I escort you to your chamber?"

"This will be my chamber now—you will allow them all to believe that I have run away. The boy will stay with me until she is born. What is your name, boy?"

"Storey." His name caught in his mouth and sounded as thin as paper.

"Storey, you will be her brother. You will let her choose her own name. You will keep her safe. Even in my death, even in your death, even in the death of everyone around you, you will keep her safe."

She looked up at him again and her eyes shot straight through him. He nodded mutely.

Abern had edged closer to the woman. Hand on the wall for steadiness, he lowered himself down next to her, knees popping. She allowed him to part the tears of her dress and examine her wounds; her eyes remained transfixed on Storey.

"M'lady, I will do your bidding," Abern said, "whatever it will be. Only allow me to dress your wounds. It is in the interest of the child."

She nodded. "He must not know," she said quietly.

"He will never know, m'lady."

Lady Gomery's hands shot up and she grabbed Abern's gray, stubbled face and pulled it close to her own. He rocked forward, off balance, and nearly fell onto her.

"Not never," she hissed. "He will know when the time is right."

Abern pulled himself away and stood up, shaking his head emphatically.

"Your every wish, m'lady. Your every wish." He backed up, grabbed Storey on his naked shoulder, and they left from the chamber together. Outside the room, he spoke back through the doorway. "I will return as soon as I am able."

Secernere – Present

"Put these on," Storey said, handing Aurora a stack of clothing, "and tuck your locks into this hat. From afar, you must give the appearance of a man. Go into that stall; I'll not watch."

She followed his instructions and came out of the stall in the holey woolen trousers and button-up muslin shirt, crossing her arms over her chest. Her breasts felt exposed beneath the thin cloth. She fought a rising blush.

"Oh!" Storey said. "Here." He handed her a matching woolen vest. She turned and put it on.

"Thank you," she said quietly.

When Storey deemed it had been long enough, the two walked out into the bright sunshine.

"I beg of you," he said, "take note of this feeling. It may be some time before you are outdoors again."

Aurora's heart darkened.

"This prospect of hiding must be strange for you," he said. "You must be accustomed to a certain degree of notoriety that attends a title."

Indeed Aurora had not allowed herself to dwell on the prospect of hiding; the very thought of long periods of time in closed spaces made her shudder.

"I was notorious for all the wrong reasons," she said. "And anyway, my reputation must not precede me very far; you still do not believe even in the existence of my manor."

"Walk beside me, dear Lady. I am not leading you by a leash."

They walked together in silence, staying near to buildings, and crossing wide open spaces with quick steps. Soon, they came upon the manor house, and Storey led them around the edges of the building to an entrance at a far wing. He produced a key, unlocked a small, nearly imperceptible door, and gestured for Aurora to enter.

"Here?" she whispered harshly. "Is this not where Lord Gomery himself would stay?"

"Indeed," Storey replied. "You shall hide in plain sight. Do not question it, unless you prefer the stable."

As Storey closed the door behind them, the sunlight was blotted out, and the room before them was coal black until Aurora's eyes adjusted. Slowly coming into view was a long dark corridor, with low ceilings and unlit lamps along the walls.

"Walk slowly," Storey said. "There is light enough if you walk slowly."

Through the walls, she could hear distant sounds—the din of a kitchen and the motion of people moving through rooms. Aurora's mood darkened further as they exited the corridor into the open space of the mansion, and she observed the walls around her. Storey was not playing guide. He did not introduce the generations of frightening men painted in portrait who stared down from the high walls, nor did he explain the absence of women. He did not identify the taxidermied heads of animals that did not live on the same continent as Fairgos, Mitoch, Nulle, and Barlavia. He did not explain why the house was so enormous, but felt so empty, nor why every door they passed was closed up tight. They walked for what seemed like miles, but still they remained in the manor house, which grew colder and darker as they progressed. Each dark panel of wood on the wall seemed more neglected than the previous. Cobwebs in the corners became denser; dust on the hand railings grew thicker. The hall was quieter and louder at the same time: while the noises she'd heard from the kitchen and rooms had faded, the silence in that wake left space for all manner of creaks and moans from the building itself.

The farther they walked, the slower Aurora felt she was moving, like she was struggling to wade through a bog. She was at least three paces behind Storey by now, but he did not seem to notice. His own strides had become more purposeful and hurried, as if he was running out of time.

Passing yet another closed door, Aurora heard a heavy thump inside the room, like a body had fallen against a wall. Quickening her pace, she joined Storey's side and found herself clenching his arm.

"Are there others in this part of the building?" she asked.

"No."

"What was that noise?" She looked up at Storey's face, but he only stared ahead.

"It is but house sounds," he said. "This is the oldest part of the manor. You will grow accustomed to it with time."

But Aurora knew there was nothing about this arrangement to which she would ever grow accustomed.

❧15❧

When Aurora's mother, Lady Inna of Cavalcata, died twelve years earlier, Lord Cavalcata locked up her bedroom forever. He sent for a large order of giant white sheets, which he draped over all the furniture, covering everything but the bed, the large painted portrait of her in her wedding gown, and a single wooden chair. He demanded that the staff no longer attend to the room, and that it should be locked at all times; he would have the only key. There were many unused rooms in the enormous manor house at Cathendria. Most of them had been covered over with similar sheets, and were neglected by the staff unless they were required for a large party of guests. But none of them were locked. In fact, nothing in their home had ever been locked. Aurora's father valued trust and believed that it was a positive cycle: the more he demonstrated trust in his staff, the more they would demonstrate their own trustworthiness. No servant was ever caught snooping; any cause for curiosity had been removed. Nothing of value was ever found missing; the servants were never in want. And if they needed something extra, they knew they could but ask for it. Locking Lady Cavalcata's boudoir was a sign of changing times at Cathendria. The sign of great changes within the Lord Cavalcata himself had begun months earlier.

Shortly before she turned nine, Aurora was already beginning to test her boundaries. Part of this included eavesdropping on as many adult conversations as she could get her ears around. Cook, for one, grew tired of catching Aurora sneaking around the kitchen, and so she took the girl under her wing, thinking it would be more productive for everyone if Aurora was an overt and active participant in the kitchen activities. This friendship did not please Lord Cavalcata, but he had other issues weighing on his mind.

Though he hid it well from friends, guests, and servants, Aurora noticed the slight changes in his personality. And so, in the autumn of that year, she abandoned all her other eavesdropping locales—the kitchen, the laundry, the garden, the servants' quarters (if she was feeling especially bold)—and began to trail her father on a regular basis.

This new investigation took an enormous amount of patience on the part of the young girl. Her father traveled often. There was, after all, a fresh war. However, lately, his trips were shorter, and the spaces between them longer. He was haunting the house more and more, as if something were keeping him there. It did not take Aurora long to realize that something was her mother. Never very strong—at least not since Aurora had been an infant—she now appeared to be weaker and more tightly tethered to her bed. The servants spent a great deal of time bringing food, drink, hot compresses, cold compresses, salves, poultices, and whatnot up to her bedroom. When he could, Lord Cavalcata would stop them on the stairs and take the laden trays up to her himself. More often than not, the trays that entered the room loaded with food would return the same way. Cook would let Aurora have her pick of the leftovers, then use what remained in preparation of the next meal.

The problem with trying to eavesdrop on Father was that he did not speak much. He had always maintained a stolid reticence, reserving the hottest of his emotions for his work. Even in scolding Aurora or wayward servants, he always seethed just below the surface. This was much more frightening.

But of late, he said even less. There was less scolding, to be sure, as if he did not quite notice what was going on around him. This worked to Aurora's advantage as a sneak, but hurt her as a daughter. Even when he was visiting his wife, they spoke in low, sad murmurs, or said nothing at all.

Then the doctors began to appear. It was not strange for Doctor Trush to be present. He may as well have lived on the estate for as often as he visited Lady Cavalcata. Following Aurora's birth, the Lord and Lady had begun trying to have another child, hoping for a male heir to manage the estate after his father's eventual passing, take his father's place in governmental affairs, and carry on the Cavalcata title.

But the first pregnancy caused Aurora's mother great difficulty, and ended with a bloody stillbirth. Aurora had been too young to remember this firsthand, but it was one of the many stories she'd picked up from her investigations. Despite the complications and her weakened state, Lady Inna had bravely asserted her desire to continue trying. She understood the importance of the male heir to their name, but as well understood her husband's underlying desire to have a boy to raise in his own image.

One of the most darkly memorable utterances Aurora had picked up from the adults was from one of her mother's ladies-in-waiting: "If only they could have a son, then they might have some success in finally turning Aurora into a daughter."

But then there were more complications: two more still births and then an ectopic pregnancy that Trush said destroyed any chance the couple had of conceiving another child. The silent mourning in the house the day that news was delivered was as if a family member had died. It was like a son had been born, lived for many years in the loving light of family, and then passed away suddenly to the despair and torment of sister, father, and mother. There remained a ghost of someone who had never existed.

Weakened from the inside out, Lady Cavalcata seemed never to recover. Trush was a near constant presence. But the year Aurora turned nine, Trush ceased to tout his own medical omniscience. It was obvious to anyone who spent more than the length of a meal at Cathendria that the Lady had taken a turn for the worse—a turn for the end. And so new doctors began to arrive. At first, they were Trush's colleagues from around the country. They brought black bags full of special tools and unusual medicines and very, very large bills of service—but none of them brought answers. Then arrived doctors from other countries, even doctors who did not even speak their language. But the shrugging shoulders and the shake of the head was universal: no one knew how to save Lady Inna of Cavalcata.

A doctor from Ekanta had just been sent on his way, and Aurora had staked out a prime spot from where she could hear every murmured word in her mother's bedroom. Aurora had grown bolder as her wardens had grown more distracted, and she now approached invisibility—if she ever was visible to begin with. This time, her father had not even made the effort to close the door all the way, and Aurora could see slivers of both her parents through the opening. Her mother, of course, was in bed, tucked among the bedclothes like a tiny white pearl inside the fleshy mound of an oyster. Her skin was as translucent and shining as a pearl—and nearly as white. Beside the bed, pacing in and out of Aurora's sightline, was her father. He, too, was pale. And he'd grown thin. Often his own meal trays— which more and more he took in his study or in the Lady's bedroom—went as untouched as his wife's.

He was crying. He appeared not even to have the energy to wipe the tears from his face. Aurora had never seen her father cry and the sight disarmed her. Her mother, too, was crying, though her sobs were angry and frustrated in the face of her husband's stoic and silent tears.

"This *thing* is eating me from the inside out!" The exclamation had all the force but none of the volume of a shout, as if it had come from a tiny woman just a palm-width tall. "It has grown out of my very heart. I can feel it now. From the outside, I can feel it. Give me your hand."

"No," said Lord Cavalcata very quietly.

"Give me your hand!"

"No!" the Lord ejected, as if punched in the stomach. "I do not want to feel it!"

"Then look at it!" The Lady tore aside her chemise, exposing her left breast, which appeared deflated and empty. On the inside of the breast was a visible lump coming up from the valley, like a plum tomato just beneath the surface of the skin. Icy blue veins emanated from the center of it, mapping the skin of her breast like rivers on a plain.

Aurora gasped and her father snapped his head toward her. For a moment, it felt wonderful to be caught: it was the first time he had looked right at her in an eternity. But in just two steps he was at the door, slamming it shut. Aurora flew to the keyhole and pressed her ear against it.

"It is my pain," her mother said. "The pain at all this loss— it's built up around my heart, squeezing it, taking the very life from me. No one could live after all this loss. No one would want to. What you see is my pain, surfacing."

"Do not say such things," Lord Cavalcata replied. "We know it is cancer. It is cancer and nothing more. That very fact has been confirmed by doctors the world over."

"*Nothing more?*" she raged. "It is only my death!"

"I . . . I cannot abide this."

"Abide what?"

"I cannot listen to you say that. I am not prepared . . ." His voice dropped off.

"Not prepared? You are not prepared to hear me talk about

it? Or you are not prepared for me to die?"

"Inna . . ."

"You are never going to be *prepared*, Vadim. I have been dying for almost a decade, and I am still not prepared. You are never prepared to die, and you are never prepared to let the one you love die."

Then she, too, broke off, and Aurora could only hear her mother dragging deep ragged breaths into her taxed lungs. Then there was only silence. Aurora ran back to her own room so she could cry without anyone hearing her.

After that, no more doctors came to the house, not even Doctor Trush. In fact, no one came to the house, and no one left it either. The usually bustling household fell silent. Everyone continued in their normal duties as best they could, but now did them very quietly. It was like everyone in the house, Aurora included, felt if they were quiet enough, they might disappear completely and Lord Cavalcata could be alone to grieve as he needed to.

When Lady Inna of Cavalcata finally passed away, it happened without surprise, display, or remark—and as it should have been; for everyone, save Father, it was as if she'd already died. Aurora did not visit her mother after the door had slammed before her. She did not feel like a member of the Cavalcata family; rather, she was an observer of a couple deeply in love and deeply in pain. And at the root of that pain was the fact that Aurora was not a boy. If she had been born the right gender, there would have been no decade-long tribulation of star-crossed pregnancies. Her mother would not have been weak; she would have been the strong, vibrant woman who gave birth to her first child while bathing alone in the river, without even leaving the water. She never would have succumbed to the cancer. And the Lord and Lady and Heir Apparent Cavalcata would have lived and loved happily ever after.

But it was not so. Aurora was a girl, her mother was dead, and her father was a ghost.

❧16❧

The place Storey now led her was cold and still. Down the long empty corridor with blood red walls, Aurora thought of the way Cathendria had been at the time of her mother's death. The feeling shook her on a level almost too deep to comprehend. Sudden sadness, and an intense feeling of irrepressible regret sunk down upon her with overwhelming weight.

She had dropped Storey's arm and fallen back a half-step behind him. Each step she took was heavy, like she was dragging something chained around her waist. The hall ended at a door, and she knew in her gut that behind it lay their destination, and she knew in her heart it would be a place of terrible loneliness.

She almost stopped him. She almost grabbed him by the arm once again—not out of fear of bumping bodies against closed doors, but out of the fear that she might go crazy locked up in a room all by herself. She could tell him everything. Maybe he would understand. Maybe he would think of a new idea.

But she did not grab his arm, and she did not stop him, and

then they were at the door and he was opening it and she was walking through.

The door opened into a narrow, dim stairwell with two flights of stairs, each ascending in either direction. The stairs themselves were only wide enough for one person to pass at a time. If one met another while going up—which seemed quite unlikely—one would have to turn around and go back. Storey began to climb the stairs on the left.

"Follow me."

Each step groaned under his weight, then creaked again under Aurora's. The snaps and pops of the wood echoed through the hollowness of the walls, and for a moment, Aurora saw a vision of all the planks and stones crashing down around them.

Storey glanced back over his shoulder. "You should be able to move around without worrying about the sounds you'll make. This part of the house is very noisy."

At the top of the two flights they'd traversed was yet another labyrinthine corridor with four doors near the end, two on each wall. The walls were bare wood—no portraits, no animal heads, no tapestries, no candelabras. The wood smelled like it had gotten wet and never quite dried, like the underside of a tree felled long ago. Like rot was imminent.

"In here." Storey opened the last door on the left and entered. Aurora held her breath and followed.

She exhaled as she saw that her new home was not what she had imagined—that being something akin to a rat's hole, with a pile of wood shavings for a bed. Indeed, it was a step up from the stable. In size, the room approximated that of a large carriage. The roof sloped down from a height half again as tall as Storey, down to waist-high wainscoting. A dormer window allowed some sunlight to filter onto a simple, narrow bed. A wooden table with a matching chair took up the space in the opposite corner, a chamber pot tucked discretely beneath. A pitcher and basin sat atop. Next to them was an oil lamp and a small, cracked hand mirror.

"Bad luck, I know," Storey said. "But only for the one who broke it, I think," he said.

"Who broke it?"

"Me."

A threadbare rug covered a bit of floor in the center of the room, and a burly wooden trunk was the last of the furnishings. It might well have been a castle.

"The bed has fresh linens on it, but don't expect them to be laundered again before you leave. The water in the pitcher is fresh. The trunk is empty, but I may be able to pilfer a few garments for you. And, there is nothing below, so you can just . . . throw whatever you need to out the window."

Aurora blushed, but appreciated his discretion.

"As for food, I will tell you right now, it won't be of the sort you have been eating."

"That's all right."

"I will bring you what I can, when I can. I suggest you practice rationing."

"How long, Storey?" she said. She wasn't even sure what she was asking.

"Until I can find a way, Lady."

She sat on the bed. It was hard, and the stuffing in the mattress crunched beneath her weight. "Will you tell me why—why . . . everything?"

"Will you tell me who you really are?"

"I am Inna."

"Then no." He walked out of the room, then turned around to face her. "I will return when I can, with food and perhaps something to occupy your time." He paused. "When you were not cooking and laundering and performing other servantly duties at Peregrine, how did you occupy your time?"

"Swim in the river, and ride horses. Walk through fields of wild flowers and climb very tall trees so I can see for miles. Play chess on the top of a tree stump. Find wild herbs and put them on roasted chickens and watch the sun rise from the top of a hill."

"You can see the sun set from here," Storey said.

Aurora looked outside and seeing that her view of the sky was halfway obfuscated by the towering stone wall, her heart fell. It was so fitting that her only view from this miniature wooden cell was another wall. She was a self-made prisoner trapped in a holding within a holding.

"It will suffice," she said.

"It is said, we shape clay into a bowl, but inside is where we put our food. We take stones and build walls, but it is inside of them that we live. We work with substance, but emptiness is what we use. I hope you will find usefulness in your own emptiness, m'lady." He paused. "I am going to close this door," he said, "but I will not lock it. It locks from the inside, and I suggest you do just that. I will not lock you in. You must trust me that you should not leave this room, not for anything."

She nodded. "Storey? Thank you."

He bowed his head to her once, closed the door, and was gone. Aurora heard his every step down the hallway, down the stairs, and then down the corridor two floors below. His footfalls faded, but the house continued to bump and thump and creak, like a restless dreaming giant.

Aurora stood in the middle of the room, unable to move. The violent trajectory of her recent life had plummeted her forward with such intense momentum. Now that she had finally reached a destination, albeit a temporary one, it was as if she'd hit it with the force of running into a stone wall. Her vision of the future seemed blocked by that same stone wall.

How was it, she considered, that she had moved from the care of one man to the care of another, in the span of mere days? Perhaps she was not missing out on her twenty-first year as a Fairgosian noblewoman. Even if her father had lived, it would have been the same eventually. She would have been married off—handed off—to another titled lord, Kynton or someone like him. She would move to a new estate, take on a new name, and with age and wear have less and less desire to cause trouble. Eventually, she would cease to be, existing only to bear children to carry on the new, faux name forced upon her. Would it kill her, like it killed her mother?

Once Storey got her to Nydia, maybe she would make that her home. Even a schoolteacher or a washer woman had more freedom than a titled noblewoman of Fairgos. She stared at the wall outside her cranny of a window.

Without having to worry about horses or waterwheels, Aurora's mind wandered back to her father. Had she her druthers, she would have become a spinster, staying with him as long as life would allow. But he was away so often, would she not have been building only a life of solitude for herself?

As entrenched in the war effort as he was, he could have been away even more often. He probably could have—and should have—taken up permanent residence in the capital, March, like others of similar responsibility and rank. Instead, he went so far as to hold important meetings at Cathendria so he wouldn't have to travel. He must have undergone great remonstration for leaving his station in favor of home, in favor of his daughter.

Aurora realized suddenly that her father was not leaving home to spend time on work. He was leaving his work to spend time with her. In that light, the sheer amount of time he spent at home—playing chess, reading poetry, wasting energy on equally puerile pastimes—it seemed ridiculous, gluttonous. How could she have resented it so strongly that he had to leave on short notice when they were supposed to be on holiday? Every day he spent with her was a holiday for him. The lives of hundreds or thousands of men were at stake when he was called away. The country was at war, for God's sake!

At last turning away from the window, Aurora lay back on the bed and stared up to the sloping attic ceiling. She felt like an indulgent, spoiled brat who had unconscionably demanded her father's presence for no other reason than to quell her own insecurity. Like she honestly *deserved*, as some sort of *reward*, that he show his love by staying at home with her to eat pomegranates. But really, he had loved her all along, with a hidden intensity that outweighed his sense of duty and loyalty to his own country.

She felt a wave of nauseating depression wash from the center of her heart out over her entire body, then crumpled forward, shaking with tears. He had died thinking she did not recognize his sacrifice for her, feeling regret at being absent instead of pride at being summoned away. He had died without his own daughter knowing just how very much he cared for her with the deepest of loyalty and love.

With her arms wrapped around herself, she tried to still her body and her thoughts. Despite the fear and anger, the regret, the many questions that clung to her mind like flies on rotting fruit, she could not deny that she had returned to Secernere because she had been asked to. This was the end of selfish Aurora, the needy child. Someone else needed her, and there was more to do than wait.

Squatting in the tall grasses, Cort lifted one of the tall suede boots from the ground and examined it. He'd never see its equal in quality and beauty, but the heels were worn low and the leather was supple, broken-in. Indeed these were the boots that made the tracks from the Cathendria manor house.

But he could not discern the scene. Though the grasses were crushed and matted, there were no signs of a struggle, only that someone had lain down. The dress that paired with the boots had been violently torn open; he found buttons on the ground as far as two yards away. But without a struggle, this was no rape. Why would she strip in the middle of a field?

From there, the tracks changed. He found only the imprints

of her toes and the balls of her feet, with long spaces between the strides. She was barefoot, and she was running.

"What were you so frightened of, m'lady?" he whispered to himself.

He followed the tracks on his hands and knees, searching for any sign that she was being chased by man or beast. But there was nothing so fresh as her own tracks. It was confoundingly clear that she was alone. The tracks ended at a large flat rock that protruded out over the river, and no tracks retreated. It was obvious: she had gone in. The river was still flooded since the most recent storm, and the water was ugly and raging. What on earth would have possessed a woman of sound mind to jump into such a maelstrom? Surely, it could not be suicide.

He shook his head, as if disagreeing with the idea would make it untrue. He would never, could never, approach his liege with news that his betrothed had taken her own life. But he didn't believe it himself. There had to be another explanation. All he knew for sure was that she had gone into the river. The body, dead or alive, had to be somewhere, and he would find it.

He needed a boat.

❧17❧

Aurora had watched the sun set, then rise, set again, then rise once more. Two days, and Storey had not returned. It was quite plain that no one else, not even odd Abern, knew Aurora was living, barely, in the tiny hidden room, and that she was starving, thirsty, and possibly starting to go mad. She'd lost the will even to think about the reason she had returned, and her mind was suspended somewhere between surviving and what comfort death would bring. When the knock on the door finally came, she rose from her bed, walked to the door, unlocked it but did not open it, then returned to the bed and curled into a ball on her side.

As she watched, the door opened and Storey entered, carrying a sack. His face was weary, his eyes bloodshot. Aurora said nothing, and neither did he. Setting the sack on top of the trunk, he pulled out the wooden chair and waited. Lifting her head just an inch, Aurora nodded, and Storey sat down. She continued to watch him. Storey stood once more, removed a piece of bread from the sack, and handed it to Aurora. He then filled her pitcher with water from a jug. Not moving from her side, she ate, greedily. Forcing herself upright, she brought the pitcher to her lips and drank with relish.

Storey sat again.

"Nydia has been burned to the ground."

Aurora swallowed and watched him.

"A Fairgosian squadron crossed in from Ekanta." He rubbed his hand over his eyes. "Ekanta . . ."

"They are a neutral people," Aurora said.

"I think neutrality is an idea that cannot exist in our world," he said. "It is said, when we lose our way, war-horses breed in the border lands." He looked so very sad, personally hurt that Ekanta had been extorted into a role in the war. "Nydia was a civilian town—trades and craftspeople. I believe this very chair on which I sit came from Nydia. It is no strategic stronghold. This attack, this great burning, it was retaliatory."

"When in war, how can one not deem all strikes to be retaliatory?"

"Fairgos' initial attack could not be called retaliatory," Storey said. "It was prompted by nothing. Their leaders hate ours. Someone decided to take hateful action."

Once again, Aurora forced herself to remain silent in the face of confusion. For what she knew, the Fairgosian attack was prompted by a clear threat from the Mitochian government. The first attack over the border was to preempt worse violence. Storey's perspective was the first she'd had the opportunity to hear about what the other side of the border experienced.

"But what I meant," continued Storey, "was the fact that they *burned* Nydia—I believe it is directly tied to the burning our army conducted in Fairgos."

Aurora's spine tingled. "Burning?"

"Yet another plot dreamt up by Cashel, the master of strategy. He believed the whole color of the war would change if only he could rid himself of his counterpart in the Fairgosian army."

"Exactly what role does Lord Gomery fulfill . . . ?"

"What manner of remote household do you come from, Lady, that you honestly maintain that you do not know who Cashel of Gomery is?"

Aurora continued to stare.

"No man has more power in this country right now! He is the royally appointed war strategist. He is the army general who does not fight. He is the chess master. He moves our nation's daughters and sons about as if they are pawns, and he does so from his own study and from inns and from comfortable suites at court. He basks in the credit for all the victories and when he fails, he denounces his own officers then slaughters them in public.

"He is our nation's greatest monster."

And his counterpart was Aurora's father.

The room began to spin, and she felt nausea rise in her throat. She lunged to the window, threw up the sash, and vomited down the side of the building.

"Oh my God!" Storey rushed to her side. She felt his hand on her bending back.

"I am all right," Aurora mumbled.

"I do not visit for two days, and when I do come I give you moldy bread and tell you horrific war stories," Storey said. "I would be sick as well."

She withdrew into the room, and dragged her sleeve across her mouth. "It is nothing. I think it has been too many days since I last ate."

Storey's expression was of genuine concern. "A thousand apologies, m'lady. I . . . I simply cannot find an excuse to come up here more often, not to mention the missing food." He sank back into the chair. "And now with the incident at Nydia . . . Nydia was my only solution. I know not what to do with you. I know of no safe place for a strange woman."

"But here," Aurora said.

"No. Here is the *most* dangerous place for a strange woman."

"Perhaps . . . the war will end soon."

"The end has been a possibility since the beginning."

"Do you believe Mitoch will be the victor?"

"In such a war, no one will be the victor." Storey sighed deeply, then pressed his hands to his knees and pushed himself into a standing position. It appeared painful for him to do so. "I cannot stay. I'll leave this sack. It contains more food—I pray it doesn't make you sick as well—and there are also some more clothes. I shall return . . . when I can. Meanwhile, I think it would serve us both to think hard about this predicament. The longer you stay here, the more danger we are both in."

Storey always seemed to be leaving. And Aurora always seemed to be alone. She was also always hungry and tired and sore and sick. She imagined being a prisoner in a legitimate jail might have offered more comforts. But every occasion she found herself reflecting on her own misery, she would remember that she was here to help someone who was weaker than herself. In this world of war, where masses died in a single day, Aurora could take solace in the needs of a single, tiny girl.

Aurora napped at sunset, then forced herself awake a few hours after darkness had settled on Secernere. She lit the lamp, unlocked the door, and for the first time since she'd been put in this room, stepped outside of it. The lamp threw phantoms of orange light upon the wooden walls, and upon the four identical doors at the end of the corridor. She had no plan, but the doors offered sufficient first steps. Checking the latch to ensure she wouldn't be locked out, she shut her own door with a soft click.

Without taking a step, she was already close enough to the door across the hall to take hold of its handle and push. Locked—no surprise. The house was bumping and thumping, as it did every night. The floorboards beneath her creaked. Stepping close to the next door, she leaned forward and placed her ear against the wood. She heard nothing. She tried the door, and it too was locked. At the fourth door, she repeated her listening, but the door only returned silence. She tried the latch and it unexpectedly gave way. With a whine, the door opened to a long, black hallway.

Aurora reached the lantern into the hall, but it only lit the walls enough for a few steps. She entered. The lamp lit a small section around her, and as she crept forward, the hall behind her enclosed itself in blackness. Step by step, she moved forward, her destination unknowable while her past disappeared.

In the flickering lamplight, a door appeared at the end of the hall. This was as far as the corridor went, and if Aurora was to explore any further it would be through that door. A massive thump pounded the wall to her right, shaking the wood, and Aurora jumped. The lamp wick flickered, threatening to go out. She pressed her ear to the wall. Farther away, there was banging, stepping, the small and larger noises of things running into other things. Or people running into things, or things running into people. These were no house noises.

Taking deep breaths to quiet her pounding heart, Aurora moved to the door. She stopped and listened. The lamp waned to a low glow, then perked up again. She listened. Giggles. The laugh of a little girl came from behind the door. Aurora pressed her ear against it. Yes, the laughing was distinct. Stooping down, she held her lamp close to the keyhole and tried to peer through. Nothing but darkness. Slowly, she pushed at the latch. It did not give: locked. The girl was humming now. The tune was an old nursery rhyme Aurora remembered from when she was young, a child's ballad about peaceful people in Ekanta playing together in fields of flowers. Aurora hummed a bar to herself; it was the same tune.

She stood and placing her fingertips upon the door, lightly tapped. The humming, the laughing stopped. She tapped again.

"Little girl?"

Silence.

"Little girl? It's me . . . from the forest. I have returned to Secernere."

Silence. Aurora tried the latch again.

"I cannot help you if I cannot find you," she said.

Only silence. Aurora sighed and turned away. The house noises stopped. The thumping, creaking, the laughing all stopped. Everything was silent as she made her quiet, dark way back to the room. The silence kept her awake until dawn.

The shouting, and more so the pounding on the gate door, could be heard from the stable. Placing the tack he had been mending on the ground, Storey stood slowly and listened. He could ignore it. The people outside the gate knew not whether anyone was within. The walls were high and thick; the gate door on the north side was the same. Eventually, they would tire of pounding and their voices would grow hoarse from shouting. Some of the stronger, younger men might try to scale the wall, only to fall, maybe dislocate their shoulder or snap their forearm. They would scream in anger at the door, but they knew not who would or would not hear their pleas. Easily enough, Storey could just wait. He could just do nothing. No one else on the property even had the mind to consider opening the gate to strangers.

Cashel was away again, a lucky thing. He would have opened the gate brandishing a sword, slicing and stabbing at the crowd until they dispersed and ran in fear. He would have killed the biggest of them and hung him on the gate as a *no trespassing* sign.

Even as Storey saddled his horse and buckled the belt under its massive belly, even as he pushed his foot into the stirrup and swung his leg over the horse, he knew he could just wait. He could ride the horse to the mill storehouse and pick up the week's grains. As he kicked the horse's ribs and began to move forward out of the stable, he thought about taking the corn to the coops where it would feed the chickens and ensure the con-

tinued supply of eggs. The sky outside the stable swirled with
blacks and grays, continuing to threaten the rain that had been
promising itself all day long. He would then take the flour to
the kitchen, where it would be baked into rye loaves to feed
the staff. From the kitchen, he would gather the putrid scraps
and bring them to the pig pen, where they would turn to slop
for the swine. They would feast on pork chops, bacon, and
ham over the winter. He thought about all of this even as he
approached the gate and the shouts ringing in his ears were
almost deafening in their urgency, even though probably only
a dozen or so people were outside the gate.

He dismounted the horse and tethered it to a ring in the
wall, then used both hands to force upward the enormous rust-
ing latch of the gate. Grasping the metal handle, he contracted
almost every muscle as he pulled the door open. Inch by inch,
the massive, cumbrous door crept open, revealing a huddling
mass of bedraggled refugees. The pleas turned to cheers.

A little boy, no more than five years old, ran through the
doorway and wrapped his arms around Storey's knees. Storey
reached down and stroked the boy's greasy, matted shock of
hair as he surveyed the small crowd. It was mostly men, as he'd
expected, maybe ten or so at first glance. Some of them were
injured. An older man had a bandage wrapped around his head
covering his right eye. A young woman clung a raggedy bundle
against her bosom: a tiny sleeping infant. The rest were children, both boys and girls. Their faces were nearly black with
dirt and soot. Storey scooped up the boy and held him as he
walked out of the gate. The boy let his head drop to Storey's
shoulder.

A tall, muscled man emerged forward from the group. His
shoulders were slumped as if carrying a weight greater than the
pack on his back, but he put his best effort toward holding his
head high.

"Sir," he said, his voice like the bark of a tree, "we come
from Nydia. Our homes have been burned to ashes. We have

lost three men on this journey already. We seek asylum."

Murmured echoes of his plea emerged throughout the group.

"Please . . . asylum . . . nowhere to go . . . starving . . . children."

Storey handed the boy to the waiting arms of an older man, then held up his hands in placation.

"I am sorry. I cannot express my regret with words, believe me that. But there is no asylum here."

Angry shouts of protest rebutted him.

"Please!" he shouted.

"Look at your walls!" shouted one man. "Look at your land! There are riches here enough!"

"What kind of man would turn away his countrypeople in a time of war?" said another.

The group surged forward, and Storey put up his hands in impotent protection.

"Wait!"

The infant woke and began to cry. The woman smoothed its head against her bosom. She looked up at Storey. "Have you no soul? We are people."

"Wait!" Storey repeated. "Please. I will bring what supplies I can. But we have not the accommodations for more to live with us."

"We shall sleep in the stables with the horses," said the first man. "We need little. Only a chance at life."

The crowd piped up again: "Please . . . only a little . . . you'll hardly know our presence." And once more: "The children."

"You must wait here," said Storey.

The man's face darkened and he took another step towards Storey, poking his finger into his chest. "What if we storm in? There are more of us than you."

Storey batted the man's arm away and took his own step forward. Staring right into the man's eyes, he said in a low intense growl, "If but one hair of yours crosses the threshold into my land, you, the woman, and the children will get nothing from us."

The man backed away. Turning to his companions, he said, "It is all right. Let us wait. Everyone, please, just be calm."

Storey pointed at the man again, watching him as he backed away through the gate. He pushed the door shut and jammed the latch into place with a screech of metal against metal.

"Dear God, help us in these trying times."

Storey marched into the kitchen and threw an empty sack onto the table. Abern was washing potatoes alongside the cook, a once-fat man grown leaner in recent months, so that his skin hung loose around his jowls and paunch. Both men turned as Storey demanded, "What have we got to eat?"

"We sup in three hours," the cook responded. "Though do not expect a rich meal."

"There are refugees outside our walls. They need what food we can spare."

"We can spare none," the cook said.

Storey looked to Abern, who responded by opening the large door of an upright pantry. Within were rows upon rows of empty shelves. A deflated sack of flour hunched in the corner, and several jars of preserved fruits and vegetables stood next to one another in a weak line. There was not much more.

"The others are much the same," Abern said.

"Where is our food?" Storey asked.

"We will be able to bake a few loaves tonight, with whatever the mill provides us," said the cook, "but the cupboards are nigh bare."

"I don't understand."

"Nydia," said Abern. "Supply routes ran through that town. Since the incident, no transports have been able to come this far. Until another post is established, we are on our own—and we were struggling to begin with after the summer's drought. We cannot feed strangers. In fact, we will be lucky if we are not forced to add some of our staff to the lot of refugees outside."

"Is there *nothing* to spare?"

Storey stormed around the room, throwing open the cupboards and yanking open drawers. He turned to the two men by the wash basin. They only stared at him.

"Then I shall eat but broth for the next week. My meals will go to them."

With a sweeping motion of his arm, he emptied the contents of one cabinet into his sack, followed by another.

"And we'll slaughter one of the hogs tomorrow. It has been too long in any case." Abern made to protest, but Storey's expression stopped the words before they left his mouth. "We might all eat broth for a while."

As he left the building, he found the rain had finally begun to beat down. The ground beneath the pounding horse hooves became mud that splattered his boots and trousers. With dark storm clouds crushing the horizon, the sky was nearly black. He was soaked by the time he reached the gate. Behind it, the shouts rose in response to the pounding hooves.

"Open it! Let us in!" came the calls. "We beg of you!"

Storey dismounted. Gripping the underweight sack in his fist, he imagined the group smashing forward onto him as he opened the gate. If they rushed him, he would not be able to keep them outside. There were not enough staff at Secernere anymore to help him wrangle even such a small crowd.

"Please!" they shouted. "Help us!"

Storey swung the sack in a wide circle, around and around, letting the bag go at the apex of the arc. It flew up and sailed over the top of the wall.

He rode his horse away fast enough that the hoof beats drowned out the screams.

❧18❧

Aurora startled out of heavy sleep to the sensation of a hand on her shoulder. She turned abruptly and saw Storey standing over her.

"Hello," she said, her voice groggy. The sun was very high in the sky.

"You did not lock the door."

She wiped her eyes, crusty and sticky; she had cried herself to sleep again last night. "I'm sorry—I forgot."

Returning from another late night exploration of the maze of corridors in her wing of the house, she'd had nothing on her mind but the laughing and singing that seemed to sound from behind every door.

"Probably better that way, since you failed to answer when I knocked." He sat in the chair.

"You were knocking?"

"You were sleeping very deeply. Were you dreaming?"

"Was I talking?" Aurora sat up in bed, gathering her bedclothes around her lap.

"You were struggling against something. I almost did not wake you."

"Is it very late?"

"After noon," Storey said. "Do you feel well? Have you been sleeping quite a lot?"

"More than I've been awake." She rubbed her eyes again. "Little else to do."

Storey produced a bag and emptied its contents onto the table before him. "I hope to remedy that. I know we are both frustrated that we've found no solution to your predicament. Perhaps some levity will help the time pass more quickly for you." He patted the items in front of him. "Books. Just a few for now; I could not take very many at a time. I will bring more when you finish these."

"I have already finished the one on top."

"The Bible?" Storey asked. "You have finished the Bible?"

She smiled. "Why so surprised? It is a good story."

Storey laughed and shook his head.

"What, have you not read it?"

"No," he chuckled. "I have not."

"Can you . . . read?"

"Of course!" He tried to mask his indignation.

"My apologies. But it is not very common in my household. The only servants who could read were the ones I taught myself. Most were not even interested in it. I was only going to offer to teach you."

"If only we had time for such lessons."

"Who taught you?" she asked.

"My mother, when I was a boy. She died when I was young."

Aurora glanced down at her hands. "As did mine," she said.

"We all have our trials." He was silent for a moment, then gestured again at the items. "A few scraps of paper and some charcoal, for writing or drawing or what have you. I was able to get my hands on some embroidery thread and a needle. The thread is coming unraveled and the needle is dull. But perhaps you'd like to stitch a violet onto your pillow. And—" From underneath his chair, he produced a flat, squarish piece of rough cut wood and a box full of little wood chips. "I remember a mention that you play chess."

Aurora looked at him skeptically. "How can I believe you can read, but do not know what chess is? That is . . . kindling."

"No," Storey said. "It is a chess set. You must not only see what things are, but what they can become." He reached into his pocket and produced a folded knife. "You left this in the Friesian's saddlebag. Keep it close this time."

Aurora accepted the knife and teased out the blade.

"Careful," Storey said. "Unlike the sewing needle, that *is* sharp. Very sharp."

"It is not a very ladylike thing to be able to whittle."

"That is exactly why I thought you would be good at it."

Aurora smiled despite herself.

"It would do well to pass the time?" he asked.

"Yes," she nodded, continuing to smile. "I . . . thank you."

Storey nodded. "It is August, you know; we do not just keep kindling laying around. It was an impressive feat for me to gather all that wood. I trust you'll do right by me in making a respectable chess set."

"Of course."

"Perhaps I shall have time for a lesson or two in that game."

Aurora nodded. "I hope so. . . . I hope you'll not think it inappropriate of me to say, but I do treasure my time with you. I have not known loneliness till this room."

"I hope you'll not think it inappropriate that I dragged you into the woods within the first hour we met."

"Not at all."

"I have come to enjoy your company, as well. It is a welcomed and strange respite from every terrible thing that happens outside this room." He was at the door. "I will return when I can."

This statement was his farewell and had become familiar to Aurora. She found hope in it, when there was scarce other place for such hope to live.

The coming days passed in a similar fashion, Storey arriving unannounced at irregular intervals. Sometimes he bore food; sometimes he did not. He was beginning to look thin in the face and shoulders. Through his open shirt collar, she could see his protruding collarbone. But he said nothing of it, so neither did she, accepting what he brought as though it were a feast.

Aurora left the books untouched as she worked on nothing but the chess set. Somewhere inside, she believed that if she created a game that could only be played by two people, if she had a pastime that required a partner, it would somehow enable Storey to spend more time with her. She worked her fingers raw and her knuckles rigid with soreness, carving each tiny piece as perfect and symmetrical as she could. Storey had the forethought to bring two varieties of wood to differentiate the battling kingdoms. Pale Mitoch and dark Fairgos. Aurora worked through the soft pine pieces first, using them to practice her skills. When that set was complete, she began on the rosewood. It was harder, resistant to the details like miniature crosses on the bishops' tall hats. Her favorite pieces were the knights, which she carved as horses.

She managed to complete all thirty-two pieces without even nicking her fingers, impressed with her ability to pick up the new hobby with ease. She lay the slab of wood across the table, and stood above it, stabilizing it with one hand as she dug with the other to carve out a pattern of sixty-four squares. The knife cut into the wood, then gave way, skipped across the slab, and drove into the meat of her palm. In sudden blinding pain, she shoved her face into a pillow to muffle her shriek. A rush of dark red blood beaded up, then poured from the wound. The blade still stuck in her hand. She eased it out, hissing at the pain, and immediately pressed her bed sheet to the gushing wound. The blood spread though the cloth like a blooming rose as she pressed against the cut as hard as she could, willing the flow to stop.

When she finally removed the sheet, she saw that the blood had stayed, but that the gash was wide and deep. If she did not close it, it would never heal properly. She picked up the unused embroidery set and moved back to the bed, into the sunlight. For a moment, she stared at the horrifically large embroidery needle, with its wide eye staring back at her. It would have to do.

The embroidery floss was thick enough to sew up a goose, so she unraveled a length of narrow thread. She threaded the needle with the black floss, then placed the point at one end of her gash. Pressing lightly, the blunt splinter of metal would not go through. She grit her teeth, exhaled sharply, and pushed harder. Her face found the pillow again as she cried out. She drew the thread through the openings and made a knot best she could with only one hand, then continued onto the rest, making four stitches in total before snapping off the length of thread. Finally, she tore a long strip of fabric from the sheet and tentatively bandaged her wounded hand. It throbbed with pain, as if fire were pulsing out of it. Suddenly lightheaded, she lay back on the bed as the room began to spin.

Once again, she awoke to Storey standing over her, shaking her.

"Lady! Wake up! What happened?"

Bleary eyed, she looked up at him and struggled to comprehend what he was saying.

"All this blood! What happened?"

What was he saying? Then she remembered. "I cut myself," she said groggily. "With your knife."

"Why?" he exclaimed.

She laughed quietly. "It was an accident."

Holding his arm for leverage, she pulled herself into a sitting position. She unwound the bandage and offered up her hand for his inspection. He winced slightly, but tried to hide it. She had washed most of the blood away, but the gash itself was still a dark, clotted red, and the black stitches were grotesque against her pale palm.

"It's not that deep. I'll be fine as long as the stitches hold." She looked up to meet his eyes, but saw he was looking elsewhere.

"You've finished . . ." His voice was full of wonder. Already, he was holding one of the tiny queens up in front of his eyes. "These are beautiful."

One by one, he picked up and examined every piece in silence, then placed each back in its exact position.

"Almost finished. Otherwise, I would not have had cause to be playing with that damned knife this morning." She motioned to the ruined board.

Storey picked it up off the floor. "I don't think I would have chosen to paint the squares with my own blood. But, you are a unique woman." He smiled. "Does it hurt?"

She nodded. "Yes."

Storey sat down beside her and took her hand into his own, holding it in his lap. "It is said, if you realize that all things change, there is nothing you will try to hold on to. If you have no fear of dying, there is nothing in life you cannot do. Trying to control the future is like trying to take the master carpenter's place. When you handle the master carpenter's tools, you will surely cut your hand."

"Where does that come from?"

"Just something I learned as a young man."

"It sounds very wise."

Storey nodded slowly. "It is wise. I know many wise ideas, but I am not a wise man. A wise man does not need to talk to prove his point."

"Need we stop trying to control our futures?" she asked.

"It would be easier to do had I more trust in those who already control it. It is said to be patient with your friends and your enemies both . . . but I find it so trying."

"The master carpenter . . . is that God?" Aurora asked.

"I suppose it is to some."

"To you? Do you believe in God?"

"No," he said. "Not the way you do."

"How do you find peace then?"

"I don't."

Aurora watched her hand in his hand. It was rough and calloused, tan on the back and white on the palm, just as hers. Pine and rosewood. They sat in silence for a long while. She concentrated on the feeling of his skin against hers and it made her pain fall away.

❧19❧

Two more days had passed since she'd seen Storey. She had made the food last. Even the smallest of morsels could sate her belly now; her body no longer filled her clothes. The hours she slept became short, sporadic. Day and night had scant meaning anymore. It was a new moon, and after the sun went down, a black blanket eclipsed her room. In the blackness, she could not read her books, nor carve at wood (loathe as she was to pick up the knife again), nor embroider something other than her own flesh. Aurora had given up sneaking out of her room for any further mesonoxian excursions. The reality was that she was chasing a ghost. The songs, the laughing, the thumping—not to mention the horse and note—remained unexplained, and Aurora began to feel quite sure she was losing her mind.

Tonight, she sat cross-legged in the middle of her bed, conjuring memories and fantasies, as if she were having a séance with ghosts from her own life. She held her hands beneath her shirt, fondly stroking her fingers over her ribcage. It was a curious sensation. The darkness offered no perception of depth; she had only the memory of the size and shape of the room, and it seemed to get smaller and smaller as the night went on until she held herself still as furniture, fearing to bump against the walls if she moved at all.

The volume of the house increased with the volume of darkness, and Aurora began to concentrate on the noises all around her. In her mind, she tried to picture very vividly that a bat was fluttering and thumping against a window pane. It was one room over and one story up. If the sound was a bat, it was nothing else. She then created in her mind a picture of a tree outside, its leaves blowing viciously in the stormy wind, which is what undoubtedly caused the wall beside her to crackle and shake.

But she could not picture what could cause the regular, rhythmic bumps that moved back and forth, back and forth, other than an actual human being walking around within the house. It was no clicking of claws on four legs. It was no scampering of rodents. They were undeniably human footsteps, slow and methodical.

Aurora rose from her bed, holding her arms out in front of her, and took cautious, abbreviated steps until her fingers touched a wall. She then meticulously made her way around the perimeter of the room, pressing her ear to different spots on the walls, trying to locate the source of the footsteps. The steps, which did not cease nor diminish nor lose their rhythm, sounded precisely the same from every wall. Moving back to the center of the room, she discovered that there, the footsteps were loudest. Then, all at once, they stopped.

Aurora froze in her position and waited. They would start again, she was sure of it. She waited until her body ached with stillness, but there was nothing. She sat back on her bed. The wind had stopped. The bat had retreated. She heard nothing but the sound of her own breath entering and exiting her nostrils. Hugging her arms around herself, she pressed her fingers into her ribs, where they fit as if into a mold.

In the dark, where she could only hear her breath, and only feel her body, she barely recognized herself and was overcome by the very certain notion that she could no longer stay here. She was an animal gone wild in a cage, ready to break out by whatever means possible.

As he navigated his bateau around a sharp elbow in the river, Cort saw a beach that would have been the perfect campsite—had he not, just an hour before, left his camp to start the night's journey farther north. Once crossing into Mitoch, the only safe travel was that conducted under the cover of night. The previous day's campsites, chosen for their coverage and inaccessibility, brought fly-infested swamp, wolf-riddled forest, and otherwise miserable conditions. This site was tauntingly perfect. A steep slope walled in one side to keep out the creatures. The beach was flat, and he imagined sleeping inside his tent without awkwardly curling around tree roots or fighting the gravity of sloping, uneven ground. His only work to prepare the site would have been to move some washed up tree branches out of the way of the tent and to create a bit of camouflage for himself. But it was not time to camp.

As he began to steer his way around the bend and move on, the flat-based bateau abruptly caught the bottom of the river, which was exceedingly shallow on this side. The rocky plane of the beach submerged into the river at a low, flat angle, then dropped off into a deep crevice below the water's surface.

"This is it," he mumbled.

The topography was conducive in every way to catching debris that floated down the river; this explained the tree branches on the bank. The angle of the bend aimed the detritus straight to the eastern side of the river, where it then caught on the shallow ledge and washed up on shore. This beach would have trapped an unconscious body like a fish in a net.

Cort jumped down, splashing into the deep section of water and anchored the boat there. With precise movements, he climbed up onto the ledge, where the water rose just inches above the soles of his boots. He lit a small lamp and held it close to the ground. Here, the river would have washed away any tracks or marks, but—yes, there it was. A yard beyond the water line were evident drag marks, as well as a set of man's footprints and a set of paw prints circling and pacing. The soft silt of the beach had preserved them perfectly, even though the shallow depth of the marks indicated they were weeks old by now.

Closing his eyes, he pieced together the scene: The body caught the ledge and washed up on shore. She was either dead or unconscious, because she left no tracks of her own. There were no signs of blood or struggle; the animal had not been violent. It was likely a medium-sized dog following an undeniable scent, and it led the man to the body, who dragged her farther onto the shore. Then, as evidenced by deeper footprints and the disappearance of the drag marks, he lifted her, into his arms or up over his shoulders, and carried her up the slope. It seemed an impossible feat, even for an especially strong man. But the evidence was there that he had done just that.

"I found you," Cort whispered. "Devil be damned, I found you."

Cort noticed now, at the top of the slope, a soaring wall rose up into the sky. There was an estate here. The very thought of who might live here—who the strong man could be—turned Cort's blood cold. His passage into Mitoch had not been an easy one, even for a trained military scout. How did she pass the border undetected? If she was even alive, could Lady Cavalcata have passed as a Mitochian? Would she have known to? Or was she now a prisoner . . .

Connecting the path from here to wherever she was now would not be a simple task, and could not be accomplished in the coming night. Though the trail was hot and the campsite tempting, Cort returned to the boat and paddled back upriver to an ugly, ragged, and completely inconvenient campsite, where he set up a camouflaged lean-to and settled in for the night.

The footsteps began again for the third night in a row, and Aurora had come to expect them. But it did not make the new routine any less disconcerting. The steps were the same—plodding, methodical. Was someone sleepwalking? Or were they pacing in sleeplessness? Was it even a person at all? Storey had more than one time assured her that no one lived in, or even visited, this wing of the house. Aurora had not mentioned the footsteps to him; she had heard his excuse about *house sounds* enough times to already know his response. The question suddenly occurred to her: if someone else *was* living on this end of the house, and Aurora could hear them, could they also hear Aurora?

Though she'd already made up her mind to leave at first opportunity, the thought that she might be discovered before she was prepared was disturbing, but it became positively frightening the longer she pondered it in the dark. Could Lord Gomery really be as dangerous as Storey had made him out to be? She struggled to remember whether Storey said that the lord was away or back at the estate. What if those footsteps belonged to him? Could he hear her? When she dreamt and cried out in her sleep, did he hear that? Aurora's breath quickened. Could he hear her breathing, too?

Would he really kill her on sight before he even exhaled?

Every movement she made suddenly seemed amplified to a deafening volume. The friction between her trousers and the bed sheets on which she sat sounded like sandpaper rubbing together. She shifted her weight slightly, and the bed creaked with the sound of a thunderclap. As she turned her head, her hair brushing against her shoulder was like a forest rustling in the wind, and she heard her vertebrae crackle like a log being split. Paralyzed by the notion that the sheer loudness of her body's sounds would draw someone to her room, she sat in bed as still as a statue for the length of the night.

As the misty purple veil of dawn pulled off the sky to make way for the daylight, a heavy cloak of slumber fell over Aurora. She immediately fell into a dream. As she watched from her bed, her chamber door opened, and the little ghost girl entered the room.

"You finally found me," said Aurora.

The girl sat down on the chair at the table and began to line the chess pieces up into neat rows of eight.

"Is this a game?" she asked.

"How did you know I was here?" Aurora asked. In the corners of her eyes, the room was blurry and melting. The girl, too, moved in and out of focus, like smoke that dissipated then reformed.

"Teach me to play."

"Why will you not visit me when I am awake?" Aurora asked. "I've been looking for you. I came back for you."

"You *are* awake."

❧20❧

Secernere – Twelve Years Earlier

True to her morbid prediction, Lady Gomery passed away, dying as she brought the infant daughter into the world. Abern delivered the child, assisted by Storey, who had grown exponentially stronger and more mature in the five months he had been at Secernere.

Storey cradled the tiny thing in his arms and gently wiped her clean with a soft cloth. No more a pure creature than this had come into the world covered in blood; even she had caused another's death. For what felt like the thousandth time, he wondered at the remarkable violence of this place. But his wonderment had become detached, objective curiosity, and was no longer the horrifying pain he had been forced to come to grips with in his first days at the estate.

The baby—now called only that—had cried for just a short time, then fell to silent observation of the dark, strange world around herself. Storey shushed her and stroked the blond down on her head. Abern bent forward, sopping up the bloody mess around Lady Gomery's body. When he'd taken care of the most of it, he rocked back on his heels.

"Yet another to bury," he said. "Storey, I think you're of age to help me with this task. I am getting to where I cannot perform such an endeavor alone."

Storey nodded. "And her?" he asked, looking down at the baby.

"I will find something suitable for a cradle. She will have to be fed cow's milk, poor thing." Abern balanced himself on Storey's shoulder and stood. "She will be fine while we do our work."

Once the baby was well settled and cushioned from rolling around, Storey followed Abern out of the chamber to the cattycorner door.

"Before we bring the body, I will show you our destination."

Abern unlocked the door with a long skeleton key, and they entered a narrow stairway that was darker, tighter, and evermore claustrophobic than any of the labyrinthine pathways Storey had so far explored. At each cramped landing that marked the start of a new switchback in the staircase, the air was chillier, wetter. It was evident they were descending below ground. Abern walked slowly, as he walked everywhere slowly—but Storey was neither in a rush to arrive at their destination.

At last they reached the bottom, a flat, damp cavern with stone walls and packed-earth floor.

"We have a way, yet," said Abern in a low voice. "Follow me. It is simple, but pay attention. This place will be your duty now."

"What place is this?" Storey whispered.

"We are going to our graveyard."

"Is there not a cemetery outside?"

"Yes," said Abern. "There are plots for the Gomery family. But this is *our* graveyard, for those who die of different circumstances, and whose final dignities must be conducted in secret."

"Is my . . ."

Abern nodded. "Your mother is buried here. Your father, too."

"I do not have a father," said Storey.

For what seemed like leagues, they walked in silence down a corridor that never seemed to change. Then all of a sudden, the odor of decomposition overwhelmed them, and Storey recoiled. Abern was already tying a kerchief around his face, and he handed another to Storey. Soon they came upon a large room with body-sized mounds on its floor. There were so many.

"Which one?" asked Storey.

Abern moved toward a pair of graves near one wall and motioned to the farthest.

"She is here."

Storey fell to his knees before the grave. Five months had passed, and he'd barely shed a tear. The wonders and horrors of his adoptive home at Secernere had busied his mind to such an extent that he hadn't the capacity to feel the full weight of his loss.

But here, in front of the unmarked pile of dirt that held her remains, in the midst of the foul stench of death that assaulted his every sensibility, in the crushing dark and suffocating closeness of the walls, he finally succumbed to the emotion. He sobbed uncontrollably, then fell to his side curled in a ball and continued to cry.

"Mother . . ." he moaned.

Somewhere behind him, Abern took a step backward and hid himself in a shadow.

Secernere – Present

Aurora dragged her hand across her eyes, rubbing away the fog and bleariness. Had she slept at all? Was she still asleep?

The girl did not seem to find it strange that Aurora would question the reality of her existence, which, despite hearing the girl speak, she continued to do.

"I am awake. . . ." Aurora said to herself. "Am I awake? Where . . . Who . . ."

She rubbed at her eyes again. A heavy, sandy weight lay right behind them, pressing at her brow from the inside. Sentences did not make sense in her head, and she could not force words out of her mouth.

The girl sat pleasantly behind the row of pawns and royalty with her dainty hands folded in her lap, her legs crossed at the ankle. She had the perfect mannerisms for a little girls' tea party, but her ragged scrap of dress betrayed her. Reaching up, she poked one of the pawns forward with her index finger, then looked back up at Aurora.

"Teach me?" she repeated.

Aurora shook her head, as if to loosen the sleep and madness from it, then twisted her hands up into her hair, gripping it as if to hold her head steady. She let her unfixed gaze roll loosely over the blanked on the bed and said very slowly, "Yes. I will teach you the game."

She disentangled her fingers and ran her hand back over her hair, smoothing it, then looked at the girl, trying to focus on her face. It moved and changed, puzzle pieces of an eye, a mouth, a nose shifting over the white plane of skin. Then Aurora's eyes fixed, and the movement stopped.

"But with special rules." Woozy, she stood and pulled the table toward her. "You sit on the chair across from me, and I will sit on the bed. Oh . . . we do not have a board."

She was beginning to feel more fully awake now, and yet the girl remained in the room. She was real. They both were. And here they were together, in hiding at Secernere.

Aurora retrieved the nub of charcoal from the trunk, then drew the sixty-four blocks of black and empty squares onto the table. Setting each piece in its place, she explained their names and how they moved across the playing field. The girl nodded in mute comprehension until Aurora explained the movement of the queen.

"Why do both queens go wherever they wish?" she asked.

"Both sides are equal; each piece is equivalent to its counterpart on the opposite side," Aurora said.

"But it is not so," said the girl. "All queens do not have the same power. Nor do all kings. Where there is balance, no war exists."

Aurora had no explanation at her disposal for this.

"I think," she said finally, "the imbalance is not in the pieces, but in the minds of the players."

The little girl nodded, satisfied.

"Now," Aurora went on, "the special rules are, if I capture one of your pieces, I get to ask you a question. If you capture one of my pieces, you get to ask me a question."

"Very well."

"You must *answer* the question you are asked."

"I understand. Shall I go first?" The little girl moved a pine pawn two spaces forward. "Light and dark. Like us. Your enemy is the shadow that you cast yourself."

They played through several turns in silence, and Aurora found herself astounded at the precociousness of the girl's approach. She could hardly believe—and for the most part did not—that the little girl was entirely unfamiliar with the strategy of chess. Finally, Aurora captured one of the girl's pawns.

"Who are you?" she asked, instantly regretting the vagueness of the question.

"Dymphna," was the girl's equally vague reply.

Aurora sighed in frustration, as much at herself as at the little girl, then relegated herself to her own rules and motioned for Dymphna to take her turn. She did, and captured one of Aurora's sacrificed pawns.

"How did your father die?"

"What?" Aurora exclaimed. Perhaps this girl really had heard her through these walls, was an eavesdropper like herself. Or could she read minds? "How did you know that?"

Dymphna stared at her blankly, as if she could not understand the question unless it had been asked post-capture.

Aurora took a slow breath to restrain herself from sweeping all the pieces to the floor. Again, she vowed to play by her own rules.

"He died . . . in a fire."

The girl's diaphanous eyes seemed to see right into Aurora's brain. She did not dare attempt the detailed lie she had constructed for Storey's benefit. But likewise, she did not want to give away the truth to someone she still had no reason to trust.

Another capture, another question.

"How did you know my father was dead?" Aurora asked.

Dymphna rolled a captured pawn between her two hands. "My father is dead, too."

The answer was both cryptic and crystal clear. Aurora immediately recognized the sadness in the little girl—the cold detachment and matter-of-fact nature that accompanies grief before strangers. Aurora felt a kindred sorrow with her.

Several more moves and Dymphna gained another piece, this time a knight, and another question. "Who are you hiding from?"

"I am hiding from Lord Gomery."

"Why?"

Aurora echoed the girl's previous quizzical look, and saw the tiniest glimpse of a smile play at the corner of Dymphna's eyes. Dymphna motioned for Aurora to move. She yawned widely as she swept a bishop across the board in a long move and gained a question.

"Were you the one I heard walking last night and the night before?"

"At night, I am sleeping."

Damn, Aurora thought. Another non-answer and the perfect opportunity for a follow-up question, if only one could be asked.

Knight takes bishop. Aurora became aware that she was losing to this girl.

"What is your name?" Dymphna asked.

"Lady Inna of Venclova."

The girl calmly stood. "I do not want to play if you are going to lie."

"I beg your pardon?" Aurora mustered as much false indignation as she could.

Dymphna just looked at her, shaking her head ever so slightly in disappointment.

"Aurora."

The girl sat again and motioned for Aurora to take her turn. Aurora began to play aggressively, making bold moves to capture more pieces, at the expense of her strategy.

Rook takes bishop.

"Who are *you* hiding from?" she asked.

"Everyone."

Rook takes knight.

"Why have you shown yourself to me?"

"Because I know we will keep each other's secrets," Dymphna said.

Queen takes pawn.

Aurora was not sure what question, no matter how well crafted, would garner the answers she sought. The girl herself was not probing for information from Aurora; rather, she was asking questions that revealed what she already knew. Was it meant to keep Aurora off-balance? Was it an odd display of power? Was this girl a witch?

"Why did you ask me to come back?" Aurora asked at last.

"I have never known anyone like you before." Dymphna moved her rook into a position that left her king wide open.

"Are you sure you want to do that?" Aurora asked.

169

"When two great forces oppose each other, the victory will go to the one who knows how to yield."

Dymphna stood, pushed in her chair, then left the room, closing the door gently behind her. As if the girl really was a ghost, Aurora keenly felt her presence in the room for hours later.

Storey arrived at twilight.

"I really must not be spending enough time with you," he said, sitting down at the table, "if you are playing chess with yourself."

Aurora jumped up and began to arrange the pieces. "I was just . . . making sure they . . . worked." She glanced at him, but he was not listening. Reaching to upright the toppled king, she bumped into his shoulder. "Oh!"

"It's all right," he said, standing. "I am in your way." He moved to the trunk, where he set down a bulging sack.

"No, it's just that . . . you are so thin." She reached toward his shoulder, then pulled back, staring into his eyes with concern. She reached again, and this time gently squeezed his collarbone. "Storey . . ."

He pulled himself away from her grip. "I am fine."

"You are not fine. Look at your face. Have you seen it?"

She grabbed the hand mirror and held it up to him. He waved it away.

"I have only discovered I do not need to eat as much as I thought I did."

Aurora snatched the bag and overturned it onto the surface of the trunk. Enough food to last her three days or more tumbled out. Pears, apples, hunks of cheese wrapped in cloth, dried sausages, loaves of bread. And she already had food saved up from the previous day.

"You have been giving me your food?"

"Not all of it."

She forced the food back into the sack, all but one loaf

of bread. She broke off a large piece and shoved it at Storey. "Eat."

He shook his head and took a step back. "It is for you."

"I have enough. I have too much. But you . . . how do you even have the energy to do your work?"

He shrugged. Aurora again thrust the bread toward him, and this time he took it, biting off an enormous piece that puffed out his cheeks while he chewed.

"Thank you," he said through the food, a few crumbs spitting from his mouth.

Aurora pressed the entire satchel of food against his chest, and he was forced to hug it to himself so it would not fall. She caught his gaze and held it. "You take this with you when you leave."

He began to shake his head no.

"*You take this with you when you leave.*"

This time, he nodded.

"Will you sit while you finish?" She pulled the chair out for him. He obliged and sat down, continuing to chew his food like a cow with a mouthful of cud.

"Have you really been getting enough to eat?" he said, after swallowing the last bite.

She thought about the way her fingers fit into her protruding ribs. "Of course."

"Do you need new books?"

"I've not finished the ones you already brought."

"Clothes need laundered?"

"No."

"Is it getting too cold here at night?"

She paused. "About the nights . . ."

She wanted to be precise in her words. The urge to ask him about the little girl was overwhelming. But Aurora remembered Dymphna had said she was hiding from everyone. And, more poignantly, she recalled the phrase: "I know we will keep each other's secrets." That was the very nature of their bizarre bond. She would not betray Dymphna, but she could only ignore so many questions that needed answering.

"I have been hearing things."

"I know what it's like in this wing. It creaks at night. We have heard it together."

"No, that's not it." She paused, struggling. "Is there . . . is there someone else hidden in the house? Someone you keep here, like you keep me?"

An even more pressing question ran through Aurora's mind: If she continued to remain locked up in this room with no safe escape, would she someday end up like the girl—gaunt, pale, . . . strange?

Storey laughed darkly. "If only you could understand how mad that notion is. Do you think I have a whole harem of pretty girls I'm storing up in different rooms around the manor? I don't let any of you leave your rooms because you might run into each other and get jealous." He laughed again. "Actually . . . that's not a bad idea . . ." He rubbed his chin in mock consideration.

"I do wish you would take me seriously," Aurora said. "I heard footsteps last night, and the night before. Pacing. Sometimes singing. I have . . . I believe . . . there is another person, or people, living in one of these rooms."

It maddened her to play these games, when there were so plainly proof points at her disposal. She wanted to scream, *I know about her! I've seen her! She's beaten me at chess!*

Aurora was never one for bluffing games, where knowledge, facts, reality were of no consequence in the face of fictions and sleight of tongue.

He stared at her, concern in his eyes. "M'lady . . . I know it has been days, many days now, since you have been outside of this room, but . . . it frightens me that you would invent companions. Maybe what you heard was someone cleaning."

"In the middle of the night?"

Infuriatingly, he shrugged.

She shouted inside her head, *I am not mad!* But there was no reason to press the issue further. Though she did not believe a word coming from his mouth, neither was she convinced he knew the truth. However, someone was bringing Dymphna food. Someone had to bring her fresh water, and even clothes. As dingy as that rag of a dress was, she had not been wearing it forever. Maybe no one visited her, but someone was keeping her alive.

"So are you going to teach me this game, or are you content just to play it against yourself?"

Aurora nodded absently and set up the pieces. There was already a game being played here, and she was certainly not playing it by herself.

❧21❧

Storey's first indication that something was very wrong was the total silence that met him upon opening the door to Abern's chamber. Even in sleep—especially in sleep—the man was a cacophony of body noises. The sneezing and coughing, snorting and snoring, burbling and gurgling, even the creaking and popping of worn-out joints and ancient bones: the man was never silent. Though the noises and emanations of the human body sometimes repulsed him, nothing nauseated Storey so profoundly as this silence.

Floorboards creaking beneath him, each step forward was a thunderous echo in the rabbit's burrow of a room. Storey followed the flicker of his low-lit lantern, and as he approached his friend's bed, the amber glow cast across Abern's face. Bundled in his bed, gnarled hands lying on the blanket over his body, he appeared to be sleeping. But even Abern had said himself his only peaceful, restful, silent night of sleep would come when he was dead.

Dead, he was. And Storey had known it before even stepping foot into the room.

Setting the lantern on a small table, Storey sat in a chair near the bed and placed one of his hands over Abern's cold fingers. The hands looked nearly gray in the dim glow, and the fingernails had turned a bloodless white. Abern had been ailing for as long as Storey had been living at Secernere, but since no doctors could visit, Abern suffered without reprieve, and without vocal complaint. His body complained on his behalf, rather boisterously, but there was nothing to be done. Of late, they had all done with less, and Abern was no exception. Storey, the cook, and some of the others tried to sneak extra spoonfuls onto Abern's plate, but the man would never eat more than his share. If he had an extra bite of bacon, or a spare crust of bread, if his plate was ever fuller than another's, his leftovers went back to the kitchen to be made into another meal.

Storey's conscience burned painfully. If not for his own agenda, Storey thought, if not for his own underhanded actions, there would have been more to go around. Stealing food from the kitchen was tantamount to murdering Abern with his own hand. He was as guilty as any villain in this death.

But as he thought of the vibrant life and untapped potential that he was sustaining within these very walls, and looked at the gaunt and weathered countenance of Abern, the poignant guilt in his heart lessened to a dull ache. Food or no, Abern had little future as it was; had he known Storey's plans, he'd have given up what he had anyway. Though he was not strong enough to fight for a cause with his body, Abern offered everything he had to give—and that was stronger than any sword blow. Even with another bowlful of broth or one more slice of bread, the situation Storey encountered now would have been no different.

Storey whispered, "I am sorry, my friend." He squeezed the cold hand. "I am sorry you could not live to see the better future that will surely come. But I know death was as welcome to you as sleep to a man after a hard day's work. It is said, he who holds nothing back from life is ready for death. You never held back."

Storey wiped the tears from his eyes.

"After the death of my father, you were my father. After the death of my mother, you were my mother. In the absence of a real brother, you were that too. I will miss you more than anyone I have ever known."

Still holding onto his friend's hand, Storey cried quiet sobs until his lantern had nearly burned through all its oil. Standing, he leaned forward and placed a dry kiss on Abern's papery forehead.

"Sleep here in your bed a while longer, my friend," he said. He tucked the bed clothes in tightly around Abern's body, as if putting a child to bed. "I will bury you at dawn as one of my own family."

"Dymphna is such an usual name."

Aurora was sitting across from the girl at the hand-drawn chessboard. She had seen Storey four times since she had last seen Dymphna. His visits were usually very late in the evening, but he had finally found a way to spend more than just a morsel of time with her. They too had played chess during each visit, and even though Storey learned the concept quickly, his skill was eclipsed by the virtuosity with which Dymphna played the game.

Since Aurora had carefully explained that the object of the game was to put the king into checkmate—and *not* to allow your opponent to do it first—the girl's win percentage had all but reached one hundred. Aurora wondered again if the girl could read minds, and whether she was using that talent to her advantage. There was no question rule this time, and the conversation was running free, as much as it could with the strange, reticent little girl.

"Who named you?" Aurora continued.

"Check," Dymphna said.

"Did your mother give you that name?" Aurora moved her king out of harm's way.

"Aurora is an unusual name." Dymphna did not look up from the chessboard.

"Yes, it is. I was named after the river." Aurora motioned to the window. "That river out there beyond the wall? The Calder? It is called something else in . . . other countries.

"It is called the Aurora River in Fairgos," the girl said.

"Yes, that's right. And I was born in that river."

"In Fairgos?"

"I said in the river." Aurora refused to lie anymore, fearing discovery from the intuitive little girl, but did not always feel the truth was required. "I do not think Calder is a nice name for a baby girl."

Dymphna shook her head in agreement.

"Besides, Mitoch was not at war with Fairgos when I was born. We were both peaceful countries, and there was no disgrace in naming me after the river in their country." Aurora captured Dymphna's queen and tried to mask her triumph as she continued her story. "My mother was in the river, bathing. She liked to do that in the hot summer months. She was eight months pregnant, but that did not stop her. In fact, she told me later that floating in the water eased the discomfort I put on her joints.

"But the long walk from the manor house to the river must have caused her to go into labor too soon. While she was in the river, the contractions started to get very close together, and she realized she would not get back to the house in time. And then she made a very strange decision, one that I think predestined the course of my life: she did not get out of the river to deliver me."

"Witches do that," Dymphna said. "They have their babies

in river or lakes, because that is what the womb is like inside—full of water."

Aurora nodded. The comparison to a witch was unfair, but she could not deny that her mother's choice was unconventional—so much so that it was never spoken of in their household. This was the first time Aurora had ever told anyone the truth.

"She thought it would be less traumatic for me to enter the world that way. So out I came, underwater, and then she scooped me out of the river and I took my first breaths of real air. Then she made a wee nest of grass and leaves and laid me in it while she finished bathing."

Dymphna expelled an uncharacteristic giggle, and Aurora saw her smile for the first time. "She finished bathing?" she laughed.

"Yes, she absolutely did! And I can hardly say I blame her. She was a bloody mess after that, and so was I. She did not want us to return to the house with both of us so untidy. She wanted the entrance of the new Lady of Cavalcata to be elegant—and it was."

Aurora smiled, remembering the story her mother had told her so many times while tucking her in at night. The late Lady Inna had once been strong and proud, had always thought she was built for having a brood of children. But fortune did not afford her that talent.

"I named myself," Dymphna said.

"Oh!" Aurora was surprised: an even stranger story than her own. "Is that a custom in this area?"

Dymphna shook her head. "No. It's just . . . there was no one else to do it."

"Oh." Aurora tried to keep her voice neutral, but the girl's own phlegmatic manner of speaking made her statements all the more heartbreaking. "Why Dymphna?"

"Dymphna was a saint, a noblewoman. She lived on an island in the West in the seventh century. She had a beautiful mother. But when she was sixteen, her mother died and her father became mad with grief and loneliness. He vowed to scour the world in search of a new wife, but she had to be beautiful inside and out, as beautiful as his dead wife. Alas, the search failed. There were no women in the world as beautiful as Dymphna's mother—except Dymphna. In his madness and grief, he sought to make Dymphna his new wife."

Aurora watched, fixated on the girl as she recounted the story as simply as if it were a favorite fairy tale.

"She was very frightened, so she fled with her confessor, Saint Gerebernus, who was a very old priest. They went to another country in the East and hid in a chapel. But her father and his spies tracked them down, and then her father arrived as well. When Dymphna and Gerebernus were discovered, her father's soldiers slew Gerebernus, and then her father begged Dymphna to return home with him. When she refused, he raised his sword and decapitated her."

Dymphna moved a rook forward and knocked over Aurora's king.

"Checkmate."

Secernere – Hours earlier

His crooked spine aching from his too-hard bed, Abern shifted for the thousandth time that night. His empty belly growled and contracted within him, and his innards writhed with indigestion from the day's early meal of scraps. His lungs felt full of phlegm, his heart full of black bile. No position offered respite from the pain his body produced from the inside out. Another hungry, sleepless night would do nothing to help him heal from this latest sickness.

As he began to wake, Abern became aware that someone was in the room with him. He heard breathing and the subtle creaking of the floorboards. With painful difficulty, he pulled himself onto his elbows, peering out into the black.

From across the room came the voice.

"So happy to see you awake, Mister Abern, that I may offer my farewell in person." It was Cashel, his voice disembodied in the darkness.

"My lord." Abern fell sideways as he expelled a juicy cough. He righted himself. "If you please, I'll light a lantern."

"Not necessary."

Abern waited for more, but Cashel said nothing.

"So you are taking your leave of us, my lord?" Abern said. "Is it not the middle of the night? I have difficulty telling time of day anymore. My quarters do not have a window."

"You do lately spend quite a lot of time in your quarters," Cashel said.

"It is my ailment, sir. It worsens."

Abern listened as Cashel rose and slid toward the bed, dragging the chair with him. Its wooden legs scratched and screeched across the floor. He was nearer now as he spoke.

"Much about our situation worsens, my friend. The cupboards run dry. More of the servants have left under cover of night. I, too, will soon leave once again to attend to my armies, who have similar problems, as they run low on supplies and numbers of defectors increase by the week."

Abern coughed again and peered out into the darkness. He heard Cashel's breath but still saw nothing except the black vacuum of his chamber.

"It is said, my lord, the balanced world adjusts excess and deficiency. It takes from what is too much and gives to what is not enough."

"I could not have stated it better myself," said Cashel's voice. "A man who eats food when there is near none, but contributes no work when there is much to be done—what adjustment would the balanced world make in that scenario, Mister Abern?"

Abern struggled to sit up farther.

"Let me tell you a story, Abern. One of my regiments was traveling north toward a rendezvous and they had many miles to cover in just a few days. This required them to march continuously for hours in the morning and many more hours after lunch, every day. Two of the women in the unit were having great difficulty keeping up, and together were slowing the pace to the point where the rendezvous would not be met.

"Now, don't misunderstand me: I value the cohesiveness of a military group. A team can only be as strong as the weakest member, and in every continuum, there are extremes of greatness and of wanting. Being the weakest was not a condemnation of these two women.

"Indeed, one of them, Demine, is a tremendous swordswom and is as well a beauty with good humors. Demine's slow pace was very much due to an old knee injury that she could not ignore under such strenuous exercise. But it was also partly due to a particular weakness in her character. Like all women, she has an enormous capacity for love, but myopia taints her caring. She tends toward a desire to ensure the happiness of a singular individual, rather than being mindful of what is best for the group. This is precisely why I argue that women are not equipped to lead nations. For all Fairgos' evil, they have it right in that regard.

"Due this flaw, Demine latched onto the second woman, Borodin, whose own slowness came from a much less respectable place. Demine became quite obsessed with watching over Borodin, keeping her company, and encouraging her as her energy and will flagged.

"Borodin had qualities of which neither she nor I can boast. She was fat, lazy, disrespectful, and generally a poison to the unit. Not only was she having a potent negative effect on Demine—a promising soldier—but her attitude was affecting morale all over her unit. The other women began to complain about the impossibility of the rendezvous. In their eyes, Borodin and Demine were the evidence, rather than the cause.

Spurred on, Borodin began to complain loudly of other perceived injustices: too-small rations, worn-out uniforms, dull or broken weapons—as if she were the only one facing these trials. All this, while marching more and more slowly, and eventually refusing to march at all. Demine, in the solidarity of alleged friendship, refused as well.

"This could not go on, Abern. A soldier is a part of the machine that is the unit. A unit is part of the machine that is the army. One soldier refusing to function can bring down her unit by simply neglecting the duties of her rank. But more than neglect, Borodin had put herself in a position to lead by example and was on the eve of bringing the entire unit to a screeching halt. We are at war, Abern, and this was treason.

"At first I beat her, then progressed to the cat. But I soon realized this would not solve my problem. Abern . . . you know intimately my passion for carnal justice. Messy deaths prove points. Blood stains prompt memories when time would fade the lessons. However, in the field we kill treasonous soldiers by breaking their necks. This is so no blood spills on their uniforms, because those uniforms can be worn by others. We waste nothing in the pursuit of the good of the whole.

"She screamed as I came to her." Cashel sighed ruefully. "The weak ones always scream."

Before Abern's eyes, the room began to spin. He searched, wildly scanning the room. Found nothing.

"Sir, allow me to light the lamp." He began to cough uncontrollably. "Please, Cashel. You needn't do this. . . . Cashel, I held you as a baby."

"Then you know more than any that I entered this world covered in blood, and I feel no remorse at my role in it. Farewell, Mr. Abern. It is for the good of the whole."

Abern took his last breath and did not have time to exhale before the pillow was over his face, and his lungs gave out, his brain gave out, his heart gave out, and he was dead.

❧22❧

$\mathcal{D}$espite the heat even at dusk, the moist ground beneath the oleander where Cort sat was cool against his thighs and buttocks. The wall, too, was cool through his sweat-soaked shirt as he leaned against it. From this spot, he was well hidden and could look out through the expanse of the wide, flat demesne while he gnawed a salty piece of venison jerky. Though the estate was dangerously open, with few trees and widely spread buildings, Cort had so far seen no one during his exploration. He wondered if in fact the place had been abandoned.

The livestock appeared to be in the initial stages of malnourishment, and there were far fewer horses than stalls in the stable. No doubt, the estate was suffering the effects of the war. However, there were no signs of invasion, no buildings destroyed; the costs remained indirect. But even indirect consequences could be cause enough to seek shelter elsewhere, closer to a town, or nearer the capital.

Swallowing the last bite of his supper, Cort rose to a crouch. Then, establishing he was still very much alone, he stood and began his trek around the perimeter of the impressive wall. In a practiced, almost unconscious procedure, he ran his fingertips along the stones as he crept forward, shaded and covered by the lush, soft-leaved oleander. The bushes grew up against the wall to a height half again as tall as he, for as far as he could observe. It was perfect cover for his exploration.

The sun began to set, lowering the demesne into slow, gray darkness. Cort would progress with his investigation in a calculated pattern toward the interior-most buildings, which he would reach under the cover of night. If he concluded that indeed the estate had been abandoned, his next task would be to decipher in which direction they had gone, then follow. He continued to have no reason to believe Aurora was dead, and if she wasn't, she would be with them.

He stopped.

Until now, the wall had been just a wall. Where his fingertips lingered, an inconsistency in the stonework told him that this wall was not simply a wall. As he looked closer, he saw no difference in the stones. He continued to feel around the area until he found the seam.

It was an opening of some sort—a door.

He groped around the edge until he had discerned the entire perimeter of the door, but he could not decipher how to open it. No handle was apparent, no latch or lever. Then, pressing his shoulder against the middle of the door, he pushed with simple brute strength, and it gave way reluctantly. He pushed the door in far enough to accommodate his body, and squeezed in.

The interior facet was wooden. Cort tested the large iron latch to ensure he could open the door from the inside, then closed it behind himself. Whatever manner of concameration he had entered became oppressively, tangibly black. He held his hand before his face and could not see it. No light crept within the wall. Rummaging through his pack, he retrieved his lantern and lit it, pouring a pale yellow glow over what he now saw was a narrow stone corridor.

The passageway appeared endless in both directions, leading into imponderably dense shadows. Traveling down the passage to his right would take him back toward the mill, where he had entered. The left-hand path would move toward the cluster of buildings surrounding the manor house, so he began to walk in that direction.

The air trapped within the wall was thick with the smell of earth and worms, and it was as cold as an October evening. Cort withdrew a coarse wool sweater from his pack and pulled it on. The interior walls were separated by the width of two men, who would brush their shoulders if they passed. The ceiling was only a head higher than Cort, and the ground was hard packed dirt. For as far ahead as he could see (which was really no more than a few yards), the walls were plain stone, just as the outside, with no sconces or torches along the path. It was on the inside as it was on the outside. He passed no additional doors.

He walked for a considerable distance without observing any change in his surroundings until, abruptly, the atmosphere around him became irriguous with the odor of decay. Again, Cort opened his pack, this time retrieving a kerchief, which he tied around his mouth and nose as he moved forward. Before him, the corridor opened into an eye-shaped apartment that widened gradually to about twenty feet across, then narrowed again at its farthest end. The ceiling was taller here, dome-shaped, but the floor was still merely earth. Three torch sconces hung on the walls on either side, and in the center of the room was a stone pedestal topped with a bowl of water. Cort held a match to one of the torches, illuminating the chamber, including five large mounds of dirt along one wall. It was a row, almost surely, of five graves. Each was marked with a single white stone.

Another four graves lined the opposite wall, and Cort approached them. Three of the graves appeared to be many years old, the mounded dirt the same dry color as the floor. But the grave on the end, dark and moist, had been dug this very day; a shovel, caked with earth, leaned against the wall like a skinny, loitering vagabond.

He did not take even pause to consider before his hands were around the shovel handle and he was digging into the fresh dirt, throwing it aside with urgent haste. The odor was nearly more than he could bear, even as he breathed through his mouth. Soon enough, he exposed a shoulder of the corpse, wrapped in a white shroud, and he dug around it with his hands, exposing the head. Supporting the skull in one hand, he carefully unwound the shroud. The greenish-blue skin of the chin became exposed first, and then it was evident: the corpse was an old man, probably died of old age. It was not Aurora.

"Praise be to God," he whispered, letting the body fall back to the ground. He roughly shoveled the dirt back onto the body. "Lord, forgive me for the desecration of this final resting place, as I hope you have forgiven all sins of those who lie here."

This body was fresh. Either they had fled the estate very recently, or they were still here—somewhere.

Cort extinguished the torch in the funerary chamber and continued down the unchanging corridor. He walked for at least a hundred yards before he saw another door, identical to the door through which he had entered. It would have been brash to try the door from the inside, so he continued to walk.

All at once, the blackness before him opened up as the tiny flame of a candle moved toward him. Holding it was a ghostly girl, dressed all in white. Cort froze. The girl froze. Her sharp intake of breath reverberated against the stones. Cort opened his mouth to speak, but she was already running. She ran by him, and air as cold as death moved around Cort's body when she passed. Goose bumps rose on his skin, but the chill went much deeper. Her candle blew itself out as she ran, but she did not stop. Cort, in silence, watched the white apparition disappear down the corridor until the blackness swallowed her whole.

Yes, they were still here.

Aurora's knife slid into the soft molding near the floor, carving a slash to mark the end of her twenty-sixth day in the room. Storey had been visiting every day, but she hadn't seen Dymphna in four. She traced over the twenty-second mark and wondered where the girl could be. Her story, the one about her name, had given Aurora nightmares. What was it about the legend that the girl found so familiar? Was it the hiding? Was it being hunted?

Aurora wondered what could be keeping her frequent visitor away for so many days in a row. Maybe she was sick. Dymphna's pallor and frailty were her most distinguishing characteristics, and Aurora wondered whether the girl were succumbing to an illness, perhaps one that had plagued her all her life. The thought made her heart hurt. She'd never before felt such a peculiarly pure bond with another person—like they needed each other, like each couldn't be entirely whole without the other.

As she continued to poke her knife at the wall, a strange, pointed odor seeped in low along the floor and poked her nostrils. Something was decaying. Gagging, she stood to escape the smell.

Her thoughts turned dark. Dymphna was hiding in the house and no one knew about her. If she died, what would happen to the body? She shuddered, and returned to her bed, huddling her arms around herself as the light withdrew from the room. She tried to picture a large greasy rat, lying dead in the floorboards. If it was a rat, it was not Dymphna. If it was a rat, it was not Dymphna. The nightmares continued into another long eventide.

The next morning, Dymphna reappeared at last. She seemed always to appear, never to arrive. When Aurora awoke, the girl was already sitting at the little table with the chess pieces set up in front of her on the fading, blurry board. Aurora never heard

187

her footsteps. As she pictured it, Dymphna hovered above the ground and transpired herself through walls like a wisp of winter breath through a scarf.

"You have not visited in a long while," Aurora said. She did not move from her prone position on the bed.

"I was frightened."

Aurora bolted up. "Frightened of what?"

"Frightened of a man whose face is hidden."

Aurora thought of the first and only time she'd seen Cashel, everything but his face. They were frightened of the same man. She wanted to choose precise words and see where this conversation would lead, but her brain was still emerging from the fog of slumber.

"I have missed your company," she said.

"You have other company," Dymphna said.

Aurora had not mentioned Storey. But Dymphna was bright enough to discern that someone had been taking care of Aurora, as Aurora had assumed of the girl. Storey could not be a secret; there was no point in holding back now. "Yes, Storey. He is the one keeping me here. You know Storey, do you not?"

"I know no one."

"How do you eat then?"

"I put food into my mouth and I chew it."

Aurora wanted to feel joy and relief that Dymphna was back, but instead felt frustrated, cross. So many times she thought they were past such semantic jests, but Dymphna would always confound her at the most inopportune times.

"Dymphna . . ." Aurora began haltingly. "I know we have talked many times and you have told me much. You are a wise and wondrous girl. But I still do not understand why you feel you must keep yourself a secret from everyone here. If you do not know your caretaker, if you do not know the man who has locked you up, or the reason for it, why do you think it is important that no one see you?"

"People see me. But no one knows I exist."

"And you wish to keep it that way?"

"Yes."

"But why?"

The girl was silent, considering, or trying to recall the words she wanted to say. It was a rare moment that she didn't have a quick answer on her tongue.

"It is said . . ." she finally began. ". . . Must I value what *others* value? Must I avoid what *others* avoid? Other people have what they need, but I alone possess nothing. I alone drift about like someone without a home. Other people are bright; I alone am dark. Other people are sharp like a sword; I alone am dull like a ploughshare. Other people have a purpose; I . . . don't know. I am different from other people. Other people are unknowable to me, as I am unknowable to them, and that is the very foundation of violence and strife."

Someone so young, so small—she had such heavy thoughts on her frail shoulders. Aurora's heart broke.

"Who would make violence against you?"

"Cashel," she said darkly.

"But you are only a girl." Aurora felt herself growing more anxious with each parcel of knowledge Dymphna allowed. The girl knew no one, yet she knew enough to fear Lord Gomery?

"He would believe I am a threat to his power."

The terrifying and powerful Lord Gomery that Storey had warned her about with such gravity—this man was afraid of a little girl?

Maybe she *was* a witch. Or maybe Lord Gomery believed so. Only a girl who displayed supernatural power could possibly put that kind of fear into such a singularly dominating leader. Aurora had read about them in dozens of books, and her father had known too many associates who had fallen because of the predictions of a witch woman.

Aurora didn't believe in magic, but she did believe that the power of suggestion was enough to drive a man to a demise of his own creation. She dismissed the thought. Dymphna was no witch. Even in her most cunning riddles, she exuded the complete and utter innocence of a child. She never been tainted by the shadows of human nature.

While Storey spewed his platitudes as if to comfort himself, to excuse actions misaligned with his thoughts, Dymphna quoted her own with the wholehearted faith that only the guiltless can maintain.

"Is that who you were frightened of these past days? Cashel?" Aurora asked.

"No."

Aurora realized it did not matter. For a child, the cause of fear was inconsequential against its symptom.

She shifted toward the middle of her bed, and patted the space beside her. The little girl looked at her, her eyes wide. Patting again, Aurora nodded in encouragement. Dymphna approached like a skittish animal and gingerly sat on the bed next to Aurora, who looped her arm around the girl's frail shoulders. Dymphna's cool detachment dissipated into the air as she melted in Aurora's embrace.

For the first time since being held by Kynton, Aurora felt the warmness of physical human connection. She also realized, as plainly as spoken word, that the girl had never before felt that connection. As Aurora felt tears forming, Dympha circled her arms around Aurora's waist and snuggled into the crook of her arm, closing her eyes in contented relief. Though they were both thin and boney, the embrace was as soft and comforting as a down blanket in the cold of a long winter night.

Aurora smoothed the girl's pale hair. "Have I ever told you about my home?" she whispered.

She felt the little girl shake her head against her stomach.

"It was called Cathendria. Do you know what that means?"

Again, the girl shook her heard no.

"It means House of Purity," Aurora said. "Like water is pure. Like a soul in heaven is pure. Like a little baby is pure."

"Cathendria," whispered Dymphna.

"Dymphna, I was wondering . . . I was thinking . . . I might like to give you a name, since you had no one to give you one. I think it might be time for you to have a new name."

The girl twisted her head and her watery blue eyes peered into Aurora's face with expectant wonder.

She was so innocent, so pure.

"What do you think of *Catherine*?"

The little girl's face broke into a genuine smile, an expression of happiness Aurora had never seen on her before. She squeezed her arms around Aurora and mumbled into her flesh.

"Yes. Catherine. I will be called Catherine."

Snuggled there, in every way like a newborn in Aurora arms, Dymphna—now Catherine—soon fell asleep, and with her head leaning backward against the wall, Aurora also let herself doze. Soon the sleep became deeper, and when she awoke hours later, Catherine was gone again.

❧23❧

"He is a deserter!"

Kynton reeled at the word. That any of his men would put Cort in such a category . . . He took a breath and tried to remain calm. Even seated at the head of the table in a majestic March auditorium, he did not feel so much a leader as a criminal being dissected by a prejudiced jury. To maintain tranquility would be his greatest chance to rise above the swirling turmoil of his harried band.

Farhan jumped in. "It is well known that the first to accuse a fellow of desertion has fancied such an escape himself."

The first man leapt to his feet, but Kynton raised a mollifying hand. Unspoken was his agreement with Farhan's statement. The overzealous vilification of his friend among the council made it clear that desertion was exactly the notion on many a man's mind.

"The last we are is each other's enemy," he said. "Let us treat each other with this truth in mind."

Volker paced the room, playing the part of the prosecutor

before his stacked jury.

"You mean, let us treat *you* with this in mind," he said. "First of all, you say he did not defect. You claim, rather, that you sent him—our lead scout, one of our best men—you sent him deep into enemy territory. Second—"

"I did not *send* him anywhere, Volker."

"*Second* of all, you executed this action without the consent of the council."

The men around the table nodded and mumbled in assent.

"And now, *now* you want to send *another* scout to find the first scout, who was chasing after a *woman*?"

Volker was expressing an energy level higher than Kynton had seen in him before. The man was angry. Moreover, the men were angry.

The covert plan between Kynton and Cort had betrayed their trust, and rightly so; since losing Lord Cavalcata, the men felt keenly aware of the part played by each and every man in the workings of the leadership. In the absence of one component, the machine began to shake and shudder. In the absence of two, the machine screeched out as gears stripped themselves and threatened to stop working altogether. Now Kynton would ask of them to separate off yet another part?

"You misunderstand. . . ." Kynton attempted to remain passive, his voice quiet, even as Volker's irritation heightened toward rage. Volker had been chomping at the bit to usurp Kynton's station for years, and this budding opportunity had him almost manic.

Kynton fixed his eyes outside a window behind Volker's shoulder, focusing on a rabbit-shaped cloud that floated through the blue sky.

"Yes, we misunderstand!" continued Volker. "What you tell us is clearly the raving of a man of unsound mind. It is no wonder we misunderstand!" He turned and appealed to the men of the council. "Some of us have come to the conclusion that it may be time for new leadership."

There, it was out. The threat was verbalized, and it hung in the air unanswered like the cloud outside. Kynton knew he was losing the ability to control his men, and even worse, his ability to inspire in them courage and loyalty and the motivation to carry out his plans. Since the burning at March and the loss of Cavalcata's guidance, they were men lost, fumbling toward morale that was creeping just out of their grasp.

He moved his gaze away from the cloud and looked at each man's face in turn. This time, they were not nodding assent. They were not speaking any words at all. They did not meet his gaze, nor did they look at Volker. Some may have been ashamed to have broached the subject of removing him from power. It was likely many had not yet come to agree with the blustering, ambitious Volker. Either way, Kynton still had a modicum of power and honor. It would be all he had to work with.

He stood, then pushed in his chair until the back butted against the table's edge. He walked to the window and looked outside, his hands clasped behind his back. The rabbit had changed to a toad. He turned and looked at his men, then motioned to his chair.

"Cort's chair stands empty. Would you have another be empty as well?" he said. "I understand very plainly Lord Gellert would not hesitate to fill my chair. But I will leave another chair empty, because, fellows, I will not follow Lord Gellert as my leader. If you choose a change in leadership, I will leave this council. I will don the uniform of an enlisted man and find a campaign fighting deep in the heart of Mitoch. I will go solitary into the unknown of their wild, wooded land because I want to find my beloved Cort and my beloved betrothed. If, as a leader of a country's army, I must relinquish the very rights for which we fight—for friendship, brotherhood, love, and family—then that is not the manner of army I wish to lead.

"I understand that it sounds simply mad to spend any time at all on the death of a mere two in the whole of the nation. But for whom do we fight if not for the few? Do we not fight for the mother who has already lost her son to this war? Is that not our Cort's mother? Do we not fight for the daughter who lost her father to this war? Is that not our own Aurora of Cavalcata? Do we no longer fight for the fallen?"

"We choose to have no more fallen," said Volker.

Kynton slammed his palm onto the table. The men flinched.

"Then we shall lay down and expose our bellies to the Mitochian army as the defeated!" He pointed at Volker's chest and lowered his voice to a growl. "If you choose to have no more fallen, then you choose not to be at war. This war, my friend, will be won by the deaths of our men, and by our own deaths. The cause for which Cort gave up his life is no less honorable than that of Lord Cavalcata or any others of the fallen!"

Kynton looked around and again addressed the room at large. "That is why, this time, I will not allow for a single man to go alone into that wilderness. I have designed a campaign that will lead us to the heart of the country, to the very area I believe to house Cashel of Gomery, the villainous architect of our would-be demise. I know not if we will find Cort or Aurora on that path. But I know that with the defeat of Gomery will come the advantage that will make us victors in this war. It is with that success I will reap vengeance for their deaths. I will personally lead this campaign—"

"Lord Sebastia, you cannot—" It was Farhan who interrupted.

Kynton cut him off, pointing his finger this time at his detractor. "I am the general of this army, and I will lead and I will fight if that is my choice. If I die leading this campaign, then you will be granted your wish of an empty seat and you may fill it as you see fit."

He glanced to Volker, who was staring fixedly at a spot on the floor in front of him.

"If you wish not to hear me out and offer second to my motion, then you may leave now. But have faith that this campaign will proceed, with or without your second."

He looked at each man's face. "Go. Leave now."

He looked at Farhan. "Go." Farhan subtly shook his head.

Kynton looked at the downcast eyes of Volker of Gellert. "Volker, go." Volker did not move.

Kynton pulled out his chair and sat in it, then leaned forward over his folded hands.

"Good," he said. "We shall begin."

Before Storey had even fully entered the room, Aurora was already speaking: "We need to talk."

Storey deposited a sack of supplies onto the trunk and did not even look at her. His underarms and chest were damp with sweat, and dirt streaked his jaw.

"It is not the time." He made to leave.

The darkness that gnawed at Storey's soul and mind seemed to grow stronger by the day, as he increasingly withdrew from their interactions. It was coming to a portentous head, and something—Aurora could not discern what—was on the horizon. She only knew the nauseated feeling that flooded her chest when she saw his sunken eyes and hollow clavicle. Despite every slashed knife-mark in the molding, she knew that time was not something they would have forever.

"No, Storey. I have questions and I need—"

He turned and glared at her. "*It is not the time.*"

She jumped to her feet and pressed her face to within inches of his.

"If I left it up to you, it would never be time to answer my questions. I should walk out of this room right now and get myself killed, as you tell it, and then my death would be on your conscience because you never fully explained—in *detail*—the gravity of the situation into which you have relegated me, and which I did not understand enough to keep myself safe."

"If you do not believe me, what, pray tell, has given you cause to remain in this room up to right now? Is the bed just too comfortable to abandon?" He spat the words.

Aurora did not back down, her fists clenching themselves into tight balls. "Tell me, what has Lord Gomery done that has made you so frightened of him?"

"*I* am not frightened of him."

"But—"

"However, *you* should be frightened of him."

"You talk about him as if he is evil, and yet, you have never explained why you feel that way. I know he is a part of the war, a war of which you do not approve. But playing a part in a war does not make someone evil." Even as she said it, she knew she was not speaking entirely about Lord Gomery.

Storey shoved the door closed behind him, then leaned up against it with his arms crossed.

"Twelve years ago, Cashel discovered his father was having an affair. Cashel's reaction was to run the man through with a sword. He then withdrew the sword and used it to slice open the jugular of the mistress. As the both of them writhed in pain, bleeding out into the floorboards of this very house, he wiped the sword on the tablecloth, went out for a horseback ride, and left the whole bloody mess for the servants to clean up." His voice was even, as if he were describing the weather outside. "Suddenly struck with insanity, his mother fled, never to be seen again."

Horrified, Aurora could not respond.

"I witnessed everything. I was twelve years old."

"Oh God." The fear she felt at night, which nearly always seemed ridiculous and unfounded in the light of morning, returned with almost paralyzing force. She knew suddenly, with as much certainty as if Storey had said it, that Cashel had killed many more than the war called for. There truly were ghosts haunting this manor.

"We have lost numbers of servants, let go because we

could not afford to keep them on, or sometimes even to feed them. We've lost them to desertion, when they were fearful they would get on the wrong side of Cashel's sword. We've lost them to old age and disease." He paused, swallowed. "And not one of them has ever been replaced with anyone new to this estate. While Cashel has charged me to protect Secernere from strangers, my work has been to protect strangers from Secernere. We have had no visitors, guests, messengers, merchants, boarders, or beggars enter the gates in more than five years. Until you."

"I don't understand," Aurora said, almost to herself. There was a quiet desperation in her voice. She backed away from Storey and sat on her bed.

"We did not have any swimmers, drowners, or floaters, either. He slays all, Lady. All strangers. All unfamiliar faces. All men, all women—women, with extreme prejudice. Fairgosians, with worse. If you are not his sworn and proven ally, you are his enemy, and if you are his enemy, you are dead."

Aurora's mouth was dry, and she found she could barely speak. She whispered, "Why?"

"Why what? Why the paranoia? He is frantically afraid someone will take away his precarious ounce of power."

"How could that happen?" she asked.

"Do you mean in the reality of the world? Or in Cashel's paranoid reality?"

Storey took a deep breath.

"After . . . the incident, Cashel enlisted in the army. There was violence deep within him that surfaced occasionally, but the war tapped pure bloodthirst. He went on a number of consecutive tours, only returning to Secernere at intervals of many months. He fought on the front lines, killed platoons' worth of Fairgosian soldiers.

"But what changed everything was an illicit trip to our eastern border, near the mountains. He was tailing a scout who he thought was working as a double-agent. After murdering the scout, he took over gathering intelligence. Cashel interviewed landholders, peasants, trappers, and slave traders. He talked to everyone—he didn't care who they were. In the end, he had gathered enough information to provide the Queen with precise technical navigation instructions that led to Mitoch's first real battle victory, when otherwise we easily would have lost. At the end of his term, he was going to re-enlist—he wanted to keep on killing things—but the military and government wanted to hire him in a different capacity, as a strategist and consultant.

"Ambitious little monster, he saw the opportunity to get more out of this than just a new job. Even though he was the only Gomery child, he had no access to his mother's accumulated wealth. Outside the army, he was no one. His title would not be legitimized unless he married, which he had no desire to do."

Aurora struggled to keep up with the tale, but the details were tangling into a knot that became tighter as she tried to work through it.

Storey continued. "He struck some kind of secret deal with the government. With his position in the military would come what is essentially noble status. He now has claim to the Gomery title, the accompanying power—and the money. I believe, however, the money was what he only *thought* he wanted. As he rose through the ranks to even greater claims of authority, he found he was accumulating social and civic power. And that turned out to be his true heart's desire.

"The Gomery fortune diminishes. He is letting Secernere fall to disrepair and debt. But I think he cares not about Secernere. Secernere does not allow him to be anything. What power does he have as a miller or a horse merchant? But as long as the war goes on, he has all the power of a woman. If the war ends, whether in victory or defeat—"

"He will go back to being no one," Aurora said.

Storey nodded. "It is said, give evil nothing to oppose and it will disappear by itself." He continued, "Cashel has designs to change the complexion of the government, to enable men to share the power. But really, he doesn't want to share power—he wants it all to himself."

All the power of a woman. The phrase echoed through her head like a holler down a well. *All the power of a woman.* The revelation was dizzying. She tried to hide her raw shock. In Mitoch, the women ruled.

This simple premise was not in any book she had ever read.

"I think I understand. . . ." she said.

"It comes down to a very simple but dreadfully sinister idea: the longer Cashel stays in the war, the more power he gets. The more power he gets, the longer he will wage the war. None of his strategies, none of his campaigns are forwarding us toward victory or truce; they only further embroil us. I cannot understand why no one sees that. They just allow it to continue!" Storey crossed the room and dropped into the chair. Leaning forward, he took his head in his hands. "The madness of this life has no end."

"Why does he return to Secernere at all?"

"It is just more paranoia," Storey said. He lifted his head. "He worries some sister or aunt or cousin will appear to claim Secernere and the title and all his holdings. He comes around as often as he can spare the time just to check up on the few of us who remain here, to make sure we are not hiding any female strangers on the premises."

He laughed darkly.

"If someone with legitimate claim were to turn up—without Cashel killing her first—she would have legal rights to pull him from his position. Typically, anyway. War changes everything, does it not? I do not think the government would allow such a thing. It would be ludicrous for them to relinquish their omnipotent Cashel of Gomery just for the sake of legal propriety. Besides that, it would create a power vacuum only to be filled by another ruthless killer, man or woman, so the scenario is useless to those of us who seek peace. Barring a Fairgosian victory, the only solution—the outlandish fantasy that it is—would be for a Gomery woman to lay claim to his position and prove that she could end the war."

All this time, Aurora had convinced herself the paranoia belonged to Storey. But as each fact laid itself bare, on overblown tale of a ruthless, deluded overlord became frightening truth. And she realized with horror that she—Fairgosian nobility, a woman hiding within Secernere's walls—was the very target of all Cashel's wrath.

Staring down at her hands, which lay in her lap as if they belonged to someone else, she whispered to herself, "I cannot stay here."

"What was that?"

She looked up at him, her eyes glistening, her face and body slack with exhaustion. "I cannot stay here."

"Ah, so you finally come to the conclusion I have been drawing for you all along."

His attempt at levity was transparent, and neither even tried to smile. They were quiet. Anxiety hung between them, tangible and pendulous. No house sounds now.

"Storey . . ." Aurora finally broke the silence. "I am Fairgosian."

❧24❧

I know," Storey said.

"What?" Aurora jumped to her feet.

"I said, I know you're Fairgosian."

"But—" she stammered. "How?"

Storey waved his hand. "Your hair, your eyes, your accent. Your lies. Your confusion at everything that is common knowledge in Mitoch. I marked you as a foreigner the moment I saw you."

Aurora huffed at his dismissiveness. She was a *proud* Fairgosian lady . . . was she not? She wasn't so sure anymore what she was.

"It was, of course, possible that you were from some remote border town in the south where they speak with pseudo-Fairgosian accents, and that perhaps some far-back strange relative of yours contributed to that dark complexion. Maybe your home was secluded enough that you actually had *not* heard of Cashel of Gomery and the tales of his wartime heroics. But do you know what finally confirmed everything for me?"

Aurora shook her head.

"The Bible. It was the matter-of-fact way you told me you read the Bible—and the way you were surprised I have not."

"I don't understand."

"Do you think a people like us, like Mitoch, would use such a book as our sacred text, a book wherein women are the root of evil in the world? Where God is the patriarch of all the universe? Where he gives the gift of a son, and all his son's followers are men? Governments, monarchies, entire religions employ such a text as the sacred 'Word of God' for their own sinister purposes, not the least of which is to keep certain groups—like women—in subservient roles. How is it that your God made women to be the creators of life, but he himself is not woman? It makes no sense."

Aurora felt her face go hot. "You don't even believe in God! How dare you suggest that you understand his ways!"

"What I believe in is older than God."

"Whatever you believe in, it is the devil's work." Aurora retreated to the bed and pressed her back against the wall, hugging her knees to her chest.

Storey chuckled contemptuously. "You represent your government very well."

"What?" She remained indignant. With his mocking, accusatory tone, Storey was proving correct her every suspicion that revealing herself as Fairgosian would only bring animosity.

"Tell me why our countries are at war," he said.

"You know very well why we are at war."

"No," said Storey, "I want to hear your version."

She had read the King's *Declaration of War*. She had read everything she could. She should have known these answers. But the daughter of the Royal War Master to the Fairgosian King and His Army stumbled. She tried to recall the speech. *I am a new leader in an old country.*

"Mitoch . . ." she began awkwardly, waving her arm in front of her, as if to indicate she was talking about *this* Mitoch and not some other one. "Mitoch is a backward country. Fairgos desired to bring our progressive government to your people to help your country thrive in this modern world."

"And so your armies *attacked*? What sense does that make?"

Damn. She had to think. What were her three proof points?

"We had to be assertive ..." Aurora began.

"Aggressive, you mean."

"Mitoch was a threat! A clear and present threat that we had to eliminate. We had to attack. . . . We had to maintain our nation's security and autonomy."

"What was the threat?"

". . . It was clear they—you—were preparing for war. You were going to attack us because you hated how we prospered."

"Go on."

"You were ... building up your army. Stockpiling weapons and armor."

Damn. Her words thudded out like wrong notes, falling dully, wrongly, impotently on her ears.

Storey laughed again. "Now you are just making things up."

"All right then, if you know so much, *you* tell me why our countries are at war."

"I think you overestimate what knowledge means, m'lady." Storey stood, crossing his arms over his chest, and paced while he spoke. "Nothing in Mitoch changed. There was no *stockpiling*. Our people were quietly going about our business being a peaceful nation. Though you seem educated, it is evident that no one ever told you the truth about Mitoch, and it is no wonder. When did you begin your studies, as a girl?"

"I was twelve ..."

"And you can't be more than, how old?"

"I recently turned twenty-one," she said.

"All right, so you are twenty-one. Happy birthday. The war has been going on for over a decade. I have no doubt that your government forbade it to educate children about their enemy, or at least to educate them in the truth. So let me put it very plainly: Mitoch is a matriarchy. That means—"

"I *know* what a matriarchy is."

"Would you not believe that a country where women are the governors, where women hold titles of nobility, where women hold all the wealth and power—would you not believe that we are a nurturing, peaceful, quiet country?"

"Of course I cannot say for sure," Aurora said in a low voice. She felt unprepared to make any logical leaps, now that it appear she knew far less than she thought she did.

"So you think we would build up an army and threaten our neighbors for no reason, stockpiling weapons and brandishing our broad swords like so many—" He grabbed his crotch.

She turned her face from him. "Do not be crass."

"Your country was the one that changed, m'lady. It is said, to be free of sorrow, you must look back upon your roots and find your mother. Not so with Fairgos. A new king came to power; are you old enough to remember?"

She nodded, still not looking at him.

"This new king was very much like Cashel: he was frightened of losing his power. It unnerved him to rule a country that bordered a country where men would have no power in their government. He was afraid that the women of Fairgos might rise up and demand rights, wealth, power, self-ownership. His sister, had he one, might steal his throne."

"That is a ridiculous notion."

"Of course it is!" exclaimed Storey. "But who is to keep in check the ridiculous notions of a king? No one. And so he wages an unfounded war. So he spreads lies and misinformation about the evil country of Mitoch. I am sure you heard quite your share."

He sighed, then continued. "A generation of children have grown into adulthood without having truly understood who it is they are fighting, or why. There will be no truce."

"I have heard talk of re-unification!" Aurora said. "Is that not peace?"

"The myth of the return to Sangeva. Re-unification under one leader. And who do you think that one leader would be? It will not be the Mitochian queen. It will not be a queen at all. Your government wants the security of a total win. They want to absorb Mitoch into themselves until we no longer exist. Under Cashel, my government wants the security of an ongoing war."

Storey let his words hang in the air, and Aurora was silent for a long time before she responded.

"If men have no rights or wealth or power or self-ownership in Mitoch, then your country is no better," she said petulantly.

"Oh, I am not defending Mitoch at all! In many ways, we are just the same. This entire conversation began because of the Bible. We have our own version—it is called the Thema. We have a God, too, but he is a she."

"The Thema, is that from where you get your wise sayings?"

"No." He spat the word. "The Thema is social propaganda masquerading as religious text, just like the Bible. The best that I can say about it is that it has, for the most part, aided us in remaining a peaceful nation—until this war, of course. People who are very much afraid of death will practice morality if they think it will bring them eternal life."

"If you hate the ways of Mitoch as much as you hate Fairgos, why do you even stay here? A country like Ekanta would welcome a man such as yourself, would it not?"

"Ekanta is safe, peaceful, but it is no utopia. Nowhere is. What kind of man would I be to flee a nation so mired in turmoil?"

"As if your presence makes a difference here?" Aurora said. "As if anyone really matters to anyone else? No one's presence—or absence—makes any difference. We all fancy ourselves to be the center of the world, and none of us are. The world spins and spits us out, dumped off at the bend in the river. There is no one to miss us." She was crying. "We are

God's pawns. One may become a queen, but the other faceless seven are sacrificed in anonymity."

Storey sat beside her on the bed and took her hand. "It is not for us to know what difference our actions will bring about. It is said, the wise woman acts but does not expect. When her work is done, she forgets it—and that is why it will last forever."

"I cannot even act. I am trapped here. I came here to try to help, to matter. I wanted to be more than a consumer of history books."

". . . I know that feeling well," Storey said. "You—we—will act when the time is right, and that time is soon. I feel the trajectory of the world moving toward the inevitable. We will be a part of it, whatever happens."

Aurora stared at her hands, as if answers lay in the creases of her palm. "I heard you praying once. . . ." she whispered. She parsed the words out tentatively, like her own secret prayer. "That first day, in the barn. You leaned up against the door, and I heard you pray."

"And?"

"If you do not believe in God, who were you praying to?"

Storey was silent for a while. His gaze withdrew to something deep inside himself and his eyes lost their focus.

"It's been many years since I lost God," he began. "But who to pray to has been an idea I have struggled with every minute since then. I often talk to him by mistake, forgetting that I am talking to no one."

"I don't understand."

"A person is raised with God as the invisible advisor, the imaginary friend. She is someone who is constantly present, unflappably forgiving, all knowing, and all understanding. How could one not want to pass every thought, every decision through the gates of her advice, in every circumstance? More than that, who else can one turn to during life's most trying challenges, those which are unfathomable to any soul-bearing

207

human? When we cannot understand each other, when we cannot even understand ourselves, from whom can we possibly seek guidance other than our own God?"

Aurora whispered, "No one."

"No one," Storey repeated. "Exactly. . . . So when we kill our god in the deicide that occurs when reality is fully realized—the deicide that is enlightenment beyond the fiction our parents and governors deliver to the innocent minds of the children, the poor, the weak, the dumb, the lost, and the otherwise vulnerable, impressionable, empty vessels—we have *no one* left to provide us with guidance or understanding. The painful irony is that God has *never* imparted us with guidance or understanding."

". . . But the Bible . . . It advises us on every aspect of life," Aurora said. She coughed. "Or the Thema."

"God did not write the Bible or the Thema. Man did. Woman did. The Bible is not God. Besides, the Bible exists out of time. It existed before you were born and will continue to exist long after you die. And it will always say exactly the same thing. What kind of advice is that?"

"It is timeless advice."

"But the trials of humans are not timeless. They are firmly rooted in our time—now. The characterization of people today, the changing landscape of culture and our governments. The weapons we use in this war we fight."

"This war is not unlike other wars."

"Ha." A wry smile crossed his lips. "You do speak a truth there. But," he continued, "do we each not feel as if we are the first and only to live? That we are in bright color, and everyone else is pale, as if viewed through gauze? These history books you consume, are they not in only two dimensions?"

He waited for an answer which Aurora did not have.

"I don't understand," she finally said. The repeating words rung loud and pathetic in her ears. She had never in her life felt so dumb, so witless as she did since arriving at Secernere.

"You said earlier that we each fancy ourselves to be the center of the world. That's what makes the idea of God so insidiously intoxicating. It's not exceptional wisdom out of an ancient book. It's how the idea of God makes you feel so special.

"Tell me if this is familiar. When your father died, you felt as though you were the first, the only woman whose father had died so young, so tragically. When thinking of your father, you only identify as a daughter. You do not think of yourself as an independent, individual woman . . . a person. You perpetually think of yourself as young, a child. His child. You are only a daughter. Even as he aged, he didn't, because you were aging too. Everything was relative. He only looked different—especially when you went for so long without seeing him—"

"Stop it," she whispered.

"Sometimes, you would see him anew. He would be grayer, his lines deeper. But you would still feel like the girl, the daughter. Powerless against the father's omniscience and omnipotence—still a child."

"Please. Stop."

"And when he died, you felt like no one had ever hurt more. You felt like no daughter had ever loved a father more. No father had been more perfect, even in all his imperfections—those flaws that were so easy to explain away. When he died, it was unduly violent, untimely early. It was entirely unfair, unwarranted. You were the only daughter in the entire world to lose a father . . .

"Never mind that he was someone's husband. Never mind that he was a friend to many. Perhaps he was someone's lover. He was a son, too. He was a client, a colleague, a patient, a lord, an overseer. He was so much more than a father—but not to you. *You* were the only one to lose him, and you felt it more than anyone, ever."

"You're goddamned right I did!" she screamed. Tears dripped from her jawbone. She pushed herself as far away from him as she could.

209

"Now replace your father with God."

She dragged the back of her hand across her eyes and tried to will away the fresh hate she was feeling for this man.

"Think of all the things God is to you. Think of your personal relationship with God. Think of every intimate detail of your life you have prayed about. Think of every privacy you could not have completely to yourself because of the constant and watchful presence of God. Think of what you shared with God on the day your father died. There is no intimacy deeper than what we have with God. There is no stronger love."

"You're right about that."

"Now imagine, instead of your father dying, it was God."

She stared at him as his face shifted from beautiful to grotesque and back again, as if each of her eyes saw a different side of him and wouldn't focus into a unified image.

"He is gone, and there is no one left to replace him. He's not like a lover; you cannot go find a new one. He is like a mother, a father—but so much more. When he is gone, he is gone. The hole is so much deeper, so much more immense than you can possibly begin to imagine."

"But if you don't believe God exists, then you can't believe he ever existed. So how can he die? This is not at all like my father. Curse you for even making such a comparison!"

"But I did believe, as much as I believe I have arms, legs, and a heart that beats in the silence of the night."

"And one day you stopped believing."

"It came upon me suddenly. . . . It felt like I was remembering something, only to realize it wasn't a true memory, but a dream. Suddenly, God was not reality, but rather a false memory. He was there and then he was not there—and I realized he never had been."

"But why?"

"Did you ever ask why is God? Why would you ask why isn't God?"

Aurora felt bitterly aware that every time she had ever asked why anything, it was for reasons petty and self-serving. She felt self-obsessed, foolish. Indeed, she did feel like a child, not just a child to her father, but a child to the whole of the world. Trust and innocence became naiveté, and virtue became flaw.

Storey placed his hand on the bed between them, attempting to close the chasm he had opened.

"The day God died for me, I have never felt so alone. You don't know what it means to be alone until you kill your God."

She thought she knew what it was to be alone in the whole of the world. This idea crushed her. She felt the physical weight of it on her heart, pressing down on her brow, squeezing her shoulders together. Aurora again rubbed away her tears, then looked into Storey's green eyes and took his hand again. "You don't have to be alone anymore."

He rubbed his thumb across the back of her hand and squeezed it lightly. He leaned forward, and Aurora could feel the hot breath from his nostrils cooling the moisture on her cheeks.

All at once, he pulled her toward him and pressed his lips to hers, so briefly. Then he was standing, walking, closing the door behind him. He was gone, and Aurora could still taste him.

❧25❧

Secernere – Twelve Years Earlier

Abern sat on the edge of young Storey's bed, putting himself nearly at eye level with his charge. He reached his knotty hands up and gripped Storey by the shoulders, which had filled out with the muscles of a hardworking farmhand. He looked deeply into Storey's eyes with his own leaking, rheumy brown gaze.

"Your presence at Secernere . . . it has brought immeasurable value to . . . this estate, to my fellow workers . . . and to me. You must understand that. Do you?"

Storey nodded, his eyes moving back and forth, roaming over the complicated topography of Abern's seasoned face.

"I want you to stay. No matter what happens today, know that *I* wanted you to stay."

Storey nodded again, his quelled anxiety growing once more.

"But it is not my decision."

"I know."

"Lord Gomery returned last night, and he will give us audience following supper this evening. I do not know if he will guess who you are. And he does not know that I have kept you here all these months while he has been on duty with the military. I know not how this conversation will pass. Do you have the knife I gave you?"

Storey patted his pocket, feeling the silhouette of the folded blade. He nodded.

"Despite your manly mind, you are still but a boy, and because of that I do not believe you are in any danger. But do not hesitate with that blade, should the need arise. That is not my wish for the conclusion of this conversation, but we will deal with the consequences when we come to them. I have learned much from you, Storey, as I hope you have learned from me. I have come to see you as my own son."

Abern squeezed Storey's shoulders, then brought his hands back to his lap, knitting his fingers together.

"As well," he continued, "you have been a wonderful surrogate to the infant. I see your bonds growing as brother and sister. And I have faith that your wiles will allow us to continue to hide her, as long as is necessary. However, for you to continue to be a productive member of this estate—my veritable right hand—you may no longer hide.

"And thus you will meet Cashel."

Storey stood just around the corner of the doorway, listening, peeking at what he could. Abern entered the room, bowing as deeply as his crooked back would allow anymore, and greeted his lord.

"Good to see you, old man," Cashel replied. "Please, give those old bones a rest."

"Thank you, m'lord. What news of the conflict, sir? Has it yet been quelled? Are you home for good?"

"Not hardly." Cashel sighed. "I fear a war has come to our lands, Mister Abern. Nigh a year has passed since the attacks; the fighting yet continues. It does not serve any longer to call it merely a conflict."

"A shame, sir. I thought I had lived long enough to avoid such times in my life."

"I think I should like to talk of other things," said Cashel.

"Indeed, sir." Abern hesitated.

"You had something in particular about which to speak with me?"

"Yes. . . . You'll forgive me. I am unsure how to begin."

"Allow me: Omit the tedium, and begin with that of the most import."

"Indeed, sir." Abern appeared in the doorway and gave a slight nod to Storey, who followed him inside the chamber. Rather than offering any sort of introduction—tedium, Storey supposed—Abern merely stood the boy in front of himself, with his hands on his shoulders.

Cashel, though still quite young, appeared much older than when Storey had first viewed him five months earlier. The pale, gaunt man sat behind a large escritoire with his hands folded on the desktop in front of him. The room was a library or office of some sort. Storey had never seen so many books in his life; behind Cashel they stood stacked up to a ceiling that rose to the height of three men. A fire crackled from the far end of the long room. For several moments, the three were silent, and Cashel's eyes moved slowly from the young boy to the old man and back again.

"What is your name?" Cashel finally said, addressing the boy. Storey provided only his given name—as he'd been instructed by Abern—and Cashel asked, "What is your house? Who are your parents?"

"I am orphaned, sir. And I have no title of which to speak."

Cashel squinted his eyes. The corner of his mouth twitched. "How did you come to visit Secernere?"

Storey swallowed and allowed himself only a half-second to mentally recount the tale he had practiced with Abern.

"My parents were fishers, sir. They were killed by Fairgosian pirates near the border. I escaped in their boat down the Calder in search of haven. This estate was the first I came upon. I sought shelter in your great walls, and Mister Abern was kind enough to offer it."

Storey felt an affectionate squeeze on his shoulders, but as he glanced up at Abern, he caught a darkness flashing across Cashel's eyes.

"And what is your purpose now, Mister Storey?"

"I wish to be a hand here, sir, my lord." Storey bowed and kept his head lowered as he awaited a reply. "I seek your formal permission to stay."

"How old are you? Twelve or so?"

Storey briefly lifted his head. "I am recently thirteen, sir."

"We are not usually in the business of taking in strays. The preparation for war has put hard times on all." Cashel paused.

Again, no one spoke. Storey dared not to look up. As he stared unblinking at the thick, magenta carpeting beneath his feet, he saw again all the blood spilled before him, and he felt an aching in his heart. He loathed to supplicate to this man, and felt the uncomfortably conflicting emotion of wanting Cashel to deny him. The very idea of serving Lord Gomery and of living out his life at Secernere Manor disgusted him. Abern and the infant were the sole reasons for him to stay. In Abern, he had family, something he thought had been irrevocably torn from him. And in the little girl, he saw a future. That he had nowhere else to go was no dynamic in his thought. He'd as soon take his chances in the mountains.

He squeezed his eyes shut and mentally recited a comforting mantra: "I know that I do not know. I know that I do not know." This was another of his mother's teachings: "It is said, when a people think they know the answers, they cannot be guided; when they are able to unravel their knowledge, their way will become evident to them."

Storey needed now, more than ever, to be guided. He could not make this choice, but only have it made for him.

Cashel finally spoke. "...But you look strong."

At this, Abern took his opportunity. "Indeed, sir! He is developing a stronger back than any here, and has quite a magical touch with the horses. He has proven useful in the stables, the mill, the fields—anywhere assistance has been required. In your—" Abern began to say "mother's," but carefully stopped himself. "In the absence of a household head, and in the absence of those who have recently . . . taken leave . . . young Storey's fortuitous arrival and willing aid has been most welcome to we in lowly service." Now, Abern bowed, too.

Cashel again stared hard at the boy. It was an eternity. Storey felt his every pore scrutinized.

"Do you have brothers, Mister Storey?"

"No, sir."

"Neither have I," said Cashel. "Nor have I parents. It seems we have much in common." There was another long moment of silence.

Then Cashel slapped his hand atop the desk and stood, the loud crack of sound reverberating throughout the room.

"Very well. You shall have a place at Secernere and I will teach you my ways."

Storey and Abern both rose, and Abern gave the boy a hearty slap on the back. Cashel rounded the desk and offered his hand to both men in turn.

"My gratitude a thousand times," whispered Storey.

"Indeed!" cried Abern. "Mine as well."

Cashel nodded, gripped the boy's shoulder, and shook him. "In our absence of family, perhaps we shall make apt brothers to one another."

Secernere – Present

On his way to the kitchen, Storey heard footsteps trotting up behind him in the corridor, and he turned to see a red-faced Cashel jogging toward him. Reaching him, Cashel hooked his arm around Storey's shoulder and he smiled broadly, falling into step. Storey glanced him over and saw that his white shirt was darkly stained with red clay—or was it blood? Cashel's blond hairline was beaded with sweat. He was breathing heavily, as from exercise, while he spoke.

"I know, my friend, how remorseful you are to be tethered here instead of a part of the army." He heaved. "We have been blessed with a unique opportunity."

Storey continued toward the kitchen without responding.

"Come on, now, I have something to show you." Like an impatient child, Cashel tugged lightly on Storey's shoulder.

"I am occupied."

"Whatever it is, I am positive it can wait. This is an absolute once-in-a-lifetime experience for you—and for me. We can finally bond as brothers."

"I don't think so."

Cashel stopped walking and pulled on Storey with enough force to stop him in his tracks. Storey sighed with exasperation, and turned to look directly at Cashel, his arms crossed. Cashel's gleeful face had turned dark.

"Then it is not a request," he said.

Storey swallowed hard. "Very well."

Cashel turned on his heels and began to walk in a hurried gait that made him appear ready any second to break out into a run. Storey followed, marching down the corridor as he fought the burning tension spreading throughout his shoulders.

Cashel looked backward, a smile once again cracking his pale face. "He's in the wine cellar."

Hours earlier

Cort did not even turn around. As the thunder of horse hooves approached him from behind, he began to run. But even as he stretched his long legs as far as they would reach, pumped his arms, hungrily gulped breaths of air into his burning lungs, he knew there was nowhere to run. The horse was upon him; Cort only heard it. He felt the butt of the sword handle crack into his skull, then saw black. He never even glimpsed the rider.

When he regained consciousness, he slowly opened his eyes and saw that he was someplace very dark. He could not see much, and what he could see—flashes of barrels, shadows on a bumpy stone wall—was tinted deep red, like blood. The pain in his head, his shoulder, and his wrists overwhelmed him with nausea. He felt like a hot poker was forcing itself through the space between his eyes from the inside out. He tried to move, but discovered he was bound. His shirt had been removed and he stood bare-chested, his knees weak and rubbery.

Slowly lifting his head, he saw a shadowy form move in and out of his field of vision; he could not enable his eyes to follow the figure. He tried to speak, but only sounds came out.

The dark form was moving toward him. As the man stepped into the wavering, bloodshot light, Cort saw that he was every inch the Mitochian soldier: tall, blond, near translucent pale skin, and eyes that burned with anger.

"So glad you could join us," the man said.

Cort struggled again to find his voice. "Please . . . I am on a search-and-rescue mission. Civilian."

He hardly glimpsed the man drawing back his arm before he felt the closed fist across his jaw. Turning his head to the side, he spit a red glob to the floor, then cleared his throat.

"Let me go," he said huskily, "and I will return to my country. I am not here as a soldier."

The man flapped his hand as if trying to shake the sting out of it, then laughed. His voice was a cartoonish impression of an idiot. "Oh, very well, sir. A thousand apologies for tyin' ye up here. I hadn't the foggiest impression ye was on a civilian mission. That just changes ever'thin'."

Cort felt a blinding white heat pierce the side of his abdomen and he cried out from the pain. He saw the man withdraw a short dagger from his body and watched as the blood poured out. In a flash, the man had stuffed the wound with some kind of leaves that stung like boiling water, but quelled the bleeding.

"Cannot allow you to lose too much blood and pass out again. What would be the fun in that?"

"Please . . ." gasped Cort. "Torture is a violation . . . the treaty . . ."

"Do you know why I enjoy fighting your people with such relish?" the man asked, strolling in casual circles around his prisoner. "Because you are such cowards. You—an armed man, dressed to hide, and carrying military colors—trespass on *my* land, and you want to tell me that *I* am violating something?"

He poked Cort's chest with his finger.

"What? An international law? The rule of your god? Even though you are obviously a soldier, you can plead that you are not and that makes me dead to the rights of any noble landholder?"

The man stabbed Cort in the gut again, this time on the opposite side. Again, he stuffed it with the searing leaves. Holding the tip of his bloody dagger beneath Cort's chin, he lifted Cort's face so the men were looking each other in the eye.

"No soldier under my command—and indeed that is every soldier in the whole of Mitoch—would *ever* deny she was a soldier, especially to protect herself from torture, as you call it. They would sooner die than deny their true blood. Your cowardice will only create a worse situation." The man sat down on a barrel and proceeded to wipe his hands clean on a rag as casually as cleaning up for suppertime. "Tell me, who are you

219

here to rescue? What makes you think he is here?"

"She . . ." whispered Cort. "She is only a girl. She's a civilian. She is no worry of yours."

"You would lead the Fairgosian army right to my doorstep!" the man shouted with sudden rage. "Only a girl. As God is only a girl!" He spat. "Only a girl."

In two steps, he had crossed the room and he struck Cort across the eye socket with the back of his hand. Cort felt the skin on his cheek split open.

"You are only a girl," the man said. "Who is she? She must be important for a soldier to risk his own life for her. I thought the entire premise of your country was that women are *not* important."

Cort did not respond.

"I said *who is she?*" the man yelled, spittle flying from his mouth and landing on Cort's face.

Cort remained silent.

Two strikes—one to the stomach and one to the sternum— came in quick succession, and vomit expelled from his mouth at the force of the blows. He coughed and spat, trying to clear his mouth of the awful taste.

"You answer me when I ask you a question!" the man shouted. Then, in a calm, level voice: "Trust that you will know when we are done with our conversation. It will be when you see your god's face crying as you are pulled down into Hell."

❧26☙

The door creaked shut behind them, and it closed off all light from filtering into the cavernous cellar. Storey followed Cashel down the dank stone steps lit only by a low lantern tucked into a wall sconce. The strong odor of mildew muddling with fermented grapes assaulted his nostrils, and the walls were wet and cold against his shoulders as he brushed their roughness.

Cashel was jogging down the stairs with a jovial energy; Storey plodded behind, taking each step as carefully as if he might slip off to his death. When they reached the floor, Cashel lit a torch, throwing tiger-like orange and black stripes across the stacked wooden barrels of wine, across the rugged stone walls, across the puddled floor, and across the half-naked man tied to an upright beam in the center of the room. He looked like a battered martyr of Fairgosian mythology.

"Who . . ." Storey breathed the word like an injured growl.

"Because I cannot bring you to the war, my dear friend, I

221

have brought the war to you."

The man's head hung down below the level of his shoulders. A wet moan escaped his parted lips.

"Cashel . . . what in God's name . . ."

"It's a Fairgosian! Living and breathing! Well, more or less. I thought we might have a bit of fun with him." Cashel's white grin flashed like the snarling mouth of a wolf.

"It appears you have already had some fun with him."

Storey could not tear his gaze from the hideousness of the scene laid out before him. The man had been stripped to the waist, and there were stripes of bloody gashes across his glistening torso, as if he had been clawed by an enormous bear. Blood caked his hair and ears. Dark bruises splotched his shoulders and chest. His arms had been wrenched toward his back to bind his hands behind the beam, and one of his shoulders was obviously dislocated. The ropes across his wrists cut into his skin, and he bled from his forearms where they rubbed against the splintered wood of the beam.

Worst of all were two black holes in the man's sides that had been stuffed with grass or leaves of some sort. Gooey congealed blood oozed out of them like mud. With his long, thin limbs, he looked like a hideous scarecrow.

Storey wanted to run to the man, cut him free. He would throw him over his shoulder and carry him out of this hell of Cashel's creation.

But he was frozen to the spot, impotent, left only to stare and swallow the bile back down his throat and be once more horrified by the thought that Cashel's life was as valuable as any in the country. Storey's only hope, the key to his plans, was to keep Cashel alive, and to keep him trusting and friendly. But he had never, in his most hellish of nightmares, considered that he would be recruited to assist in the torture of a fellow member of the human race.

He cleared his throat. "Ah," he said, mustering the pretense of insouciance best he could. "You have been interrogating the fellow. What have you learned so far?"

Cashel approached the bound soldier and withdrew a short dagger from a hip holster. He dragged the tip of the dagger across the man's chest, though did not draw blood.

"Come over here, Storey!"

Storey took a step closer.

"You are a man, just as I," Cashel continued. "We both have masculine urges of the kind we must suppress in our country."

He handed the dagger to Storey, who accepted it reluctantly.

"Tell me you do not wish, in the darkest corners of your heart, to know how it feels—" He stepped behind Storey and reached around his body to gently grasp his hand, speaking softly in Storey's ear. "—to know *exactly* how it feels to push this blade just ... hard ... enough ..."

He guided Storey's hand, dagger between his fingers, so that he dragged the blade across the man's chest again.

". . . to pierce a man's skin."

Storey's muscles twitched and vibrated, shaking his body despite his every effort to hold still.

"To break through this frail shell we wear, this thin, nearly transparent rind that separates us from our environment." Cashel pushed Storey's hand forward, and the blade plunged into the man's shoulder.

The prisoner groaned again, and a bloody bubble inflated then popped on his lips.

Storey pushed back against Cashel and stepped away, letting the dagger fall from his fingers and clatter to the stone floor.

"No." He waved his hands. "No. Cashel, you are the warrior. I shovel dung, remember? I leave this to you. . . . I would not know where to put the knife. I'd likely kill him before you were done with him."

"As you wish."

Cashel's hand flashed forward. Grabbing a shock of the man's hair, he ripped his head backward, exposing a battered face that was both collapsed and swollen, like a rotting peach.

Cashel reared and struck a backhand across the man's face. Spatters of blood and a tooth flew out of his mouth and fell to the floor.

"But you do not know what you miss!" Cashel reared back and struck again. The man's head fell forward, unconscious. "I shall wait until he wakes up again. There is no pleasure otherwise."

Storey backed away until his heel hit a cask and he stumbled back onto it in a sitting position. His hands rubbed at one another frantically as he tried to keep the rest of his body from shaking. The skin of his knuckles felt clammy and raw. He didn't know where in the room to look, so his eyes darted around, failing to focus.

"No, of course not."

"While I wait," Cashel began, "I will tell you what I know. This man was like a wilting flower at my feet, petals crumpling and folding before I even asked one question or raised one fist. Upon finding him sneaking like a rat through the brush, I grabbed him by the back of the neck and threw him up against the stones. He begged for his life then fell to his knees like a woman. I told him no. His next tack was to protest that he was on a civilian search-and-rescue mission. But—" He strode to a barrel and retrieved a scrap of royal blue fabric. "—he was wearing this." Shaking the folds from the cloth, he held it up for Storey to view: it was a kerchief emblazoned with the silver crest of the Fairgosian royal army. "A Fairgosian scout."

Cashel leaned down and retrieved the dagger, proceeding once again to taunt the man's torso with its sharp tip.

"A civilian search-and-rescue!" He laughed as if the statement were clownishly ludicrous. "My first thought was, at least this man has gumption enough to *try* to lie to me. But I took him down here, and as we proceeded through our conversation, it became evident he was telling me the honest truth."

He dragged the dagger down the man's chest, stomach, and onto his pants, where it sliced through the brown fabric.

"Remember that man we slayed at March, in the inn? That singular hope of the Fairgosian people? As it turns out, the War Master has a daughter."

Cashel's voice was sing-song as he said it, and he flitted into a little pirouette. He brought the dagger up to the man's cheek and pressed, letting a purplish bead of blood form on the silver sheen of the blade. Then he drew the blade across his tongue.

"This daughter has gone missing into the wilds of Mitoch— can you imagine?" He mimicked a lost little girl, holding his fingertips up to his surprised, o-shaped mouth and batting his eyelashes. The torch flame danced in his eyes, and he smiled with a wide open mouth. "And the daughter was betrothed to the general of the Fairgosian army! How perfect is that!"

He was practically jumping up and down with glee.

"Oh, Storey, my friend, my brother . . ."

He moved to where Storey sat, grasped his shoulders, and pulled him into an upright position. Storey's legs felt like columns of water beneath him. His unfixed eyes lazed toward the floor, drunk.

Still grasping his shoulders, Cashel said, "Can you only imagine the things I would do to that little minx if I were to find her?" He laughed. "Oh, the things."

Taking a few paces away, he turned back toward Storey, sweeping his arm around the room.

"And do you know the best part? If she is indeed alive, as this soldier so intently believes, then she cannot be more than a few days away from here! How can you not be amazed by the lucky fate of that!"

"Fate, yes," mumbled Storey. "Lucky fate."

Cashel pointed at Storey's chest with the dagger. "I am going to find her, I promise you that. I am going to take some of those goddamned bloodhounds and a horse, and I am goddamned well going to find her. Have no worry, my friend. I will bring her back here. I know *she* is an experience we can certainly share." He looked to Storey, awaiting a response.

Storey rubbed a hand over his face as if he could change his expression that way. He forced a rueful smile.

"Sir, a thousand apologies that I cannot revel in this right now at your side." Storey forced the words out of his mouth in slow deliberateness. "But I fear I am succumbing to an illness of some sort. Nothing serious, but the dampness of this cavern worsens my humors."

"Yes, of course, my friend," Cashel replied. "Please, go, rest. I shall need your assistance in the morrow as we prepare for the hunt."

Storey climbed back out of the cellar. With each step, he felt like another stone was pulled down from the walls around him and placed on his aching shoulders. The nightmare of Secernere was built upon his breaking back, and he still knew not when he could shake off those rocks and bring the walls crumbling down. How many more white stones would he lay before he could seal off that grave room forever? When could he open the walls to invite the hungry and tired inside? When could he stop hiding innocents within the walls, and when could he stop hiding within the walls of his own body?

The daylight was near blinding as he exited the cellar. He thought of the Fairgosian myth, trying to remember correctly. Wine turned into blood. He couldn't remember why or how, just that it did, and for some reason it was good. The barrels in that cellar might as well have been filled with blood. More blood had been spilled down there than wine drank in this sober place. More souls crushed than grapes.

Grinning broadly, Aurora merrily snatched up a pawn and waved it above her head like a trophy. "My question!" she sang. "What is your favorite color?"

Dymphna considered, rubbing her pointed little chin with her white fingers, her brow furrowed. "The color you see behind your eyelids just before you fall asleep."

Aurora closed her eyes and tried to discern what colors floated there, behind her eyelids. She saw dark red with dancing stripes of blue and green. She turned her face toward the window and a white square appeared.

Dymphna giggled with delight. "No, silly!" she laughed. "Before you go to *sleep!*"

Affecting a noisy snore, Aurora collapsed onto the bed, dead asleep. Dymphna squealed and jumped on top of Aurora, shaking her and giggling. Aurora's eyes popped open and she stuck her fingers into Dymphna's ribs, tickling her. Dymphna twisted and tried to tickle Aurora in return, and they both exploded into irrepressible laugher. Aurora finally caught her breath, and she held Dymphna—Catherine—in her lap, running her fingers through the girl's fine hair.

"I have a serious question for you," Aurora said.

Dymphna, still under the control of her own riotous laughter, twisted out of Aurora's grasp and ran back to her side of the playing board. "But you have to capture a piece first!" She choked out the words between giggles. "And it is not even your turn!"

"Please, Catherine?"

Dymphna expelled an exaggerated sigh and stomped heavily back over to the bed, cuddling up to Aurora. "All right. . . ." Her faux dejection was utterly adorable and Aurora squeezed her close.

"If I were to leave here—"

Dymphna pulled away. The mirth drained from her face, and she shook her head emphatically. "No!"

"Shh . . . Catherine . . ."

"You cannot leave! You cannot!"

Aurora sighed, unsure of how to proceed. "Please . . . just allow me to finish. It has become too dangerous for me here. My friend, Storey, who I have told you about—he has revealed some dark secrets to me about this place. I am going to leave. I have to. And it will be soon."

"No . . ." Dymphna moaned. Her face became red and splotchy and tears were welling up in her eyes. One spilled over and streaked down her cheek in a glistening rivulet.

"Catherine, I want to know if you would come with me."

Dymphna's eyes widened. "Really?"

Aurora nodded.

"But where would we go?"

"I don't know yet. I hope Storey will help me devise a plan. I think Ekanta would be a safe place for us."

Dymphna's eyes sparkled and she began to sing, "Ekanta, the beautiful country of peace. It is where I visit before I wake from my dreams. I wish we could learn from their glorious ways. I wish I lived in Ekanta all of my days."

It was the lullaby Aurora had heard through the locked doors so many nights ago.

Dymphna dove back into Aurora's lap and encircled Aurora's neck with her arms. She nodded with a serious finality. "Yes. I will go with you."

Aurora hugged the girl tight, feeling the same joyful tenderness as when she had first embraced her. "My Catherine, we will both be safe. I promise you."

Pulling back, Dymphna looked up at Aurora. "Now may I ask you a serious question?"

"Of course!"

Dymphna pointed gravely at Aurora's chest. "How old do I have to be before I get those?"

They both broke up into peals of laughter, doubled over beside each other on the bed, gasping for air. Aurora held her aching sides and giggled as tears rolled down her cheeks, when a shock ran up Aurora's spine and she clamped her hand over Dymphna's mouth. The girl's eyes looked at her questioningly, but Aurora only placed her finger to her lips. Dymphna nodded.

In the next moment, the stomp of heavy boots came roaring

up from the corridor below them—someone running up the stairs. Storey's footsteps were always light and slow. He never ran up the stairs. The stomping continued, amplifying with each step. Dymphna looked pleadingly at Aurora. Aurora's eyes darted around the room. Under the bed, out the window, inside the trunk: but it was too late to hide the girl. She pulled her close in a protective grasp.

"No matter what happens, stay behind me," she breathed.

With a piercing crack, the chamber door flew open.

❧27❧

Heaving ragged breaths and red-faced with anger, a sweat-covered, bloodied Storey crowded the doorway before them. His eyes flashed. "Dymphna! Home, now!"

He pointed out into the hall. The girl remained frozen.

"*Now!*"

Without looking at Aurora, she ran to the door, squeezing past Storey's immense frame. Her tiny, muffled footsteps sounded down the stairs.

Storey stepped inside and slammed the door behind him. The room vibrated.

"You . . ." He pointed at Aurora, his eyes narrowing to slits. His voice was a roar. "You would bring this house down around us!"

Instinctively, Aurora retreated on the bed as far as she could. Her back hit the wall, and she pulled her knees up to her chest, holding her hands out as if Storey might strike her.

"I don't know what—"

"Enough of these lies!" Storey thrust his hand out and

grabbed Aurora's wrists, wrenching her to her feet.

"You're hurting me!"

She was crying. He swung her around, slamming her back against the door and pinning her arms above her head by the wrists. She writhed and struggled against him.

"Tell me your name," he growled, his face inches from hers.

"Inna—"

"Tell me your name!"

She twisted her face to the side, ashamed, and whispered, "Aurora. Lady Aurora of Cavalcata."

Storey tore his hands from her and turned away in disgust.

"This house will come down, and we will be crushed by every stone of this wall."

She watched him.

"Cavalcata," he spat. "Cavalcata!" Turning on his heel, he pointed an accusatory finger at her. "You are the *daughter* of the man we assassinated at March."

Tears streamed down her face as she nodded.

"But more than that—you are *betrothed* to the general of the Fairgosian army?"

"What?" Aurora dragged her hand across her face, swiping at the tears. She shook her head. "I am betrothed to no one."

A muscle between Storey's nose and mouth twitched. "I warn you, Lady, one more lie from that red mouth of yours, and I will—"

"I am betrothed to no one!" she shouted.

Storey stuck his fingers into his hair and pulled at it. "Because of your lies, the very army of Fairgos is on its way to Secernere."

"No. That is not possible. . . ."

"It is possible!" He stepped toward her again and she flinched. "This very day, Cashel captured a scout who was here, looking for *you*."

"It isn't possible!" she cried desperately. "They wouldn't

231

waste manpower searching for a woman. . . . They would have lost my trail at the river. . . . How would they get through the wall?" Her eyes frantic, she searched his face. "It isn't possible."

Mixed emotions flashed across Storey's eyes as his anger and affection for her seemed to fight each other. He took a deep breath. The anger ebbed, for a moment, and in forced calm detachment, Storey explained both what he had heard from Cashel and what he had seen with his own eyes. When he finished, Aurora was sobbing and shaking her head as if to make it all go away by the sheer force of her denial.

"And beyond that," Storey continued, "your fraternization with Dymphna has put all three of us in peril."

Aurora looked up. "You knew?"

"Of course I knew. I know everything that occurs at Secernere."

"Why have you hidden your knowledge of her? And why do you hide yourself from her?"

"I do not hide myself from her—I have raised her! And what I choose to tell you and to keep from you is my business."

"But she told me . . ." Aurora let her sentence trail off, knowing she had never understood—and could never fully understand—the words that came out of Dymphna's mouth. "Never mind. I just—I am so confused!" Frustration forced more tears from her eyes. "If her visitations were so perilous, why did you allow her to continue?"

Storey sighed heavily, rubbing his eyes, and he finally sat. The anger was gone now.

"I am many things to Dymphna, but I could never be her mother. The changes I have seen in her these past days outshine every book I've made her read, every lesson I've taught her, every practiced idiom I've drilled into her head. I have made it my life for the past twelve years to groom her into a leader for this country. But because of that, she lost the innocence of childhood—and that would have been the most powerful trait of all. But you . . . you have brought that out in her."

"Who is she . . ." Aurora whispered in awe. "Who is she really?"

Storey lifted his head and looked into Aurora's eyes. His irises shone bright green like the meadow after a thunderstorm, and glistened with the rain drops there.

"She is the Way," he said. "The path to peace. She is the luminousness that will be inside all of us, and will make us all like little children." Tears began to pour from his eyes, falling from his jaw onto his chest and onto the table. "She alone can stop this war. She is the Way. But without a mother . . . she was incomplete, unbalanced. It is said," he went on, "when you find the mother, you will be free from sorrow."

Aurora continued to stare into his eyes, but could not speak.

"I am so sorry I came here in anger. The danger you have brought does not matter. We have found you. We have found the mother."

All at once, Aurora felt like the room had exploded like a bursting star, leaving no walls around her and no floor beneath her. Her head spun; she was floating and spinning in airless space. Her mind scrambled to find some way to be grounded by gravity. She began to shake her head back and forth, first slowly, then with more vigor.

"No . . ." she said. "No . . . no, no, no, no." She stared at Storey with wide, dilated eyes. "I do not know who you think I am, but I am not her. . . . I am no one's mother. I am not—I do not fulfill some prophecy. I am no one."

Storey came to her side and took her hands. The weight of his body beside her on the bed and the touch of his hands almost brought her back down to earth. She felt gravity again, but she was still dizzy. She was still shaking her head back and forth.

"I am no one. I've never mattered."

"Please, look at me."

She opened her eyes. Storey's gaze was soft and misty as it moved over her face. There was joy and awe there, relief and hope. There were emotions he should never have had about her.

"Do not mistake my meaning. It is not a prophecy. I do not believe such stories."

Aurora felt mingled relief and disappointment. "Then what do you think I am?" she whispered.

He squeezed her hands. "Twelve years. It has been twelve years since Dymphna was born here, and only a few months longer that I have been living at Secernere. All this time, I had been waiting for something; I know not what. I have been unwise. The wise one sees things as they are without trying to control them. But me, I plot and plan. I perfect every idea and orchestration. And yet I have been paralyzed by inaction. If you had not come, I would still be waiting, maybe for years.

"It is said, there is a time for being safe and there is a time for being in danger. Cashel knows you are nearby, and we are in danger now, yes. But that is the impetus for action."

Aurora continued to search his eyes, hoping to find answers there. His every word was confounding; built into sentences, they became positively indecipherable. Who was he? Who was Dymphna? Moreover, what was Aurora's role in this other than to have brought this danger to their doorstep?

Instead of asking any more questions, she leaned forward and kissed him.

But it was more than that—more than the first tentative kiss of affectionate tenderness they had shared. Aurora felt blood rush from her head through her body, and she pushed against him. He responded by pushing back, his hand encircling her back and gently lowering her onto the bed. Running his hands over her face and through her hair, they continued to kiss each other deeply for what seemed like an eternity.

Then Storey let his mouth release from Aurora's, while keeping his forehead pressed against hers. He ran his fingertips down the side of her face. Aurora finally opened her own eyes, blinking like she was waking from a dream, and found herself looking into his perfect green gaze. He stared back into her eyes, then kissed her on the corner of the mouth, then on her forehead, then pressed his forehead to hers once again.

"I promise you," Storey said finally, his voice smoky, "this is the last time I will say this: I will return when I can." He pushed himself up and moved to the door.

"Storey, wait—"

"There has been enough waiting. It is time for action. We will leave here soon."

Aurora sat up, the reality of the situation dawning on her. "But where will we go? How will we get there?"

"It is said, opportunities multiply as they are seized. If we act now, our answers will follow."

It took nothing more than hearing her father's words come out of Storey's mouth to make her ready for whatever came next.

❧28❧

Secernere – Six Years Earlier

𝒞andlelight danced over black words printed on pale paper as Storey drew his finger across the first line. The tiny girl sat beside him, barely indenting the bed with her meager weight. Her paleness gave her a spectral quality, and her body seemed fragile to the touch, her bones birdlike. Her hair was thin, too. Never thickening much from the fuzzy down with which she was born, it hung to her shoulders like pale pieces of straw. But her mind—her mind was sharper than the axe Storey used for splitting firewood, and quite as robust.

She read the line haltingly, but clearly and without mistake. "In the days that followed, rep . . . resent . . . atives from the gov- ern . . . ment . . . including the woman who would become Lady Milena of Bratus and the first Mit . . . och . . . ian queen, signed the documents that would give the country of Mitoch its inde . . . pendence."

"That was very good."

Storey was beyond impressed, recalling his own slow progress. But he withheld exuberant praise. To grow the seed of pride inside this girl was not his goal.

"Milena. That is a beautiful and noble name. She was our first queen, and the mother of all our queens to follow. Have you yet thought of a name for yourself?"

"No," said the girl. She did not elaborate.

Storey sighed. He would not give up on fulfilling Lady Gomery's strange wish, but he was growing weary of having nothing to call her but *girl*.

"With your new reading skills, you will soon learn many new stories and ideas. I have no doubt you will soon come upon a name that suits your fancy."

"I wish to know all names," she said. "I wish to read all books. I wish to know all knowledge."

Storey was beaming inside. "Excellent. We will start immediately."

They sat in the loft of the mill together, side by side, Storey reading *Revelations of the Feminine Spirit* and the girl reading *Cordrey's Religions of the World*. He glanced over and saw that she was on the chapter about monotheism in Fairgos, and he nodded in approval.

It was a bold move, sitting with the girl in the daytime, but Cashel was again on duty away from Secernere, not due home for another day; the miller, Misko, almost completely deaf. The sunshine was delightful as it shone onto the pages of their books.

By now, the girl was reading voraciously, her interest in books outweighing that of normal conversation, eating, or even sleeping. Storey was aware that the girl's lack of socialization was having the unintended effect of making her . . . strange. He could think of no better term. She was not unpleasant, nor did her company make him uneasy. But the ways she communicated to him, and the ways she garnered information from him, were foreign, creative, and unlike that of any person with whom he had ever shared words.

He remembered how he struggled when, just days ago, she had posed with the simplest set of words, the most difficult question anyone can ask or answer: "Why am I?"

It was a frightening moment for him, the realization that she *was* because he had made her. But he was unworthy to be her creator, her teacher. And his insufficiency made him feel false, empty.

That abrupt philosophical curiosity had appeared because, as is so often the case with children, death had entered the picture. In the loft of the mill, Dymphna had settled into a comfortable nest of straw only to place her hand upon the silky cold feathers of a dead pigeon. The presence of the pigeon was confounding to the girl firstly because it was a wild animal, which did not interact with humans, and secondly because it was a bird, and birds belonged in the sky and not on the floors of lofts. As she held it in her hand and talked softly to it, Storey watched the realization move across her face like a late afternoon shadow. The wild animal was not interacting with her, the bird was not flying, because there was something very, very wrong.

"It's broken," she said. She held it up to Storey in two hands, like it was a toy that had stopped working properly.

Instinctively, Storey took it into his hands as if it was in fact a toy and he could mend it for her. In his hands, he felt that it actually was broken: the bird had broken its neck; it probably flew too fast through the window and hit the opposite wall. Its head limply lolled from side to side. He petted it absently as he spoke. He had never touched a bird before. The feathers were smoother than he would have imagined.

"This bird is dead," he said. "Do you know what that means?"

"No," was the heartbreakingly simple answer she gave.

Storey breathed in and out for a while; he needed to do some breathing before he answered. The girl was patient. She understood.

"You and I are alive," he said finally. He had come upon the conclusion that the simplest way to define death was to describe it as the opposite of life. "Every animal we see outside is alive—every bird, every squirrel, every fish in the river, every bug that flies around. A living thing moves around. It breathes in and out. It eats food and drinks water. It thinks thoughts and asks questions and wonders about mysteries."

"Even bugs? Bugs think thoughts?"

"Yes, they do. They wonder, 'where is that little girl whose blood is so sweet like candy? I'd like to give her a bite today!' " He lightly pinched her arm and she squealed in delight. "But living things cannot live forever."

"But the world lives forever. Why do its creatures not?"

Storey thought about the Fairgosian religious belief that human lives were cut short as a punishment from their god for being arrogant. He was enraged at the idea that a god would create lives only to take them away as punishment.

"It is said that all things must be in balance, so there cannot be life without death. If things lived forever, everything and everyone would get very old and the world would become very crowded, and soon there would be no room for anyone. The world is very big, but it also very small. Like you."

"I am not very big. I am only small," she said.

"You are big inside." He placed his index finger lightly on her forehead, then on her breastbone. "You have a whole universe in here, and in here."

He went on, "The world lives forever because it has no needs of its own. It is present for all beings. And so every living thing gets a certain amount of time to have a piece of the world to use for what they need. If things lived forever, they would use up all the world."

"People die so that other people can be?" she asked.

Storey nodded. It was not a one-for-one ratio, he knew; the mathematics were fuzzy. But the idea was sound enough, simple enough for the child.

Dymphna reached toward him and scooped the pigeon into her own hands. She examined it with a look that was partly affectionate and partly clinical. "When you die, you can't move, and you can't see or hear or feel anything anymore?"

"That's right. It's like being asleep."

"Can you wake up? Can you stop being dead?"

Again, more religious dogma entered his head—the idea of the afterlife. That, through a god, no one ever really had to die. It was a comforting thought so powerful that it placated and subjugated masses of people. The majority of people in the world did not even know that they would eventually die.

"No," he said. "When something dies, it is dead forever."

"Why am I?" she asked.

To Storey's bald look of empty retort, Dymphna launched into a barrage of questions. A child's clarification: stating the same thing many ways.

"If I am here, does it mean that someone else had to die? Where did I come from? Why am I here? Did I exist before I can remember? What happens after I die—will someone else come? Will they be like me? Does everyone have to die? Do you have to die, Storey? Will I be alone then?"

Sometimes Storey wondered if religion had been invented to answer the questions of children. But he could not, would not, seek answers there. The answers religion offered were, at best, indecipherable cryptograms. At worst, outright lies. However, though he rejected riddles and lies, neither could Storey tell her the complete story—ever.

"I found you when you were very small, still a baby," he began. "When creatures are brought into the world, they are very small. Sometimes their eyes are not open yet. You were so little with no one to look after you, so Abern and I took care of you and fed you and made sure you would grow up strong."

"Were my eyes open when I was born?" Dymphna asked.

"Yes. Human babies are born with their eyes open, but we are not born with our minds' eyes open. It can take an entire lifetime for us to completely open our eyes and begin to see what is really around us."

"But why?"

"Why what?"

"Why would you take care of me if you didn't even know me?"

"Because you needed us. When we ignore the needs of a stranger in favor of caring for ourselves, we are really ignoring ourselves. And I think . . . we needed you. I needed you. There is much to be learned from the newborn baby."

"I thought babies didn't know anything yet."

"It is said that the newborn baby is supple and soft. A new plant is pliant and bending. The newborn baby represents Life and represents the way we should always approach life, to be supple and bending and soft. If we lean hard against the world with stiffness and power, we are only representing the ways of Death."

"I am trying to learn, Storey," Dymphna said slowly.

She said this frequently. Though it often seemed she was so full of questions that they would never stop, sometimes she revealed a self-conscious fear that having questions was a sign of weakness. She would say, "I am trying to learn, Storey," and then ask a particularly difficult question. Storey wished that he could make her understand that asking hard questions was an emblem of wisdom. But self-awareness was not among his lessons for her. The lessons of the self could only come with knowledge, experience, and the immovable movement of time—not from another who barely understood himself.

"I am trying to learn, Storey. But I do not understand. If Life and Death are equal in the balance of the Way . . . if death happens to all living things, then why is it bad?"

This question hurt his heart. His mind flashed to his moth-

241

er, buried within the walls of Secernere. Storey would never be able to articulate any good that had come out of that murder. So much had changed, and all of it for the worse. He could not articulate any good that had come from any of the murders Cashel had caused. Death had been a plague on Mitoch in such an unnatural fashion that it flew in the face of everything the Way stood for.

But it was a valid question. It was a good and true question. He would answer it with the goodness and truth it deserved, even though his own human weakness caused him to struggle with believing in that truth.

"Death is not bad," he said. "If someone calls something beautiful, then something else can be called ugly. If someone calls something good, then something else can be called bad. But if we follow the Way, those labels disappear and we only see things in terms of their existence in balance with everything else. Just as night follows day, death follows life. Both the Thema and the Bible say, 'There is a time for living and there is a time for dying.' While we live, we must be lively. We must be green like the shoot, turning our leaves upward to the sun. Life is good when we do not let the idea of death interrupt. Death is good when we do not let ourselves cling to life when it is impossible.

"Our knowledge of death should bring us comfort instead of fear. But we must never confuse knowledge with understanding. We must always know that we cannot know, and understand that we cannot understand. Unravel your knowledge, and there you will find the truth."

Dymphna nodded, her pale blue eyes filled with the paradox of innocence and wisdom.

"I know that I cannot know." She paused and looked down at the pigeon in her hands. "But I will always wonder."

"You should be the queen," Storey whispered to himself so quietly that Dymphna did not hear him at all.

Today, he gazed at her again, thinking the same thoughts.

She was so tiny, but so regal in her innocent wisdom. Noticing his gaze, she turned and looked up at him. She did not smile—she never smiled—but her countenance was serene and comforting. He did smile, vaguely, and she turned back to her book.

Storey knew he could not bring her happiness, but neither did she know its opposite. She was on the path to becoming a master—that was all that mattered. She needed no other person to bring her contentment. It was said, if you look to others for fulfillment, you will never truly be fulfilled.

Downstairs, the millstone disengaged and stopped turning for the first time in several hours. The grinding had dissolved into the background of white noise, and the sudden silence was jarring to their peaceful rendezvous. The girl looked up at Storey again, questioning, but he only shook his head and put his finger to his lips. He heard the heavy mill door thunder open, and thick boots crunched across the floor.

"Misko!" It was Cashel's voice, its normal timbre amplified aggressively. He was home early, and he was in a furor.

In a flash, Storey grabbed the girl and pulled her onto his lap, smashing a rough hand against her mouth. She froze in his arms.

"Misko!" came a second cry.

"Here, sir," Misko said. His shuffling gait moved across the floor.

Straining his every muscle, Storey shifted as silently as possible to look down at the scene through a crevice in the loft woodwork. He saw the fat Misko, dressed in dirty brown clothes and thick leather apron. Then Cashel entered the field of vision: he took quick, striding paces right up to Misko, but did not stop when he had reached the man. Instead, his forearm shot up to Misko's throat and pushed the fat miller up against a beam. Misko shouted in pained surprise, but the pressure on his windpipe cut the noise short. His pudgy hands flew up to Cashel's arm, pulling at it. But Cashel did not relent. Shoving his face forward next to Misko's, Cashel began to shout directly into Misko's good ear.

"Do you know what happens to those who steal from me?"

Misko gasped and sputtered, but could not reply. He forced his head to shake side to side.

"It is not wise to perform an act without fully understanding the consequences!"

Cashel released his arm, and Misko's hands flew up to his throat, massaging his windpipe. He coughed violently and bent double, still shaking his head. Forcing out the words in a rasping, injured voice, he said, "I don't know what you're talking about, my lord."

Cashel reared back his right arm and swung his heavy fist across Misko's soft jaw. The man crumpled to the ground. Storey pulled the girl even tighter. She expelled a tiny grunt, her face pressed against his body. Storey felt his heart beat hard against her as his eyes remained glued to the scene below.

Misko remained prone, shielding his face with his two forearms. Cashel toed him in the ribs.

"Get up!" he shouted. "I said, get up! Face me like a worthy adversary instead of a cowering man! I killed ten Fairgosians on my way home yesterday and they all showed more honor than you."

Misko only curled his body tighter into a fetus-like position, moaning. Cashel crouched down beside him and again pressed his face close up to Misko's.

"Did you think I wouldn't discover the truth? Did you think I would not know? Over two hundred kilos unaccounted for? Did you think that because I was fighting a war I wasn't also paying attention to the business of Secernere?" Cashel's shouts turned to a low growl as he continued. "Tell me, to whom did you sell my property? Who has it? Who?"

He reached forward, grasping Misko's arm and slowly peeled it from his face. The fat miller's expression was sheer terror. Tears streamed down his face. Already his jaw was sickeningly swollen. He continued to shake his head.

"I don't know what you're on about, my lord. I promise! Please, please don't hurt me no more. I have two little girls. I only sold what grain I was s'posed to, and to what customers I was s'posed to. I gave you all the gold I got. There's no two hundred kilos missing!"

Cashel sprung to his feet, took a few steps back, then, running at Misko, kicked him squarely in the ribs. Storey heard the horrible crack all the way from the loft. Gripping the girl, he carefully started to slide back against the wall. The floorboard below him gave an awful creak that shattered the naked air. Cashel's head snapped toward the loft. Storey froze.

"Please . . ." Misko beseeched, his voice failing.

Cashel's attention was immediately drawn back to the man moaning at his feet. He began to shout again, and Storey took the opportunity to move all the way against the wall. He didn't want to watch anymore. Shifting his arms, he further buried the girl's head. Blinded her, deafened her.

Soon there was no more shouting and no more pleading, only the blunt smacks of flesh against flesh until the miller didn't respond at all. Cashel clapped his hands together as if to rid them of stable dust. Muttering profanities under his breath, he finally retreated, his business taken care of.

Storey approached the library door and found Cashel sitting beside his large desk, rubbing his eyes. It was like a reprisal of that morning so many years before when he had first asked permission to stay at Secernere. Only this time, Storey had been the witness to an hours-old murder committed by the very man who had summoned him. The girl was safely tucked away in her hiding place and seemed no worse for wear, but Storey could not so soon shake the horrible sounds.

He crowded the doorway, but did not enter. "You sent for me?"

Instead of replying, Cashel threw an open ledger-book at Storey, its white pages flapping before it slapped down at Storey's feet. Storey looked from the ledger to Cashel, but said nothing.

"I need to have you start taking care of this sort of mess." Cashel groaned with exasperation. He gestured at the ledger-book. "Go on, pick it up."

Storey obliged and flipped through it for show.

"Misko. Stealing from me—"

Storey choked on his own saliva for a second, then turned the noise into a throat clearing.

"—but not any longer. Look, look at it. It's all in there. Look at the entries starting on the fifth page through the end. You do know how to read numbers, do you not?"

Storey's eyes narrowed but he did not answer. Cashel's condescension came so naturally that it seemed almost jovial. Storey looked at the clumsily penned numbers; each digit had been written with painstaking purposefulness, like a child's handwriting.

"I do not see the problem." His stomach churned as he forced his voice to remain conversational. "Everything seems correct."

"Who taught you mathematics?"

Cashel shot up and strode to the doorway. He ripped the ledger-book from Storey's hand, flipped to a page, and jabbed his finger at a column.

"Right here, idiot. Look down here. Two hundred kilos of rye just goes missing off the books, and the money for it is not accounted for." He slammed the book shut and threw it onto his desk. "I will not allow thieves to steal from me. Everyone here tries to take advantage because they think my head is gone—completely taken up with war notions. But they are *wrong*." He tapped a forefinger against his temple. "There is plenty in here to go around. I don't miss a thing."

Storey calmly walked toward the desk. "So you will be

turning Misko over to the Guard then?" He cleared his throat again, and picked the ledger-book up off the table, thumbing to the numbers in question.

"Of course not! Those bunch of small-minded fools. I've moved all the guards with a thimbleful of intelligence into commanding positions in the army. The ones left are the very dregs of our society. Sad really. Not fit enough even for the army, yet we trust them to keep our citizens safe from criminals. But what else to do in a time of war? No, I would never allow the Guard to take any part in Secernere justice. We do well on our own. Problems do not recur."

Storey coughed again, and motioned to Cashel to join him. "I beg you, have a second look. The math is perfect. No two hundred of anything is missing."

Cashel jabbed the page again. "Right there!"

Storey squinted, then saw the problem. He nearly vomited. "That is a six, not an eight."

"Let me see that!" Cashel snatched the book away and pressed his face to the page. "Huh. Hmmm." He began to nod his head. "I suppose you are right. My wise Storey. That could definitely be a six."

A man was dead because of sloppy handwriting. Storey choked back the overwhelming desire to kill Cashel with his own bare hands at that very moment, instead taking three deep breaths. In his head, he repeated, *Violence, even well intentioned, always rebounds upon oneself.*

But there were so many more reasons he had to keep Cashel alive. It taunted him every day. If Cashel died before the girl was ready, there was a chance his position would be filled by someone else and break the tie of the Gomery bloodline to that power. The girl would be just another landholder, and no party to Storey's vision of a peaceful future. Cashel had to be kept alive until she was ready . . . until Storey was ready. If they would ever be.

"So Misko is innocent then," Storey said aloud.

"Misko's gone," Cashel said dismissively. "He was lazy, stupid, and deaf to boot. Abern will find me someone else to work the mill. Oh, that reminds me: we lost another today."

Storey did not comprehend the statement outright. The simple phrase could have referred to another horse taken by infectious anemia, another customer who could no longer afford to do business with the estate, another servant who had deserted them. Secernere lost things like a man with a hole in his pocket.

"Just a skivvy," said Cashel derisively. "Abern found his quarters emptied of all his belongings this very afternoon."

"The fourth this month," said Storey. The staff were fleeing like rats from a flood. "Do you know why?"

"I would imagine it was because I had him dispose of Misko's body." Cashel sighed and collapsed into his chair, swiveling back and forth like a hyperactive child. "Men are not men here. It sickens me. Were they not needed to tend Secernere, I would send every man in our service into battle, just so they would know what it is like."

"But we do need them here," said Storey. "All of them. Our staff grows thin, and there is more work than ever."

"Then I imagine I know how you will respond to my next proposition. Will you sit? You make me nervous pacing the room like that."

Storey reluctantly lowered himself into the hard-backed chair before the giant escritoire. His knee bounced up and down. He reminded himself to breath, and silently recited another dictum: *let your heart be at peace, even as you watch the turmoil of other beings.*

For some long moments, Cashel simply watched Storey, and Storey found he could meet Cashel's eyes for no more than a split second at a time.

Finally, the tension grew too much, and Storey prompted, "What did you say about a proposition?"

"I have watched you grow from a frightened little boy to

a man. A leader of men. I know what it means to be a leader, and so I can recognize the quality in you. That is why I would be remiss in my duties to the Queen if I did not offer you an immediate officership in the army. You are exactly the kind of person I need in command, and I know you would only grow stronger under my stewardship."

"But, sir—" The uninvited flattery Storey felt deep in his bosom surprised and disconcerted him. "An officer? I—I am but seventeen years old, and . . . I am a man."

"You are of age to make the decisions that will guide your life. No one but God can know where these decisions will lead, but it is our gift to do the choosing. And of course I care not that you are a man. It is a testament to the gamut of my control that I can appoint anyone I choose. The more of your ilk I can appoint, the better off we all shall be."

"I don't know what to say," Storey replied in all sincerity.

"Say nothing until I give you your other two options. You, of course, have the option to stay on at Secernere. Now that you are an adult and you have proven your worth, I will offer you a salary in addition to your normal provisions of food and shelter. It is nothing compared to what you would receive as a commissioned soldier, but it would be some gold to store away all the same. Since Abern, you have been the most competent, motivated, and loyal man I have ever had on my staff. Abern shall, someday—someday soon I expect—not be equipped with the necessary faculties of his station. I will need someone to take up his mantle as steward of Secernere. You are the man for that job as much as any other I could hope to find in this country. That is why I offer you the option to stay here and take care of my estate as my trusted first man."

"I don't know what to say," Storey repeated dumbly.

"Your third option is to desert." Cashel paused, again staring into Storey's darting eyes.

Storey swallowed hard. He did not attempt to speak. He was not even sure he had heard Cashel correctly.

As if cued, Cashel began again: "Storey, I have grown to love you as my brother. I do not wish our lives to part. But I am a fair man. And so I offer you the option to defect from Secernere, from me, just as the other cowards have. They are not above you. They cannot choose some path that is not available to you. They receive no freedom that you do not already own. Granted, I would slit their throats if I ever found them, but that is not my point. You arrived here accidentally, remained here voluntarily. The choice of whether you continue to stay shall be made in a deliberate manner. While I love you, you are not beholden to me or my house, not indentured, not enslaved, in no way coerced to staying in my eyesight, employ, or empire. I am a fair man. If you leave, I will miss you, but only God will judge your decision."

Storey opened his mouth to speak, then closed it again, knowing he would only thrice repeat himself.

"I do not expect you to make a decision right here, Storey."

Storey exhaled.

"In fact, take one month. You have until I return again in thirty days, and then I will demand my answer."

Storey lay in sleepless contemplation for the twenty-seventh consecutive night. He was nowhere closer to a decision.

It was indeed loyalty that Cashel perceived in Storey, but the loyalty was to Abern, to the hapless staff of Secernere, and to the nameless girl, whose role would more clearly define itself only with time. The loyalty was to his dead mother and to the pursuit of the complicated and inequitable justice he sought in her memory. What Storey felt about Cashel was so much more difficult to understand.

But tugging on that loyalty like a dog straining his lead was the idea that he could just walk away. With impunity from Cashel, without judgment from God (for he did not believe in her anymore), and without the disdain of the omniscient soul of his mother (for he did not believe in an afterlife), he could just walk away. And away from Secernere, there was nothing but possibility—the possibility of inner peace, happiness, fulfillment, even love. Secernere offered nothing but more of the same, and perhaps the worse. The worst. Storey shuddered to imagine what the worst might actually be. But he knew that if he left, the girl was not cargo he could bear.

And finally: the army. The position in the army officership was what presented the most difficult moral dilemma. While he would gladly fight for his country, he loathed the idea of fighting *this* war. He loathed the idea of acting in any capacity to increase Cashel's burgeoning influence. But Storey loved his country and he loved his country's people. Could he help free them from the tyranny of an unjust war by stepping into the proffered role? Was his plan for the girl just a fool's errand, when the real opportunity lay here?

He threw his shoulder to the side and tossed around in his bed. No position was comfortable. He hadn't had a full, restful night's sleep in weeks, and he felt like his mind was hiding under a fog.

He heard a creak on the floorboards outside his room, and he froze. Squinting toward the door, he watched as the latch lifted slowly, and the door opened a small ways. A tiny figure, nearly glowing white, slipped into the room and closed the door behind her. She silently crossed to Storey's bed, lifted the quilt, and climbed in with him. He crushed himself to the wall to give her space, and she snuggled up against him.

"Storey," she whispered, "I have a name now. Whenever we are together, you can call me Dymphna. Dymphna and Storey. Brother and sister."

He closed his arm around her frail frame and sighed. He would stay.

❧29❧

Secernere – Present

On his way to the stable, Storey concentrated on walking slowly, coolly. The sun, now of the September ilk, beamed gloriously with the jollity of ignorance to the happenings of the land it illuminated. A sun that understood would be dimmer, twice as shy to rise in the morning. But maybe today was not so bad, as Secernere days went. The prospect of final escape after so many years had latched itself onto every fold of Storey's brain, like a spider building an increasingly intricate web from corner to corner. He had been imprisoned by his own designs, but, in Aurora, he had been delivered a key.

He had counted on being alone in the stable, and groaned to himself as he saw Cashel through the doorway. Immediately, he constructed his rationale for visiting the stable and braced himself. Cashel saw Storey and beckoned him closer. He had a dark, serious expression on his pale face.

"I nearly lost my wits, Storey. Do not ever let me lose my wits like that again."

"It was not my place, sir. . . ." Storey hedged. Where was this going?

"No, no. It is your place; it should be your place." He spoke slowly and gravely. "You are my brother and I need you to correct me when my selfish passions lead me astray. In any event, I was coming to collect you shortly." Cashel swung a heavy leather saddle onto a horse.

"Collect me, sir?"

"We are leaving Secernere."

"*What*?" Even cool Storey could not mask his unqualified shock.

"This can come as no surprise, can it? We cannot remain here as living targets to be hunted down by the militia that would invariably follow a Fairgosian scout."

"Cashel, you know I always plead ignorance to the ways of military strategy, but why would any militia follow into territory from which a scout has not returned with information? Or . . . did you let him go?"

Cashel laughed. "I suppose I could have let him go, to draw them here, into a trap. . . . I always knew you had a military mind, my brother. A terrific idea, had I time enough to gather the appropriate men and arms. No, what remains of him is still down in the cellar. Before we leave, I will finish the job, and likely have you take his body to the river."

He paused his activities and looked off to the distance.

"I sometimes imagine there, somewhere along the unknown northward path of the Calder River, there is a bend where the bodies of my enemies gather like a log jam. I would set such a sight aflame and watch them burn like they do in Hell as we speak these very words."

"You know I do not believe in Hell."

Cashel resumed saddling the horse. "Your non-belief does not cease its existence."

"Neither does faith alone make a thing true."

With a small nod, Cashel allowed the assertion, and continued his work in silence.

"You are wise, Storey. Always so wise. . . . I should have spent more time learning from you, instead of . . ." He trailed off in thought.

What had he to teach Cashel, Storey wondered, especially after all this time? What had he to teach anyone? For years, he had viewed Cashel as the architect of the long war, and Dymphna as the path to its end. But while he had groomed Dymphna by his own measure of ideal leadership, Storey could not deny that Cashel, too, had innate qualities of a true leader. For all his evils and missteps, he was courageous, decisive, ambitious. In many ways, he was young Dymphna's foil, and her match. They were two sides of a coin.

It was funny, it a melancholic way: Cashel fantasized about brotherhood with Storey, when Dymphna was a truer sibling. *But never the twain shall meet.*

"So we are leaving?" Storey said at last. "All of us?"

"All of us who remain."

"And where shall we go that will accommodate such a troupe?"

"You speak as if our numbers are great as they once were. I do not think we shall put a strain on any host. In any event, I plan to lead us to the estate of an associate in the east. He has a guest house for me, and servant quarters enough for you all. It will only be a few days. From there, I shall be able to gather a unit of men to accompany us back here and secure the premises once more.

"Consider it a holiday." Cashel turned and caught Storey's gaze. "I want to be gone in the next twenty-four hours."

"Then, sir, if you will permit me leave, I shall begin preparations right off."

Again, Cashel silently nodded, and Storey jogged off toward the manor house.

This news of a compulsory exodus was a deeply troubling notion. *All of us who remain* did not, of course, include among the numbers the one and a half women who waited in the walls of Secernere. Yet Storey would not leave Dymphna alone, not even with Aurora, if there was even the slightest chance the vile military—Fairgosian, Mitochian, he cared not which—would arrive with swords of every nature.

In his chamber, Storey dropped to his mattress, running his hands back and forth over his head. The room in which he had dreamt, planned, schemed, meditated, and ruminated for twelve years, the four wooden walls that seemed to breathe with his every secret thought—the very essence of that room had been packed into a threadbare sack that crouched beside him, along with his meager belongings. Once painted with the outpourings of his soul, Storey had stripped it bare of all that hope and meaning so that he could take the best and worst of it with him wherever he went. It was now just a room, and if Storey had his way, he would never return to it. Standing, he heaved his sack onto his shoulder. It felt light on his back; all the weight was in his head.

As expected, he found Cook in the kitchen, hunched over the wash basin. Storey winced at the sight of his narrow shoulders; the man was slimmer than ever before. And standing alone without the company of an oft present Abern, the lone, bowed figure seemed to be the very embodiment of the demise of Secernere.

Storey tapped the doorframe with his knuckles. "My friend."

Cook turned slowly, withdrawing his hands from the water and wiping them dry on his dirty apron. Deep, dark circles cupped his tired eyes and he nodded in acknowledgment. His slack expression did not change.

"Has the news yet spread?" Storey asked.

The man cocked his head. "What news?"

"I thought as much."

Storey explained Cashel's mandate and watched as the man's eyebrows rose upward and created deep creases across his forehead. Cook was silent, his mouth opening and closing like that of a fish. Finally, he found the words.

"The army?" he choked out. "Here?"

Storey nodded gravely. "I . . . Pardon my hesitation, my friend. I do not know the easy way to say this." He took a breath and continued. "It is true, is it not, that had you somewhere to go, you would have left this place by now?"

Cook coughed, and the cough turned into a bluster. His face turned red and he vehemently shook his head no. "Sir, I—I am a loyal, honorable man. I would never—"

Storey held up his hand and attempted a reassuring smile.

"No, no. I am not here to pass judgment on you. I know you are an honorable man. You have shown more than loyalty to us by your presence here, even now. But you must understand that at this moment, everything has changed. We are facing danger of the kind we have not yet known. These stone walls have protected us, in a way—until now. The war from which we have mercifully been sheltered now marches toward our doorstep. I only seek the truth from you: have you someplace to go?"

Cook shook his head sadly. "You were correct the first time, Mister Storey. Secernere is my home, for better or worse. I have nowhere else, no one else." He continued rubbing his hands on his apron.

"Then heed my words. It is vital that you follow Cashel's every order, his every idea. Do what he says, go where he goes. Stay with him, and you will be safe. He will do whatever is necessary to save himself, and so you cannot go wrong by following him."

"But, what about you?" Cook's hands were ringing furiously now. If Storey had frightened the man nearly out of his wits, so be it. He needed to express the gravity of the situation.

Storey could not save everyone. So often, he felt he could not save anyone. But right now he had but one charge that mattered.

Even in your death, even in the death of everyone around you, you will keep her safe.

No—two charges now. Aurora had become an inextricable part of Dymphna's life. He would have to keep her safe, too.

Swallowing, he put on his familiar mask. "I am not going with you—"

"But Mister Storey!"

"I am so sorry, my friend."

"Where are you going to go? What are you going to do? After what you've revealed—you cannot be staying here? Are you?"

His eyes were opened so wide, Storey could see the whites completely surrounding the miniature brown islands of his irises. He stepped toward the man and gently placed his hands on his shoulders. They shook beneath Storey's fingers.

"I wish I could tell you. I wish, even more, that I could be by your side during this trial. But I am needed in a different capacity. . . . I have a mission."

"For the army?" Cook whispered.

Storey nodded, solemn. "It is a secret, so I cannot explain. But—" he held a finger directly in front of Cook's face. "—no one must know that you know, not even Cashel."

"No! Of course not, Mister Storey!"

"I promise you that everything will end in the best of ways. You will be safe, I will return, and we will enjoy a peaceful future such as we have never known. Just, give me your word, please, that you will do as I say and follow Cashel away from this place."

Cook drew his shaking hand up to his forehead in an awkward salute. "You have my word, sir."

Storey squeezed Cook's shoulder in solidarity, then left without another word.

He visited each of the remaining Secernere servants in turn, the few there were, telling them the news. Most of them took it with the same incredulity and fear as Cook. In response, he gave them the same advice to follow Cashel, and the same vague tale about a secret mission.

This task finished, he returned to the stable, thankful to find it empty but for its equine inhabitants. He wandered down the corridor, pausing to gently stroke the velvety muzzles of each horse. He wished he could take all of them, or turn them into the wild. They snorted affectionately, but an anxiety lingered in the air—as if they knew something large was looming.

As he touched his Friesian—the horse he would ride away from Secernere—he leaned forward over the stall door and whispered the plan into the animal's ear. The horse blustered and nodded his giant head. Storey patted the horse's cheek and said, "Good boy." He moved to smaller chestnut he had planned for Aurora and explained her role in the escape. She gazed back at him and lazily blinked her long-lashed eyelids.

Storey sat down on a wooden bench near the door, from where he had a good vantage of anyone coming up to the stable, and waited for the sun to go down. A dog crossed his view.

Damn. Those blasted hounds are loose again.

He stood and called to it, and it came to him. In its jaws, it held a bone almost too large for the young dog to manage. It dropped the bone at Storey's feet and panted, smiling proudly as only dogs can. White and brittle, the bone still had traces of dirt from wherever it had been dug up. It was as long as a man's thigh.

There was no time to take the dog back to its pen. He threw the bone out into the falling darkness as hard as he could, and the dog bounded after it. Finally, now that night was providing its cover, he could put it off no longer and crept silently up to Aurora's bedroom.

Standing outside the door, he was unable to bring himself to open it. He simply waited, breathing quietly and rehearsing the actions of the next hour.

Aurora's voice, groggy with sleep, slipped through the door: "Storey?"

He took one more deep breath, placed his hand on the latch, and entered.

❧30❧

Aurora felt only half rested. Laying on her bed in the darkness, she had sought sleep, but every tiny noise yanked her back to full wakefulness. She had dressed and packed, wanting to be prepared when Storey arrived. But when she finally heard him outside, she knew she never could have prepared herself for what was coming next. Nothing in fact, she mused, could prepare anyone for anything. Life was very much like tumbling down the steep slope of a mountain.

Storey was but a black mass in the doorway, standing just outside the threshold as he had many times before.

"It is time. Are you ready?"

She sat up and nodded. Her head felt heavy, cloudy. She stood and grasped the pillowcase in which she had stuffed the few things she could call her belongings. She felt the weight of her knife in one pocket and the carved pine queen in the other.

"Is it safe?" she whispered.

"As much as it can be. We will travel through the tunnels; no man ever goes down there if he can help it."

As Storey led the way by torchlight, down the cold rock stairs into the bowels of Secernere's wall, Aurora's thoughts continued to drift back to her bed—when it was only the two of them in the whole of the world.

He had smelled like hay, spice. Nature. His body had been heavy on top of hers, like it might crush her. Or like it would envelope her and she would simply disappear. His body radiated heat. Sweaty, moist in spots, his scent still clung to her clothes. His mouth had tasted salty, his fleshy lower lip like tender steak in her mouth. She absently licked her lips at the thought.

Watching his hulking form descend the stairs, she longed to reach out and grasp him from behind, press her body against his hot, broad back. She wanted to feel it all again. But she resigned to follow him, fixating on the whiteness in the flame that flickered at the top of the torch he carried. As her feet struck the earthen floor, she knew she had to start thinking about something else, anything else.

"Tell me about Dymphna."

"What do you wish to know?"

Storey led, and they proceeded forward on silent footfalls, the torch throwing vicious shadows on the uneven mortar and stone.

"Everything. For all she's said to me, she's told me nothing. *You've* told me nothing. Who is she? Where did she come from? Are you kin? And what did you mean when you said she is *the way?*"

Aurora took a few quick steps to catch up and began to walk beside Storey, nearly jogging to keep up with his long strides.

"She is Cashel's sister. Full-blooded sister." Aurora gasped and looked at Storey's face, but he only looked straight ahead. "And therefore, she is the heir to Secernere: all its property, wealth, and prestige—indeed, its very power. Cashel's power. Cashel does not know she exists."

"How is that possible?"

"Cashel lives in a world of his own construction. Also, I'm very good at hiding things." He glanced at her with a small smile.

"You've been hiding her for her whole life?"

"Twelve years, if you can believe it."

"Because Cashel would have killed her if he knew who she was."

The smile was gone. "He would kill her even if he didn't know."

"What about her mother?"

"Dead." Aurora felt a pang.

"Her father?"

"Dead."

"What happened?" She almost didn't want to know.

"Cashel happened."

Inwardly, Aurora shuddered, and the pair continued in silence for a ways. Finally, she asked, "What now?"

"What do you mean?" Storey said.

"Dymphna. Being the way. What does that mean? What are you going to do with her?" Aurora struggled to ask the question neutrally, but there was an unfamiliar intonation in her voice. Suddenly, she knew very clearly what the most important thing in the world was, and it wasn't home and it wasn't herself. It was the only person to whom she had ever mattered.

Perhaps he could have brushed off the question, but they had come too far for that. Nevertheless, Storey had never before had to articulate his plans for the girl. He had never had to articulate the girl herself. What she meant to him was ineffable. To even attempt to answer to the curiosity—the intrusiveness—of a third party when there had only ever, ever been two . . . Aurora's tone was protective, accusatory. It stabbed at the seed of fear inside him which, season after season, tried to germinate and grow, but which, season after season, he tried to wrench out by the root.

"I have . . . plans for her," he said pensively. He sighed deeply to beg Aurora give him pause.

In his dreams, Storey imagined that his country—that his world—was led by Dymphna, that tiny innocent child. He had been preparing her all her life for the role, whether to success or failure.

She had, on one hand, only ever known war and danger, hiding and anxiety. She was wrapped in a shroud of non-existence, only knowing Storey, herself, and some indiscernible destiny for which she knew she was being prepared but did not fully, or even partially, understand. But on the other hand, she knew only peace and love and the simplicity of the Way. Storey had been selective in her education, the history, philosophy, religion, and literature he imparted to her.

But while he was playing at teacher or parent, setting out plans for her and designing a destiny unbeknownst to her, was he really playing at being a god? He fixed his eyes on the darkness ahead of them in the tunnel, the black just beyond the light of the torch.

To Storey, a god was a hateful thing. Storey had lost his god, and the god that remained for others was arrogant and felt nothing but contempt and embarrassment at his creation. Instead of being the path to true peace of the soul, the idea of god rent the soul. Believers were left with confusion, wondering from where their awful ache and longing came.

Storey was terrified at the idea of playing god.

He had not actually created the little girl, formed her from mud or a rib. But he fully acknowledged that he had created her spirit and her intellect and her belief system. It was naïve to suppose that a baby was born an innate nature that will form on its own whether the child is raised by a king or by wolves. The baby is nothing without parent—natural or surrogate, mother, father, or both. Even the knowledge of an absent parent could have as much effect on a child as the company of a present one. Storey knew this truth intimately.

That is why Storey never told Dymphna the true history of who she was or how she came upon her situation. As he had so delicately couched it in his raising of her, she had no situation at all. She did not realize there were other children in the world who had lives different from her own. She did not realize that children usually had two loving parents. Storey had taken every pain to impart to her that she was normal and that her life was normal and that her future would be normal—even though in his own design it would be absolutely extraordinary.

It was a cruel duality that he forced himself to ignore. Even in the innocent simplicity of her questions, Aurora was forcing him to confront the question of Dymphna's own humanity, divinity, morality. And his carefully manicured belief structure shuddered.

"I have been planning it for years," he said finally. "She must be presented at court as the legal heir to Secernere and the head of the household of Gomery. I have made contacts in Ekanta who can aid me in this process."

"Then what?"

"Then she shall have the opportunity to claim the property and title, and to pronounce what she wants done with Cashel."

"She is but twelve! How can she make such a decision?"

"I have been her teacher and guardian since she was a baby. She knows the right decisions to make. She has had her whole life to prepare for this role."

Aurora bristled, feeling her affection for Storey recede like a wave from the shore. Dymphna was a person—a child. She was not some cog in a machine of Storey's design. A machine created to bring down his enemy for legitimate, but abstract, reasons. But again, she quelled the emotions that clawed just beneath the surface of her composure.

"What about Cashel?" she argued. "Has he not enough power and influence—enough success—that even the Queen herself would be hesitant to take it from him?"

"I don't know the answer to that. I've not seen a man rise to such power in all my life; I'm not sure any of my generation has, and the Government may not know at all what to do with him.

"That's why I'm going to have him killed."

Aurora gasped. After a moment, she said, "If that was what you wanted all along, why haven't you done it yet? Surely it would be an easy task within the emptiness of Secernere."

Storey was quiet once more. She could sense he was retreating into his mind again. In fairness to his consideration, she walked beside him in the silence.

"I cannot," he said finally.

"But in your mind, is he not the most evil man in all the world?"

"You don't know the whole story." His tone was one of frustration, as if he was hiding something but no longer wanted the burden.

Aurora was frustrated herself at everything that had ever been kept from her, at everything she had believed that turned out to be false. She didn't know the whole story of anything.

"We've lived side-by-side since I was a boy," Storey said softly. "He gave me a home. He is my enemy, but he is also my brother. The power of murder is not in me . . . not for him."

They walked again in silence for a while. The pathway under the wall seemed to stretch for leagues. A rat scampered across their path and disappeared into the wall.

Finally, Aurora said, "What if you didn't kill him? If he was still alive when Dymphna went to court?"

"It's too uncertain, as I said. However, by the letter of the law, Dymphna has the legal right to marry Cashel off to a woman of her choosing. It should then be the new wife's decision whether to allow him to continue his brutality. And I doubt any woman would. So I imagine he would be relegated to taking care of the household, as any husband."

"Your country does not make sense to me," said Aurora.

"Nor yours to me."

"I cannot imagine a place where a woman could control a man in such a way. I cannot even imagine a woman would want such control."

"Because you equate control with masculinity?"

Aurora hesitated, feeling set up. "Perhaps."

"I imagine you controlled your father in your own way, whether by guilt, coquetry—"

"Shut up." Aurora stopped walking. Her skin burned. She clenched her hands into fists. "Stop. I've given you much leeway, but if you ever mention my father again . . ."

His eyes were downcast. "I'm sorry. I . . . think not positively of fathers."

She began to walk again. "Then think not of mine. Tell me of what you know, not of what you do not."

Storey switched his torch from one hand to the other, running his free hand over his head. ". . . I was saying, one can lead without controlling. One can show another the way without force or domination. This is how women have led our country for hundreds of years. A woman choosing to remove Cashel from his role would have different reasons than you likely suspect. Just think of an example in the reverse: Imagine a single, unmarried woman rising to a position of political influence in Fairgos."

"I don't know that I can." Aurora chuckled softly. "All right, I'm imagining it."

Fleetingly, the image of her mother flashed into her mind: alive, well, strong—and powerful. She then replaced that image with herself, making decisions that affected her countrymen, ruling over some county or even an entire region. Queen of the whole country. She all but laughed again at the ridiculous notion.

"Now imagine that she gets married," Storey said.

Married. If her father had lived, if she were still at home, preparations for her own wedding would have been well under way by now. He would have given her the most glorious celebration Fairgos had seen in a decade. The idea of the wedding mortified her. But the marriage . . .

The pictures popped into her head in rapid succession, quick as a blinking eye. First she imagined Storey in that place at her side. She flashed through images of a happy household together, Dymphna—Catherine—maturing under their guidance, perhaps their own baby on the way. The household she imagined was not like Cathendria; it was not like Secernere. It was a humble hovel near the water. The Aurora River maybe, or even the sea. Any power she had, she would surrender it for a family.

A moment later, Kynton entered her mind for the first time in days, replacing Storey as her imaginary husband. With him at her side, they ruled together as a powerful couple, from the high vantage of a castle tower. He would not usurp her power, only add to it. With his strength and her compassion, they would make Fairgos great once more.

Then, she imagined a third future. She imagined her life as it was for many women of her station: her father choosing a suitor for her with all the care he'd taken in choosing a tutor. For so many women, marrying was just another business deal made by people who cared little for them except as collateral. A strange man entering her life, one who had no care for her other than what money and power he could put his hands on— the image of having any power whatsoever burst like a bubble, and suddenly she was giving direction to the maids and playing the harpsichord at parties.

Aurora caught Storey watching her in his periphery. He

must have seen the subtle change in her expression.

"Now imagine that the woman is a man, living in Mitoch."
Storey had made his case.

"I understand," she said.

They continued on in silence again, until such a potent
stench entered her nostrils that she could not withhold com-
ment.

"What *is* that?" she cried, drawing the inset of her elbow
across her nose.

"Our cemetery." Storey handed her a kerchief, and she
placed it up to her face. "It won't be long until we are past it."

In minutes, they entered the cemetery space. Aurora felt the
inexplicable need to stop and observe what she saw there, even
though the decaying air was overwhelming. She remembered
the enormous stone monuments she'd seen in the graveyard
outside. These white stones were mere pebbles by comparison.

"Who are they?" she whispered.

"Servants who have died here—those who we could not
bear to send down the river as Cashel would request. Abern
is here."

"Oh!" She found herself beset with stinging grief for the
man with whom she was hardly acquainted. "I didn't know. . . ."

She turned to look at Storey, but he was rushing to a messy
grave in the corner. He kneeled down. Turning his face to her
briefly, she saw that it was contorted with anguish and streaked
with fresh tears, but he was already looking back at the grave. He
began desperately to scrape the dirt together with his bare hands.

"Who would do such a thing?" he cried.

Best she could, Aurora suppressed the urge to gag and went
to Storey's side. But all her will betrayed her when she caught
the glimpse of decomposing face exposed through the dirt. She
turned and vomited against the wall.

"I'm sorry," she whispered, dragging her sleeve across her
mouth.

Storey stood and gently rubbed her back. "We should keep moving."

Aurora nodded, grateful for the opportunity to leave this place.

Farther down the next corridor, as the smell began to subside at last, Storey finally said, "That was Abern's grave. Dug up."

Aurora gasped. "How horrid!"

Storey gave a casual wave of his hand. "It could have been the dogs. The miller's daughters often leave them out by accident."

"I'm so sorry. I know he was your friend."

"I suppose it could have been worse. My parents are buried there, too."

"You parents served here?"

"No, not exactly." He did not explain further. Still nauseated, Aurora did not say anything.

Eventually, the passageway began to rise in elevation until they exited through a door. They climbed a steep flight of stone stairs, passed through another door, and then entered an anteroom. As Storey pushed through another door, he said, "This is the mill, where Dymphna stays."

The door opened into the same spacious building by which Aurora had returned to Secernere. Filtered through the sunlight, the air was flocked with dust motes and smelled acridly of fresh grain. Piercing the air were the fierce barks of dogs—more aggressive and frightening than the friendly yelps Aurora had heard while trapped inside the coach weeks before.

Looking across the length of the wooden building, they immediately saw a pack of four dogs, hackles raised, barking viciously up at something in the loft. Cowered in the corner was Dymphna, terrified.

Then, entering through a side door near the dogs was the man Aurora recognized immediately to be Cashel, Lord Gomery of Secernere.

The instant Aurora saw all three strange characters together, their history was immediately evident. Dymphna and Cashel, though many years separated their ages, were nigh unto twins in appearance. They shared the same white hair, translucent skin, and watery glowing eyes. But Cashel was also obviously linked to Storey. Though their coloring varied, with Storey's green eyes and auburn hair, their shared features—deep-set eyes, high cheekbones, broad round shoulders—revealed them as brothers. But not symbolic brothers.

Blood brothers.

❧31❧

Twelve Years Earlier

Though Storey had never known him, never met him, he'd long lived with a keen awareness of the existence of his father, an imagined figure to fill the hole where he stored the phantom pains of paternal love amputated above the joint. When pressed for answers about his father, Storey's mother only ever answered, "He is unknowable," and the conversation would end. But now—now, he would be known.

The previous Sunday, Storey had witnessed his mother's own revelation that brought them to this present. They sat together on a hard wooden bench, as Storey read aloud to his mother. He read to her every day for one hour, and she likewise would read to him for one hour; Sundays were set aside for readings from religious and spiritual texts. A pleasant breeze meandered through the open window, and outside a robin sang. It was spring, and Storey was happy.

At a certain point, his mother stopped him and said, "Storey, please read that again."

He obeyed. " 'Those who amass wealth and lock it up will only themselves be imprisoned.' "

She sighed a deep sigh. "Once more, please."

Storey read the line again, then looked to his mother.

"I have been a fool," she said.

Even as a veil of sadness pulled itself down over her face, his mother was still the most beautiful woman Storey had ever seen. She was true royalty, even if she didn't have the blood to prove it. Storey often told her that when she got to heaven, she would be a queen there. Her reply was always to kiss him on the forehead and say, "We are already in heaven."

Storey continued to watch her face as it grew tight around the eyes, then tears fell. Neither her mouth nor her voice changed as she met his gaze and went on.

"My son, it is said, those who strive too hard to get into heaven will never reach it. In all my efforts of goodness and holiness, in my striving to be a good mother in the way of God, in my endeavor to lead you toward the Way, I have suffered great imperfection. And in this, you have suffered.

"I have tried to protect you from the truth, when the truth is the only thing that will nourish you. You can never grow into the fullness of your being if you are not fully nourished. Storey, I am sorry."

She took his hands. He looked at the gleaming surface of her wet eyes, then willed himself to look into them, behind him, to find the meaning that her words were not quite conveying.

She continued, "Our wealth ... This—" She motioned around the room.

Storey had not, so far, considered what they had to be wealth, but rather the customary accoutrements for a small family in their town who were sufficiently independent of servitude or serfdom under a lordship. They had what they needed, nothing more, but nothing less. They seemed to have exactly enough not to be owned by another person. It certainly was not wealth. But he nodded and listened anyway.

"—It comes from your father. He has sent me money every month since I was first pregnant with you, on the condition that I tell no one—not even you—of his existence or identity."

"Why?" Storey blurted out. "Why would he not want to be known by his own family? Is he not proud of us?"

"Do not desire the accolades of others, Storey."

"But, even my own father?"

"It is said, you are held captive by those whose approval you seek. It will only lead you away from your path. Do you understand?"

He did not, but he nodded nonetheless.

"The reason he asked this is that he is a nobleman—Lord Gomery—and he is married. Such news as an illegitimate son would damn him in our society. But, Storey, our love affair began many, many years before this marriage. He was not Lord Gomery then, but Lord Landwin. I knew him simply as Paul.

"We were so in love, but we could never wed. I was a servant of his parents' estate. He is entitled. When his parents chose for him a wife, he had no choice but to marry her, though he did not love her. They married, joining their households. We continued our affair with practiced secrecy . . . for years. But when I became pregnant, everything changed. He asked me to go away, that he would pay me to. And I did, because my love for you—even in my belly—was stronger than my love for him could ever be . . . especially after he made such a request of me. It was then that I began to study the Way to find peace.

"I took the money for many years. I've taken the money your whole life. I thought it would protect you. But the teaching is true, as it is always true. Read it again."

" 'Those who amass wealth and lock it up will only themselves be imprisoned.' "

"And so we are imprisoned here, in this hovel built on lies. We are not free to go as we please, because you are not free to seek your father. Storey, the teaching is always true. I am so sorry that I have strayed from my path in this way."

She began to weep. Reaching up, Storey took her in his arms—mother and son were nearly the same size now—and hugged her with all his strength. She shook against him, trying to speak only to be cut off by her own sobs.

"Shh," he soothed. "That which is perfect may seem imperfect."

That wasn't what he wanted to say. He wanted to say, "I love you and I forgive you." But he knew his mother would only be comforted by the words of the teaching.

She pulled away, a dim but genuine smile on her wet face. She tilted her head as she gazed at him, lightly running her hand over his head, then down his shoulder and arm.

"My son."

She heaved a sigh, cleared her throat, and was at once composed again.

"Now. While you should not and shall not seek his appraisal or approval, it is not wrong in any way that you should seek your father, the man. Every person needs to understand their beginning so that they may understand their path. I think we should go to him."

Storey's heart leapt. His breath stuck in his throat. But his mind caught up. "What will happen to the money?" he asked.

"It will stop," she said simply. "I know not how such a meeting as this will end. But the future is not ours. It is said, trying to control the future is like trying to take the master carpenter's place—"

"—When you handle the master carpenter's tools, you will surely cut your hand," Storey finished.

This time, she smiled warmly. "Yes. The only injury we two shall do ourselves is not to enact this venture thusly. It is not far, and the way is safe."

"Now?" Storey breathed.

"Now."

Now was now: after half a day's journey along routes heavily fortified with Mitochian soldiers, they had arrived at the strange and massive manor called Secernere. Storey's mother had entered the receiving parlor, and Storey had been obliged to wait in the anteroom. He waited and tried to be patient, repeating mantras and prayers to keep himself calm—until the shouts began.

He hurried to the doorway. It was ajar just enough to allow him vantage of the unfolding scene.

His mother stood in the center of the room like the tallest tree in a forest—steadfast, wooden. Her polar opposite was another woman who was crumpled in a heap on the floor, weeping wildly. Her white-blond hair spread around her like a puddle. Her dress appeared as if it had been heaped on the floor without anyone in it. Her face, even contorted in anguish, was bloodless—the color of fresh milk. Storey guessed her to be the cuckolded Lady Gomery, and his heart went out to her. Whether or not the couple married for love, that was a woman whose heart had been broken.

Then Storey saw him: the cause of all this. The cause of Storey's very existence. Lord Gomery. Lord Landwin. Paul. Father.

He stood in profile to the scene, not looking at his wife, not looking at his mistress. His arms were crossed on his broad chest. Storey felt as if he were looking into a crystal ball, seeing his future self in every physical detail. Father.

A door banged. Suddenly, a fourth character entered the stage. He was a younger man, just a few years older than Storey himself, and a fine and exact mixture of his two parents. Storey watched, horrified but entranced, like a play was beginning. This new character shouted.

"What in hell's name is going on here?" he demanded.

"Leave, Cashel," said Lord Gomery, not looking at his son.

"Who is this woman? Why is Mother crying?" The young

man called Cashel was by now red-faced, his breathing already audible and quick.

"I said leave, Cashel!" Lord Gomery unfolded his arms as if to make himself appear larger. He stared down his son.

"And *I* said, what in hell's name is going on!" Cashel shouted. He pressed his face up at Lord Gomery's. Indeed, the son was quite as large as the father.

Lord Gomery feinted as if to attack, but did not move his limbs. The two stared.

Storey's mother spoke. Her voice was like a bell ringing out over a yard. It cut through, and everything in the world seemed to fall silent, except Lady Gomery's wounded howls.

"I was Lord Gomery's lover," she said.

"So?" demanded Cashel.

"He has a son."

Somewhat reluctantly, Cashel left the immediate orbit of his father and turned his malevolent attention toward Storey's mother, a marble column. He growled, "Yes: me."

"No," she said calmly. "He has another son. You have a brother."

Storey automatically pressed himself flat against the wall, taking a sharp breath. Then, with silent care, he returned to his dangerous eavesdropping.

Cashel watched her through slits of eyes. A slow grin spread across his face and he laughed. Predatory eyes still on Storey's mother, he said, "Is this true, Father?"

"This is no business of yours, Cashel," his father said. "You are a child."

"It doesn't matter. The mere sight of Mother on the floor like that tells me it's true." He turned to the disrupting visitor. "How long has this been going on?"

"It ended twelve years ago," she said.

"Cashel, I command you go to your quarters!" But Lord Gomery's imposing presence was diminishing.

"You command me?" Cashel once again pressed near his

father. "You would make a cuckold of the head of this family, my precious and beautiful mother, then tell me it's none of my business? I don't think you *have* any command right now."

He stooped to the floor and rubbed his hand over his mother's back; her wails had quieted as she watched the exchange in trepidation.

"I did not come here to disrupt this family," said Storey's mother.

"What did you expect to happen?" Lord Gomery cried.

"My son deserves—"

"Your son is your son, and your son alone," he said. "He has your name, he lives in your household, and you will give him away when his time comes. He is your son. You can never prove he is mine. A child can only ever be traced to the mother."

He stopped, seeming to be through with his speech, only to start again, as if finally saying all the words he had waited twelve years to speak. "It was your *choice* to have a child. You couldn't even afford him. There was never a reason for you to bring forth life from a relationship that was dead."

Storey could not see his mother's face, but he knew this had hurt her deeply. He saw that hurt reflected in the eyes of the only man she had ever loved, whose own pain at speaking the untrue words lingered like a ghost that only Storey could see. He was a desperate, weak man, impotent in the face of the destruction he had caused.

"In that light," began Storey's mother quietly, "I will press this issue no further. I do not know what I expected from this meeting, but this certainly was not it. I will no longer take up your precious time."

She turned and Storey glimpsed the pain he had imagined.

Cashel placed his broad body between her and the door.

"Who gave you permission to leave? You're as much a party to this as my whore father."

Storey's mother took a step back.

"Well, Father, I guess the good news for me is that a girl

bastard didn't show up. Just another worthless boy, right?"

"Cashel!" This from the crumpled mother, now sitting fully upright.

"I'm sorry, Mother, but this is a conversation that needs to be had."

Cashel turned back to his father. But rather than continuing the conversation, he reared back his arm, threw it forward, and punched his father cleanly across the jaw. Lord Gomery fell to the ground, his mouth bleeding at the corner. Cashel stood over him and spat.

"And you—" In two quick strides, he was upon her. "You don't know what you expected? You should have expected the worst, you bitch."

The hand that had just leveled his father flew up to her throat and he choked her against the door through which Storey was watching. It slammed in his face, the weight of his mother's struggling body just on the other side of it. Tears began to stream down his cheeks. He pressed his hands against the wood of the door, trying to feel the heat of his mother, trying to feel her life. Trying to let her know he was there. But he could not save her; he was too small.

A scream: Lady Gomery begging her son to stop.

Muffled but close to the door, Cashel's voice pierced through: "I'm sorry, Mother! But women don't always get to be right! This woman fornicated with *your* husband and all you do is cry about it? She made a baby with *your* husband, with *my* father. She wants him, what, to be a father to him as well? What next, a husband to her? She expects nothing except everything. Why are you so weak?"

The door shuddered. The wood vibrated with labored and terrified breaths.

"Why are women so weak?" he cried, then quietly, barely audible, just a whisper through the door: "Let me show you what strength is."

ᴥ32ᴥ

ℐn the mill, revelation shown starkly in the faces of every character while the dogs punctuated the scene with anxious barks. Cashel saw the little girl first, and he stopped as suddenly as if he had run into a glass pane. He had flames in his eyes as he took in her every feature.

Then he turned toward the movement in his periphery— Storey and Aurora. Storey might have been invisible, and Aurora might have been an angel or a monster for the incredulous look on Cashel's face. He stared hard at her.

From the loft above, Dymphna screamed, "Storey!"

Cashel's eyes snapped back to the tiny girl, his gaze burning. For only a split second, Aurora saw it: he was imagining how he would kill her.

She screamed, "Catherine!"

Cashel returned his stare to Aurora. His eyes were wide, his jaw slack. As he swiveled back and forth between Dymphna and Aurora, a multitude of emotions crossed his pale face: shock, fear, pain, anger. Hatred.

Storey stepped in front of Aurora. She grasped the back of his shirt, holding him like a shield.

"You know her. . . ." Cashel said slowly. He took a step forward.

Storey involuntarily glanced up to the loft, and the instant he did, Aurora knew it was a mistake.

"You know them both." Cashel shook his head slowly back and forth. Muscles in his brow and at the corners of his mouth twitched, betraying his competing emotions. "No women at Secernere for so long. Now two at once. And you know them *both*."

"You *are* brothers. . . ." Aurora couldn't help whispering into Storey's ear.

"Hush!" he hissed.

Cashel took another step toward the couple on the floor, continuing to stare at Storey. "You have betrayed me, haven't you. This is your betrayal."

"Cashel—"

"The Lady Cavalcata, I presume. The War Master's daughter. When you should have led me to her, you hid her from me . . ." He spoke slowly, as if puzzling out the answer to a riddle.

Aurora tightened her grip on Storey.

". . . And the one in the loft?"

"Cashel, what about the army? Why are you even here?" Storey's voice trembled.

"Who is she!" Cashel yelled. Then softer: "Why does she look like me?"

"Cashel—"

"I loved you. You, my only family. My brother." Cashel's voice was shaking now. "You betray me!" he cried. "Be at least honorable and define your deceit!"

Aurora suddenly pushed off Storey's back, ran to the ladder that led to the loft, and began to climb. The dogs ran at her and nipped at her heels as she launched herself up into the air, escaping their snapping jaws.

Cashel lunged toward her. Storey grabbed Cashel's shoulder, held him, and threw a hard punch at his cheek. Cashel staggered backwards, punch drunk, and Aurora scrambled into the loft. Dymphna ran into her arms. Aurora had never clutched anything so tightly.

Below, Cashel had regained his senses and Storey stood ready for him. They stood eyeing each other.

"I don't want to fight you, Storey."

"I don't want to fight you either."

"Tell me who she is!" Cashel's voice broke, and he cleared his throat to mask it. "She is no daughter of Cavalcata. She is no Fairgosian. She is of Mitoch."

"She is of Gomery," Storey said. The tremble in his voice was gone.

Cashel's fist shot forward. It caught only air as Storey dodged. "There are no women of Gomery."

Frantic, Aurora surveyed the loft area. There was nothing. No windows. No back way out. The only escape was down the ladder.

"You're wrong. She is born of the same loins as you."

"Impossible!" He jabbed, and again caught only air. "My mother is dead, childless but for me. I was the one who found her body in the Calder Forest . . . half eaten by wolves."

"She is dead, yes," said Storey. "But she died in *my* arms. *I* put her body out for the wolves, to hide the fact that she had recently given birth to a child."

This revelation knocked Cashel back the same as a punch. As he staggered, Storey bent and speared his head into Cashel's gut, running him into the wall. Cashel jerked his knee upward, smashing into Storey's cheekbone. Storey stumbled back. Blood spilled from a gash in his face.

Dymphna gasped, and Aurora shoved her hand over the child's mouth, muffling the cries.

281

"Storey, you bastard, I loved you!" Cashel screamed. He was crying now. "Who is she!"

Storey spat blood onto the straw covered floor. "She is our sister."

Their eyes were locked.

"Heir to everything you have."

"*Our* sister . . ." Cashel whispered. "You . . ."

"And me, the bastard brother who's grown up big enough to see her on her way to court."

At this moment, Storey was indeed the biggest presence in the room. His shoulders were tense and bulging; his voice was clear and strong. Cashel had shrunken, breaking under the weight of deep betrayal. His eyes were wild. They seemed to struggle between looking at Storey and deep into Storey, as if trying to find the meaning that lay somewhere in his soul.

"Then you really are my brother," Cashel whispered. ". . . I knew it from the day we met."

"I may share your blood, but we share nothing else," Storey growled. His muscles rippled beneath his clothes as he prepared to attack again.

"Why!" Cashel cried. His eyes still glistened with tears. "My Steward of Secernere. My brother. I gave you everything."

He yelled and surged forward, slamming his fist into Storey's gut. Storey groaned and stumbled backward, bent double.

When he stood again, his face was red with anger. "You took everything from me!"

Cashel squeezed his eyes shut for just a moment. "Your mother . . ."

"You are the devil." Storey lunged, pushing Cashel against a wall. He pressed his forearm hard on Cashel's throat.

Cashel coughed, struggled. His face inflated, puffy and red, and his eyes began to bug out. Finally, he shoved Storey on the shoulders and set him tripping backwards.

He rubbed at his throat, coughing. "All these years—why didn't you just kill me?"

Cashel ran forward again. Storey dodged. They both slowed and stared hard at one another.

"Your mother gave me the gift of a little Gomery girl," said Storey. His chest heaved as he drank in ragged breaths. "Even as a boy, I knew it would be my life's work to raise that child so she could stop the violence you rain down upon everything." He glanced up at Dymphna and Aurora. "The future of Mitoch is in that loft."

"Then the future of Mitoch is *dead*. And so are you."

Cashel roared and dove at Storey, knocking them both to the ground. There, they wrestled, throwing punches and grappling with the ferocity that defined them as enemies. As brothers.

What Aurora saw was the unraveling of the fiction Storey told her, and told himself. His rage did not grow from Cashel's violence against the world. It came from his violence against one. Truth, she realized, was more like smoke than stone.

Aurora knew only one thing for certain now, and that was that she had to see Dymphna delivered to safety, no matter what.

Her fear fell away, and she screamed.

"Storey!"

Dodging fierce blows, Storey heard his name. The call was so unexpected that he did not even turn and look. But when he saw Aurora's thin, weak arms precariously holding the little girl out over the loft edge, he shoved Cashel with all his might, as far away from him as he could get.

"You're crazy!" he shouted. But he knew she wasn't.

"Catch her!"

Dymphna didn't scream. She didn't frown. She didn't struggle in Aurora's grip. She only stared down at the hard mill floor so far below, her pale blue kitten eyes completely encircled in white.

Storey ran to the spot beneath the girl and had barely opened his arms before she was falling toward him. There was a long, slow moment and he could not comprehend the quickness or the vastness of what was happening. Then her body connected with his arms, they were together, and then they were on the ground.

He rose, holding her with all his strength, and ran. He did not look back.

He had to get to a horse. They had to ride far away, in any direction at all.

His heart tried to fly back to the vision and memory and desire of Aurora, but his mind smothered that flame. Aurora had been sent for a reason. She had been sent to save Dymphna. She had freed them and there would be no more reason for her to be with them. He ran and did not look back.

His arms burned with the burden of the girl, waif that she was. His legs ached as they pumped and propelled them toward freedom, propelled the country, the world toward freedom. He pictured a crown being placed upon Dymphna's head.

He ran. In his mind, Dymphna was dressed all in white. It was not the soiled, thin, gauzy white of the tattered dress she wore today. It was satin. It was studded with oyster pearls, quilted with silken thread so fine the knots were invisible. Spotted ermine fur rose up around her face. She giggled as it tickled her white cheeks. A heavy cape gave mass to her boney shoulders and fell to the floor, pooling around diamond-soled shoes. Tiny heels gave her height. Her creamy hands were folded in front of her. They were like ripples in milk, shifting yet still.

He ran, and Dymphna sat in a throne. It was gold and ivory and stood twice as tall as she. It made her miniature, made her enormous. Her smallness was her purity. There was no room in her for evil, only the perfect benign love of a saint. The love shone out of her brighter than the sunlight reflecting off the satin of her robes or the glint of diamonds and pearls. She was the Way.

❧33❧

urora's muscles had been burning, screaming in pain—
but letting Dymphna go was agony. It was the most excruciat-
ing thing she had ever done. Storey had stolen away with the
little girl like she was the last hope of the world. And maybe
she was. He didn't even look back. That she had done the right
thing was a notion Aurora clung to like a shipwrecked sailor to
splintered flotsam.

Now she and Cashel were alone. He was still coming around
from Storey's last attack. She stared at him, the living myth.

For Aurora, Cashel of Gomery was hope turned to terror.
She had fought so hard against Storey's notion of Cashel as
villain, clinging to him as the last vestige of a salvageable life.
Now that she had seen his eyes, she knew his wickedness. Indeed, his rage might have been as personal as Storey's, but that
only made him more dangerous.

As he stared toward the barn door through which Storey
and Dymphna had escaped, his gaze flashed remorseful, almost
longing. He must have known he was too late to catch them.

But suddenly, Aurora saw him change. Everything about his sullen, crushed demeanor morphed into something entirely different. He stood taller, straighter. His face was cold like iron. He had completely shut off his emotions. Strangely, he looked patient, entitled, smug—as though, if he just waited, Storey and the girl would come back to him like homing pigeons. Like there was nowhere else for them to go except back to the world that he owned so singularly. Like Secernere had the gravity of a black hole.

Suddenly, the most terrifying thing about Cashel of Gomery was his overwhelming confidence that, even in the wake of his most unexpected betrayal, the future would be of his own making; that he would be subject and not object.

He turned his self-satisfied attention up to Aurora. His flashing eyes echoed those of the carnivorous dogs that growled and barked below. With Dymphna, his look had the intensity of a bonfire—huge and hot in a way that would completely engulf. With Aurora, his look was smoldering coals. He wanted to roast her slowly and savor it, charring her black like an animal on a spit. His fear of Dymphna gave immediacy to his hate. But Aurora was no threat.

For Cashel, Aurora of Cavalcata was prey.

But when she should have been terrified, the oddest emotion began to well inside her: she was envious of his manic, single-minded fearlessness. It was her mind, her never-ceasing, ever tick-tocking, logical mind that saw the situation from all sides. She predicted all outcomes, including those that terrified her. But if she only saw what she wanted—like Cashel did—she too could be brave. She sought the little kernel of courage inside her and willed it grow from green bud to plump red fruit. She would be subject; he would be object.

She had the higher ground, twenty feet of air and just a tiny ladder separating them. She felt a smug sneer play at the corners of her mouth. Focusing on the singular desirable outcome, Aurora began to feel the sense of inevitability that must have given Cashel his power.

Though she was safe, however, she was also trapped. Inevitability did not serve them both. One of them had to be wrong.

With her legs swinging out behind Storey's back, Dymphna bounced along in his arms like a bag of flour he might have run from the mill to the kitchen. She clung to him, her face nuzzled into his chest. He felt her hot breath moisten the fabric above his heart. He brushed his hand over her hair and pushed her head hard against him, steadying her as he ran.

There were two horses packed and ready to go. The front gate in the wall was unfastened and stood open enough to let them squeeze through. It hurt him to leave Aurora behind. It sickened him to leave her with Cashel. But after all, who was she? Just a stranger who found herself in the wrong place at the wrong time. Secernere was always the wrong place. Storey had done his duty in taking her far into the woods and pointing her in a direction away from Secernere. She chose to return. She even admitted that she came back to save the little girl. And in the end, that is what she'd done. Anyway, she seemed like a resourceful girl.

The strangest thought that entered his head was worry about what would happen to Cashel. Storey had spent the past decade talking himself out of killing Cashel. Now, it could happen any one of a multitude of ways. Did Aurora have it in her to murder, if it came to that? In the face of Cashel's worst, could she remember to keep him alive?

And at any time the Fairgosian search party—or even the army itself—would arrive at Secernere. Cashel had not fled as he had been warned to do. Unlike with Aurora, there was no question of whether a Fairgosian soldier had the fortitude to kill him. Storey wondered whether the Fairgosian army even knew they were tracking toward Secernere and the grounds of Lord Gomery. It would be a sweet surprise for them when they found out.

They reached the giant oak where Storey had tethered the horses. He let Dymphna slide down to the ground. She smoothed her hands down over her dingy frock, wiping away the wrinkles, then bravely brushed at the tears on her cheeks.

There they were: two people, and two horses. Storey lifted Dymphna onto what would have been Aurora's horse, shortened the stirrups to Dymphna's tiny feet, and threaded the reins into her fingers. He untethered both horses, then hoisted himself onto his, swinging the animal round to face the direction of the mill. He stared for more time than he had.

Dismounting his horse, he grabbed Dymphna and placed her atop his. He pushed her forward in the saddle, then returned to the other horse and let the stirrups back out again. He leapt into the saddle behind Dymphna, kicked his heel, and together they began to gallop towards the front gate.

To leave the other horse wasn't to save Aurora. But to have taken it with him would have been to guarantee her murder.

Cashel stood, a slow smile spreading across his face. He pawed ineffectively at the dust and hay that clung to his long black coat, then reached up and extracted a length of straw from his yellow-white hair. His grin widened to bare his teeth, and Aurora glimpsed a canine mouth, incised fangs glinting in the sunlight. She tried to harden her face as she glared back at him. She knew the longer she could keep him there, the farther away Dymphna could run. What would his game be?

"Lady Cavalcata," he said, bowing. "Now that we are free of distractions, at last we can be formally acquainted. I am Cashel, Lord of Gomery. You may call me Lord Gomery. Or you may call me sir. You may even call for help, but it won't do you any good." He laughed at his joke. "Your man Storey has shown his true colors: he is a traitor and a coward."

"I think you're quite more agitated over Storey's 'true colors' than I am," she said. "Besides, what makes you think I need help?"

He laughed again. "I have your friend."

Aurora's heart sank. *Kynton.*

"No," she breathed.

"He's in my cellar. Well, some of him anyway." He paused, but Aurora refused to react. "Scream now?"

"Why aren't you going after Storey?" she asked.

"Women don't come to Secernere very often. And never has one so alluring as yourself graced us with her presence."

"He shall travel very far while you stand here talking. Do you not care?"

"You are very beautiful indeed. I like your dark skin. We shall have a hell of a time entertaining one another."

"Do you understand what it means that you have a sister?"

"Of course I understand, you bitch!" His smile snapped away. "Do *you* understand?"

"Of course."

"Yes, I'm sure you received a worldly, nuanced education about Mitoch from your ever-so progressive country. Even as nobility, you're still only a woman. I'm sure people in your country only ever refer to you as Lord Cavalcata's *daughter*—never as your own person. Isn't that right? I wonder if that has changed now that he's dead."

She flinched at this.

"We're both nobility," he went on, "and we're both nothing—except that I've found a way to be *something*." He lifted his arms. "Do you see what I've built for myself? This, with no help from anyone?"

Aurora allowed her eyes to leave Cashel's face and glance around the mill. The millstones were covered in dust, torpid boulders unmoved for ages. Grain, black with mold, collected in the corners where walls joined. No one worked here anymore; this was nothing more than pitiful refuge for Dymphna. The manor house was just as morose, cobwebs filling the vaulted ceiling. In the orchard, the fruit putrefied upon the mangled roots of the trees. Aurora knew intimately how bare the pantry was.

But the bleakest mark of the failed estate was the same as that of Cathendria: all the people were gone. With them went their energy—their souls and the life they breathed into stone. Without the people, an estate was just a dead thing ready to rot back into the ground.

"You're right," Aurora said steadily. "It's so much more than I have of my own."

His fiery eyes shot back to her. "Shut up. . . . Come down here."

"No."

He didn't break his gaze as his fist crashed into a nearby beam. When he withdrew it, dark blood was running down his knuckles. A black drop fell to the floor, landed in a bit of sawdust, and turned to a maroon paste. "I said come down here."

"You can order Storey around because he is your boy. But you are nothing to me, and I am nothing to you."

Her eyes flicked toward his wound. He grinned, then waved the back of his bloodied hand at her. "How about you bleed next, Fairgosian? We'll see if it's the same color."

She could not restrain her disgusted wince.

"There's nowhere for you to go, my lady."

"I am content to stay here for as long as necessary." Even if Cashel stupidly climbed the ladder, she could just kick him back down, easy enough. "I've lived in must less luxurious circumstances."

"The Fairgosian War Master's daughter? I have a hard time believing that."

She sat down and scooted forward, letting her legs dangle

over the edge of the loft floor. "As a matter of fact, the conditions at Secernere are quite spartan over all. Even for a Mitochian man, I expected quite more."

He squinted up at her.

"I have been here for almost a month now, and I swear it gets worse by the day. On my very first day here, Abern fed me pomegranate arils on a silver spoon. Now I am lucky to gnaw a cheese rind. It's really not much to brag about, as you are so wont to do."

His face betrayed growing confusion, then anger.

"You sound insane." He forced a laugh. "Do you know that about yourself? Is 'gnawing a cheese rind' some Fairgosian aphorism?"

"I have been living in a room at Secenere for, oh, I think it has been nearly thirty days—" She touched each of her fingertips, counting.

"What?—"

"—You can see the marks I made in the molding. You probably know the room, just a bitty one in the back of the manor house—"

"—No—"

"—Storey has been clothing me, feeding me, and keeping me company all along. All right under your nose." She let her feet kick back and forth like a little girl on a swing.

At this, he jumped at her. But his swiping claw of a hand was comically shy, and she laughed.

Suddenly, he was on the ladder. Aurora scrambled to her feet and stood at the ladder's summit. His massive hands grabbed rung after rung, his towheaded crown bobbing up towards her, and it no longer seemed an easy thing to kick him off. The closer he got to her, the bigger he seemed. The bigger he was. He was a soldier made strong and enormous by punishing drills and generous rations.

Adrenalin surged through Aurora's shaking body and every inch of her skin felt like exposed nerve. She really was trapped.

She was skinny and weak not at all equipped to fight him off. Her plump red courage was withering. She took a step backward.

One bloodied hand rose up and grasped the top rung of the ladder.

Aurora sprung forward and stamped her foot onto his fingers as hard as she could. She heard the cracks. Through the thin sole of the ill-fitting boot, she could feel almost every bone in his hand. The proximity to his open mortal flesh sickened her.

He shouted and yanked at his hand, but she had it firmly beneath her foot. They were at another, more gruesome impasse.

Then, anchoring himself under by the trapped hand, Cashel roared in pain as he snatched at her ankle with his free hand. She was too quick. She lifted her foot from his hand. Caught in the momentum of his frantic grab, Cashel's body tipped backward and he flailed wildly to catch the ladder. He missed. He fell toward the mill floor, seeming to drift like a leaf from a tree. When his body finally hit, a hard slapping sound vibrated the mill.

Aurora's breath caught in her throat. She stared for ages waiting for his body to move. The dogs surrounded his body, burying their noses between his legs and in his armpits.

Then Cashel expelled a long, low moan. His head swiveled from left to right, then back. His eyes were still shut, his mouth hung open. Blood trickled from the corner of his lips. One dog yelped and jumped back as if kicked. It again leaned forward and nuzzled at Cashel, then uttered a low whine. Cashel moaned again.

The ladder remained the single exit. Down the ladder, over Cashel's prone body, and through the gaping door. But still she felt paralyzed. The soles of her boots stuck to the floor with dried blood, but fear rooted her to the spot.

She thought of Dymphna.

The fear flew away. She was half-climbing, half-slipping

down the ladder. Her breath was coming fast and shallow. Each time she inhaled, she wasn't sure she would get enough air into her lungs. Her head spun. A dull roar flooded her ears, and she could hear nothing.

The dogs stared at her. Their eyes all looked like Cashel's eyes. But the dogs were nothing. They were just animals. Instinct outweighed thought and it was their weakness. A few more rungs and she would be among the dogs, among animals. On the same plane as Cashel, close enough to touch him. Close enough to hear the breath steam out over his teeth.

She was on the floor. She had to step over the devil to make her escape. Blood spread out around Cashel's head like a sick halo, and his breath sputtered like a something with a hole in it.

One of the dogs barked. Then another. Then all of them were barking, as if to wake their master. One of them snapped its jaws and caught Aurora's calf, one sharp tooth punching through her trousers into her flesh. She yelped. Cashel's eyes popped open, and they were on fire.

"You bitch," he seethed.

Suddenly Aurora's feet were out from under her. Cashel held her ankles. He was sideways, leaning on his shoulder and she was falling. Then she was on the ground and he was standing. His forearm pressed down on her neck. He panted through red teeth and specks of blood and tissue spattered onto her cheek. She gasped, breathing in whatever he was breathing out.

"I'm going to make you watch while I kill Storey, and I'm going to make him watch while I kill you. And I will just let you imagine what I'm going to do to that horrible little brat you call my sister."

His hand was in the air. His hand was a fist. It smashed down and she saw black.

"Why have we stopped here?" Dymphna asked.

Storey dismounted, then helped Dymphna to the ground. She looked up at the canopy of trees and slowly spun around. He remembered how Aurora had spun in this spot, disoriented, frantic. Dymphna was curious, serene.

"I have been here before," she said.

"You've never been here. You've never been anywhere."

"Yes, I have," replied Dymphna. "I have been here, to this very spot. I remember that tree, because the limb is low enough for me to reach. There's a cave back that way."

Storey was already tethering the horse to a low branch that, broken at its joint, bent down to the ground. Dymphna pointed to their shared horse, which snorted and shook its head as Storey tugged on it.

"I rode *that* horse, while I was holding onto the other horse. I brought it here for her. I tied it to that limb, and then I rode the other horse back home."

"You brought a horse to Inna? I mean, Aurora?"

Dymphna nodded.

Storey dropped the reins and stared at her. Aurora had been telling the truth all along. "What? Why? What? You can't even barely ride a horse, let alone— How did you even— . . . Why?"

"Why did *you* bring her out here *first*?"

"Haven't I taught you not to answer a question with a question?"

"Have you taught it to me if I haven't learned it?"

Storey grimaced. "I brought her out here to save her. Just like I brought you out here to save you."

Dympha watched him, unconvinced. "It does not matter who is in the woods and who is at Secernere. The danger is not here and the danger is not there. The danger is in being alone. The only way for we three to be saved is for all of us to be together."

There was as much logic as love in her assertion. In these flashes of stark wisdom, Storey felt the most pride and the most terror at what he had done. He felt helpless to ever teach her anything again.

"And that is why we stopped. I am going back for her. I will have to leave you here, but it won't be for long."

Dymphna nodded, then sat down on the tuffet of moss that had served as Aurora's pillow. She had heard what she wanted to hear.

"Remember the cave back there? If you hear anything louder than a sparrow, you run. You run and you hide in that cave until I return for you."

As he and his horse flew through the woods once more, Storey began to think that perhaps he had succeeded with the girl after all. Instead of asking questions, little Dymphna now made wise declarations. The answers were coming from inside of her, instead of from Storey. The pupil had eclipsed the teacher.

∂34∂

When she regained consciousness, the first thing Aurora noticed was the smell. The room's aroma was a complex recipe of odors that at once intrigued and repulsed her. The air was damp and thick, moist. Humid. She smelled mildew, cavelike wetness hanging in the air. There was an astringent, pointy scent, like fruit about to turn. Maybe wine. A lower, baser odor aroused something primal and protective from a deeper place in her mind. It was layered in two: the lighter top layer was like iron or rust, mixed with the sea—blood; the bottom layer was thick like flesh, and it was rotting. There was deadness here. Not death, yet. Not the end of the life of a living thing. But deadness, that which takes a thing over one piece at a time; a cumulative process that culminates in death, all the while filling a room with odors signifying something no person is meant to know.

Aurora let her eyelids part but found it was as dark as when she had them closed. What shadowy objects she could see by the flicker of a wall torch spun in her vision, compounding her rising nausea.

She was tied up. Backed up against some sort of wooden pole or beam, she was bound by rope around the shoulders and hips, and her hands were tied together behind her. Her body throbbed and pulsated with pain; she'd been beaten, raped. Yet she had no inclination to scream or even to be scared. She still grasped that red fruit of courage—or was it irrational bravery? With it came the feeling of inevitability she'd experienced in the barn, and it was growing in intensity. Upon waking here, she felt very strongly—almost *knew*—that Dymphna and Storey were somewhere safe and that Kynton was alive and nearby. The fact that she was in a cellar, bound and severely injured, *but not dead* signified to her that Cashel, too, was present somewhere near. And that meant he would be discovered in the scene of his crime that was all of Secernere.

With time, her dilating pupils accepted more light. Form, shape, and depth crystalized before her. She determined with more certainty that she was in a wine cellar. And she was not alone. When she heard a low masculine groan seep out near her, she realized the source of the smell of impending death. There was a man here with her, somewhere just out of her periphery. The groan was pain. It was abandoned fear given way to exhaustion. It made no acknowledgment of Aurora's presence. The man, she guessed, was also tied up, also beaten. The hollowness and defeated tone had its own timbre of inevitability, but it was not linked to courage or the premonition of justice. This man foresaw his death. She did not call to him. If any consciousness remained in him, she could not bear to discover that it was Storey or Kynton.

Then she remembered what Storey had so frantically relayed to her just that day: Cashel had captured a Fairgosian scout. This man could be no other. The revelation added to Aurora's certainty that she could perceive both the present and the future just by sheer will of mind. She felt impenetrable. She willed Cashel to return to the cellar-prison so she could murder him with her thoughts.

Sure the man was no one she knew, she felt more prompted to speak to him. Perhaps not all humanity was gone. A protective emotion rose up in her like a fountain and she struggled against her bindings. She wanted to go to him. The rope scratched into the exposed skin of her shoulders and she gritted her teeth against the pain.

"Hello?" she called quietly. No sound came in return. She tried again. "Hello?"

Nothing.

"My name is Aurora." If this had to be a one-way conversation, so be it.

Suddenly a loud, tremulous, bubbling utterance came from the man. It was indiscernible as words, but the emotion said everything.

"You know who I am. . . ." Aurora whispered.

Aurora hadn't believed it when Storey said they had sent a scout on her trail. She refused to believe she was important enough to warrant the whole of another person's time spent on finding her—especially when she could have been anywhere. Further, she denied that there were time, energy, or resources for anyone—even Kynton—to think about one lost woman when thousands of soldiers succumbed to the fight every single day. But that universal, languageless tone of emotion confirmed everything her humility would have argued. He knew who she was, and moreover, he had been sent for her.

"Can you speak?" she asked. "It would mean more to me than anything if you could tell me your name."

She waited. In the silence she felt the thick of his effort. Finally: "Cort . . ."

"Cort."

He was struggling but continued. "Son of the Ellis family, in the capital."

"The capital of . . ."

"Fairgos.

Unexpectedly, Aurora began to weep. Hearing the name of

her country broke her heart in two halves: one side that would live there forever, and one side that could never return. She made no effort to rein in the desperate sounds and cried openly for what felt like a very long time. It abated finally, tapering off into infantile gasps and hiccups.

"M'lady." His voice seemed stronger now. "I would kneel before you if I were not so bound. I knew your—"

"No. Please, no."

He had the heavy accent of someone who had lived in March his whole life—caricature of the tinge of accent that sometimes clung to her father's speech after he had stayed at court for months at a time. It was bittersweet melancholy to hear her father's ghost in just those few words across the low light of the cellar. But if she could have nothing else right then, she only wanted not to remember who she was. She did not want to be reminded of her status, of her father, of her empty broken home. She didn't want to hear her title, or worse, the anonymous *m'lady*.

Cort pressed on. "M'lady, are you hurt? Who brought you here, was it the tall blond man? I do not know what to do. I was sent here—"

"Shush, please!" She said it more harshly than she had meant to. But he quieted.

"M'lady . . ."

"Cort, I promise I will call you Cort, if you promise to call me Aurora."

"Yes, m'lady . . . Aurora." Her name sounded on his lips like a foreign word, one which he struggled to pronounce correctly, with just the right accent and intonation so that he would not confuse a greeting with an oath. It did not sound beautiful. It sounded strained and uncomfortable. They were both tied in ropes in a dark cellar, awaiting death, but their classes put a wall between them such that they could not even be human together in this time that was more human than any.

"Cort . . ." She squeezed her eyes shut, took a deep breath, then opened them again. "I want you to know that I am fine. I am safe."

Cort needed to make no sound to tell her how ridiculous her words were. Neither was fine. Neither was safe. Their captor, that devil, could arrive at any moment. Or not arrive. Neither option fared them with a better fate.

Aurora sighed in exasperation at her impotence. In her mind, she had seen the future for herself, for Dymphna and Storey. She had not anticipated another character. She did not foresee that her heart would open up and surge toward him, even though they were strangers, even though he was dying. She could not have guessed the overwhelming ache to know that a man was almost dead and the blame rested entirely on her titled, noble shoulders.

"Listen," she said, willing the frustration away from her tone of voice. "I want you not to worry any more about me or whatever mission sent you here. This will in all likelihood not make sense to you, but there is something larger at work here than you or I. I take great regret in the fact that you were sent here because of my foolish actions. When I jumped into that river, I did not realize how far the ripples would travel. I can hardly fathom that you are here with me, my fellow countryman. My brave soldier. I know you not, but you will forever have a place in my heart for what you have done. I promise you I will make it my life's work to reward you when we both escape this place. And I do believe we will both make it out of here, alive."

This last was a lie. She did not believe at all that this man would ever go anywhere again. And with Storey gone and Abern dead, this man would not even have a dignified burial in a proper cemetery. He would be tossed into the river like sewage.

"I hope I do not sound unkind or ungrateful. I just . . ." she trailed off.

She realized that she was perpetuating this wall between

them. Her words, her little speech, was full of the same kind of clichéd rhetoric her father used when he talked to his soldiers. He employed complicated, flowery vocabulary to distance himself, to firmly establish his leadership and their follower-ship. Words could create a podium behind which to stand, a platform from which to look down at an audience, even when everyone was—and should have been—face to face on equal ground.

"I'm sorry," she said finally. "The truth, Cort, the truth. The truth is that I have been trapped at Secernere for nigh unto a month following the worst tragedy of my life. I had a chance to escape, but I ruined it. I betrayed myself, and also you, and whoever sent you. We should not be here now. It is my fault, and I simply cannot bear to spend any more time thinking about every mistake I've made that has led to this situation. I cannot bear even to think about my own name. I just want to forget everything. Please . . . I just . . ."

In her ears, the word *I* rang out so loud. Could she never stop being a selfish spoiled brat? In every aspect of her life, her consciousness turned inward. She looked out of her head through her two eyes, and no matter where she was, she was the dead center of everything. Could she just once stop talking about herself and what she wanted?

"Does it hurt you to speak?" she finally asked.

"Not any more than it hurts when I do not speak." Every word screamed that he was lying. But it was himself to whom he was lying, not to Aurora.

"Cort . . ." It felt good, in a way, to say his name, as if speaking it brought them closer by millimeters. In life, she would never have been able to call him Cort. *Cort* put cracks in the wall. ". . . will you tell me about your life?"

He coughed, and his lungs burbled. "What do you wish to know, m'lady? . . . Aurora."

"From where do you hail? How did you find your way into the army? Has it made you happy?"

"I was born and raised in the capital. My father is a black-smith there. I am the only son in my family, and I have eight sisters."

"That is wonderful . . ."

"It was difficult. So many mouths to feed, and we were poor for a very long time. But yes, it is wonderful. Have you brothers and sisters?"

"I haven't." She was crying as she listened.

"God smiled upon us. When the war began, my father was contracted by the army to shoe all their horses. It was under those circumstances that I met Lord Sebastia. He was then only a Major. We became friends. Kynton."

"Kynton . . ."

"He never once asked me to join the military. Because I helped my father in support of the army, I was exempt from conscription. I joined out of loyalty to Kynton. If you'll forgive me, m'lady, it was never about Fairgos. I love my country. But men do not fight for countries. Men fight for other people."

"Are not countries made of people?" Aurora asked.

"A country is only an idea. Many people may think they share the same idea and call it a country. They cling to the idea because it is a fabric, a casing that holds things, people together. But the truth is, no two people have the same idea. Fairgos is not the same to you as it is to me. Country is a gray, blurry thing. For some, it is a dream, an achievement to be reached. For others, it is a barrier to their dreams. For most, it is simply taken for granted. No man fights for country. He fights for his mother. He fights for his wife. He fights for his parcel of land that grows corn in the summer. He fights so that he can one day stop fighting and return to a home where he can try to achieve a little happiness.

"Countries do not fight each other. Men fight each other. And they only fight so that they can stop fighting and go home. It is the most horrific irony in the world."

"And yet here you are." Aurora's misery grew into a dull

ache. The bruises and wounds on her face and body flamed up with renewed pain. She found that she very much wanted to die.

"Aurora, I want you to know something." Cort's voice was abruptly weaker. It was as if he had only a bagful of words and he had spent so many of them on that speech he needed to make. Now he was reaching down into the very bottom. "I volunteered to come here, to find you. No man sent me on this mission but myself. I came to find you because Kynton loves you very much. Kynton is my brother, and I love him very much. Please feel no guilt. It was my duty and to my very honor that I came here. If I die here, it will not have been in vain."

Aurora wanted nothing more than to look this man in the eyes. But there were only words and the short and long spaces between the words. So she only said, "Thank you" and then they were silent.

Nearly unbearable hunger pangs came, but with patience they went away. What didn't go away was the thirst. Aurora's mouth squeezed in on itself, sticking with dehydration. Her tongue felt woolen. She wondered for the first time how long Cort had been here before she arrived. If she felt this broken, how could he even begin to endure?

Time passed much in the way it had when she had been locked away. With no sunlight, no visitors, no food, there was no way to mark time. Time felt like an unnatural construct. Like war. As Storey would say, like religion. As Cort would say, like country. Was nothing immutable? Maybe love.

"Cort?" At first it came out as only a hoarse croak. She coughed and tried to clear her throat. "Cort? Cort, how are you?"

He moaned in response, but it was faint.

"Cort, we are going to be fine. I know it. Kynton and the army are on their way to us. You must know they are tracking you. I know Kynton must feel the same love for you as you for him. He is coming to find you."

He moaned again, but even now it was just a shadow of the sound he'd made before.

"I heard it earlier: Lord Gomery himself was preparing to flee. He knew they were on their way. If he is full of fear, we should be full of hope. They will be here soon, and we will be freed. We will feast and drink wine and celebrate. Cort, please endure."

But the more Aurora said without response, the more she felt as if she were talking to her own conscience. Speaking aloud the lies she was telling herself sent shivering cracks up through the foundation of denial she had built.

Still he made no sound. He was close to death.

"Cort, our country has been built upon the backs of men like you. You are an eternal flame of pride for Fairgos. It is because of you that we will win this war and build a stronger future for our children. You have helped ensure that we have a home to which to return when this is all over. I would never have you kneel before me. Sir, if my hands were not bound behind my back, I would salute you.

"I hope you will pray with me."

She let her head drop into a bow.

"Dear God, we are but humble human beings. We do not dare to attempt an understanding of your ways, even during our most trying of times. But in this test we face, we feel darkness and we feel fear. We feel confusion that this can be a part of your plan. We know you have the greatest of plans for us, your children, even as we know that we cannot know them. We do not ask that you explain your mysterious ways to us. We only ask that you give us the strength to face our plight with the knowledge that we are not alone. Give us the strength to stand up to our trials, to see light where there is darkness, and to see hope where there is fear. Remind us that when our time on this earth is done that we will come home to you and live forever in your kingdom of love. In your name we pray, Amen."

A thin gray whisper floated through the air and passed in front of Aurora's face, and she felt it like a cold draft: "Amen."

❧35❧

She could only tell that hours had passed because the torch on the far wall had begun to burn low, the flame flickering tenuously. She fixated on it so her mind would not be consumed by the terrifying blackness that would surround her when it finally went out.

Back at Cathendria, she thought she knew loneliness. Long nights in the cell at Secernere have proved her wrong, proved she knew nothing at all. She considered what Storey had said to her about his loneliness. Was she truly alone if she had God? Did she have God? The prayer she had made with the soldier was for his benefit only; she hadn't believed she was actually talking to God. She wasn't sure she could recall the last time she had prayed and it felt truly like she was talking to anyone other than herself.

"Dear God," Aurora whispered. She waited. The man made no reply or sound. God made no reply or sound. "Here I am. What would you have me do? Is this really what you have planned for me, this succession of comically gross misfortunes? I pray of you, help me understand your ways. Give me the strength and the courage to overcome my trials."

She laughed miserably.

"For thine is the kingdom and the power and the glory. But what is *mine*? The imprisonment and the impotence and the humiliation. If the devil returns to this cellar and rapes me again, God, will you give me the strength to overcome that trial? Will you send down an angel to wipe away my tears and sew back together what has been torn apart?"

She began to weep. As her shoulders heaved upwards, the ropes burned into her skin, cutting her.

"I am so afraid, God. I have never been more frightened in my life. I hate you for doing this to me. I hate you for letting Storey plant doubt in my mind. I hate you for not answering me. Ever. I hate knowing that I don't have a choice about whether you exist, because even if you don't, you still do. Like Storey said, you will never not be. You won't be different. Only I will.

"If I die tonight, will I be delivered into your arms? Has Heaven set a place for me? When Storey and Dymphna die, will they go to hell because they don't believe in you? How can it be Heaven if Storey and Dymphna aren't there too?

"I know that I cannot know your ways. I know I am so tiny and human, and you are Great and All Knowing, and there is no way for me to comprehend your plan for every living thing, for all living things, for all the universe. But how can I continue my faith in such times? You have abandoned me."

Her sobs became wails and echoed off the wet stone walls. They drowned out the dripping that was water, or wine, or blood. The man she could not see made no sound. He couldn't. He was dead. The flame on the torch appeared to be sucked into a vacuum, not like it was going out but that it was going somewhere else. It disappeared into itself, became a glowing ember, then finally turned black. The open cellar became a closed casket. Aurora screamed and raged against her bonds.

✼

Periods of lucidity became moments, then slivers of moments. In the time between, Aurora let herself fall back onto an increasingly comfortable cushion of imaginings and fantasies. She looked out a window and saw the sea. A laundry line sliced across the bluest of skies, and the white linens blew like sails. They were clean and pure like the clouds. Dymphna ran across the yard, chasing a yellow butterfly. She had grown tan after days playing in the sun. She had grown thicker, muscular, like Aurora had been at her age.

Aurora called to her. "Dymphna! Come in! Come in here now! Storey is here to visit us. Come see Storey.

"She just hates to come inside anymore. Please, won't you sit down? I am so pleased you are here. We have both missed you so much."

"Aurora?"

"Oh, don't wait for me. Please, sit while I finish preparing our meal. Dymphna! Come now! There will be another sun tomorrow!"

"Aurora!"

He was shaking her. Why would he not just sit down?

"Aurora! Where are you?" Storey cupped her face in his hands and steered her to look at him.

"Dymphna is coming. You will see her soon."

"Dymphna is in the woods waiting for us. I have come back for you."

"Storey?" The sunshine faded to a deep black-orange. The clouds turned steel gray then grew together, and the sky covered over with stones. The green sea shrunk into two lakes. Then two ponds, then two pools, then two puddles. They contracted even further into two eyes. Her eyes focused and she saw that she was staring into the sea green eyes of Storey.

"We have to hurry! Cashel is right behind me."

"Storey!" Her eyes felt swollen with tears she couldn't cry

because she was too dried out.

He moved behind her and began to work the knots that bound her hands. When they were freed she jerked them forward and rubbed her aching wrists. The caked blood looked black in the low light of Storey's torch.

"Where was I? Where am I?"

"It's all right. We are still in the wine cellar. Just hold on, I almost have these knots." She felt the bonds around her shoulders slacken, then fall to the floor. Storey was fumbling around her feet.

"Storey...there is a man..." Remembering she could move now, she turned to see her companion.

"He's dead," Storey said plainly. "Let's go."

Aurora stepped out of the ropes now pooled around her feet and turned fully toward Cort, son of the Ellis family. His face had been beaten so severely that it was barely recognizable as a face. She could not tell if he was handsome or hideous, but he looked beautiful and noble. A rough shadow of beard covered his chin and cheeks. One eye was swollen shut, and the other was closed as if he was only sleeping. His head hung.

"Aurora!"

She took a step toward the rope-bound body. "Storey, we have to—"

"No!" He grabbed her by the forearm and tugged. "There's no time!"

Not feeling her body but merely inhabiting in, she let herself be turned away. Storey took her hand and pulled her up the first few stone stairs toward the dark door, where light peeked in underneath.

Then the light broke in two and the door slammed open with a deafening snap. Standing there, a hulking shadow with light streaming in around his form, his enormous hand pressed flat against the open door, was the monstrous Cashel.

Aurora began to scream. And she continued to scream. She screamed to deafen herself and screamed as if it would blind her to every nightmare that was opening itself up before her. Storey grabbed her and wrapped himself around her, with one hand smothering her mouth. She continued to scream, though the sound was muffled, and then it subsided. Her breath heaved in and out, sputtering wetly past Storey's tight hand. Her eyes stared wildly. She struggled against Storey's hold, wanting to escape, to run, anywhere—even though there was nowhere to go. Cashel blocked the only exit.

In three quick steps, Cashel was running down the stairs. Storey spun so that Aurora was behind him, then turned to face Cashel. Without breaking stride, Cashel raised a booted foot and kicked his heel directly into Storey's sternum. Storey expelled a pained breath as his body shot backwards onto the stone staircase. He continued to flop like a ragdoll down the floor, where his body crumpled into a fetal position and ceased to move.

In another fluid movement, Cashel leapt onto Aurora and sent them both crashing down. They tumbled as a pair down every cold hard step until they landed on the floor beside Storey. Cashel fell on top of Aurora with his crushing weight, and she thought she might never take another breath. Storey's face was only inches from hers. His eyes were squeezed tight and he grimaced against his pain. But he was alive. She turned back to see Cashel, also just a breath away from her face. His eyes were on fire with rage.

Cashel lifted himself from her chest, and Aurora heaved in a hungry breath. He sat on her pelvis and leaned forward. Aurora gasped out a weak "No," and his hands were around her throat. He squeezed.

"Storey!" Cashel shouted. Tears were streaming down his face. "Storey, open your eyes! Watch her die like you watched your mother die! Do nothing and watch the bitch die!"

She thrashed, kicking her legs and flailing her arms. The light was being sucked out of her, dampened like the torch. Darkness seeped in around the corners of her vision. She couldn't let it end this way. This wasn't her future. With a burst of strength she lifted her pelvis enough to turn sideways. As she rolled, she felt a pain shoot through her hip. There was something hard between her body and the stone floor.

Then she remembered: the knife.

It is sharp. Very sharp.

She wrenched herself in the other direction, plunged her hand into her pocket, and withdrew the knife just as she was slipping out of consciousness. Her hand flew upward and the blade slid easily into Cashel's side, beneath his ribcage. He fell sideways, his hands leaving her throat. She rolled onto her side, gasping and coughing. As Cashel dove at her again, he caught him with the knife again, this time in the gut. She withdrew it then stabbed him in the chest.

He collapsed backward. His body was strewn across the bottom few stairs, arms spread wide, his chest exposed. Still choking breaths into her stinging lungs as best she could, she crawled on her knees up between his legs. Kneeling before him, she plunged the knife over and over again into his chest. She began to yell as she stabbed. She brought it down again and again until she felt a hand on her shoulder, gently holding her back.

She fell backward against Storey's heated body, and he enfolded her in his arms.

"Shh," he whispered in her ear, slowly rocking her back and forth. "Shh. He's dead. Hold still. He's dead. It's over."

❧36❧

$\mathcal{E}$ach one leg of a giant, Aurora and Storey leaned into one another and walked themselves up the staircase. Aurora had let it be known that it was murderously cold to leave Cort's dead body down there with Cashel's, but hunger and thirst overcame.

The cellar opened into the kitchen. Storey eased Aurora into a chair, propping her arms and head against the tabletop. She was like a straw-filled dummy. Blood, bright red turning dark, was splattered all over her vest and shirt. Her hands and wrists were covered in blood too. Some of it was hers; most of it wasn't.

At the sink, Storey pumped the tap handle. The effort sent agonizing waves through his chest and biceps, but he breathed through it. He heard the glug and gurgle of water coming up the pipe, then it splashed cold into the cup. Lifting Aurora's chin with two fingers, he placed the cup to her scaly lips and let the water trickle into her mouth and down over her face. She drank gingerly at first, then took bigger and bigger gulps. When the cup emptied, Storey filled it again and brought it back to her. This time, she pushed herself upright and took the cup into her own hands and poured the water down into her throat. They repeated the ritual once more, then Aurora set the cup on the tabletop.

Wordlessly, she lifted her hands toward Storey, showing him the carnage there. Her eyes pleaded to him with a muddle of dread, disgust, and helplessness. He nodded. His hand gently under her elbow, he helped her to her feet and guided her over to the sink. She held her hands beneath the spigot as Storey began to pump. He grimaced and gritted his teeth against the pain. Icy water splashed out over Aurora's hands. She rubbed them together, hissing and gritting her own teeth. The pale red water ran down the drain, away from them. He pumped, and she washed. She washed until she could see the pink of her own flesh again and the water ran clear. She then cupped her hands beneath the flow, brought a handful of water up to her mouth, and drank again.

Storey continued to pump. Aurora lifted a hand and placed it on his arm. Her touch was ice cold; the skin was soggy and pruned. He stopped pumping.

"This water comes from the river," Aurora said.

Storey nodded.

"It tastes like home." She touched Storey's shoulder, then hobbled back to the chair on her own, gently lowering herself into it. "I suppose we cannot stay around here to take a bath and a long nap." She chuckled softly and stared down at the floor. One of her hands gripped the table as if for balance, and the other hung limply in her lap.

"No," Storey said quietly.

"Dymphna."

"Yes."

"Is she all right?" Aurora continued to stare at the floor.

"She can take care of herself."

Aurora nodded. "You?" She turned to Storey.

"Well enough."

"What happened?"

Storey gazed at her and watched her image become transparent until he could see the table and the wall through her body. She flickered like the flame on a candle, like a ghost.

"It will not improve your situation to know," he said.

She did not question him further.

Storey made a final round through the manor house, collecting what scraps of food he could find, and filling two discovered canteens with water. He packed the rations into his horse's saddlebags and lifted Aurora onto its back. Climbing up behind her, he reached around her body to take hold of the reins. She pressed her back into his chest, and he could feel the heat of her body through his clothing. She tilted her head back into the nook of his neck.

"Are you ready?" he whispered.

"We should have buried him."

"Who? Cashel?" He spat the name like a curse.

"The man in the cellar. He was the scout from Fairgos."

"I know."

"He was a good man," Aurora said.

"No man is truly good or truly bad."

"To me, he was a truly and completely good man. How he lived the rest of his life is no matter to me."

"That's an awfully selfish way to view the world."

"I am a selfish person," she said. "And I shall repent by acquiescing to leave without burying him, even though it is what I selfishly desire."

"Fair enough," Storey replied, and they began their plodding marathon back through the woods.

Aurora had not been outside for this long since she'd last traveled through these woods. The month had changed; it would be September now. The air seemed cooler and the sun seemed lower, but it could be just that she didn't remember the way it was before. It would be another month or two before

314

the leaves began to change color then drop to the ground. For now, they were still green and vibrant, upturned toward the feeding sun, oblivious to their brown and ragged futures.

Her head nestled in Storey's shoulder, she found herself drifting toward sleep again, and once again trying to avoid it. If Storey could not sleep, she would not either.

"This is now my third trip on this path," she mumbled, yawning. "Each has been so very different."

"Ah, let's see," said Storey. "For one, you were mostly unconscious, also struggling for the end of it. You had quite a dirty mouth on you that day."

She bumped her head against his collarbone. "Oh I certainly did not."

"I seem to remember that you called me a—"

"If I called you anything, it was because you deserved it."

"And then, the second trip . . . I know nothing about the second trip. Dymphna told me yesterday that she brought you a horse."

"So it was her then," Aurora said. "At that moment when I woke to find a saddled horse beside me, I was quite positive magic existed."

"Doesn't it?"

"No."

After a period of silence, Storey said, "Are you glad you returned to Secernere?"

"Glad . . . I don't think gladness enters into it. The note told me *you must return to Secernere.* And so I did. I do not always do what I am told, but I always do what I must." She sighed, then yawned again. "In any event, it is all for the best, as we are so close to being reunited with our Dymphna. And Cashel is gone."

"We will have to find a way to explain that. Otherwise, Dymphna may face not the role of a leader, but imprisonment for fratricide—Wait."

"What?"

"Did you hear something?"

"We are in the woods. I have heard lots of things."

Storey tugged on the reins and halted the horse. It snorted and stamped on the ground before growing still.

Aurora fidgeted in the saddle. "What—"

Storey raised his hand to quiet her.

The entire forest was still. No trees rustled, no wings flapped, no predator or prey snapped a twig under scampering claws. The horse breathed and Storey breathed and Aurora held her breath.

Then all of a sudden, a thunder of hoof beats—a herd of horses, it sounded like—filled the silence. Dead leaves on the ground rustled under heavy boots. Storey's horse reared up halfway, and Storey caught Aurora around the waist to keep her from falling to the ground.

Before them were four mounted soldiers, three of whom had drawn swords. Five more soldiers stepped out from behind trees in all directions surrounding the couple, and they were aiming crossbows squarely at Storey's head. Right off, Aurora recognized the Fairgosian military uniforms. The solider who had not drawn his sword pulled his horse to the front of the group. It was Kynton.

Storey raised his hands outward. When Aurora did not do the same, he grabbed her elbow and lifted it upward.

"Do not touch her!" commanded Kynton.

Aurora felt Storey's racing heart pound through his shirt.

"It's all right," she whispered to Storey. "It's all right!" she called to Kynton. "I am all right!"

Kynton moved his horse forward again. Threatened, Storey's horse balked. Aurora grabbed the saddle horn to keep balance, and Storey grabbed Aurora's shoulders.

"I said, do not touch her!" Kynton yelled, then drew his sword.

Storey's hands flew upward again. Aurora wavered on the horse.

316

"Stop it!" Aurora screamed. "He is my friend! He is no threat!"

Kynton sheathed his sword, dismounted his horse, and signaled his men to stay still. The crossbows and swords remained pointed at Storey. Kynton approached their horse. His face was hard and angry, and his gaze did not waver from Storey's face, even as he grabbed Aurora by the waist and pulled her to the ground.

As her feet hit the ground, Aurora felt dizzy and lightheaded. Everything was backwards.

"Kynton," she said softly. Perhaps she could bring down the volume of the whole situation if she only whispered. She placed her hand on the horse's neck to steady herself.

Kynton snatched her by the shoulders and swung her out of reach of the horse, as if he were removing her from some immediate danger. This motion was too much, and she collapsed to the ground.

"What have you done to her!" he yelled. "You'll hang!"

He knelt and helped Aurora to her feet.

"Please," she said. "Stop. He is not our enemy."

"Look at your face," Kynton said, finally lowering his own voice. "And your clothes. Why are you dressed like this? Where did all this blood come from?"

He held her at arm's length, and she listed in his grip. Staring into his swarthy complexion, she remembered his face but did not recognize it. He ran a finger over her jawline. She was sore there, swollen, and she reflexively turned away from his touch. Kynton turned and yelled to one of the crossbow men.

"Take him into custody!" He turned back to Aurora. "We have an encampment near here. I have fifty men with me. We will all return there and sort this matter out."

Aurora watched helplessly as the five foot soldiers swarmed Storey and wrenched him from the horse. They were like a pack of wolves taking down a deer. Storey did not resist, and their aggression did not match his passivity.

"Dymphna," Aurora said.

"What did you say?"

"There is a little girl. . . ."

Kynton nodded. "Yes, we found her."

"Is she safe? Is she well?"

"As well as a white Mitochian urchin can be," Kynton said. "She is at the camp under watch of guard."

"Guard? She's just a little girl!"

"Oh, my dear Lady Cavalcata." He again made to touch her cheek, and she turned away. "In Mitoch, little girls are soldiers."

Her stomach turned over.

Kynton put his arms around her and pulled her into a tight embrace. She felt like every bone in her body would crack under the pressure.

"I missed you, my lady. I have thought about almost nothing but you in every day you've been gone. I praise God that I have found you."

Peering over Kynton's epauletted shoulder, Aurora looked for Storey. She saw him within the cluster of soldiers, bound as she and Cort had been, his head hanging. She could not see his face. She only wanted to see his face.

❧37❧

As Aurora peered into the encampment in the waning light of early dusk, she saw a decimated forest landscape. Brush and branches had been hacked down to make room for the tents of fifty men. Pup tents for the soldiers; larger pavilions for the officers. The largest of all, she imagined, was for Kynton. A wide swath had been totally cleared of all vegetation. At its center was a bonfire pit and a small fire onto which soldiers were just beginning to throw sticks and logs. Makeshift seats surrounded the fire—cylindrical sections of freshly cut trees that had not yet dried enough to be firewood.

Aurora rode in front of Kynton on his enormous steed, even as Storey's horse walked behind them empty of a rider. Despite wearing trousers, she was obliged to sit sidesaddle. Storey walked along the ground as well, tied like a dog on a leash to one of the mounted soldiers' horses.

A soldier near the fire caught sight of them and called to his companions. One by one, the small army emerged toward them, cheering and clapping. The conquering hero, Kynton beamed at them. He raised a triumphant fist.

Kynton dismounted and helped Aurora down, and a soldier was already leading his horse away. Other soldiers were patting his shoulder and heartily pumping his hand in congratulations. Aurora was bumped and jostled all around by the flocking crowd. She felt her breath and pulse quicken. She searched for an escape route, but found no opening through the bodies. She began to shake her head back and forth. *No, no, no.* Her breath came faster. Her heart squeezed. In the midst of it all, she felt her hand grabbed. Kynton squeezed it affectionately and leaned his face toward her ear. "Come to my tent. We have much to talk about. I will have dinner brought to us."

"I need to see Dymphna first, the little girl." Aurora pleaded with her eyes.

"Whatever for? Who is she?"

"I just need to see her. Please."

"Whatever you desire, my lady."

She was led to one of the smaller tents close to the center of the encampment near the bonfire, but not so close to the officers' tents. Outside, two soldiers kept guard.

"Go get food," Kynton said to them. He pulled the flap aside and held it for Aurora to enter.

The scene inside made Aurora's heart well with joy. Dymphna was sitting on a stuffed rucksack across from a teenaged soldier, who sat cross-legged on the canvas floor of the tent. Between them was a chessboard balanced precariously on a split log. Tiny pewter chessmen fought each other on the board—but most of them were crowded together in a pile beside Dymphna. The two were totally entranced in their game. Aurora wanted only to watch them, for just a moment. But no sooner had they entered than Kynton was yelling.

"What the hell are you doing! Get out of here!"

Both heads snapped to the tent flap in surprise. The young soldier leapt up, toppling the board to the floor. He averted his eyes and hurried from the tent, mumbling apologies as he passed, huddled and mortified.

"Aurora!" Dymphna cried in delight. Aurora fell to her knees as Dymphna jumped and ran to her. They hugged each other, laughing and crying. Aurora rocked the little girl back and forth; she never wanted to let her go again. Through the roar of blood rushing in her ears, she vaguely heard Kynton say something and the tent flap fell closed.

Aurora finally pulled away from the girl and held her at arm's length. "My little Catherine, I have missed you so."

"I never knew so many people existed in the world!" Dymphna exclaimed.

Aurora laughed, tears still streaming down her face. "Are they treating you well?" she asked.

"Yes!" Dymphna nodded emphatically. "Mostly. Some of the men are not very nice. But most of them are like Storey. They just want to teach me things and take care of me. And I have never had such wonderful food!"

Aurora sighed, relieved. Perhaps little girls in Mitoch were soldiers, but they were still little girls. She was glad to hear that even across borders men wanted to protect little girls, and little girls just wanted to play.

"What's happening next?" Dymphna asked. She had no idea she was a prisoner. She was beaming in excitement over what was just an excursion to her, a new adventure.

The truth was, Aurora had no idea. She had clung to inevitability as a savior; but as they all crashed here together in the woods, she realized that fate was neutral, at best. Everything good about this situation was tainted by old prejudices, old habits, and old hates. The world was the same as when she'd left it.

"I still need to figure that out," she said at last. "You just sit tight, yes? I am going to go talk to Kynton for a while. He is the leader of these men."

"When can I see Storey?" There was such unknown complexity in her innocence.

"Soon."

Outside, Kynton was waiting only steps away. He had given her privacy, but no more. His protectiveness was a feeble mask of his mistrust for Aurora's judgment. Her umbrage at this grew by the minute. With the most genuine smile she could muster, she beamed at Kynton. She saw his face soften for the first time since the night her father died.

"Thank you," she said. "I am all yours."

The light was nearly gone now. The bonfire blazed hot and cast ragged quilts of orange and black across the faces of the soldiers. Even after a decade of war, the men seemed jovial. Their camaraderie was lively, tangible. Because they were with Kynton, they had to be the best of the best. Aurora could also tell this was not a search-and-rescue party. Somehow, they knew that they were on their way to Secernere, and they knew what waited there for them. They knew not, however, that Secernere was already a dead place.

"I have a dress for you," he said. He lightly placed his hand on the small of her back and directed her toward his tent. "It is yours. When we discovered you were missing, I took it from your closet. I knew that wherever you were, you didn't have anything nice to wear." He chuckled. "I have never even seen you properly dressed."

His eyes glinted flirtatiously and Aurora burst into a violent coughing fit. She calmed herself, and acquiesced. He had given her visitation with Dymphna; she could give him his damsel in a dress.

Inside his tent, which was profanely more spacious than Dymphna's cell, Kynton unlatched a large bag, and pulled a rumpled green gown from within. It was glittery, shiny, bawdy, and enormous. She had owned that dress for years and never worn it. It was obscene that some poor horse had to lug it over the hundreds of miles from Cathendria to Secernere.

A more welcome sight was a large bowl of water, wash rag, comb, and shard of mirror. Kynton saw her eyes light up and seized on it.

"You are pleased!"

She smiled her inscrutable smile again.

"I will give you your leave. Perhaps then we can talk for a while?"

"Yes, of course, my lord," she said.

As he disappeared, Aurora relished solitude for the first time in as long as she could remember. She stripped off the trousers, shirt, and vest, and surveyed her naked body. The ropes had left scabbing red burns around her ankles, wrists, and shoulders. Purple bruises splotched the skin all across her body, like the patterned markings of a strange jungle animal. She lifted the mirror to examine her face. It wasn't her looking back. It was an apple that was two days past ripeness. It was a mask. Her features were swollen, blue, yellow, and green. Her eyes were red. Her hair was a matted nest. But the most horrifying was her neck. The shadow of Cashel lingered: the distinct prints of hands embraced her neck in the black of broken blood vessels. Seeing physical evidence of the pain she felt did not shock her as it once would have. She merely felt numb.

She washed as best she could with the freezing, still water, then dragged the comb through her hair and twisted it into a long plait. Standing naked and shivering in the middle of the tent as the moisture evaporated into the air, she waited for as long as she felt she could. Then she put on the dress and returned once more to the patient Kynton.

An enormously broad, unaffected smile spread on his face. Aurora saw a flash of his handsomeness there and remembered the beginnings of a crush she'd had on him, even at her darkest hour.

"You look stunningly beautiful, Lady Cavalcata." He bowed.

"Thank you, Lord Sebastia." She curtsied.

Maybe it was the dress that let her forget for the blink of an eye everything that had changed since then, that she had changed. Maybe it was the shine of the brass buttons on Kynton's uniform. Maybe it was being outdoors and smelling food cooking on an open fire. But then the moment of nostalgia for Fairgos was gone and a great resolve came over her.

They sat near enough to the fire to be warm in the cool air, but away from the crowd of rollicking soldiers. They had only been seated briefly when a soldier arrived and quietly handed them brimming bowls of dark, meaty stew. Aurora smiled to the man and accepted the bowl. She resisted her desire go slurp it down directly from the bowl, and instead took small spoonfuls as fast as was ladylike.

The dress made her feel ridiculous.

While the soldiers laughed and carried on, Aurora and Kynton began to speak in quiet tones.

"Were you kidnapped?" Kynton asked.

"No." She took a spoonful of stew, tasted it pensively, then swallowed. "I think I tried to kill myself."

"That is a ridiculous notion," Kynton huffed.

It could have been a ridiculous notion. It could have been the truth. For Aurora, it was a barometer of how honest she could be with this man whom she realized she did not know at all.

"Of course. You're right. I lately have many ridiculous notions from which I've been endeavoring to tease out the truth. I merely tried to go for a swim, and I ended up washed away."

"How horribly unlucky. But it is a relief that your disappearance was not related to the war."

"Why?" How could anything about this situation be a relief except that she was safe?

"I . . . I would have felt responsible," Kynton said. "I don't know that I could bear the thought that I wasn't able to protect you." He patted her knee. "But now I know I could not have protected you from going for a swim."

"Aha." Aurora continued to eat.

"You have been gone for so long. How have you survived all this time in Mitoch? Where did you stay? What did you eat? You must tell me everything."

It will not improve your situation to know.

"With time," she replied instead. "I am just so close to everything right now. I do not wish to recall every detail. You understand, don't you?"

"My lady, I have made a career of soldiering in a time of long war. I understand completely."

Kynton took a bite of stew and anxiously glanced around the camp. He fidgeted with the spoon in his bowl.

"I really must ask, however," he said, "who *are* those people? The little girl, the man you were riding with. I would ask how you could be so careless with foreigners like that, but it obvious you have affection for them, and they for you. I just do not understand."

"Indeed, I do need to talk to you about them. . . ." Aurora said. She knew what end she had to reach, but wasn't sure what tack would take her there.

Kynton placed his barely touched food on his lap and turned toward Aurora. A stonier look of concern had replaced his awkward flirtatiousness. Aurora bought herself time by slowly finishing her food. Unbidden, Kynton handed his own bowl to her and she ate that too.

"I'm sorry," he said quietly. "I have rushed everything since we found you. I can't imagine how hungry you must have been, how tired you are. It's only that . . ."

Aurora gently touched his hand. "Do not fret. I understand. For you, life has passed almost as normal. The resolution of your patience has ended with finding me here. I understand that you have so many questions for me, that you desire to build, or correct, the story of how these past days were filled for me.

"But you must understand that, for me . . . I saw no resolution. I had resigned myself to a certain unknown and unkind fate. I had not prepared in my mind to share the story with familiar faces when I was rescued. After the first weeks, I did not dream of rescue."

"I wish I could have let you know that I did not rest a day, that we were on our way all this time." He looked down at his hands. "I saw you in my dreams, you know. We talked. I told you everything was going to be all right. I had hoped . . . Oh, it was foolish."

"You had hoped what?"

"I had hoped that you had seen me in your own dreams, and that you heard me assure you. I hoped that we had met there and that you knew you would soon be safe."

"You would not know to look at me now . . . though, here in the dark, I'm sure my face is shadowed enough that you can imagine . . . but I have been very safe, up until a few days ago. That man with whom I was riding, his name is Storey. He was a farm hand at Secernere, the estate of Lord Gomery—Wait, no, just hear my story."

Kynton's face had turned dark and hard. Suitor was now soldier, with no gray area. "I *knew* we were close. How far are we from there? Is that bastard there now?"

"Please, just wait," she said firmly. She set her empty bowls on the ground and looked sternly at Kynton. "Storey was an enemy of Lord Gomery's as well. In fact, he has been plotting his subversion for many years. Storey is a friend of Fairgos. He had been taking care of me ever since I landed on the shores of Secernere, barely alive."

"I cannot believe such a tale."

"You must believe it, because it is the truth. I have been safe. I have been sleeping in a bed every night. I have eaten every day. I have had enough company to keep my wits about me. It was all because of Storey. He was protecting me from Lord Gomery while we tried to find a way to get me back home."

"But all of this!" He motioned at her battered face and neck. "The blood all over your clothes! When we found you in the woods, you looked near death—both of you did."

"We had finally tried to make our escape. Lord Gomery tried to stop us."

"Those marks on your neck, they're his."

Aurora nodded.

Kynton stood in a rage. "Oh what I will do to him!" Several faces turned toward them, flames flickering over their craggy features.

"Shush now." Aurora took his hand and gently pulled him back down to the log. "There's nothing that can be done now. He is dead. He lays dead in the wine cellar below the kitchen. I care not what you do to his body, but you are a man of God and I trust you will let that be your guide."

"Dead? How?"

"Listen to me. If I tell you what happened, it must remain a secret of you and of your men."

"What, why?"

"Do you trust every man here?"

"With my life," he asserted with conviction.

"Then you will promise on their behalf and for yourself that you will not tell what happened."

"If it is the only way to find out, then I will promise, for myself and every man here." He placed his hand over his heart.

"Storey killed him, in trying to protect me."

"Why must that be a secret?"

"What if it had been a servant at Cathendria who was discovered to have slain my father, to subvert the war?"

"He would be hanged for treason."

"Yes," said Aurora. "For one, Storey was my savior and I owe it to him to promise the safety of his life, if I have any control to do so. I do not wish to see him hanged, by our country or theirs. But there is more to this than selfishness. Would it not fare better in the public court of opinion, in Fairgosian society, that you, General of the Fairgosian Army had descended upon Secernere with such a small but powerful group of your best men, and you had singlehandedly slain the man who has been the perpetuation of this war? Would you not desire every man, woman, and child in our country to believe that it was Fairgos who eventually dominated over the evil Lord Cashel of Gomery—and not that Mitoch had merely collapsed in upon itself?"

"There is no honor in lying…." Kynton began. But his voice betrayed that even he did not believe what he was saying.

"I am not talking about lying. I am talking about taking control over our own history when we have the opportunity. The history that breeds patriotism in the next generation is not necessarily the detailed truth of every occurrence, but the essence of the truth that is at the *heart* of events. Do you understand what I mean?"

Kynton was gobsmacked. He stared at her, his round mouth hanging open in a compressed *o*. His brow formed a flat, straight, thick line over his eyes. His nostrils flared into black holes. There was surprise, shock, and revelation in his face—and Aurora knew that these emotions were not directed at the content of her words, but rather the deliverer. She watched Kynton's knowledge of her fall apart. Even in her green dress with her combed hair tied in a tidy braid, she was not and would never again be the woman he wanted her to be. She was something more, but also something less.

Slowly, he began to nod. Some connection in his mind had come apart; it sparked and shone in his eyes.

"Yes," he finally said. "I understand what you mean. My men will take Secernere, and with it, we will take Cashel of Gomery. This is our opportunity to see peace in our lifetime."

"Yes."

Kynton began to stare at the fire. Much more interest lay in its fiery center of coals than would ever again exist for him in Aurora.

She felt the release of his bindings, and it was more freeing than her escape from the wine cellar. Had any Fairgosian woman ever worked toward creating disinterest in such a man as Lord Kynton of Sebastia?

"Will you release Storey? He has no worth for you."

Kynton nodded. "What of the little girl? Who is she?"

"She is an orphan, stowed away on the grounds of Secernere. I plan to take her as my own child."

"Such a pale white Mitochian girl . . . You will be shunned."

"Not where I'm going."

He turned and looked into her eyes. She saw the moment of heartbreak that he had been resisting with his honed military stoicism. In a flash, it was gone.

"I shall grieve that I will never have the chance to get to know you, Lady Aurora of Cavalcata." His apology was tacit admission that he never really knew her in the first place. Aurora appreciated this honesty; it lessened the burden of leaving him.

All the weight of the night sank onto their shoulders like blankets piled onto a winter bed. They sat in silence and let the pops of the fire and the sparks of men's laughter fly out over top of them. But they did not partake. Neither of them felt sadness or regret, only inevitability.

The reverence was broken when a soldier emerged running from the darkness and stood heaving before Kynton.

"Sir—" he huffed and tried to catch his breath. It was the young chess-playing soldier from Dymphna's tent. "—the Mitochian, the man, he's escaped."

"What!" Kynton stood, and the boy shrank.

"There was some confusion about whose turn it was to eat. . . . I just, I'm sorry, sir. Wasn't anyone's fault, sir. I think I got him in the arm with an arrow. He's run off into the woods. Should we be going after him, sir?"

Aurora reached up and gently placed her hand on his arm.

"No," Kynton said. "Let him go. We'll be taking Secernere tomorrow. Lady Cavalcata has enough intelligence to tell us just how to do it. We needn't waste the resources on a mere farm hand. It is too dark to track him, anyhow, and he'll be long gone by morning. Go finish your meal."

"Thank you," Aurora whispered.

The boy jogged back to camp, undoubtedly cheering inside at his lucky break, and they were alone again.

"Listen to me," Aurora said. "I will tell you everything you need to know to get to Secernere. From here, it's easier than you could imagine. The company has vacated the premises, and Cashel is dead. It will be the easiest and most gloried mission your men will ever know. But you must let me go as soon as we are done speaking."

"My lady, I will grant you every wish I can, but it is pitch black out here. These woods are strange to you."

"They are not strange to the horse. I have no time to linger." She knew she could not conceal from Kynton that she was going after Storey, but there was no need to speak the name aloud.

She explained the path back to the Secernere demesnes and laid out what she knew of the grounds, including the kitchen with the wine cellar below. She talked about the hollow wall and what lay beneath it.

"It sounds like a prime point of fortification for the war," Kynton said.

"I think holding Secernere will make all the difference," she said. ". . . There's one more thing."

"What's that?"

"Cort."

"You know Cort! He found you?? Is he alive?" Not even when she had emerged in the dress had Aurora seen such light in his eyes.

"I'm so sorry."

Kynton rubbed his huge tan hand down over his face. "Oh no," he whispered.

She lightly gripped his arm. "I'm so, so sorry."

"Where is he?"

"You will find him in the same place as Cashel." Her throat clenched. "You must be prepared for the worst. We had not time to give him a proper burial."

His other hand rose to his face and he held his head, rocking it back and forth. Aurora knew they had no more to share. She leaned and placed a light kiss on the top of Kynton's head and squeezed his shoulder. Without looking up, he reached his hand toward her, touched her knee, then let her go forever.

Aurora spoke a few brief words to the soldiers who guarded Dymphna, and they put up no argument. Inside, Dymphna was sleeping inside a cloth bag. She was on her side, curled like a comma. Aurora lay down beside her, draping her arm across the girl's body. She whispered into the girl's soft blond curls. "Catherine?"

Dymphna stirred, then turned her face toward Aurora, sleepy, but grinning.

"I know you are tired, but it's time to go."

"Where are we going?"

"To collect Storey first, and then . . . I do not know yet."

Dymphna reached up and brushed a stray hair behind Aurora's ear. "It is said, a good traveler has no plans and is not intent upon his destination."

"I like that," said Aurora. "We will know when we get there, won't we?"

Dymphna nodded heartily. She yawned, stretched, then sat up. "Often, the journey *is* the destination."

The woods were so thickly black that the trio of horse, girl, and woman felt no movement as they swam through. But they were moving, forward into the journey of destiny. The horse knew the way.

Dymphna dozed softly in Aurora's arms. Exhausted herself, Aurora held onto wakefulness by holding onto the vision of Storey. She knew he was on his way back to Secernere, like a moth to a flame. *You must return to Secernere.* He knew no place else.

At Secernere, they would meet once more and all three would be together at last. They would say goodbye to that place and it would not be the end, but their beginning.

Acknowledgments

Writing, by its nature, is a solitary activity—but only on its face. There is a reason almost every book you pick up has an acknowledgments section: we may write alone, but we don't create in a vacuum. Writers are the products of all the love, support, and advice we've received along the way. Every person who has touched us—no matter in what small way—has also touched our writing.

I dedicated this book to my parents, but I must also thank them here. Whether I was painting naked winged angels on the walls of my bedroom, shooting comedy sketches on VHS with my New Jersey cousins, or scribbling stories in spiral-bound notebooks that would never see the light of day, my parents encouraged and cultivated my every creative whim. When I told them I wanted to be an artist when I grew up, they never said an ill word about it. When I read Toni Morrison's *Jazz* at age 16 and decided I was destined to be a writer, they accepted that too, with the same support as if I'd wanted to be something much more practical, like an optometrist or court clerk. Their consistent support and love is what has allowed me to grow into the writer I am, and to continue to grow.

Of course there are many others. Thank you to all my English teachers—and all teachers—for the work you do. And it *is* work, some of the hardest there is. Thank you especially to Mrs. Huller, who in eighth grade taught me that all great characters must have flaws, and to Mr. Gant, who in eleventh grade gave me *The Sound and the Fury* and turned everything I knew about narrative fiction on its head.

Thank you to Madison Smartt Bell, my creative writing professor at Goucher College, who recognized in me an ear for rhythm, and nurtured it with expert criticism, sometimes harsh but always attentive.

Thank you to Brooke Shaden for taking photographs

straight out of fairy tales—and for taking a photograph straight out of my book before it was even written. Her work appears on the cover of the first edition, and the interior plate of this edition. Thank you also to the generous and creative designers who share their work for free, including Eduardo Recife of Misprinted Type and Caleb Kimbrough of Lost & Taken.

Thank you to the Office of Letters and Light, the creators of National Novel Writing Month (NaNoWriMo to the initiated). OLL is what got me to stop talking about writing a book and actually do it. The work this organization does for literacy and creativity makes the world a better place. Give loads of money to them. I try to.

I also need to thank a very special group of creative people. I have difficulty putting into words how grateful I am to them. I feel that gratitude in the way my heart beats a little differently when I think of them. It's how being around them makes me want to create. It's the knowledge that if I pass my ideas through their brains, those ideas will come out on the other side better in ways I could never have imagined on my own.

So thank you to Stacy Kauffman, my longtime colleague, "work wife," and friend. Stacy did me the biggest favor and honor by stepping out of her comfort zone and into the spotlight, making her screen debut in the book trailer for *The War Master's Daughter*. She also remained relatively calm when I told her I wanted to put her on the cover of the second edition. But Stacy was brave enough to walk out onto the King and Queen Seat wearing boots a size too big, and that deserves to be immortalized.

So thank you to Spencer Greer, a fellow member of our merry band of polymaths known as Liquid Squid. Thanks to Spencer for his insightful feedback on an earlier draft of the book, and serious eternal indebtedness to him for his beautiful camera work on the book trailer. I am ecstatic to be able to showcase Spence's gorgeous photography on the new book cover. I hope whenever I am in front of a camera, Spencer Greer is the one behind it.

So thank you to Ryan Stevens, an old friend who became a new friend and can now safely be called an old friend again. If he's nice I might even call him family. Ryan's mind is behind the original score that backs the book trailer. More thought was put into that brief bit of music than *anything* you will hear on the radio. Ryan puts that kind of thought into every minute of his life.

So thank you to Jessica Goodyear, my most passionate and thorough beta reader, sounding board, and cheerleader. Without her careful reading, detailed comments, and unyielding enthusiasm for the project, this book would have fallen miles short of its potential. Jes is the founder and heart of Liquid Squid and a creative force in film, having recently won her first film festival award (the first, I'm sure, of many, many more). She worked by my side on every aspect of the book trailer, including conception, location scouting, production, direction, and editing. Her creativity, drive, and energy are unflagging and contagious, so basically I want to be around her all the time.

Finally, thank you to all those I don't have space to name here, those of you who made this second edition possible, not simply because you bought the book, not because you read the book or liked the book, but because of reasons completely independent of the book itself: because you made me feel like I could do it.

I did it. We did it.

—Elly Zupko, December 11, 2011
updated February 21, 2013

About the Author

Elly Zupko is blessed to be able to write things down for a living, most of them true. It's the making things up part that sometimes gets her into trouble. She lives in Baltimore, Maryland. *The War Master's Daughter* is her first novel.